Love Always

MICHELLE BROWN

This novel is inspired by real events and the lives of actual individuals. While the narrative may incorporate fictional elements for dramatic purposes, the essence of the story remains true to the experiences of those who lived it. The characters you will meet are drawn from real life, and the events depicted are rooted in historical reality. It is our hope that this blend of fact and fiction will both engage and enlighten readers about the remarkable stories behind the pages of this book.

This book exists with my immeasurable
thanks to many people.

To my children; Travis, Miranda and Ronnie.
Thank you for your unrelenting belief that this novel
not only would exist but that it is a story worth telling.
Thank you for being my inspiration to do better and be
better in every regard.
I am so incredibly grateful for each of you.
AFNMW

To my mom, Diane; thank you for always
supporting me and believing in me. Mostest

To my family. Thank you for your patience
with how long it took to tell this story.

To Mrs. Judy Wales, my fourth-grade teacher.
Thank you for seeing my passion for writing,
even back then and encouraging and supporting me
in my efforts to become a writer.

To Mrs. Eva Olsson. Thank you for the
gracious gift of your time and the sharing of your
story. You are a true reflection of the power of not
allowing hate to rule your heart. Thank you for your
permission to include a portion of your story in mine.
The honour is mine.

Last and certainly not least, to my Nan and Grandad
for sharing their epic love story and inspiration for this
novel.

Trigger Warnings:
This story contains bad language,
references to violence, death, war,
holocaust, sexual intercourse, and
mature themes.

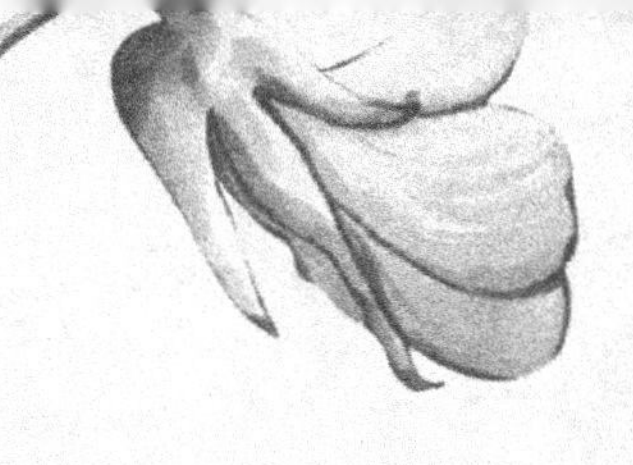

*When I saw you, I fell in love,
and you smiled because you
knew.*

- William Shakespeare

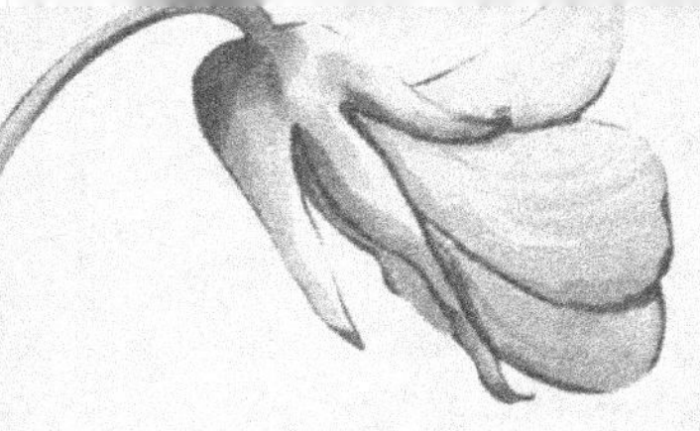

Chapter One

The enormous wooden doors loomed before her, weathered and worn from centuries of standing guard over the sacred space within. Carved with intricate designs and embellished with ornate metalwork, they exuded an air of solemnity and strength. Vivian hesitated, her heart pounding as her nerves started to get the better of her. Standing before the imposing entrance, she couldn't help but marvel at its resilience. Despite the devastation wrought by bombs and gunfire, the doors remained steadfast, silent sentinels against the tide of destruction. In their rough grain and sturdy hinges, she found a sense of solace, a reminder that even in the darkest of times, there was still beauty and depth to be found.

Taking a deep breath, Vivian pushed open the doors with trembling hands. They groaned in protest before swinging open with a soft thud. Stepping across the threshold, she felt a sense of calm.

A light breeze floated through the chapel windows. The rays of sunlight fluttered in like angel wings, soft and warm and carrying the scent of spring. The thick limestone walls had survived many barrages and attempts to disfigure the magnificent archways and main areas of the church. There was one small section of the entryway that revealed the

remnants of scorching from the 1666 Great Fire of London. But even the stained-glass windows remained intact. Those along the sanctuary depicted the twelve apostles. The main window was a combination of a kaleidoscope of colour and the resurrection of Christ.

Outside the window, a flock of tiny bluebirds found a perch among the gnarled branches of the ancient oak trees. They were twittering with excitement as they sang an accompaniment to Mrs. Rachel Witt as she played "Only Forever" on the piano. Mrs. Witt was perhaps in her eighties but looked to be in her sixties. She was small but not frail, with stark white hair and clear, azure-blue eyes. She had the determined look of someone who had survived war before and planned to do so again.

It was not the traditional wedding music she felt was appropriate, but the groom had been so insistent and sweet she couldn't refuse. He had also paid extra, and in these trying times, the money was helpful and gave her an excuse to overlook the modern song he wished her to play. She smiled sadly as she thought back to her own wedding day. Pledging her love to her groom *only forever*, just as the words in the song she was playing.

Thomas anxiously stood at the altar. The tailored dress uniform he wore accentuated his broad shoulders. His full lips lifted in a nervous smile and emphasised the deep dimples in his cheek and strong chin. Impatient to get the wedding started, he shifted his weight and watched the old woman at the piano. Her eyes were sad from an ever-present grief despite the joy of the day and the music she was playing. Thomas wasn't an old man, but he had already witnessed the brutalities of war and couldn't help but wonder if his wife would carry a sorrow like that for him one day.

He glanced at his friend beside him. They had on the same smart, Army-issue dress uniform. Karl has been his best friend since childhood. There was nothing they wouldn't do or hadn't done for each other. They had even joined up together. "Let's do some good!" they had said. Neither of their families had been pleased with their choice or the unit they eventually volunteered for.

Frontline action and being in the thick of it was what they had always wanted, and they were proud of the regiment motto, "First in, last out." Karl smiled encouragingly at Thomas as if to say, "Be patient, my friend."

There was movement at the back of the church, and everyone turned towards it. Thomas caught his breath. He couldn't believe his eyes.

She's an angel, he thought to himself.

Vivian walked towards him in a pale grey dress of the softest satin he had ever seen. It clung to her body in a way that generated a strong, raw desire in him to see the rest. Her chestnut-brown hair was rolled and pinned in place with baby's breath. Their eyes locked together, and in that moment, the sound of the piano, the birds, and the gentle breeze disappeared. All they could see were each other.

Vivian smiled shyly at Thomas as she moved towards the altar. Her breathing had become almost erratic. She could feel the connection between them, and her step faltered ever so slightly as the intensity of the moment seeped into her. She was suddenly conscious of every step she took and attempted to focus on her flowers for a moment to regain her composure. The bouquet was a simple bunch of lily of the valley, the delicate flowers fragrant and hanging like tiny bells off their almost invisible stems. They were one of her favourite flowers, and she smiled at the thought, feeling much calmer.

She decided to brave meeting Thomas's eyes once more. Fern had warned her about his charms, but she had clearly wasted her breath. His eyes danced mischievously, reminiscent of a clear summer sky before dusk, with flecks of indigo swirling in their depths, creating an intensity in his open appraisal of her. She was unsettled, and he found it amusing. He was entranced by her eyes. They reminded him of the lush forests back home in Ontario. Flecks of gold, like scattered rays of sunlight dancing across a verdant meadow, shimmered in the light, alluding to treasures hidden in their depths. He had never seen eyes of such colour. They were shining with happiness.

She reached the front of the small church and noted his matching sprig of lily of the valley on his lapel. Her eyes fell lower to his medals. It made her sad to think of the lives lost behind each of them. The families from both sides of the war who would never see their sons, husbands, or fathers again. Yet, it was because of the war Thomas was there. Their eyes met, and they felt the jolt connect them again. Neither could help but take a tiny breath to steady themselves.

Reverend Michaels, a small, balding man with a round face and bespectacled eyes, opened the ceremony. "Welcome! Welcome!" he bellowed to the few guests who were present and eager for something to celebrate. "It is during our moments of greatest challenge and despair that we most welcome a joyous occasion such as this. Today, we have gathered to celebrate the marriage of this man and woman. To rejoice in the love, they so clearly share." He smiled at the faces of the beautiful bride and handsome groom who had barely heard a word he said as they gazed at each other. "In these times, our need to vanquish evil is great. We come together today in the face of God to share in the joy of this union."

His voice faded out once again as they stared into each other's eyes. Vivian, stuck in the moment, thought of how fate had brought them together. Reverend Michaels looked at the bride and groom and asked them to hold hands. Fern turned to Vivian, handing over her bouquet. Lost for a moment, she recovered her wits when she realised everyone was staring at her. They were all waiting for her to take the flowers so the ceremony could continue. She blushed crimson, so distracted by Thomas and his piercing gaze she had forgotten where she was and what she was meant to be doing. She was the maid of honour at her best friend's wedding, but she only had eyes for the best man.

Thomas smirked at her. He too had been lost since the

moment he saw her walk down the aisle. He hadn't even noticed Fern. He heard the minister pronounce the couple husband and wife and finally broke free of the magical spell he was under just in time to see his friend embrace his new bride and share their first married kiss. In that moment, he found himself wishing he could embrace Viv in the same way. An incredible thought considering he had not even been formally introduced to her yet.

The couple turned to the congregation amidst the clapping and tears of happiness. Holding hands, they exited the church, eager to start with the merriment of the reception in the adjacent hall. Just as Thomas stepped to Vivian's side to escort her down the aisle, the jubilation dissolved. The familiar drone of the air raid horn broke through the joyful event, and everyone looked at each other in quiet panic and desperation.

"Everyone, please be calm!" the minister called out to the congregation. "We are blessed to have a large cellar under the rectory. If everyone would follow me, there is more than enough room. We shall be quite safe until this latest barrage is finished."

The guests followed the minister towards the shelter. There was no rushing or pushing. The people of England were accustomed to the air raids, and they felt protected by the thick stone walls of the church and corridor. They didn't have much time to reach the cellar, but they refused to give in to the terror of the Nazis and Hitler's reign by panicking just yet. Despite the bombing, the mood remained surprisingly light and good-humoured. Everyone was still basking in the joy of the wedding, and no one was willing to let it go completely. There were so few moments of joy during a war that the guests clung to those they had.

Making their way down the stairs, however, it became harder to keep their resolve. The all-too-familiar buzzing of bombs could be heard droning far above them. London was under attack once again. With the percussion of the first impact not too far off, their pace hastening, and Karl clutched

Fern's hand.

The floor was cobbled and uneven, and the ladies quickly removed their shoes. They were made for celebrations, not evacuations. Fern's mother struggled to keep up as she hobbled along with her cane, and her daughter looked back at her with concern.

"Leave me, my dear. I'm just fine. Slow but fine. I will be along." She was composed and unperplexed, but Karl had recognised Fern's wary expression and fell back to his mother-in-law's side and aid.

"Of course, you will, Mother Dear. I just needed to slow down a bit and catch my breath." Karl smiled broadly as he took her arm.

The minister was cooing calm prayers and encouraging the guests onward. "Almost there, everyone. I must apologise for the lack of cleanliness. I haven't had time to tidy things after the last raid." He gestured towards the floor and walls of the stairwell and hallway. The loose bricks and mortar were showing signs of fatigue given the constant onslaught of the Luftwaffe.

As they reached the final portion of the passageway, there was an incredible crash and blast from nearby. The shudder caused several loose stones to fall from the wall. People were knocked to the ground, and the floor became more uneven with fresh debris. The dust hung like a misty cloud of rain, causing everyone to cough, and the light from the lanterns dimmed. Another explosion rocked the passageway, leaving everyone grabbing at the walls for stability. Many of the larger rocks relented at being touched. Falling in enormous chunks like dominoes, they pulled people to the hard ground with them.

Fern's elderly neighbour, Jim Avery, was struck on the shoulder by some of the heavy granite. It knocked him to his knees.

"Jim!" several people cried out, running towards him.

"I'm all right." The elderly man shooed away the hands that reached out to help him up. "It will take more than a few rocks to damage this old fool." He chuckled, but there was a tense and telling tone to his voice. He was bleeding from the side of his head where one of the rocks hit him, and his hands were scratched from trying to catch himself as he fell. He tried to make light of things as he paused to gain his bearings and shake off the disorientation he was feeling.

His nephew Matthew stayed with him while he caught his breath.

"I'm right as rain now, Matt," he said. "Carry on. Carry on." Patting his nephew on the shoulder, he moved forward again towards the shelter, but they were all alarmed by the explosion. They knew it was close, very close.

Another bomb found its way to the ground and shook the passageway before people had even recovered from the last impact and rattling. The shrieks continued as more rocks and sand tumbled from the walls and ceiling.

"Quickly!" Reverend Michaels couldn't maintain his countenance. "Everyone inside, please. This way. This way. Stay calm. We will be safe here." He hoped his voice was not betraying his fear and despair. He beckoned from the doorway of the cellar, holding it open for the terrified crowd.

Karl stopped at the door, his heart pounding with adrenaline as he released his mother-in-law's arm, ensuring she was safely inside the shelter. Turning to Fern, he offered his hand and bowed cheekily. "Mrs. Gwilliam, if I may." His voice was steady despite the chaos around them.

"Why certainly, Mr. Gwilliam." Returning his bow with an equally cheeky curtsey, she offered her hand to him.

He lifted it to his lips, his gaze locked with hers. With a determined expression, he reached down and scooped his bride up into his arms, carrying her over the threshold of the shelter.

"Karl, you fool!" Fern squealed in delight, her laughter echoing off the walls. "Put me down!" But beneath her playful protest, there was a glimmer of joy and gratitude.

As he set her down, they shared a passionate kiss, their love a beacon of hope in the darkness of the shelter. Around them, the crowd whooped and cheered, eager to escape the looming threat above.

Vivian laughed as she watched her best friend enjoy the romance bestowed upon her by her new husband. But a feeling of dread swept over her as she realised Thomas was not among the congregation. *Where has he gone? Is he lying on the ground somewhere in the hallway, battered, bleeding, and unconscious from the loose rocks?* Without thinking, she turned to go back towards the chapel.

"Viv! Where are you going? Come back!" Fern shouted from her husband's arms.

"Thomas isn't here!" Vivian shouted back. "I need to go and find him."

"Don't be foolish. Get inside the cellar. You heard how close the bombs are. Please, Viv! Come back!" Fern started to pull away from Karl.

"Fern, stop! Viv, get in here! Thomas will be along. Fern is right. The planes are overhead. The bombs are underway and crashing down upon us. We all need to get inside." Karl's grip on Fern's arm began to slip as she pulled towards her friend.

"Karl, please stop her," Fern pleaded. She turned and grasped Karl's lapel, forcing him to help her friend.

Thomas appeared in the hall outside the shelter. "What is all the fuss? Why aren't you all inside yet?" He had remnants of gravel and dust on his cap and shoulders, and he was carrying two baskets with wine and the makings for a buffet.

"We were worried about you, pal." Karl slapped him on the back with a beaming smile and a glance over at Vivian.

"Were you now?" Thomas looked at Viv, who blushed again and glanced away.

"Well, of course we were," she said, trying to hide how happy she was to see him safe. "Having her husband's best friend killed in an air raid moments after their marriage wouldn't exactly make for a joyful beginning. It would cast a shadow on every anniversary they celebrated." Vivian looked at him with mock impatience as if blaming him for being so foolhardy.

"Well, I thought that since we'd all be holed up here for the next several hours, we might as well bring the celebration along." Thomas held up the basket by way of explanation.

Karl laughed. "Count on you to think of that." He took one of the baskets from his friend, put his arm through Vivian's, and pulled her inside the shelter. He shut the door behind them, and they were all finally as safe as they could be from the bombs overhead.

Thomas smiled at Reverend Michaels, whose frown turned upside down when he realised Thomas has rescued the honeymoon feast. "No use harbouring ill will towards a man bearing a bounty, eh?" He clapped his hands, and the room went silent.

"All right then," the minister announced. "Let's get some more light in here if we can and see what we can do to get this celebration underway."

A quiet murmur of relief fluttered through the cellar as the tension ebbed, and the guests realised they had made it to safety. The distraction of lighting lanterns was welcomed, and they illuminated shelves on two sides of the cellar that housed jars of preserves, medicines, bandages, and additional lanterns.

"Here, let me help you, Mrs. Witt." Vivian had opened one of the bundles housing strips of cloth and rubbing alcohol and examined the elderly woman. Gently brushing her hair out of her face, she warned, "I'm sorry, this is going to sting." She then dabbed the cloth dampened with the strong-smelling rubbing alcohol on her head.

"Pain is a good thing right now. It reminds me I'm still alive." Mrs. Witt thought back to a day, a whole war away, where as a nurse, she had tended to hurt and injured soldiers not far from a battlefield in France. It had been nothing short of a massacre, so a few bumps and bruises would not get the best of her.

"We are all certainly grateful for that." Vivian smiled more broadly, relieved to see the strong-willed woman was not going to give in to her fears or the situation. "Keep this cloth pressed on here for a bit longer just to make sure the bleeding has actually stopped." Viv placed her smooth young hand over the thinly skinned hand of her elder and showed her where to keep the pressure. They nodded at each other, a voiceless understanding between them of trust and thanks.

Turning back to the rest of the guests, Vivian noticed Jim Avery's nephew tending to his uncle.

"You see, Vivian, I am too old and gnarled for a few rocks to crack." He earned a loud laugh from Vivian and his nephew when he lifted his arm and flexed his muscles.

"Oh, Mr. Avery. I am glad you are okay." Yearning to continue to distract herself from Thomas's gaze, she looked for something else to do. "Fern, let me help you and Maeve with the food and drinks."

Opening the wine, they distributed that and the food from the baskets Thomas had rescued. There was a jar of black current jam on the shelf, and Maeve opened it. The seal noisily released with a satisfying pop.

"Here now, give us a hand, you two." Reverend Michaels held out a lantern to Karl and Thomas. The three men set the lanterns up around the shelter. "Put them on the ground, not up on the shelves in case the bombs manage to jostle us down here. We don't want them crashing down and causing injuries or a fire."

There were enough lit that the room took on a warm, romantic glow. As their eyes became accustomed to the lighting, Mrs. Witt softly sang "When They Sound the Last All Clear." Everyone smiled, and others joined in.

"Vivian, do you mind if I steal my bride away for a moment to enjoy a toast and a snack together?" Karl selected some of the cheese and what was left of a bottle of wine and guided his wife to a bench on the far side of the cellar.

"I am sure we can manage without her," Viv remarked.

"I was worried we wouldn't get to enjoy anything from our baskets!" Karl feigned annoyance.

Fern giggled in amusement and took the bottle of wine

from him. "You take such good care of me. Cheers, darling."

"Save some for me, Mrs. Gwilliam." Karl pretended to grab for the bottle. Feeling the gaiety of their private moment, they stared happily at one another. "May I have this dance?"

"There isn't any music, silly, but yes, you may," she said. The happy couple didn't care about music. They felt it and heard it in their hearts.

Noticing the young couple starting to dance, the minister called out to the guests. "Ladies and gentlemen, may I now properly present to you, Mr. and Mrs. Karl Gwilliam."

As everyone cheered and clapped, Thomas and Viv stared at each other from across the room, and she felt her pulse begin to race as he slowly approached her.

"I'm sorry I worried you." Thomas gave her a broad smile. The twinkle in his eye told her he was making fun of her, and she realised she liked it.

"You didn't worry me. I already told you. I didn't want you to go and get yourself killed and ruin my dear Fern's wedding day is all." Vivian knew she hadn't convinced Thomas in the least, but she didn't mind. She smiled up at him, enjoying how near he was to her.

One of the other women took the bandages Vivian was still holding. "Let me take those."

"Oh, thank you, Madeline. If you need anything, come get me."

Thomas had taken off his hat to reveal his light ginger-blond hair. The freckles on his nose gave him the look of a younger man. And his eyes. Oh, his eyes! The lines around them betrayed what he'd seen and the fatigue such images brought to a person's soul and body. She flushed as she wondered what he looked like under that dress uniform. Did he have the same ginger-coloured hair on his chest? Would his arms feel strong when he wrapped them around her? She shook her head to get the thoughts out.

Do you think it will be a long raid?" she asked, focusing on where they were at the moment.

He pulled out a flask and motioned for her to follow him to

a ledge so they could sit together. Thomas frowned. "They're always too long." He had seen enough of the game of war to know no one truly won.

The wine was being passed around, and the gaiety became infectious. The singing and cheering carried on for hours. Everyone seemed to forget where they were, especially Thomas and Vivian, who sat together alone amongst the crowd.

The long blast of the "all clear" finally sounded. A few of the guests had made themselves comfortable. The effects of a little alcohol and a lot of merriment had made them drowsy and content. Many had managed to create makeshift beds for themselves with jackets for blankets and each other for pillows.

"I think that was the 'all clear,' darling," Karl whispered as he held his new wife across his lap. She had a happy smile fixed on her sleeping face.

Viv was fighting sleep herself, but she didn't want to miss a moment with Thomas. Who knew if she would ever see him again. Fern had told her he and Karl were prone to volunteering for riskier adventures. Karl had promised Fern he wouldn't request anything overly dangerous from then on, but the very nature of an armoured reconnaissance battalion meant they were frequently in harm's way. Even without volunteering for extra assignments, they were always at risk, though they were currently stationed in Essex and relatively safe because of it. The assignment had allowed for greater freedoms of leave and leisure time for the men before they would be called upon to travel across the channel.

Thomas went to the door of the shelter and opened it slightly. Fresh, cool air rushed in, bringing with it the far-too-familiar aroma of cinders. One by one, the guests roused themselves. Some from sleep, and some from the temporary peace they had found inside the shelter.

Karl woke Fern with a gentle kiss. "Our guests are beginning to leave," he whispered in her ear as he helped her to her feet. "Let's take your mother home to the comfort of her own bed."

They thanked each of their guests for being part of their wedding day as they began to wander out of the safe haven, they have shared for the last several hours.

"Well, pal, I guess I'll catch up with you in a couple of days, eh?" Thomas slapped his friend on the back, shook his hand, and hugged him firmly.

Karl smiled back at his friend. "Thanks for everything, Tommy Boy. I'll catch up with you indeed. Let's go, Mum. Fern and I are going to take you home now." He took his mother-in-law by the elbow again and helped her out of the shelter.

Fern hugged Vivian and gave her a saucy smile. "Would you like us to take you home as well?"

Before she could reply, Thomas stepped up and grabbed her hand. "I thought I would walk Viv home if that was okay with her."

Vivian was so thrilled at Thomas' touch; she had lost the ability to speak. She grinned and nodded weakly, glancing back over her shoulder at her friend as she walked away with him.

Fern and Karl stood outside the threshold of the doorway into the shelter, their arms around each other's waists, grinning at the new couple as they left. He looked down into his wife's face and kissed her forehead. He was grateful for the gift, for the moment, and he hugged her tight.

"All right, you two lovebirds, let's go then." Fern's mother ripped them back to the present, and they laughed.

"Yes, Mum, you're right. We need to get you home," he said.

Fern blushed at the look in Karl's eyes. She knew what he really meant was he was eager to get his new bride home to the privacy that would allow them to fully become man and wife.

14

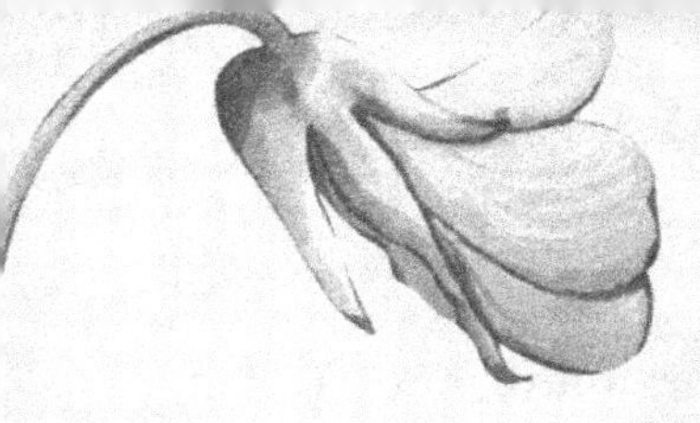

Chapter Two

"Which way?" Thomas had slipped Viv's hand through his arm and held it securely as he helped her down the steps of the church towards the street. The scent of smoke and burnt wood hung in the gentle evening breeze. Sirens could be heard in the distance as the aftermath of the bombing continued to be dealt with by the ambulances and firefighters. It was an almost daily task but thankfully, not as brutal that day as others.

"I only live a few blocks away. You don't need to take me. Honestly, I'll be fine." But Viv was relieved when Thomas ignored her protests and insisted on taking her home.

"I promised Karl and Fern, I would get you home safely. I'm not about to let them down."

"All right then, thank you. It's very kind of you, Thomas." She loved saying his name. It was like she could feel it within her body every time she did. "I'm this way." Pointing down the street to the left, they walked arm in arm.

"How is it that we've never met, Viv? I've met Fern a few times. It *is* a bit surprising you were never with her."

He was still shocked at how affected he was by Viv. His heart felt light and constricted at the same time, like he had never

experienced joy until that day, and it was all he could feel and all he feared losing.

"Honestly, I'm not sure. I've met Karl a few times as well before today. Perhaps they conspired to make sure we didn't meet." Viv laughed, but she wondered as she said it if it might be true. Fern had warned her Thomas was a bit of a rake. He always had women fawning over him, and she could certainly see why. He was handsome, but it was more his charm and the ease one felt around him that made him almost irresistible.

"That could be true." His brow furrowed briefly. "I hope we haven't ruined any nefarious plot they've had to keep us apart because, if I may be so forward, I have to tell you, Viv, I already know I need to see you again."

For the tiniest moment, her heart stopped beating. She could have leapt in the air she was so happy to hear him say that. Calming herself, she responded, "I have a shift tomorrow, but I could meet you after that."

"I'll meet you anytime and anywhere you want, Miss Vivian Waltman. I'll walk through fire if I must in order to see you again."

She blushed crimson. "I certainly hope that won't be necessary." She needed to change the direction of the conversation. "Tell me about where you're from, Mr. Thomas Cooper."

As they walked along the darkened street, Vivian could almost feel his smirk at her not-so-subtle change in topic. The rubble of the many war-torn buildings spilled onto the sidewalks and roads. They easily stepped around the debris, engrossed in their conversation and each other's company.

Thomas knew he could scare Viv off, so he took her cue. He didn't want to run the risk of her not wanting to see him again because he couldn't control the damn feelings, he already had for her. "I'm from a small place in Ontario called Ardoch, which is near Kingston. It's more of a county than an actual town. Most of my family are farmers, but that just wasn't the life I wanted. Don't get me wrong, I respect it. It's hard work. Maybe too hard for me." He laughed in a self-deprecating way. "Maybe that's why I wanted to get away. I miss it, though. It's very beautiful. Rolling hills and forests everywhere."

"I imagine it's a lot like the countryside here." She was trying to picture his world in her mind.

"Indeed. Very much like the countryside here. In fact, when I first arrived, I felt as though I were still home."

He paused for a moment.

"When I told my family I was joining up, they were not happy about it. My parents didn't understand why I would enlist when we had the farm to work. In fact, my mother was so upset, she refused to come see me off at the train." Thomas had tears in his eyes as he described how his sister had clutched him and wept.

"I'm sorry, Thomas." Vivian placed her hand on his arm as he travelled back in his mind to that day.

He could see the platform and his family as clearly as if they were standing in front of him then.

"I will pray for you every single day, Thomas. Please be careful." His sister Mary was a gentle, spirited woman with the same blue eyes as her younger brother. She doted on him, and he could do no wrong as far as she was concerned. That he was going off to fight in the war was very troubling for her. "Take this with you for luck."

She placed a small pressed wild violet from her garden into his hand. "A piece of home whenever you need it." It was attached to a small notecard with a single word written in her beautiful handwriting. *Home.*

Thomas hugged her, blinking hard to keep the tears back. "I promise to be careful. I love you, Mimi." He placed the delicate flower in his notebook before kissing her gently on the forehead and releasing their embrace.

John Henry Cooper, his father, locked hands with his son and nodded. "Thomas, I want you to know that I may not understand *why* you need to do this, but I do understand that you *need* to do it."

"Thanks, Dad. That means a lot." Thomas nodded back and reciprocated the handshake.

Fynn, his bear-sized older brother, was not a man for weak eyes. He gave Thomas a fierce handshake before pulling him into an even fiercer hug. Without a word, Fynn turned and walked away, but not before Thomas saw tears in his eyes as well.

He had never told them how in that moment, he almost changed his mind. How he wanted to tell them it was a mistake, and he would stay after all. But he knew he could not. He had already completed his training. He belonged to the 4th Reconnaissance Battalion. The lads were waiting. Karl was already on board the train.

And that's when he saw her, standing alone, away from the crowds of people. Elise. She was wearing an indigo-blue dress with a cream collar and cuffs. It had been what she called an *extravagant* gift from Thomas for her birthday.

"I don't understand why you're so angry. I thought I bought you something nice. I even had Mimi help me pick it out. You deserve fine things. You don't always have to wear drab black and brown," he had said. Of course, he regretted the last words even as they left his mouth.

She took a small step backward, injured by his words. "I didn't realise you thought I was drab and boring." He started to apologise, to try and take it back, but it was too late. She scoffed. "It's a waste of money, and we don't have money to waste. Take it back."

"I didn't mean to imply you were drab and boring. I'm sorry, Elise. That's not what I meant." But his words sounded hollow and empty.

In the end, he had refused to return it, and she had refused to wear it. How stupid they both had been.

She looked fragile, defeated, and lost standing on the platform. Her dark-brown eyes were shining with the salty flood of tears she hadn't allowed herself to shed until that moment. The indigo dress, once deemed preposterous, wrapped her in a melancholy embrace.

"So, you're leaving me?" she had asked him as she gripped the counter in their kitchen for support.

"What do you mean? I'm enlisting, Elise. There's a war going on, in case you didn't realise."

"That's not what I asked, and that's not what I meant, Thomas, and you know it. You're not just enlisting. You are running away. You don't want this life. You never have."

"You're being ridiculous. There's almost no work here. The military will give us money and a pension."

"There's plenty of work on the farm."

"I'm not a farmer." His voice was low and angry. "That has never been the life I wanted. You know that."

"Just what is the life you want then, Thomas? To be a soldier? To fight Germans? To save the world?"

"What is so wrong with that, Elise? What is wrong with wanting to feel like what you do matters? That I can make a difference?"

"You do matter, Thomas. You matter to us. You have a family right here. Make a difference for us. Fight for us."

He had no words for her. She was right. He needed more. He loved them, but he needed more. That was the last time they spoke. He had packed his bag and left for the train depot in Kingston the next day before she was awake.

Thomas leaned forward and put his hand up against the glass. Time suspended, and a shared history, a cascade of memories and unspoken words, converged on them. Her hand flickered slightly in a silent acknowledgement that she saw him, too. The train rolled and lurched slightly, preparing to move, and the indigo dress billowed lightly in the breeze, whispering a story of a love that stood stoically in their tableau of a final goodbye.

As fast as he had seen her, she was gone, swallowed up by the platform, the crowd, and the distance that separated them long before he boarded that train. His heart squeezed in his chest, and he felt saddened to know he had hurt her. He had tried to tell her joining the army was to help their family. They struggled so much financially, and he hated it. That was why she was so mad about that damn indigo dress. So, he joined, and he was leaving. He was old enough he could avoid going. Being a farmer was also a way out, but of course, he wasn't a farmer, was he? He had responsibilities there. But it was no use. They both knew it was not the life he wanted. He didn't really know what he wanted his life to look like, but it wasn't a tractor and fields. It wasn't poverty and fighting over dresses. He wanted adventure. He wanted excitement. He wanted to see the world. Didn't he?

"Okay there, Tommy Boy?" Karl asked his friend as he came into their compartment. He gave him a slap on the back and brought Thomas back to the present. The ghost in the indigo blue dress was gone.

"Oh, I will be, pal. Goodbyes are just always hard," he had replied. "Especially when we don't know how long it will be until we're home again."

"Don't worry, buddy. We'll make it back and have some stories to tell when we get here."

They had settled into their seats on the train, and then began their long journey to England and beyond. Looking out the window, watching their homes slip further and further away, he had leaned his head on the window and fallen asleep.

When he woke, the view outside had hardly changed. Farms and small towns, one after another, raced by. So much was the same, yet things were different as well. They had no idea then what they would experience. What they would survive. What they would have to live with. The lush meadows and green rolling hills of the countryside gave way to the sombre darkness of the city and the depot. The train slowed as it entered the station, giving a great smoky sigh as it settled for a brief rest.

"Well, look here, Sleeping Beauty awakes." Karl gave Thomas a warm clap on the shoulder. "We're here, Tommy Boy. Let's get these guys organised."

He remembered the excitement they had as he and Karl got off the train. They grabbed their gear and called out to the men travelling with them to start getting their belongings down from the overhead compartments and get ready to disembark.

"Make sure you have all your kit, lads. Don't want to start the first day with a march because someone was lax, eh?" Thomas called out to the younger men. He wasn't that much higher in rank, but he was quite a bit older than most of them. He had joined at a later age, which was part of the reason he could have gotten out of it as a farmer, but he wanted to serve. During their months of training, he had gained the respect of those men despite his rank and perhaps in part because of it. He already viewed them as "his lads."

The depot was surprisingly busy with the everyday normalities of life. Goods were loaded and unloaded. Men in business suits travelled for work as though there wasn't a war happening. Behind them, he noticed a group of young women laughing and giggling as they readied to board the train with their suitcases, clearly off on holiday. Their gaiety seemed a stark contrast to what he had imagined England would look and feel like after being under attack.

"Right! Let's clear out of the way and find our transport!" Thomas shouted over the din of the platform and train engines. He glanced back at the young women as they gathered to board the train, wondering how often, if ever, he would see anyone so light-hearted. He couldn't help but smile watching them. Really, what were they all fighting for if not for moments like that? He then strode after his lads, who bore an equal excitement for the adventure they imagined they were about to begin.

As Thomas shared the story of his journey to England, Vivian couldn't help but be taken back to a day at the train station when she and her girlfriends were excited to be going on *hols* together. How innocent they were back then as they giggled and tittered over young men and what outfits to wear. The station was bustling with people, including soldiers. They seemed to endlessly stream out of the train. Every new set looked the same, fresh uniforms and clean kits.

"Viv! Viv! Come on, let's go!" one of the women called out. She offered her arm to her friend still standing on the platform.

"I'm coming, Fern!" She laughed and took her friend's hand. "My goodness, I packed too much! My bag is so heavy!"

A porter appeared out of nowhere. "Here, miss, let me help." He took Vivian's bag and assisted her onto the train. As he held the suitcase up to her from the platform, he almost dropped it. Her eyes!

My God! he thought. *They're like molten amber and emeralds fused together.* Flustered, he managed to stammer, "H-have a safe trip, ladies."

"Thank you so much," they giddily said together, rushing off to catch up with their friends. Vivian was completely unaware of the effect she'd had on the poor porter.

"You two are so slow! We've already started pouring the sauce for everyone to celebrate our hols," tittered May. When she saw Fern's look of concern, she then added, "Discreetly, of course!"

It wasn't technically legal to drink on the train, but it also wasn't illegal. May was the leader of libations of the group. "We have seats over here," she pointed to an empty section.

"*Sorry*," Fern said with great exaggeration. "Viv was being swooned over again." She swiped her arm dramatically across her forehead, and everyone broke out in hysterics.

Vivian laughed as well even though she thought her friend was mistaken. "Oh, Fern. Stop." She was often naïve and thought everyone was just nice. She had no idea the effect she had on people.

Sliding into the window seat, Viv noticed a fresh set of soldiers had arrived and were getting sorted out on the platform. They shared that energy of not having seen battle yet. She wished they could keep that feeling forever but knew all too well it wouldn't last. Those men would see things that would affect them forever.

She winced. Her new sandals were pinching her feet. "I knew I should have tried to break them in a bit at home." As she looked down to rub her foot, she noticed a small notecard on the floor. There was a single violet pressed onto it with the single word *Home* written beneath. She smiled at the piece of paper and wondered who might be missing it. Placing the delicate flower in her wallet, she rested her head on the window and watched the platform begin to move away as the train set off. The darkness of the city slowly gave way to the lush meadows and green rolling hills of the countryside.

24

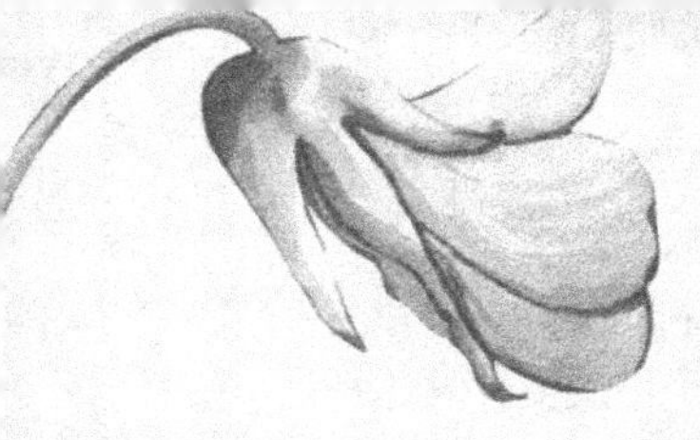

Chapter Three

The morning light was just beginning to push through the crack in the drapes. Dark and cheerless as the singed remains of many of the buildings outside, they served as a reminder of why there was a need for total blackout conditions. Vivian had recently bought a bright floral fabric to disguise the gloomy textile. It wasn't a true drapery fabric, and it didn't cover the entire opening, but she wanted to add some cheer to the otherwise depressing and oppressive tone of her room.

Her communications unit had been assigned the house after it was rented from the owners by the Auxiliary Territorial Service. They had given her consent to add her touches to the space. The other girls thought it might be a nice idea for the other rooms in the house as well, if such a luxury could be found in sufficient quantities and time made to do the work. As a result, several rooms had pieces of bright fabric loosely attached to blackout curtains like a cheerful patchwork quilt.

Vivian could feel the warmth of the early light on her face. She lay still, her eyes closed, and allowed it to soak in. There was an eagerness in her body to rise and meet the day, but she resisted it to relish the radiance for just a moment more.

The cause of her anticipation was, of course, the handsome soldier she met yesterday. Thomas. His name was like honey on her tongue, and the thought of him made her pulse quicken. She smiled with her eyes closed, picturing him in her mind. His broad, easy smile and his mischievous blue eyes.

He had walked her home last night and held her hand the whole way. They talked and talked and arrived far too quickly at their destination. Viv had wanted to invite him in—into her room, into her bed—but she dared not. The rooming house had a strict no-male-guests policy, and besides, she had just met the man.

She smiled again at the memory of the walk home and stretched, her body rubbing against the thin sheet that covered her. The familiar sounds of the other rooming house residents made their way to her. The laughter of ladies fighting for space in the bathroom and chatting in the halls filled the air. Vivian put on her robe and picked up her toothbrush and towel. Opening her door, she was immediately greeted by her friend Beth.

Beth was a warm-natured girl with black hair, pale but smooth skin, and hazel eyes. She and Vivian worked together at the communications depot and had become good friends right away. "Good morning, Viv. How was the wedding?"

"Glorious!" she announced with a little too much enthusiasm.

"Oh really?" Beth stopped and turned back to her friend. "Why, Viv, are you blushing?"

"Possibly." She playfully looked away, and they giggled together as they walked towards the washroom.

"I'm guessing it isn't because Fern was a radiant bride that you are so flushed." Beth teased her by gently pinching her warm cheeks.

"Elizabeth Ann Armstrong, don't be naughty." Viv pretended to be offended by the inference there was more to the soft colour that had risen in her cheeks. "Need I remind you that I am an engaged person?" she asked with artificial indignance.

"Need I remind *you*?" Beth quipped back affectionately. "I'm glad you had a lovely night, Viv. Honestly, you needed it. You've been so distraught with the lack of news from Aaron."

Vivian paused in the hallway, the smile on her face disappearing and the lightness she had felt earlier crushed by the weight of her guilt and shame.

"Oh, Beth, I know, and I feel just terrible. I haven't thought of him even once since the wedding, and here I was flirting with Karl's best friend Thomas the whole night. I'm a terrible person."

A sense of treachery wove its way into her being. Aaron Chieftain, her fiancé, had been fighting in the north of Africa. She'd had no word from him for many months and was worried the worst had happened. It wasn't like him not to write. She knew there were times when the soldiers weren't permitted to send letters home for fear, they might give away details about an operation that could cost many lives. She just hoped there was a delay in the mail, and she would hear from him soon.

"No, you're not, Viv! There is no harm in admiration. Who is this man who managed to take your mind off things?" Beth placed her arm around Vivian's shoulders in a comforting and matronly way. She had a kind and gentle demeanour about her. Many of the girls from the unit went to her with their stories of heartbreak for words of encouragement and consoling tea and chinwags, but they also relied on her for her common sense and ability to work through problems.

"Oh, Beth!" she said in a breathy voice. "His name is Thomas Cooper, and he's Karl's best friend. I cannot believe I've been so smitten by someone I barely know. How is it even possible?" Her eyes welled up with tears. She felt so torn and horrible to have betrayed Aaron, her childhood sweetheart, so easily.

"You haven't done anything of the sort. Having feelings, beautiful human feelings, are what help us get through each day. We mustn't feel badly for wishing for happiness. Who knows what tomorrow will bring?" Beth hugged her friend and wiped her tears with a handkerchief.

Vivian gave her a weak smile. "Thanks, Beth. I know you're right, and of course I still care for Aaron. This was just a fleeting feeling. A handsome man who gave me some attention when I needed it. It was flattering, but I'll be Aaron's wife when he safely returns home to me. He's a good man, and we've known each other almost our whole lives."

She straightened up a bit, feeling a little better about herself. She had a moment of weakness, that was all. It happened to everyone. What mattered most was she knew she was meant to be with Aaron, and she loved him, not some soldier she had just met. It was ridiculous to think of anything else.

"I best finish getting ready for my shift," she said. She shrugged against Beth who shrugged back against Vivian.

"All right then! That's the spirit. No woe-is-me business." Beth laughed and poked Vivian in the ribs affectionately. Viv then hugged her friend.

"Thanks, Beth. What would I do without you?" She continued to walk with her friend towards the washroom to freshen up. Her plan was to have a quick breakfast before rushing off to work at the communications depot. They would be busy, as they always were, after an air raid.

"The wedding was lovely. Fern looked beautiful," Viv noted.

"What happened when the bombings started?"

"Thankfully, we had just finished the ceremony and everyone, all of the guests, the minister, and Mrs. Witt who plays the organ for the church, piled into the cellar."

"Oh, my goodness! That was good timing. Was anyone hurt?"

"A few scrapes, bumps, and knocks. The cellar was about as solid as they come. The passageway gave us a little trouble with some loose stones but nothing too serious." Vivian thought about Mrs. Witt and how strong and brave she had been. "That Mrs. Witt, she's a tough one."

"I'm glad it all ended well with no one genuinely hurt," Beth said.

"Will I see you at supper later?" Vivian asked over her shoulder.

"I have an afternoon shift today. Won't be home until lights out. Hope things aren't overly hectic for all of you today, pet."

"Oh goodness! I totally forgot you were on duty last night! Is everyone okay?" Vivian stopped in her tracks at the realisation she'd been so distracted by Thomas, her feelings, and the wedding that she'd forgotten to ask how her friend's shift had gone.

"It wasn't the worst we've seen," Beth admitted with a shrug. "Always easier to tell the tolls taken in the light of day. We will prevail as always."

Vivian nodded and smiled again, calling out to Beth as she walked away, "Hey Elizabeth Armstrong, you take bloody good care. I love you, you silly sod muffin!"

Waving back, Beth laughed. "Hey Vivian Waltman, you take bloody good care, too. I love you back, you silly sod muffin!" She then went back into her room to rest. She'd had a long night and was looking forward to a well-deserved nap.

30

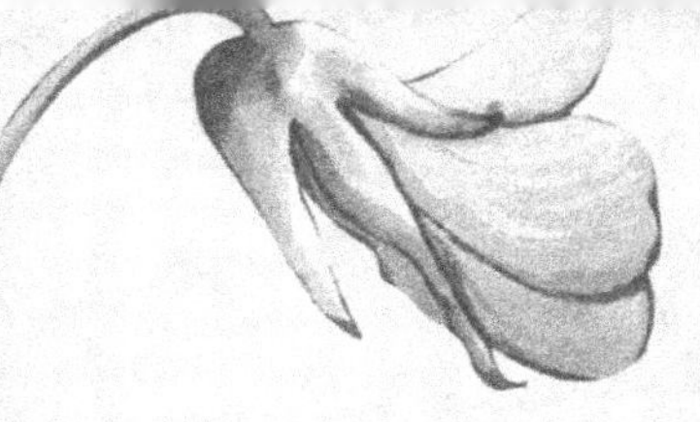

Chapter Four

The air was warm, and a light breeze playfully licked at Vivian's hair. A curl had come loose from under her cap and brushed across her forehead. She hummed cheerfully to herself as she walked along the path that wound through the park.

The trees were full and lush, and the sun was still quite high even though it was late afternoon. It danced on the leaves, making them sparkle in a way that was as joyful as she felt. As she walked, she saw couples holding hands and sitting close to each other on benches. Gentle kisses, bodies touching. It made her blush as she thought of Thomas and touching or kissing him.

The spout and body of a fountain near the entrance to the park sat crumbling and broken in large, charred pieces. Miraculously, the basin at the bottom remained intact. It seemed to be a source of fun for a family sitting beside it as their young son splashed in the water, oblivious to the missing head and torso of the statue that once stood on top.

Before she even saw him, she became keenly aware of him. She sensed his presence, then heard his laughter. Full of mischief. She could picture his face before he came into

view. His twinkling blue eyes, crooked smile, and full lips. Vivian felt herself flush again, and her heart jolted when she finally laid eyes on the man.

He was unaware of her and in the thick of a large group of children. They were chasing him, and Thomas deliberately slowed down so they could catch him. They fell down in a clatter of howls of laughter. She watched him like that. Loving the affection of those kids. Finding joy in the simple pleasure of playing in a park amidst the rubble of a village that had been targeted for destruction.

Thomas suddenly froze. He was on the ground, covered in giggling, out-of-breath children. His back was turned to her, but she knew he had become aware of her presence. Her breath caught in her chest, and her pulse quickened. He rolled over, grinning from ear to ear as he searched for her.

He couldn't believe how beautiful she was. There was a quiet elegance about her. Her skin had a warm kiss from the sun, yet it looked like porcelain. He was caught in the moment as he breathed hard from playing with the kids and from the emotions that hit him when he saw her. Her eyes shined brightly, like warm honey and new grass. He noticed the wisp of hair playing with her forehead.

"Well, there you are!" he called to her as he climbed out of the muddle. He was out of breath and unable to offer more than a wry grin.

The children tittered when they noticed how the two adults were looking at each other. They realised their playtime was over in favour of the new company.

"See you again soon, sir!" Freddy, a small blond lad shouted as he wandered off towards the swings. "Thank you for playing with us. See you tomorrow?"

"You bet! But next time I get a head start." Thomas laughed and ruffled the coal-black hair of Simon, who had lingered back. He was probably eight or nine years old, with pale skin that was covered in freckles. His strength was apparent despite the fact that he was so slight and wiry.

Simon ran after his friends, smiling and waving. The rest

of the children shouted their goodbyes, and Thomas grinned, promising to return for a rematch.

He picked a bag up off the ground nearby as he walked towards Vivian. He took her in as he approached. She was so young and innocent looking, and her eyes, those eyes, wide and bright. Forgetting himself, he hugged her and kissed her cheek.

Flustered, she pushed him away and looked around to see if anyone noticed. Her family was very conservative in that regard. "Thomas!" Vivian admonished. She smiled shyly, and he took her hand as they walked in the direction she had been going when she found him.

"Shall we find a nice spot to eat?" He gestured to the bag he had just picked up.

"That sounds lovely."

She let him lead her to the small pond in the centre of the park. As they walked, they talked about their days. She told him how it had been a busy but calm one, with a lot of calls to be made and coordinated but not with the urgency they felt while under fire.

He told her about a training they would be doing later in the week. Nothing of consequence, so she wouldn't worry. It wasn't untrue. His regiment was doing some training on driving through water and sandy terrain.

"Here's a good spot." Thomas opened the bag and pulled out a blanket for them to sit on. He laid it out and offered his hand to Vivian. Grasping it, she sat down and watched as he pulled out several small packets from the bag.

Each one was wrapped to conceal the contents. The first contained a large wedge of cheese. Vivian gasped when she saw it. She knew that alone would have taken significant resources to procure. The next revealed a tin of sardines, some saltines, and two pieces of cooked chicken.

"My goodness, Thomas!" she exclaimed at the decadence of the picnic. "How in the world did you get all of this?"

"The best is yet to come!" He grinned, ignoring her question as he pulled out a bottle of wine and two glasses.

Vivian's eyes widened, and her mouth opened. She let out a giddy laugh of delight. "Oh, my heavens. I don't believe it. It's too much, Thomas. How did you—"

He cut her off, placing his finger to her lips. "I have one chance to do this right the first time," he said, leaving his finger there as he spoke, "and I aim to sweep you off your feet, Miss Vivian Waltman." He caressed her cheek. "One last thing …" He pulled the last packet from his bag and handed it to her, nodding at her to open it as she looked at him, confused.

"What else could you possibly have?" She opened the packet and gasped. The aroma reached her nose at the same time she beheld the smooth, rich brown squares. "Chocolate! It's been a long time since I've had chocolate." She paused and glanced up at him. Their eyes locked, and he grinned happily at her. He looked like a little boy at that moment, and she couldn't help but laugh and grin back at him.

"Let's dig in." He pulled out his knife and cut some of the cheese as she arranged the fare on the napkins. Some chicken, cheese, a few saltines, and sardines. Lastly, he poured some wine into each glass.

He held his up. "To first impressions!"

She giggled as she grabbed hers. "To first impressions!"

Viv looked into his eyes again and had to immediately look back down. *I think I'll need to get used to my breath getting caught in my chest*, she thought. She prayed her face wasn't flushing as hot as her entire body was. She'd never felt so terrified yet so comfortable and trusting with someone in her life. She had never met a man like Thomas. She felt as though she had known him forever.

They ate and talked and laughed until the wine and food were gone, and they were resting comfortably on the blanket, fully at ease and happy. After relaxing there a while, they tidied up the remnants of the picnic and settled back onto the blanket.

"It's getting a bit dark. I should walk you home, Viv. I don't want to, but I also don't want to get you into trouble with your house mother." He chuckled and stood up, helping her to her feet. He held onto her hands, not wanting to break the connection to her soft skin. The electricity between them was palpable, and he could see the pulse in her throat. He wanted to kiss her there where it throbbed. Instead, he leaned down to kiss her on the lips and heard her rapidly breathe in.

She could feel the warmth of his breath as his lips grazed hers. Her eyes fluttered shut, and she tilted her chin up. Gently, tenderly, he kissed her. There was an ardour in them both they were fighting to keep at bay. He couldn't disrespect her in such a public place, no matter how much he wanted to kiss her more deeply or how much she wanted him to.

"I better walk you home before I make a fool of myself." He placed his forehead on hers as he took a moment to collect himself. His hand held her chin and cheek as he looked down at her. "Can I see you again tomorrow and every day after that?"

"Thomas …" Vivian's voice faded. She needed to tell him the truth. Tell him she was engaged. That she belonged to someone else. "I need to tell you something. It's just that—"

Thomas put his finger on her lips again to silence her. "No. You don't. You don't need to say a word except that you'll agree to see me tomorrow. One day won't harm anything. Please, Viv." He cupped her cheek and turned her face toward his. He could see the torment in her eyes.

All she could do was nod. She didn't trust her own voice.

They walked along the path towards her rooming house. The blackout rules meant there were no streetlights or even lights from inside the homes they passed on their way. Everyone kept their windows covered. The bombings had been so frequent they were concealed more than not. Easier to be missed in the dark by the next blitz.

While they were keenly aware that a bomb could be dropped at any moment, they had never felt happier than they did right then. Walking hand in hand and talking about their friends and the silly escapades of the soldiers at the camp. The pranks they played on each other and sometimes gruelling training and marches they had in full kit.

When they arrived at the rooming house steps, Thomas took Viv's hand and kissed it before holding it to his cheek. He closed his eyes and sighed. "Will I see you tomorrow? We can go to the Dorchester. Do you like to dance?"

"Certainly." She wasn't sure why she said that. She didn't really like dancing, and she wasn't very good. Having strict Church of England parents, it wasn't something she had grown up with. But she didn't care. She would swim in a lake with alligators if it meant being with Thomas again.

"I'll pick you up here at eighteen thirty hours then. Is that okay?"

"I'll be ready. See you tomorrow, Thomas." She smiled and turned, heading up the stairs. She stopped at the door. Looking back at him, she felt an urge to run down the steps and jump into his arms. Instead, she grinned and fell into the house, pulling the door behind her.

She was quickly surrounded by her shrieking housemates, begging for details of her handsome escort.

"In the morning. In the morning." She smiled, trying to pull away but laughing along with them. They all did that sort of thing to each other anytime one of them went out. It was their greatest source of entertainment.

"Boo!" They all pretended to be annoyed.

"At least tell us his name, Viv! You can't leave us with nothing when you look so, well, flushed." Marie pulled her sleeve and cupped Vivian's chin with a saucy flash of amusement in her eyes.

Vivian closed her eyes and saw his face. She smiled, and they all roared again.

"Oh, my goodness! You cannot make a face like that and not share! It would be simply cruel," Marie cried.

She pretended to huff resignation by telling them. "His name is Thomas. He's a Canadian soldier, and I met him at Fern's wedding. He was the best man."

"Oh, I bet he was. He certainly looks as though he's up for the job, Viv," Marie teased. All the girls, Viv included, laughed at the innuendo of the remark.

"Marie!" Vivian tried to sound serious, but her grin gave her away. "You will all just have to wait until I have more to tell." She smirked as she pulled away and floated up the staircase. She wanted to close her eyes and relive the evening, to dream of Thomas and see his face in her mind again.

Vivian raced upstairs with the roar of laughter following her all the way to her room. She got ready for bed in lightning time. Then, climbing underneath her sheets, she closed her eyes, smiling and sighing happily as Thomas' face swam back into her head, and she drifted off to sleep in his arms.

38

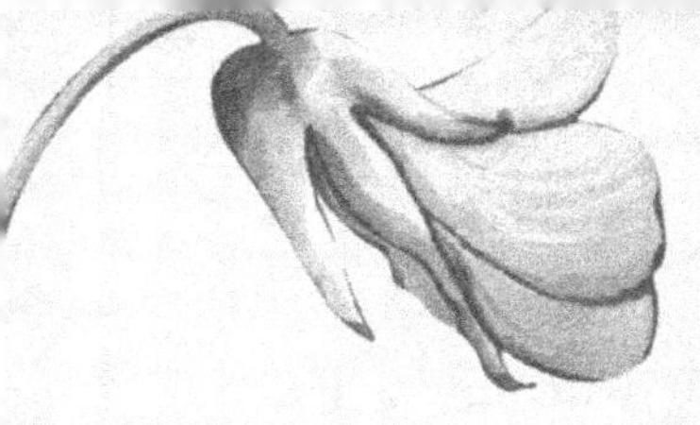

Chapter Five

The hue and warmth of twilight kissed the horizon as an exhausted Vivian approached the steps of the rooming house. Fatigue weighed heavily on her young frame from yet another night of bombings and the endless coordination and rerouting she and her shift mates had needed to do. Debris had held them at their station well past their shift, and all she wanted to do was sleep.

Fast thinking and even anticipating where they may need to send support next, had become second nature to her by then. After almost a year with the ATS, Vivian had become acclimated to the intense pressure and rapid pace that was inherently part of the job. Where lives could be lost if she wasn't able to manage her emotions.

"Focus on the task at hand," Beth had always said. "Don't think about what the locations may look like. How many dead there might be. If you focus on that, there will be a lot more dead." It was their job to minimise that.

Grateful for an extra day to recover her energy before being required to return to her post, she paused at the bottom of the stairs leading up to the black wood door. Inside, it would be bustling with the tittering of her housemates, an energy level

she was not prepared to match. She needed to afford herself a short moment to collect her thoughts.

Before she could bring herself to start up the stairs, the heavy door was thrown open, and Beth came rushing out.

"Viv! Oh, thank goodness you're home! We were so worried. What happened?" She met Vivian on the steps, hugging her fiercely.

"We're all fine. We just had to stay put after the bombing. There was too much mess about outside for us to be able to get out or for the new shift to get in for that matter."

"Are you okay? Was anyone hurt?"

"I promise, we're all just fine. It was not nearly as bad as it sounded. Not for us at least." Vivian smiled as if that would prove she really was "just fine."

Beth looked at her friend again, trying to penetrate her smile, and seemed summarily satisfied she was telling the truth. "Still, not a great shift it sounds. I guess this is our world at the moment, and we do what we need to."

"I know, Beth. Honestly, I'm okay. We do what we must, and you're right, this is our world right now. We have to keep getting up every time we get knocked down. There is no other alternative. We are not losing this damn war." To prove her point, she straightened up and stood a little taller, lifting her chin in defiance of the daily attacks.

Beth nodded in agreement. Vivian had been a very young woman when she arrived a year ago at the boarding house. She was still a kind and gentle person, but there was a strength that had grown out of what she had witnessed. Beth was a little saddened at the change, but also admired Vivian for not withering in the face of the darkness and pain as so many others had.

"Okay then, you need some food, and I'm sure no one will resent your having a bath before bed." She smiled and hugged Vivian once more.

A bath, what a luxury that was, Vivian thought as she let out a sigh. "I think that sounds perfect." As she turned to open the door, Beth put a hand on her arm.

"Viv, wait. There's something else." Beth had paused them on the top step, not wanting her to enter the house until she'd spoken to her. She pulled a letter out of her pocket and looked down at it then slowly back up at her friend. "There's a letter that arrived for you, pet."

Vivian couldn't tell what emotion her friend was feeling as she handed her the correspondence but held onto her hands as she did so. It would seem like it wasn't good news, and Vivian was instantly worried for Thomas even though she knew his regiment had not left the station. He wrote to her often, telling her about the simple day-to-day events and the funny stories of his men. They saw each other as often as he was allowed. She looked down at the letter being held tightly by them both, and she knew the handwriting instantly. The air rushed from her lungs.

"Aaron!"

Viv's breathing became rapid and erratic, and her knees weakened. Slowly, she lowered herself to the slate step, fearful that if she didn't, she would crash down upon it instead. Her hands were shaking so hard she couldn't open the letter. Gently, Beth took it from her.

With it open, she closed her eyes for a moment to steal the strength she was worried she would need to read on. She had not heard from her fiancé in almost a year, and even his mother had presumed the worst.

My darling Vivvy,

I know you must be frantic with worry, having not heard from me for so very long. I will start by saying I am okay. I am not sure if word reached you, but ten of us were taken by Rommel's men and held all this time. Thanks to our boys, we've been freed, and I will be on my way home for some rest and recovery after some debriefing and consults. I will be home to your arms soon, my darling."

Love,
Your Aaron

"Beth! He's alive. He's alive, and he's coming home." She was giddy with relief to know the man she had held dear since childhood was safe and returning home to her.

"Oh, that's wonderful news."

The two hugged and laughed and cried on the step together, still sitting on the hard slate. Vivian leaned against her friend, reading the letter over and over. As the news of Aaron's safety sank in, another realisation hit her as well. Thomas.

Sitting up, Vivian looked at her friend, her eyes flooding with tears. Beth knew the tears were not for Aaron and pulled her friend to her again in a comforting hug.

"You've no need for guilt over your time with Thomas. This is not just war but life. You are alive, my dear, and you deserve happiness."

"I'm a terrible person, Beth," She sobbed. "I thought Aaron was dead, and over these last few months I've allowed myself to fall in love with Thomas."

"Viv! Stop being so terrible to yourself. You just said you thought Aaron was dead. For heaven's sake, we all did and just didn't want to say it. More importantly, did you hear what else you said?" Beth held her by the shoulders, staring into her golden eyes.

Vivian was confused. "What do you mean?"

"You're in love with Thomas." Beth beamed at her.

"I ... I did, didn't I? I mean, I ..." Vivian tried to understand the whirl of emotions running through her body. It only took a moment for things to become crystal clear. She loved Thomas with her heart and soul. She loved him like she had loved no other, not even her dearest Aaron. "Beth, I need to tell Aaron. I need to tell him before he comes home and finds out. He deserves that."

"Yes, I suppose you do. It can wait until after you have something to eat and a good night's sleep, though. You've been through the ringer today, pet, and need to rest first."

She could only nod in agreement. Beth was right as usual. It had been over seventy-two hours since she had last slept or eaten properly. The letters could wait until morning. Arm in arm, they went into the rooming house to the boisterous and cheery lot inside.

"Hey, Vivian Waltman," she called back as they parted ways, and she walked down the hallway to her own room. "You take bloody good care. I love you, you silly sod muffin!"

Viv could not help but smile. "Hey, Elizabeth Armstrong. You take bloody good care, too. I love you back, you silly sod muffin."

44

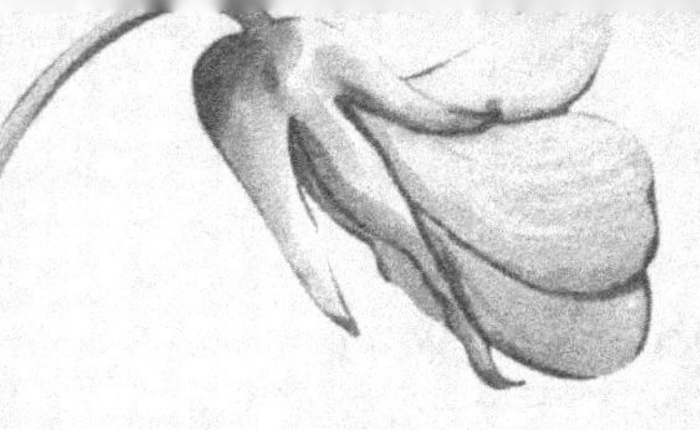

Chapter Six

Vivian woke to the quiet solitude of her room. She had completely collapsed from exhaustion and slept so deeply and soundly she was not sure what time it was. Even the turmoil of the news that Aaron was still alive was no match for the sheer physical need for her body to rest.

There was a letter she needed to write. That damn, awful letter. Before doing anything else, Vivian wanted to tell Aaron the truth. The truth that she was relieved and happy for his safety, but she had fallen in love with another man. Thomas. As much as it hurt her to think she didn't love Aaron anymore, it also thrilled her to finally admit she loved Thomas. The very thought of him brought a broad smile to her face and a flutter to her heart.

Sitting at the small desk in her room, she pulled the stationary out of the drawer. There she sat, holding the pen, staring at the paper for several minutes, unsure how to start.

My darling,

I cannot tell you how happy I am to hear that you are safe and well. I have no words for all the emotions I am feeling. I must tell you something that weighs heavily on my heart, however. I cannot allow it to continue or allow you to come home without knowing the truth. The love that once carried us has taken an unexpected turn. In your absence, I found solace with another. As much as it breaks my heart to tell you, I cannot deny my connection to this man. I must be fully truthful and tell you that I have fallen in love with him. I am so sorry for the pain this may inflict upon you. You have survived so much, and it is cruel to add to that pain. Not telling you the truth would be disrespectful to the relationship we shared. This revelation can never take away the love I held for you, my first true love.

I wish you joy and a long, well-lived life.

Love always,
Viv

The paper bore the weight of Vivian's confession. As the ink dried and absorbed into the paper, it sealed the fate of her love. How could she have done this to Aaron? He was a good man. The conflict constricted her chest, and tears fell from her eyes. Tears of relief that Aaron was safe. Tears for the loss of their love. Tears for the pain she knew she was going to inflict upon him.

Yet, despite everything, she knew she was meant to be with Thomas. She loved him, and somehow, she knew he loved her, too. The thought lifted her heart and loosened the tether gripping it. Wiping her eyes again, she took out a second set of stationary. As deeply as she needed to write Aaron to tell him the truth, she also felt compelled to write to Thomas and

tell him she loved him. She knew it was possible they may never see each other again. He could be called away and never return. But she couldn't let another moment go by
without having told him what was in her heart.

My darling,

I came to a realisation today that has lifted and lightened my heart and is giving me courage I have never felt before. In the echoes of my heartbeat, I feel yours. I love you. I cannot chance not saying it and risk you never knowing it. This is not a fleeting emotion or a delicate flower that will wither in the heat of honest examination.

I know that the future is unsure. The prospect of not seeing you again fills my heart with an ache I have never known. I feel we are kindred spirits, connected through many lifetimes only to find each other again, here in this time and place.

You do not judge my youth and lack of experience, rather you bolster me for it. Your strength and compassion have touched my soul, and I bare myself to you fully. I love you. Whatever fate intertwines us and the winds that guide our paths, I know we are meant to be together.

Love always,
Viv

The soft glow of a single lamp helped cast a warmth about the room, adding to the fervour she felt from having opened herself and her heart on the page for Thomas. Surrounded by the echoes of creaking floorboards and the muffled sounds of life outside, Vivian grappled with the realisation that her heart had embarked on an unforeseen journey—one that led to Thomas, the unexpected harbinger of love in the chaos of wartime London.

"Viv!" Beth knocked briskly on her door. "Viv! Are you up, my darling dearest? We are up for it tonight," she playfully called through the door.

"I'm up. I'm up," Vivian hollered back, laughing to herself at the way Beth could instantly lift anyone's mood. She was that person. The person whose simple presence put you at ease and made you see the brighter side of any day. Folding the letters, she put them aside. They would need to wait to be posted until after her shift.

There was a bustling of activity at the communications centre as Viv and Beth arrived for their shift. They checked in with those leaving, exchanging brief pleasantries. There was always a bit of an overlap with part of the previous shift. Their captain, Josh Hastings, felt it helped to ensure continuity in information, so no shift was ever unaware of what had transpired during the few hours before.

"Evening, everyone. Any action to report?" Captain Hastings asked.

It was the usual pleasantries. No one actually wanted to hear anything but "nothing to report" or "boring day." Thankfully, Betty smiled and didn't disappoint them.

"Nah, it's been pretty quiet. No news is good news, right?"

Beth smiled back. "Let's hope it stays that way."

Captain Hastings strolled over with a friendly smile, ready to debrief the incoming shift. He was an easy-going bloke who enjoyed the banter among the ladies. The post had been handed to him because his superior officers didn't feel he commanded the respect of his men. "Too much of a gentle spirit," he had said. Hastings didn't mind in the least. He didn't miss being asked to send men forward to face death.

The communications post required quick thinking and a calm mind. His strengths. It didn't require purposely putting anyone in harm's way. All they were to do was listen to the reports of damage and get that information to the emergency services. Occasionally, they would get intel on the incoming aircraft, but they still reported it upward. Less gentle spirited men would decide how to deal with those situations.

"Evening, ladies. As Betty said, it's been quiet. But you know how it goes in this city. One minute it's calm, the next it's chaos."

"Always keeping us on our toes, Captain." Simone chirped merrily as she, Vivian and Beth checked the logs, signed off, and swapped seats with the outgoing crew.

Captain Hastings smiled. "Wouldn't have it any other way. All right, let's get started. Viv, Beth, you'll take the primary. Betty, Simone, Mary, Sarah, you're up for support. Let's keep those lines open and clear."

"Yes, sir. Signing on. Date September 7, 1940. Weather is fair. The sky is clear."

"Thank you, Betty." Hastings turned to the table with the map of their quadrant. "Let's have a look at the status of things. Looks pretty tame. A few smouldering but intact, it seems."

"All in all, we are in good shape, sir." Betty was also checking the map for the location and status of crews and support.

The depot was quite comfortable as depots went. The girls had set up a proper tea station with no genuine argument from Hastings. Tired of the hard wooden chairs they sat on all shift, a couple of the more creative ladies had knitted and crocheted cushions. It didn't take long for Hastings to secure one for himself.

"So, Captain, any plans for your day off?" Everyone turned to listen to his answer.

"Ah, you know me, Simone. Probably just catch up on some reading. Maybe take the missus out to the pub if we're lucky."

"Sounds lovely, Captain. Wish we could join you, but duty calls," Mary lamented.

The conversation had settled into an untroubled rhythm when the air raid sirens started to blare. Instantly, the mood shifted as the team sprang into action, their training kicking in.

Sarah looked at everyone and shouted, "Here we go again. Incoming reports, everyone. Note the time in the log, Betty, sixteen hundred hours. Let's get to work."

Vivian and Beth exchanged a determined look as they prepared to face the challenges of the coming hours, their resolve unwavering despite the danger looming outside.

The air was thick with tension as Beth, Vivian, and the rest of the unit remained locked on at their posts, their fingers flying across the keys as they relayed urgent messages and tracked the locations of where they needed to send support.

"Captain, reports of high damage and injuries. Here are the coordinates." Simone handed yet another slip of paper to Hastings so he could adjust the markings on the map. Explosions rocked the building, causing dust to fill the air and debris to rain down around them. The bombs were almost nonstop and hitting far closer than they'd ever experienced before. Despite their fear, they continued their vital work, knowing many lives depended on their actions. Without them, ambulances and firemen would not know where to go first, where the worst of the damages and risks were.

Her voice strained with urgency, Beth called out to the others, "Keep it up, everyone! They can't get on without us!" The slogan for the ATS was something they called out to each other all the time, usually more for jokes than when they were truly in full gear.

Vivian nodded, feeling enlivened by Beth's words. "You know it, Beth. They can't get on with—"

Before she could finish her sentence, there was a deafening explosion. The building shook violently as part of the wall and ceiling collapsed, burying Beth and Vivian under a pile of rubble.

"Beth! Viv! Oh my God! Are you all right?! Sarah! Help me! We have to get them out of there!" Mary had been flung a few feet but had somehow not been hit or injured at all. She was able to recover her bearings quickly and set into action.

The two women frantically grabbed chunks of concrete and wood. "Carefully! Carefully!" called Hastings as he rushed to help. "We don't want to topple more onto them in our effort to get them out." His voice was cool and controlled. Moving more cautiously, the team worked together to clear away enough debris to reach Vivian and Beth.

They were able to get to Vivian quickly. Coughing, she opened her eyes and reached out to help dislodge herself.

"Oh, Viv! Thank goodness. Are you hurt? Do you feel anything?" Mary asked as she wiped Vivian's face with her handkerchief.

"I think I'm okay. Holy hell! What happened? Where is Beth? Beth!" Viv was panicking for her friend.

"We are still getting to her, Viv. Don't worry. Let's get you out of there. Can you move? Slowly. Slowly." Mary was intent on distracting Vivian and helping her get out from under the remaining rock and junk. She exchanged looks briefly with Simone. She and Moorings had managed to clear most of the debris off Beth, and her face has gone white and stern.

Helping Vivian sit up, Mary tried to keep her from going to Beth. It was pointless, of course.

"Beth! Oh, Beth!" Vivian cried out as she saw her unconscious friend. They all looked at each other. Vivian's face had become resolute as she took in the large piece of the iron support embedded in Beth's side. The look on everyone's face communicated all she needed to know.

Hastings had stopped them from clearing any more debris for fear that it would dislodge the metal, and Beth would immediately bleed out. Keeping it in place was their best chance of saving her.

"Don't move her yet, Viv," he cautioned, holding her back

long enough to point to the blood that was starting to form rivulets leading away from Beth.

Tears streamed down Vivian's face, but she needed to hold herself together. "Beth, please wake up!"

Beth weakly opened her eyes. "Viv … I'm sorry …"

Choking back sobs, she took her friend's hand. "Oh, my goodness. Whatever for? Don't apologise, Beth. Just hold on, help is on the way."

"Viv … listen to me … listen to me, Viv … you are the strongest person I know …" Blood sputtered from Beth's mouth as she tried to whisper to her friend, "Stand firm. They can't get on without you."

Tears fell onto Beth's face as Viv sobbed. "You listen to me, Beth. You are going to hold on, and you are going to be fine."

Beth smiled weakly. "Oh pet, it's okay. It doesn't hurt … Hey, Vivian Waltman, you take bloody good care. I …"

"I love you, you silly sod muffin," Vivian finished for her and kissed her forehead.

With each shallow breath, Beth's strength was fading, but her eyes remained fixed on Vivian's, filled with love and gratitude. "Thank you, Viv," she whispered. "For everything."

Viv nodded, knowingly. Her tears fell freely as she leaned in close, her forehead touching Beth's. "Thank you, Beth," she whispered back. "For being the very best friend, I could ever ask for."

As Beth's eyes fluttered closed, her hand went limp. Vivian knew she was gone but wasn't ready to let her go. Around her, sirens could be heard beckoning. Half of the building was missing, and they were looking out over the morass that was once a thriving city. She felt a searing pain and anger in her heart and howled and screamed into the darkness, the smoke, the flames, the bloody war. Roughly, she wiped the tears from her face.

"Okay, right then. Grab what gear we can that works. We need to find a safe space to report in from," she shouted over the calamity all around them. Everyone, Hastings included, blinked at her, then they shook their heads to clear them of the fog that had set in.

"She's right! Let's go!" He picked up a radio and headset from the ground beside Beth's body. Pausing, he reached down to close her eyes and placed a jacket over her for final respects. They couldn't just leave her out in the open like that. "Safe travels, Beth." It came out choked, and he swallowed hard. He needed to step up for the women, his unit.

They moved smoothly together, picking up anything useful they could carry. As they left what remained of the room, Viv paused at the door to look at where her friend lay one last time. She called out, "Beth Armstrong, you take bloody good care. I love you, you silly sod muffin!" and then clambered over the wreckage out into the shattered fragments of their city, their home.

54

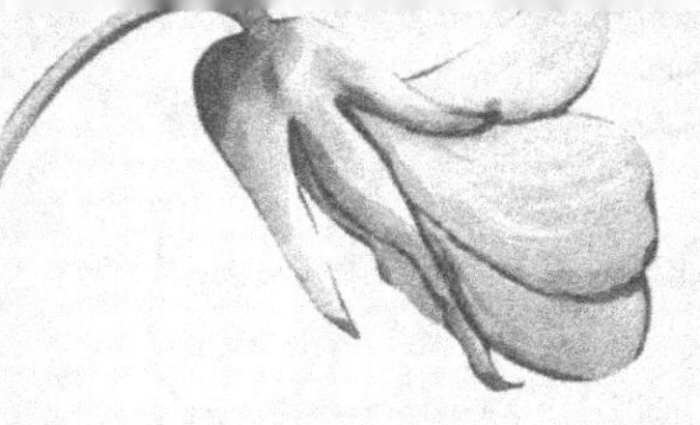

Chapter Seven

"Bombproof." That was what was said of the Dorchester Hotel. The thick, concrete walls assured a high level of comfort and safety for its guests. So far, the only damage it had sustained were some broken windows. It offered an air-raid shelter in its basement, though many of the affluent guests did not feel it should be open to just anyone and would retreat instead to the Turkish baths found well underground.

It was home to many celebrities and world leaders alike. Dance halls like the Dorchester were seen as important if not vital to the war effort. A way of keeping up morale by distracting people from the realities of war and often raising money for the war effort itself. The Dorchester didn't disappoint. It rose like a beacon from the rubble and ash all around it. It was incredibly opulent with the most up-to-date technologies and luxuries available for its guests.

"I have never been here before." Looking at the grandeur of the building in front of her, Vivian understood why so many people were drawn to it. One could feel the energy coming out of it, like a portal to another world.

"Wait until you see inside." Thomas grinned and escorted her up the steps and through the doors. The lobby was

buzzing with energy and people. Businessmen, soldiers, and women all converged together. They moved toward the ballroom where the music and laughter could easily be heard.

"My word, Thomas! Is this even real? How can all of this be happening when the world is in such upheaval?"

"It's happening *because* the world is in such upheaval, darling. We all need to be reminded why we are fighting this damn war. After-all, if we don't have anything to fight for, what's the point?"

Vivian knew he was right but was still incredulous. Thomas steered them to a table, and she was surprised and pleased to see Fern, who ran to her when she saw her.

"Viv! Oh gosh! It is so good to see you. I am so happy Thomas brought you. Sit with me. The boys can go get us something to drink." Fern gave Karl a coy smile.

"Absolutely, my dearest." He chuckled. "Let's do as we are told, Thomas, and give these two a moment to catch up. Good to see you, Viv." Karl gave her a light hug and kiss on the cheek as he and Thomas moved off and disappeared in the crowd, presumably towards the bar.

"Well, Viv. Let's hear all about Thomas then." Fern grinned broadly and gave Viv her full and undivided attention.

Laughing, Vivian leaned towards her friend and kissed her cheek. "I'm very smitten, Fern. We spend any time he has off together. I've written to Aaron and broken it off."

"What do you mean, Viv? I don't mean to be cruel, but Aaron has been missing a long time."

"I know, but I received a letter from him just a few weeks ago. He's alive. I couldn't have him coming home to reunite knowing I love Thomas."

Fern was taken aback. "He's alive?! Oh, my word, Viv, that is such good news. Wait, what did you just say about Thomas?" Placing her hand excitedly on Vivian's arm, Fern leaned in towards her friend with an enormous smile on her face.

"I said I love him. When I wrote Aaron, I wrote Thomas as

well. I told him that." She furrowed her brow slightly. "I'm hoping he just hasn't received it yet because he didn't say anything when he came to fetch me today."

"If he knew you loved him, Viv, he'd be shouting it from the rooftops. Karl told me he is absolutely besotted with you. Maybe he's waiting for the right time to say something."

"I hope you're right. Either way, I couldn't let Aaron come home without knowing the truth. I still care deeply for him. I would never want to hurt him like that, not that I haven't hurt him anyways." Vivian's face dropped in sadness. "The truth is, none of us knows what will happen tomorrow, and even if nothing becomes of us, I need to live my life as fully as I can."

"That's certainly understandable, Viv. You've been through a lot." Laying her hand on Vivian's arm once again, but this time in sympathy, she continued, "I heard about Beth. I'm so sorry. I know how much she meant to you."

"It was terrible. We all had to pull together and keep going. Leaving her there when we had to move out …" She paused to collect herself. She didn't want to turn the evening into a sad affair. "Well, it was the worst day of my life. Black Saturday they're calling it. Seems about right to me. A black day in history for certain." Vivian had pulled herself back in, harnessed her sadness and restrained it. If she opened that door, she feared she would never stop crying.

Fern saw the shift. She saw Vivian lock herself in. "Viv …" she started to tell her it wasn't her fault, that she had done the only thing she could do in that situation, but they were interrupted.

"Hello, beautiful." A young Army corporal and his friend, also from the Army, had come up to their table. The first leaned on the chair beside Vivian and looked as though he might sit down.

"We're here with our escorts." Trying to dismiss them and make it clear they were not available; Fern reached across Vivian and pulled the chair beside her closer to the table.

"Really? Where are they then?" The young man laughed

and put his hand on the back of the chair, almost daring Fern to pull at it again. His words slurred slightly, "I've been watching you for a while, and I haven't seen a single fellow. Isn't that right, Mat?" He motioned with his hand to the room and wobbled as he did so.

"Have you then? Well, you should have seen my husband. He'll be back shortly, so I suggest you go now." Vivian was getting uncomfortable with how close the man was, and she shifted away.

"I'm sure there's time for a dance before he gets back. You aren't married, are you, miss?" He turned his attention to Vivian and touched her left hand.

Vivian pulled her hand away like it had been stabbed with a hot poker. "That is not your business," she said tersely. "You have been asked to go. Please do that."

"Luke let's go. You heard them. They're not available or interested." Mat, the second corporal, had come over to his friend and was trying to pull him away. "Sorry, ladies, it's no excuse, but my friend has had a couple drinks and is just trying to blow off some steam. We're back from France for some R&R. We won't bother you anymore."

At that moment, Thomas and Karl returned and the two young corporals snapped to attention, recognising not just Thomas's higher rank of SSM but the 8th RECCE badges both men wore.

"Is there a problem?" Thomas' smile faded when he saw the two men at the table and how Vivian and Fern were visibly upset by their presence. Setting the drinks down, Karl and Thomas moved between the corporals and blocked them from the girls.

"Uh, not at all, sir. We were just leaving," Mat said in a somewhat nervous manner.

"Congratulations on having such fine women, sirs." Luke, as they now knew him, had obviously forgotten who he was speaking to and smirked at Thomas and Karl. He held out his hand to Thomas, who took a firm hold of it and stepped closer to the drunken man.

"I suggest you apologise to the ladies and go back to your lodgings, corporal. I would hate to have to speak to your CO tomorrow and let him know of your behaviour tonight."

Mat tried to intervene. "No disrespect meant, sir. Ladies, please accept our apologies if we in any way upset you. We will leave you to enjoy your evening." He reached his hand out to Thomas. "Have a good night, sir." For a moment, Thomas stared at him before releasing Luke's hand and taking Mat's.

Without smiling, he shook it and pointedly said, "Good night, corporals. Get safely back. You are dismissed."

"Yes, sir. We will, sir. Thank you, sir." Relieved, Mat forcefully took his friend's arm and quickly steered him away towards the exit.

"Well, that was fun." Fern laughed, and it broke the mood. Karl sat down and gave her a hug.

"Can't really blame them. The two most beautiful women in the place are sitting here with us. Of course they wanted to ask you to dance. I would have tried, too." Karl kissed Fern on her cheek, and everyone laughed again.

"Well, in that case, I better take you onto the dance floor, Viv." Thomas stood up, finished his drink in one swallow and held out his arm to Vivian. His blue eyes sparkled cheekily.

"How can I resist such a charming invitation, Mr. Cooper. Or should I say SSM Cooper, sir." Vivian gave him a mock salute, her eyes sparkling as brightly as Thomas's as they walked arm in arm towards the dance floor.

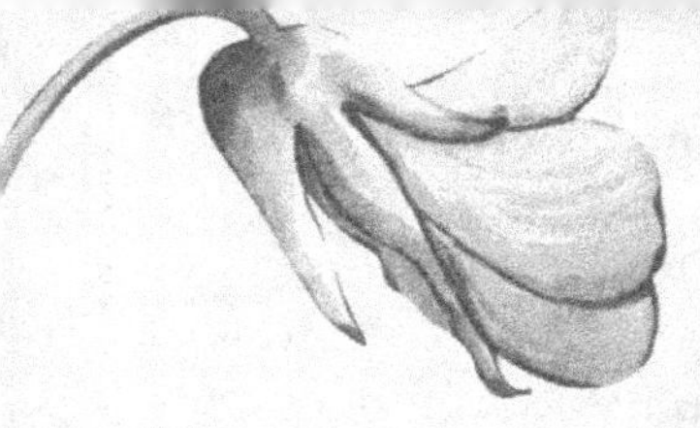

Chapter Eight

The aroma of roasting chicken and freshly baked bread filled the air as Vivian stepped into her childhood home. She smiled warmly, greeted by the comforting familiarity of her parents' cosy abode. It had been a few weeks since she'd last visited, and she was eager to spend some time with her family. Her mother, Evelyn Waltman, was tiny in stature, but no one ever made the mistake more than once of thinking she was tiny in spirit. She was a sharp-minded and strong-willed woman. She fought against societal norms and worked after having children. Her employer, Barrett's, was even giving her royalties for the enormously popular Sherbet Fountain candy she had developed for them. Her ability to combine flavours made her a fine cook and an excellent chemist. Having worked her way up to shop floor manager, Evelyn was a woman ahead of her time.

Sunday dinners with her parents had a familiar theme. Her father Wallace, or Ace as most people called him, would go to the pub until 4:00 p.m. Her mother would serve dinner at 2:00 p.m. His meal would be in the oven being kept warm when he arrived back home. That neither one of them was willing to alter their schedule was maddening to Vivian. In a

strange way, it was also a comforting reminder of the normalcy of life, even amidst the chaos of war. Despite the bombings and uncertainty that loomed outside their doorstep, the ritual of Sunday dinners remained unchanged, though perhaps a bit more meagre, right down to the conflict over scheduling. A small semblance of stability in an ever-changing world.

One thing that had changed was her brother Bryant was home and joined them for their meals. Bryant was eighteen years younger than Vivian and was referred to as a "change of life" baby. He was a loving and affectionate boy who laughed easily and loved his family very much. Because of his cognitive disabilities, he had been living in a specialised home since he was about four. One of the bombings had destroyed it about two months ago, and since housing and support were scant at best, he was moved back home. Their father was retired and could care for his son. Truth be told, he enjoyed it immensely and found enormous pride in seeing all his son was capable of. In another time, Bryant's abilities might have been viewed very differently.

"Vivvy!" Bryant hollered from the garden. "Come see! Come see!" The vegetables in the backyard had really come along, and Bryant was keen to show off his gardening skills. It was encouraged to grow as much of your own food as you could to help with rationing, but Bryant would have done it regardless. He would spend his entire day tending to the plants, checking the soil, pruning, and harvesting. He also had a goat for milk and cheese and chickens for eggs and Sunday dinners.

"Look, Vivvy! Scarlett has had babies." Scarlett was one of his hens.

"Hello, Bryant." She gave him a hug and kiss on the cheek, but he was too focused on the chicks. "I didn't realise you let a rooster into your hen house." There were five little feathered fluff balls running around the yard.

"Oh, certainly I did." He straightened up, preparing to have a serious conversation about his hens and the new chicks.

"Mattie and Shanda are not producing eggs anymore, so they'll become dinner in the coming weeks. I had to replace them if we're going to keep having eggs, and I like eggs for my breakfast, Vivvy. They're good for you. They make you strong."

It was remarkable to Vivian that Bryant understood the complexities of needing to replace his hens. Billy, the billy goat, wandered over to them and demanded some attention. After getting a few pats on her head, she chased after the hens and chicks.

"Billy! You naughty girl. Play nicely now," Bryant scolded, though he was laughing as he said it. He didn't have a harsh or mean bone in his body.

Vivian wandered over to the vegetable patch. The rows seemed very haphazard, with odd things planted beside each other, but Bryant had planned every detail of the garden. He talked to as many people as he could about when to plant different things as well as what to plant together. "It's called companion planting, Vivvy," he had told her. "I know it looks quite bedraggled, but there's a method to my madness." He had squinted his eyes, tilted his head, and held up his finger to emphasise he knew what he was doing.

"My goodness, you have a lot of tomatoes and peppers. Oh, and look at the cucumbers. You certainly have outdone yourself, Bryant."

"I have cabbages growing over here." He began showing her every single vegetable as well as the fruit vines and trees. "I'll send you home with lots for you and the girls." He puffed up his chest, very proud of himself.

"That would be lovely. They will all appreciate it very much." The girls really did appreciate it, too. Fresh produce was a real gift. "You'll have a lot of canning to do."

"I've already started. I had a lot of squash two weeks ago, and I don't like it very much to begin with. I gave a lot away, but I thought I may as well start with something I don't really like. That way, if I mess it up, I'm not wasting the foods I love."

They both laughed as he continued telling her all about what he was learning about preserving food. Vivian was impressed as usual by her brother. She knew nothing about those things and was happy to learn from him and let him be the expert.

They had been chatting in the garden for a while when they heard their father call out to them from the back door. "Vivian, my dear! Ah! It is so good to see you." He came towards them, his arms outstretched, and gave her a big hug, lifting her off the ground as he did so. Ace was a handsome bear of a man with a gentle heart and kind, warm brown eyes. He was dressed as he always was for Sunday dinner in a suit and vest with a crisp, starched white shirt.

Bryant giggled and flapped his hands. He enjoyed seeing his father happy. "Bryant, look at these chicks! Did they hatch just today? We didn't see them yesterday when we came out to check on things after that damned bombing knocked down the wee ramp for them to get in and out."

"Yes, Dad. They did. One didn't hatch though, and Scarlett kicked it out of the nest. She knew it was a bad egg."

"Animals have good instincts. Did you put it in the bin then?"

"I put the egg in the bin, but rinsed off the shell and crushed it up with the other shells for the garden. Good nutrients there."

The conversation about the chicks and eggs carried on for a while longer, teaching Vivian far more than she ever thought possible about hens, chicks, and how fast a rooster was when he got access to the coop.

"You're home early, Dad." Vivian knew it had to be quite early because they hadn't had their dinner without him yet.

"The pub closed, pet. Fred and his family decided they'd had enough of the war and packed it in. They're moving to Canada! Imagine that. So far away." Her attention perked up at the mention of Canada. "Fred's brother moved there after the Great War. He has a pub near Toronto someplace. Fred says it's in the north, though. Not sure how Fred will fare with that. He hates the cold."

"I'm sorry your friend is leaving, Dad. I hope he gets along well over there."

"Oh, he'll be fine. Fred is the sort of fellow who could fall into a bucket of manure and come out smelling like a rose." He chuckled. "But I will miss him. Damn war." His face became less animated for a moment. "On the bright side, your mom will need to think of a new way to keep me from my Sunday dinner. Speaking of which, I'm going to go in and help her." He paused as he was walking towards the rear door of the house and looked back at her, a fresh look of delight on his face. "Now there's a way I can get under her skin. Be helpful in the kitchen!"

"Oh, my goodness! Dad! You are such a terrible torment!" Vivian laughed and popped a sugar pea into her mouth.

Chapter Nine

The route home was always a little different each time. Busses found their way as close to the original route as possible, but crumbled buildings and blocked roads often required some flexibility. Vivian didn't mind. She found the trip back relaxing with the conversation and banter among the other passengers and the rhythmic bounce of the bus itself.

It continued to bound along, and Vivian could see her building coming into view. Organising her bags, she prepared to get off at her stop. Her bags were overflowing with vegetables as well as some strawberries balanced precariously on top, so they didn't get squashed.

"Thank you," she said to the driver as she stepped off the bus onto the street almost directly in front of her rooming house.

"Vivvy!" She heard her name being called. She knew that voice and only two people called her that.

"Aaron!" She almost screamed his name and ran towards him. She dropped both bags, and the strawberries on top spilled out all over the sidewalk. "Oh, my word! I cannot believe you're here." They hugged each other tightly. "Have

you seen your mum yet? She'll be beside herself."

"I have. I came here to see you first, and the girls told me you were at your family's for Sunday dinner. I didn't want to surprise you there, so I went to see my mum, had some dinner, and came back. I timed it perfectly it seems."

"You certainly did." For a moment, they simply enjoyed each other's presence. After he helped her pick up the strawberries, and eat a few as a reward, they sat on the steps, falling easily into conversation, catching up on each other's lives. It was as if no time had passed.

Suddenly, it occurred to Vivian that Aaron had clearly not received her letter. He didn't know she had broken off their engagement. "Aaron, I think there's something we need to talk about."

The tentative tone in her voice and the way she cast her eyes downward told him it was not good news. "What is it, Vivvy? You know that you can tell me anything." He took her hand and looked into her eyes. How often he had dreamt about her while in that POW camp. How often he had pictured those liquid-green, amber eyes. His breath caught in his chest. How he loved her.

Vivian almost didn't say the words. She saw the adoration in his eyes. How could she hurt him so deeply after all he had been through? But she knew lying to him was worse.

"After I got your letter, I wrote you back," she said.

"Oh! I'm sorry, darling. It probably hasn't caught up with me yet. Once they debriefed with us, we were shipped to a few different spots before they got us properly headed towards home. It was a bit of a mess and happened pretty quickly." His smile faded. It wasn't about missing the letter. It was about what was in the letter.

"Aaron, I still love you. I will always love you. You were my first love."

"But you're not *in love* with me anymore," he finished for her.

She nodded her head, tears running down her cheeks.

"Oh, Vivvy. I wish with my whole heart that it wasn't true."

Tears ran down his cheeks as well. "But the one thing I learned while I was in that camp is that we only have one life, and we need to live it as fully as we can." Tenderly, he reached up and held her face. Wiping the tears away, he kissed her gently, his lips lingering and holding onto her breath, her warmth, the velvet softness of her lips. "I will never stop loving you with my entire being, Vivvy, and I will never stop wanting the very best for you."

Then, he was gone. Vivian sat on the stairs, the strawberries resting precariously on top of the bag once again, and she couldn't help but wonder if she had just made the greatest mistake of her life.

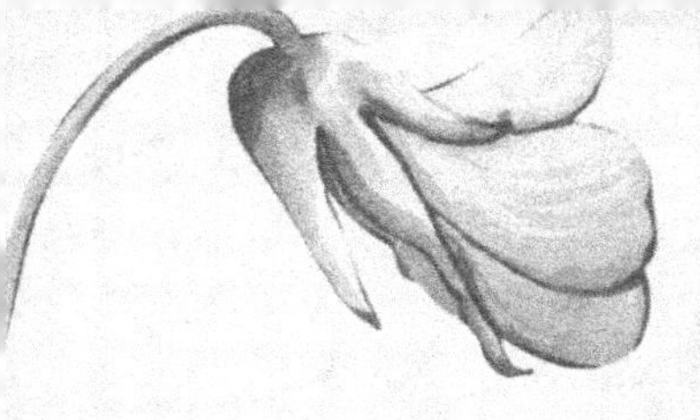

Chapter Ten

"Sir, you have a letter," the clerk called out to Thomas when he saw him come into the office.

"Thanks, corporal. Looks like it's from my girl!" Thomas ran his finger over the handwriting on the outside of the envelope, smiling and thinking of Vivian.

"Yes, sir." The corporal smiled as Thomas left to head back to his bunk and read his letter.

"Skip in your step. Hey, Coop?" SSM Oliver Robinson chuckled as he fell in step beside Thomas.

"You know it, Ollie. Got a letter from Viv. Going to go read it now then head to the mess tent."

"This must be some sort of record for you eh, Coop. How long have you been seeing that beautiful young woman now?"

"Close to two years now. I will be forever in Karl's debt for introducing us." He beamed.

"How is he? We haven't seen him since he made Captain almost that same time frame ago."

"I hate to admit it, but I haven't seen or heard from him either. He took his bride back home to Kingston and to run the training for us simple squaddies for the last couple years

now." It really had been far too long since Thomas had been in touch with Karl, but he had to admit, he preferred to limit his contact these days. Sometimes, it was hard knowing so much about your friends and the choices they make. No one wants to judge, but it can be hard to stand by and not say anything.

"Well, I'll leave you to it and see you later for some grub." Oliver patted Thomas on the shoulder, and they parted ways.

Thomas sat at his small table that doubled as his desk when necessary. The barracks were quite generous, even for a non-commissioned officer like himself. He lit a cigarette and carefully opened the envelope.

My darling,

I cannot tell you how happy I am to hear that you are safe and well. I have no words for all the emotions I am feeling. I must tell you something that weighs heavily on my heart, however. I cannot allow it to continue or allow you to come home without knowing the truth. The love that once carried us has taken an unexpected turn. In your absence, I found solace with another. As much as it breaks my heart to tell you, I cannot deny my connection to this man. I must be fully truthful and tell you that I have fallen in love with him. I am so sorry for the pain this may inflict upon you. You have survived so much, and it is cruel to add to that pain. Not telling you the truth would be disrespectful to the relationship we shared. This revelation can never take away the love I held for you, my first true love.

I wish you joy and a long, well-lived life.

Love always,
Viv

He read it again and again. How could it be true? They had just seen each other not long ago, and her last letter gave no indication of her change of heart. Thomas felt like he had been gutted with a jagged-edge blade. He couldn't breathe properly. Standing up, he paced his room, then sat down again. He had to do something. He needed to know why. What had happened? He was going to require help to do it. Picking up the letter and his pack, he rushed out of his room in search of Oliver.

"Ollie!" he shouted as he found his friend walking back toward the barracks. "I need your help with something."

"Sure, buddy. What's up?"

"It's Viv!" Thomas was frantic. He couldn't stand still, and Oliver was immediately concerned.

"What is it, Thomas? Is she okay? Has she been hurt?"

Thomas could hardly speak. Oliver guided him back into the barracks and to his room. "Thomas, sit down, and let me get you some water." He poured water from the pitcher on Thomas's desk into a tall glass and handed it to his friend, but he didn't let go of the glass, helping Thomas drink from it. "Okay, now tell me what's happened to Vivian." He squatted, staying close in case Thomas lost control completely.

"She broke things off with me." Thomas's voice was barely a whisper. It was as much as he could muster.

"What? I'm confused. You even had dinner with her family a few weeks ago. Do you think they disapproved of you and told her to break things off?"

Thomas had not considered that. He thought back to the dinner. "I don't think so. We all seemed to hit it off. I love her brother and I am sure he liked me." Hands in his face, he handed the letter to Oliver to read to see if he could decipher anything from it.

Oliver read it. "Thomas, I'm really sorry, mate. I don't know what to say." He handed the letter back. Thomas read it again and sobbed. He felt panicky. It couldn't be right. The idea of losing Vivian was just not something he could imagine.

"I have to go see her," he said.

"When do you have to leave again?"

"No, I need to see her tonight. I need to go now. I need to know why."

Oliver became alarmed. Thomas couldn't just leave without permission. He would get into a lot of trouble. "Okay, I understand that you're upset, but you're not thinking clearly right now. You need to sleep on it, and tomorrow we can go see the captain together and arrange a short leave as soon as possible."

"Oliver." Thomas' eyes were wild, his mind racing a mile a minute, putting together a plan that included him leaving immediately to go see Vivian. "It's just a few hours there and back. I can be there in about two hours, three max. I'll find out what's going on and come straight back. No one will miss me." He was so upset he was putting random items in his bag.

"Thomas! Thomas!" Oliver put his hand on the bag Thomas was stuffing with a canteen. "Thomas! Stop!" He pulled the bag away firmly. "You cannot sneak off like this. If you get caught, you will be disciplined. You are too good a soldier to risk this. Think of your men."

"Ollie, you're a good friend, and I know you're worried about me. But I'm going." He pulled the bag back and took Oliver's hand. "Just cover me for mess. I'll be back long before morning, and no one will be the wiser. Please. Ollie, please." Thomas begged his friend with his face, his grip, and his voice.

Oliver sighed. "If you're not back before sunrise, I knew nothing about it, understand me?"

"Understood." He smiled with relief. "Okay, I'm going to borrow a Jeep and go. Marshall should have closed up the store by now. I'll sneak in and grab a key."

"Thomas don't tell me. I can't lie if I truly don't know." Oliver put up his hand to silence his friend, then shook his hand and walked out before Thomas told him anything else.

Thomas gripped the steering wheel of the stolen Jeep, his knuckles white with tension as he sped down the darkening roads toward London. The weight of Vivian's letter burned a hole in his pocket, its contents echoing in his mind with each passing mile.

He ran through Vivian's words over and over again, trying to make sense of the sudden end to their relationship. The shock and confusion had quickly given way to anger and desperation, fuelling his reckless decision to go AWOL in search of answers.

You will have some reckoning if you get caught, he thought to himself.

As he drove, Thomas's mind raced with thoughts of Vivian—her laughter, her smile, the warmth of her touch. How could she just end things like this? Who was this man she had fallen in love with? How was it even possible that she loved someone else when they had shared so much together?

Desperate to find her, Thomas pulled over when he spotted a wash line with civilian clothes hanging out to dry. With shaking hands, he quickly swapped his military uniform for the less conspicuous attire, hoping to blend in as he made his way through the city.

Arriving at Vivian's rooming house, Thomas' heart sank when he realised, she wasn't home. No one at the boarding house knew where she was, but knew she was with a few of the other girls from the house and that they had walked wherever they were going. Bordering on maniacal and overcome with emotion, he set off in search of her, his steps quickening as he made his way through the crowded streets of London.

It wasn't long before he found her in the park, surrounded by friends as they sat together on blankets and benches enjoying each other's company. Relief flooded through him at the sight of her, but it was quickly overshadowed by the urgency of his mission.

"Vivian!" Thomas called out; his voice strained with

emotion as he approached her, his heart pounding in his chest.

Vivian turned towards him, her expression one of concern as she took in his dishevelled appearance. "Thomas, what's wrong?" she asked, rising to her feet. "What are you wearing?"

Breathless and feverish, Thomas reached into his pocket and pulled out the letter, thrusting it toward her. "Why?" he demanded, his voice raw with hurt. "Why are you breaking things off?"

Confusion clouded Vivian's features as she glanced down at the letter, her brow furrowing in bewilderment. "I don't understand," she replied, her voice faltering. "I didn't break things off with you, Thomas."

Thomas's heart skipped a beat as he watched Vivian's face change. "What do you mean?" he asked, his voice trembling with hope.

Vivian's eyes widened in shock. "I made a mistake," her voice was barely above a whisper. "After Beth … after everything that happened, I must have put the wrong letter in the envelope."

As the truth sank in, relief washed over Thomas, followed by a wave of gratitude and overwhelming emotion.

"I'm so sorry, Thomas. I didn't break things off. In fact, well, I love you."

Without a word, he pulled Vivian into his arms, holding her tightly as tears of relief streamed down his cheeks.

In that moment, as they clung to each other amidst the darkness of the park, Thomas knew their love was stronger than any misunderstanding and their bond would endure anything the future held for them. "I love you, Vivian Waltman." A rush and elation of joy and love flooded his body, and he sobbed with happiness, kissing her face. "I love you, Vivian Waltman!" he shouted as he picked her up and spun her around.

Her friends and some strangers passing by cheered as they witnessed them bare their hearts in front of everyone. A public testament of their feelings they needed the world to know.

"Can we go somewhere more private and talk?" he asked. There was a sudden realisation they were in a very public space, and Thomas wanted to be able to kiss her in a way that would not be appropriate in a public park.

Nodding and smiling, Vivian led him away from her friends, who cheered and whooped again.

With the weight of misunderstanding lifted and their hearts overflowing with the newfound exposure of the fullness of their feelings, Thomas and Vivian found themselves driving out of the city to the countryside in his stolen Jeep, the cool night air whipping through their hair as they left the city behind.

"Thomas, whose Jeep is this?"

Laughter sprung from his throat. "It belongs to the regiment. I borrowed it for the evening." He gave her his cheeky half smile that made her come undone every single time.

"And… the clothing?" She giggled.

"Well, these… I cannot say who owns them because I don't know."

"Oh my." Vivian started to realise Thomas may be in trouble. "Are you here with permission?"

"Ollie knows where I am." He looked at her as he drove and saw her concern. "Don't worry, my love. There's nothing bad that can ever happen now that I know you love me."

As they reached the top of a hill that overlooked the vast expanse of farmland, Thomas cut the engine and the Jeep rolled to a stop. Stepping out into the crisp night air, they found themselves bathed in the soft glow of moonlight and twinkling of the distant stars.

With a silent understanding, Thomas reached into the back of the Jeep and took a blanket out of a pack. They made their way to the edge of the hill, where they settled onto a patch of grass beneath a sprawling oak tree. The world fell away around them as they gazed out over the landscape, the beauty of the moment rendering them speechless. It was the perfect backdrop to lay their hearts bare to the universe stretching endlessly above them.

In the hushed stillness of the night, Thomas turned to face Vivian, his eyes filled with an intensity that mirrored her own. Without a word, he reached out to cup her face in his hands, his touch sending shivers down her spine.

"Vivian," his voice was barely above a breath, "I need you to know and believe that I love you."

Tears welled in her eyes as she met his gaze, her heart overflowing with emotion. "And I love you, Thomas," she replied, her voice choking with the revelation.

With a tenderness born of longing and desire, they leaned in, their lips meeting in a kiss that ignited a fire within them both, a fire that burned bright despite the darkness that had threatened to consume it.

"Thomas, I …" Vivian was nervous and suddenly overcome with emotion. She had never been with a man before. "I have never—"

Placing his finger over her lips, he nodded and kissed her gently. The hunger grew between them, as he unbuttoned her blouse, kissing her skin as he exposed it. Her heart was pounding. Instinctively, she ran her hands up the back of his head and encircled her fingers in his fine golden hair, encouraging his exploration of her skin.

He paused to look into her eyes, to seek the answer he needed. Wordlessly, she nodded and guided his hand lower. He then pulled his mouth to hers. A sharp breath escaped them both as his hand found its way inside her panties.

Shifting, he gently slid her panties down her legs. Thomas looked down at her, her eyes and skin shimmering in the golden light of the setting sun. He had never felt such longing before. Gradually, he slid his fingers up her thigh and pressed one, then two inside of her as her back arched and she moaned. Laying down beside her again, his hand explored rhythmically. He didn't want to rush the moment—not just because he didn't want to scare her or hurt her, but because he never wanted the experience to end.

He kissed her throat following the curve and her neck to her collar bone. Swirling his tongue, he savoured her pulse and felt it respond to his attention to it. Her fingers ran up his back and sent a shiver through him. As his mouth moved to trap her nipple. She gasped again, amazed at the intensity of the pleasure she was feeling through her entire body.

He parted her legs wider and shifted until she could feel the heat of his breath where his fingers were still moving inside her. When she looked down to watch him pleasuring her, he held her gaze as he lowered his face between her legs adding his tongue to his ministrations.

The trill of crickets orchestrated their lovemaking and set the tempo of their movements. Vivian's hips danced with Thomas' hand and lips.

The cresting of the waves was growing. "Thomas! Oh God!" Every sense in her body was heightened. The scent of lavender floated around them as the moon highlighted the curves of her body. Her breathing continued to be punctuated with gasps and moans. Each time he felt her tightening, he would ease back, but her hips would rise to meet him wanting and needing him to continue. She felt drunk and lightheaded from the tension growing in her body. Thomas loved how passionately and freely she surrendered to him. He brought her to the edge of blissful agony and held her there. Finally, he couldn't hold back, he needed to feel her break. His fingers and tongue worked in harmony until Vivian's body convulsed and she cried out as she erupted. Shocked, her breathing ragged, Vivian had no idea that this was part of making love. She had never been told that she would enjoy being with a man so much.

As he kissed his way back up her body to her mouth, she helped him remove his clothing. Thomas lay on his back and pulled Vivian to him. Their bodies pressed together, fitting together perfectly, soft, and delicate to strong and muscular.

Running her hands over his shoulders and chest, she felt the curls of the hair and firmness of his muscles. Working her way down across his stomach, Vivian took a deep breath and wrapped her fingers around him. His skin was warm, and she nervously began stroking him. The sounds that escaped his lips encouraged her and her confidence grew. To her amazement, she found herself being aroused from delighting him and felt compelled to move so that she was between his legs looking up at him, their mutual desire glowing in the reflection in their eyes. Tracing a line along his length with her tongue, she continued to stroke him. Vivian's movements found a steady and building rhythm and Thomas thread his fingers into her hair to try and remain in control of himself. It was a losing battle. "Vivian, if you don't stop, I won't be able to hold back."

Nervousness pushed back to the forefront, and he saw her concern over his size. "Don't worry, darling. I promise to go slowly and that it will be beautiful."

Laying her back down, he kissed her deeply as he rubbed the tip of himself on her opening. There was a moment of fear as Vivian felt Thomas begin to press himself into her. Despite how well lubricated Thomas had made her, she was still very tight, and Thomas had to pause a few times and give Vivian a moment to adjust to his presence inside her. His patience helped Vivian feel safe and he could feel her body open to him and welcomed him. Instinctively, she moved with him harder and faster, locking her legs around him.

He rolled over, bringing her with him to settle her on top of him. While he guided her hips, she leaned forward to kiss him. Having gained new confidence in her body, she sat back up, took his hands and placed them on her breasts. Looking down at him, his eyes glazed with their shared passion, she felt heat rising in her body again, and she knew what to expect and wanted it.

Thomas recognised the change and watched her face. He held her hips and met her body as they both surrendered to a thunderous completion. Breathless, they lay still for some time, savouring the sensation of the afterglow of their moment. Illuminated by the soft glow of the moon, they knew they had found their home in each other's arms. They had found a love that would withstand the test of time, a love that would guide them through the darkest of nights and into the dawn of a new day.

Eventually, the light of day started to send tiny wisps of its presence into the darkness of the night sky. They lay sheltered together under the blanket staring at the stars. Their passion had risen two more times, and Thomas knew it would rise again if he stayed much longer. He should have already been back on base. It was going to be a bit trickier to get through unseen.

"I better take you back home and get back to base, my love," he said.

She reached up and kissed his full lips and nodded.

When Thomas pulled up to the gate at the base, light was breaking the sky. It was still well ahead of Reveille, but there would be several soldiers at the end of their shift who would notice him coming in.

The private at the gate opened it without making any eye contact once he realised who was driving the Jeep. He was trying to get off his duty, not keep it forever. He understood to turn a blind eye to something that for all intents and purposes looked like it could be official business. That was in his best interests. Thomas had made it through the first hurtle.

He turned off the Jeep, and it rolled to a stop in the same spot he *borrowed* it from a few hours earlier.

"RSM! Sir!"

Thomas tried not to falter as he walked towards Marshall behind the stores' counter. "Yes, corporal?"

"Umm, sir, I didn't realise you were the one who had borrowed the Jeep, sir. I reported it to the major when I saw it was gone." Marshall looked upset. "I'm sorry, sir. If I had realised it, was you who borrowed it, I would never have said anything."

"Marshall, you did the right thing. Imagine if it hadn't been me? You'd be in hot water for not reporting it." Thomas wondered how much trouble he would be in. "Don't worry, lad. It's all fine." Thomas handed the key back to Marshall and decided it was best to go directly to the major himself. Save Marshall the worry of having to say who brought the Jeep back.

Thomas knocked on the major's door and waited for permission to enter.

"RSM, I wasn't expecting you."

"Major Grey, I was just at stores."

"Ah, yes. You've heard we had a bit of theft then?"

"Well, sir, it wasn't a theft so much as a borrow."

Major Grey looked up from his desk at Thomas. "I see, RSM." He got up and walked around to Thomas' side of the desk. "Am I correct in assuming you are the one who borrowed the Jeep then?"

"Yes, sir. You are correct. I'm sorry if I caused any confusion or concern, sir." Thomas kept his eyes forward.

"Was this an official borrowing or an unofficial borrowing of said Jeep, RSM?"

"Unofficial, sir."

"Do I want to know the details of why you needed to borrow it, Cooper?" Grey's voice softened. His RSM was not a reckless man. He was one of the best soldiers the major had ever encountered, smart and well-liked by his men and superiors.

"I am not sure you do, sir." Thomas' chin tilted down slightly. He knew what he had chosen to do would have consequences, but he also knew he'd do it again if he had to.

"At ease, Thomas. Talk to me." He sat down and motioned for Thomas to do the same.

"Well, sir, I want you to know I respect you and this regiment and did not intend for my actions to indicate otherwise."

"Okay." Grey nodded and waited.

"The truth is, sir, I received a letter from Viv. I thought she had broken things off with me, and well, sir, I lost my ever-loving mind. Genuinely lost it."

"Clearly." Grey saw where things were going.

"I snuck into the stores and borrowed the Jeep to run up to London and find out why."

"So, you borrowed a Jeep without permission, left the base without permission, and drove all the way to London and back before dawn?"

"Yes, sir. Yes, I did."

Grey stood up again and went back behind his desk. "Stand up please, Cooper." His voice was more formal, and Thomas understood he was about to hear the repercussions of his decision. He stood at attention. "Because you chose to come to me and tell the truth rather than force a formal investigation and waste people's time, you will only lose a rank to SSM for a period of ninety days or until your actions warrant the RSM title be returned to you. Any questions, SSM Cooper?"

Thomas was relieved; the punishment could have been far greater. "No, sir! Thank you, sir."

"Right, well, dismissed then, SSM."

Thomas let out a breath of relief as he opened the door to leave.

"Cooper, one more question," Grey called to him.

"Yes, sir." Thomas stopped and stood at attention again. He dared not show an inch of disrespect.

"Was it worth it?"

Thomas smiled broadly. "Yes, sir, it was."

"I figured it was since your eyes weren't all swollen, and your heart doesn't appear broken. Off you go." Grey smiled and waved his hand, dismissing Thomas.

He walked as fast as he could to find Robinson and let him know what had happened. Vivian Waltman loved him. Nothing else in the world mattered more.

84

Chapter Eleven

"Viv, are you okay in there?" Mary tapped on the door of the bathroom again. Vivian had been in and out of the restroom all morning. She hoped it wasn't catching.

"Sorry, Mary." She leaned on the frame heavily as she opened the door. "I don't know what's wrong. I just have the worst stomach bug I've ever had in my life."

"Gawd, Viv! Yer not well a'tal, are yea?" For some strange reason, Mary's accent thickened whenever she was worried or concerned. "Let me help yea back to yer bed, and I'll call the doctor fer yea."

"Oh, Mary, I don't need that much fuss. I probably just ate something that was off. I'm tired though, so bed seems like a good idea. Thank you."

Mary helped Vivian back to her room. After getting her a glass of water and a pail in case she needed to be sick again, she went to find Mrs. Lester, the house mother.

When looking at Theresa Lester, you could see she would have been a stunning woman. She still was, even with the unkindness of age and ravages of two wars. Her long grey hair was always swept up neatly in a twist. The lines around her eyes were from years of smiling, not

anger or ugly thinking. Well-earned and well-placed. She loved and cared about each of the young women who'd been assigned to her and the rooming house she managed. When she heard Vivian was ill, she knew it must be serious, Vivian was never ill.

"What seems to be troubling you, dear?" She placed the back of her hand on Vivian's forehead to feel for a temperature. There was none. The colour in her cheeks was a bit concerning, though.

"Oh, Mrs. Lester, I'm sorry to bother you. I'm okay. Just feeling poorly is all." Vivian gave her a feeble smile.

"Vivian, you are never so much as sniffly, so it is a concern when you're in the washroom for a long period being ill." She sat on the side of the bed in a mothering way.

"I've been feeling very run down the last few days. I think I just need a good rest."

"Do you have any pain, Viv dear? Headache?"

"None. Just exhausted and nauseous." Vivian sat up a bit in bed to make some room for Mrs. Lester.

Her lips pursed together. Theresa was fairly certain she knew what was wrong. She had seen it many times. "Viv, may I ask you something very personal?" Placing her hand on Vivian's, she leaned towards her.

"Well, of course." Viv felt quite confused.

"Well, umm …" There was an awkwardness to her posture and tone. "When was your last cycle, dear?"

Vivian gasped. Mrs. Lester couldn't be asking what she thought she was asking. It couldn't be true, could it? Even as the denial ran through her head, Vivian knew. She was pregnant. Overwhelmed, she started to cry.

"Oh, now, now. It's okay. It's all okay." Mrs. Lester gathered Vivian into her arms and comforted her. "I take it you've not had a cycle this month then, dear?"

Vivian shook her head.

"Well, it seems we have at least figured out why you're not well." Mrs. Lester patted Vivian on the hand and smiled kindly. "The good news is this sickness won't last much longer." Mrs. Lester hugged Vivian tightly and wiped her face with her handkerchief. "Let's put away the tears then. A baby is not something to cry over." She smiled and Vivian, who felt so much relief not to be judged by the woman she admired so much.

"Mrs. Lester, what will I do?"

"Why tell Thomas, of course, silly. If he's half the man I think he is, he will be thrilled." She stood up. "I'll fetch you some tea with a bit of ginger and toast. Help settle your stomach a bit, eh?"

Vivian's face still looked terrified at her revelation.

"You are not the first young woman to find herself in this state ahead of marriage. There are quite a number of babies born a bit too early after a wedding date." She chuckled.

"You're right, of course. He loves children." Vivian still held a foreboding in her heart, though. What if he wasn't happy? What would she do? What about her parents? Would they be happy?

"I am going to have the doctor come and just give you a check-up pet. It is always good to have a doctor confirm what women always already know."

"That is probably wise." Vivian nodded in agreement. 'Thank you, Mrs. Lester. You have been so kind and understanding." She wasn't sure if it was the hormones already beginning to run amuck inside her, but she teared up even though she was feeling great relief already.

"Oh, Vivian dear, you will be a wonderful mum. This is an incredibly lucky wee one." She gave Vivian another small hug and went to fetch the tea and toast.

Vivian felt a little better after getting something simple in her stomach, just as Mrs. Lester said she would. Mary had come back to check on her again, but Vivian didn't tell her about the pregnancy. She wasn't ready to tell anyone just yet. She needed to speak to Thomas. He was supposed to be coming in two days to visit. He had written and told her about how he had been reduced in rank. After leading the regiment through a particularly rough training, however, he had quickly earned it back. One of the corporals had been badly injured, and Thomas had gotten him to safety despite a risk to himself. In recognition of his actions, he was given two days leave and given back the rank of RSM. Two days. In two days, she would tell him he was going to be a father. Two days.

Vivian took her time getting ready for Thomas. She wanted to look perfect in the moment she shared her news with him. She washed and set her hair last night and just pulled the pins out. Her dress was a soft green that made her eyes appear larger and even more luminous. She still wasn't feeling well in the mornings, but the nausea was at least subsiding during the day, and she wasn't actually being sick anymore.

Thomas was waiting by the door when she came down the steps. He always lost his breath at the sight of her. How was it possible she looked more beautiful every time he laid eyes on her? She was positively radiant.

"Darling!" She was swept up into his arms, and he held her tight. Oh, how she had missed him.

"Viv. Oh, my Viv." He kissed her face and lingered gently on her lips. "You look so beautiful."

"Thank you, Thomas." She smiled sweetly, and he felt an urge to press her against the door and feel her body again. Memories of their night together flooded his mind. He needed to be with her again and had taken the liberty of planning a romantic adventure.

"I hope you like what I have planned." Helping her into the Jeep, which he had properly borrowed, he then jumped in his side.

"I will love anything you have planned, Thomas," she said.

As they drove along the winding country roads, the anticipation in the air was palpable. Vivian couldn't help but wonder where Thomas was taking her. After driving for about two hours, the landscape transformed from bustling city streets to rolling hills and vast stretches of farmland.

"Where are we going, Thomas?" Vivian asked, unable to contain her curiosity any longer.

His eyes flashed mischievously, and he grinned. "It's a little surprise, my love. We are almost there, I think." He had not actually been to the place he was taking Vivian. He had just been given the directions from his sergeant.

Vivian smiled. She was content to let the mystery unfold as they continued their journey.

Soon, the coastline came into view, the shimmering blue waters of the sea stretching out before them. Vivian was delighted. She loved the ocean, and it was her hope to live near it one day. A farmhouse nestled against the rugged shoreline. The wind and salty sea air had weathered it, but it was charming rather than worn.

"I think we have found our destination," Thomas said as they pulled up beside the house. Vivian looked at him, surprised. "This is my sergeant's family home. He is the only one left, and he is, of course, away. He's lending it to us."

Vivian blushed, understanding they would have the whole house to themselves, which meant they'd be alone all night. "It's beautiful, Thomas. The view ..." Her voice trailed off as she stared out over the rolling hills that led to the edge of the water. They were close enough she could hear the crash of the waves against the shore.

"I'm glad you like it." They stood there together, staring at the sea for a few moments. "I'm going to take our things inside. You explore out here for a bit."

Vivian walked down to the water's edge. There was a beautiful beach, protected from the rougher waves not far away. The smell of the salt water and the feel of the mist on her face was nice. Wanting to show Thomas, she went back up to the house to fetch him. She was greeted by the sound of a crackling fire, and a picnic feast was laid out waiting for her.

"Come sit down by the fire. It's a bit chilly out." He

wrapped a blanket around them as she leaned against him and savoured the moment. "Are you hungry?"

"I better be with all this food!" Laughing, they ate what he had set out. It was made more delicious by the company they shared together. As they caught each other up on the happenings in their worlds, Vivian felt a contentment and peace she had never experienced before and knew it was time to tell Thomas her news.

"Thomas, I have something very important to tell you."

"Well, by all means." He sat up to give her his full attention, though his manner was teasing at the seriousness of her tone.

"Well …" Suddenly, she was nervous to tell him. What if he wasn't happy about her news? "I'm … pregnant." She waited.

He was silent. It took Thomas a moment to process her words. Pregnant? His shock and disbelief quickly changed to joy. "Pregnant?!" His entire face smiled. "Vivian, this is wonderful news." He placed his hands on her belly. "We're having a baby!"

Pulling her to him, he hugged her tightly and kissed her. Then, there was a shift. She felt it, even with her eyes still closed and his lips on hers. His elation was gone. She opened her eyes and pulled back.

"Vivian …"

He never called her Vivian. Her heart sank.

"Vivian, I have to tell you something."

No! No! No! she thought to herself.

He had to say it. Before he lost his nerve again. "I have to tell you that I'm …" His eyes shifted down. He couldn't look at her. "I'm married."

Vivian felt the blood drain from her face and was grateful to have already been sitting down. Undoubtedly, she would have fainted or fallen otherwise. It was like the ground had moved away from her, and she was floating.

"I don't understand. How can you be married? We've been seeing each other for a very long time, Thomas. I would know this. I should have known this." Trying to make sense of his words was hurting her head and ears.

"I love you, Viv. I swear I do. I asked my wife for a divorce. She refused."

The roaring in her ears sounded like the surf crashing against the rocks. Nausea rose in her throat. Tears pricked her eyes, and she looked at him, the hurt, the pain of his words, born on her face like he had struck her with his hand.

"Does she know about me? About us?" Her voice was a whisper, as if saying it any louder would allow this other woman to hear her.

"Yes. I have told her. I told her I fell in love with someone here, and I want to be with you." He took her hands. "Viv, Vivian, please look at me," he begged. "I know I should have told you a long time ago. I should have told you that first night when we met at the wedding."

Vivian got up and walked to the window. She held herself up by leaning against the thick frame. The harsh reality of his marital status settled like a cold emptiness in her chest. "So, what am I to you, Thomas?" she demanded, feeling anger growing inside her. "A dalliance? A distraction? Your whore?" she spat the words at him.

"Vivian! No! I swear it. I love you. I have loved you from the first moment I saw you. I wrote to Elise that same week and asked for a divorce. I knew then I wanted to be with you."

"Elise." Vivian repeated her name and nodded. It was real. She had a name. *Elise.*

"Vivian, I'm so sorry. I was afraid you wouldn't see me anymore if you knew, and I couldn't take that chance. It just went on so long that I didn't know how to tell you anymore."

A sob escaped her mouth, and she collapsed to her knees. "How?" she cried out. "How could you not tell me?"

"Vivian, it doesn't matter. I don't care if I can't get a divorce. I love you. I want to be with you." He knelt on the floor in front of her. Tears streamed down his face. What if she never forgave him? What if he had ruined everything?

She looked at him, her face void of emotion. "How do I

ever trust you again, Thomas? You have successfully lied to me for almost two years."

"Vivian, I know it doesn't make sense, but I was so afraid I would lose you if you found out. I promise I will spend the rest of my life proving my love to you and our child." His voice cracked, and he put his head down. He looked up when he heard the door open. "Where are you going?"

"I need some air, Thomas. I need space to think."

She walked back down to the water's edge and took off her shoes and stockings. The water was cold and bit at her ankles, but she stood in it as the sand pulled out from under her feet, and the waves rolled and swirled around her. Finally, the sobs came. The hurt and anguish came. They thundered out of her like an unimaginable storm.

Her feet burned red from the cold water. As she turned to go back up to the house, she saw him standing on the shore waiting for her. The love he felt for her was as visible as the pain and fear in his eyes.

Damn him! She loved him. Somehow, they would work through things together. Somehow, she would forgive him. For the sake of their child. He didn't hesitate and strode across the sand and into the water, boots and all. She allowed him to take her hands but remained silent, his heart not beating as he waited for her to tell him his future.

Finally, she looked up at him and said, "Thomas, it won't be easy, but I'm willing to try and work this out together. Our child deserves that."

The noise that escaped him was not recognizable. It was a combination of joy and relief. He hugged her.

"I will never hurt you again. I promise you, and I promise wee Viv, too." He looked down at Vivian's stomach and placed his hand ever so gently on it.

"Wee Viv?" She finally felt some hope again for what they were together.

"Yes, Wee Viv. Our daughter. My daughter." He grinned, picked Vivian up and spun her around, dancing with her in the water and on the sand. Then he took her by the hand, and they ran back to the house, cold, wet, and covered in sand.

The next morning, Vivian woke to the smell of breakfast cooking. She was starving, and she didn't feel ill at all, just ravenously hungry.

Thomas was in the kitchen busy at the stove. A pot of tea was on the table with two large mugs. "Sorry! I hope I wasn't making too much noise. I didn't want to wake you. I wanted to surprise you with breakfast in bed." He kissed her forehead as she came to inspect the frying pan.

"The noise didn't wake me. It was the smell. It made me so hungry I had to come see for myself." She poured herself a cup of tea and topped off his mug before sitting in the chair to watch him finish up.

"I managed to get gourmet ham in a can. A special import from France." He spoke with an exaggerated French accent and gestured a chef's kiss with his hand. "The eggs are real, though. I snitched a few from the mess before I left." He carefully scooped the fried eggs and meat onto their plates and brought them to the table before sitting down beside her.

Vivian was sure she was drooling. She didn't think she had ever been so hungry in her life. She put a piece of the canned meat in her mouth. It was crispy on the outside and soft inside and could have been prime rib as far as she was concerned. It tasted fantastic.

Thomas watched with amusement as she gobbled down every bite and then sat satisfied, sipping her tea. "You weren't kidding when you said you were hungry." He laughed and put her hand to his lips. "Viv, I have been doing a lot of thinking." His mood became very serious, and she was instantly nervous about what he was going to say. "I'm going to rent this house for you after wee Viv arrives. You can't come out until after the baby is born, because you will need to be near a hospital. Afterward, you and your mom, dad, and Bryant can all move here. It's plenty big enough. Bryant can have his gardens and even more chickens if he wants."

Vivian was silent. She didn't look at him for a few minutes while she thought about his words. "Thomas, my parents are not going to want anything to do with you when they find out I'm pregnant, and you're already married. They're not going to move here with me and the baby." Her voice was quiet and calm.

"So, we don't tell them that part. What if we tell them we got married at city hall? I'm never going back to Canada, Vivian. My life is here with you and our child."

"Let me get this straight. You are suggesting that I lie to my own family?" She didn't know what to think.

"Technically, yes. The truth is, we would be married if we could be. If I can get my divorce, we will immediately get married. Everyone can just think we already are until that happens."

"Thomas, I …" Vivian stopped. He was right. Her family would never accept her or her child if they knew the truth. Once Thomas got his divorce, they would get married, and no one would be the wiser. His wife would surely divorce him once she knew they were having a baby, right? She may have been his wife, but Viv was having his child. "Okay."

"Okay? Really?" He was shocked. He thought he was going to have to sell it a lot more.

"Yes. You're right, Thomas. Once you get your divorce, we can get married, and no one has to know we never were. My parents will be happy, and I don't need to worry about being alone while I'm pregnant."

"Oh, Viv. I promise. I will send that letter as soon as I get back. This will all work out. I swear." He stood up and began hurriedly clearing the table.

"What are you doing?"

"We need to get back so I can buy you a ring, Vivian Waltman. My wife and the mother of my child needs a ring, then we can pay your parents a visit!"

Love Always

Chapter Twelve

"Mum is making a leg of mutton tonight," Vivian said. Her excitement was real. Full Sunday dinners didn't happen every week as they used to, and Thomas being home with them was a very special occasion. All of their leave had been pulled back. No one said anything, but everyone knew that meant there was something significant coming.

"Oh lovely. How did she pull that off?" Meat was not impossible to find, but it was definitely hard, and a whole leg of mutton would have been difficult to get.

"You are not the only one with the ability to source the finer things. Mum is very … resourceful." Vivian lifted her eyebrow and gave Thomas a sideways grin.

"Of that I have no doubt." Evelyn was an impressive woman. He would never want to get on her bad side. Thomas thought she might very well be the smartest person he had ever met. She knew and understood politics and business extraordinarily well, which meant she also understood the progress and lack of progress of war.

Evelyn was knowledgeable about machines and how they worked. Her passion for cooking and creating new recipes seemed quite contradictory to the rest of her skill set.

Thus, Evelyn was a delightfully complex woman whose demeanour made Thomas instinctively understand she was not to be trifled with, and by extension, nor should those she cared about.

Thomas smiled and hugged Vivian from behind as they watched her brother putter away in his garden. He rested his hands on her belly. She wasn't showing very much yet, but it was clear she was carrying his child. He kissed the top of her head. If only life could stay so simple.

She had moved back home with her parents when they found out she was pregnant, and they had quickly "gotten married." He had arranged to rent the farmhouse as promised for her and wee Viv after the baby arrived. There was no hospital nearby, so her parents had insisted she move back home while they waited for the arrival of their grandchild.

Ace was excited to be a grandad. Thomas was touched by the beautiful bond between Vivian and her father. He knew she was in good hands with her parents.

"Tommy, lad, good to see you. I didn't realise you had arrived." Ace came into the kitchen and saw the couple near the window. He was very happy for his girl. Thomas was a good man, even if he was a foreigner. At least he was from the colony, as they joked.

"Dad, good to see you. I just arrived a moment ago." The two men embraced warmly. "We were just enjoying watching Bryant gathering vegetables for supper."

"Ah yes, well, rest assured whatever he selects they will be perfect." They chuckled since they were all aware of Bryant's gifted talent for gardening. "He will be in heaven at the farmhouse."

Vivian's parents had decided it was wise to send Bryant with Vivian in the country. They didn't like the idea of her being all alone with the baby and so far from everyone. When Thomas had spoken of the enormous gardens, they realised it would be a perfect fit for Bryant to go with her. He would be able to help take care of the animals and the gardens.

Bryant came inside with an assortment of vegetables for supper. "I have some spinach for you, Vivvy. It's good for the baby. It will make her strong like you." Bryant held up the spinach in one hand and made a muscle flex with the other. Everyone laughed.

"Ev, the roast smells as though it's about ready," Ace called to his wife in the other room. One of her guilty pleasures was cheesy romance novels, and she was deeply engrossed in one.

"Right, coming!" she called back begrudgingly, putting her book down. "Hmmm, it does smell good, doesn't it?" As she opened the oven door, the heat brought out the wonderful aroma with it.

Ace carved the leg while Thomas and Vivian set the table, and Bryant and Evelyn organised the vegetables. The greens just needed a quick steaming. Evelyn spent a lot of time showing Bryant how to cook. It was something they really enjoyed doing together. Evelyn insisted Bryant learn valuable skills like cooking and basic repairs.

They sat down to a full table and an abundance of food. Thomas knew it was all for him. He had given word he was coming for three days. Evelyn decided to make it a celebration and had procured a hefty leg of mutton. Working in a candy factory gave her an opportunity to make good trades.

"Thomas, is there anything you can tell us about what you and your lads are up to?" Evelyn knew there were limitations to what he could tell them, but hopefully they could piece together enough to sort out what was going on with the war.

"I think it has gotten back here that the second front has opened up." Everyone at the table nodded. "We know that something big will have to happen. Hitler needs to be shown unequivocally that he is not winning this war." Thomas couldn't share that many regiments were already on standby, meaning they were to be ready at a moment's notice.

"Certainly so! He is a despicable man." Bryant leaned into the conversation. He had listened to many of their discussions, and he understood who Hitler was.

Thomas put his hand on Bryant's arm in an encouraging way and smiled at his brother-in-law. "We've been doing a great deal of waterproofing with bituminous. Bloody stuff is like tar and sticks to everything it touches. Takes a good deal of elbow grease to get it in all the nooks and crannies, like the seams on doors for example. Nasty stuff."

"Waterproofing …" Vivian's words trailed off. If Thomas and his men were waterproofing all their equipment, that meant they would be doing a water landing. Her heart raced. All she could think of were the losses at Dieppe.

"Yes," Thomas replied. He could see what she was thinking. Hell, he was thinking it, too. "Don't worry, darling. I will stay safe. I have to. Wee Viv will be here soon, and I plan to be around for both of you." He took her hand and gently kissed it, but Vivian was still worried.

"Well, if that's the case, it's best that every precaution is taken to make sure our equipment works when we need it to. Better to be prepared and not need it than need it and not be prepared." Ace tried to push the idea that the waterproofing was just an extra precaution, not that Thomas' regiment was getting ready for a water landing.

"Very true. You know the Army. They like to keep us busy doing silly jobs we never end up needing. Idle hands are no good for any soldier," Thomas remarked.

Ace chuckled. "No, indeed."

"Oh, Thomas, I almost forgot. I have something for you and your boys." Evelyn went to the sideboard and pulled out a box with what looked like several yellow tubes sitting in it. "My manager gave me these to give to you."

Thomas took the box and realised it was full of Sherbet Fountains. "Well, thank you, Mum. That's very generous. How do you eat it exactly?" He knew he would get a volunteer to show him.

"I can show you!" Bryant shouted in glee. The yellow paper tubes had a piece of black liquorice sticking out of the end. Bryant picked one out of the box and showed Thomas how to open the package and enjoy the sherbet powder inside. "See, you lick it like this, and stick it in and pull out the sugar."

"Wow, Evelyn! You came up with this? It's brilliant. The lads will love it. Thank you."

Evelyn smiled with pride at her accomplishment, and the royalties certainly came in handy too.

After supper, Ace and Thomas went outside to the garden to smoke while Vivian and Evelyn tidied up. Thomas had a great admiration for Ace. He was a very level-headed man with a generous spirit.

"Ace, I need to tell you something, and it's important that you do not share it."

Ace straightened up and nodded his agreement.

"There has already been an advance party and a large order to stand by. The 8th Recce isn't on standby yet. We will be next. We are only days away from history. Where we fall in that history has yet to be played out but based on what I know and from what I have heard, this will be a major shift for us. If I send word of a beautiful sea view, you will know we have started our advance."

"I won't say anything to anyone. I'm grateful for your trust, Thomas."

"I am telling you because if I don't come back—"

"I'm going to stop you right there, young man." Ace put his hands on Thomas' arm and shoulder. "You are coming home to us, to Viv, and to wee Viv. No matter what happens, you are coming home to us." Ace pulled Thomas into a fierce hug, and he was reminded of his own father and brother and the strength of their embraces.

Overwhelmed, Thomas hugged Ace back fiercely and let tears softly fall from his eyes.

"Thomas! Stop it." Vivian tried to muffle her laughter as the bed declared mutiny on the two of them crushing it.

Vivian and Thomas were cramped. They didn't dare move around too much since the bed creaked and groaned loudly anytime they shifted.

"I can't help that your bed is a traitor to my ardour." Thomas mockingly hit his hand to his chest as though being wounded.

"Well, you don't need to bounce on purpose." She giggled.

In retaliation, Thomas sat up in the bed and deliberately bounced several times, making an enormous clatter of springs and struts. They both burst into fits of laughter and fell against each other.

"You will need to stay very still then, Vivian." Thomas was still smiling and laughing, but his hands slid down Vivian's body, caressing her soft skin, and they both became still and quiet. He kissed her deeply, stifling her moan as his hand made its way to the crease at the top of her thighs, and he gently pushed them apart. His touch was teasing and exhilarating as he explored her with an increasing intensity. He delighted in feeling her body vibrantly respond to his touch.

Shifting his weight, he slid down further, kissing her throat as he moved lower. He lingered over her breasts, lovingly licking and sucking on the nipples. She arched her back and held his head. The blood was pounding in her ears as her entire body went on high alert to his touch. She still couldn't believe how good it felt to be with him. The way he touched her.

"Thomas!" She stifled her moans. "Oh my God, Thomas." She gasped as his hand intensified in its exploration, demanding more of her until she shuddered and released.

"Did that feel good, darling?" He smiled as he carefully lifted himself up and kissed her blossoming belly.

"Thomas, you know it did. You could feel me."

It was true. Thomas loved how strong she climaxed for him. For someone with no experience, she had become a very skilled lover and seemed to instinctively know how to move with him.

She placed one hand on his head and one on her mouth as his head dipped between her legs. She stifled her moans but didn't ask him to stop. It felt too good to stop. He masterfully touched her with his fingers and tongue, bringing her repeatedly to the peak of pleasure.

Thomas couldn't resist any longer, and he rose up above her on the bed. Kissing her deeply as he entered her, they both let out guttural sounds of ecstasy harnessed in whispers to try and not be heard. They moved together, matching pace and intensity, the bed strangely silent under them. Vivian wrapped her legs around Thomas, pulling him to her harder, thrusting against him. They could feel the tide building in them both.

"Vivian, I love you so much."

"I love you, too."

Thomas held her face, kissing her hard as they let themselves submit fully to their passion and love for each other.

The next morning, Vivian found Thomas in the garden with his tea. He smiled broadly and reached out to encircle her in a hug as she came towards him.

"How did you sleep?"

"Like a rock." Her face flushed slightly. "I seemed to have been very tired for some reason."

"I can't imagine why that would be." Teasing her, he kissed the tip of her nose.

"Viv, I am not going to be back for your birthday."

There was silence between them for a few moments as they both thought about how unsettled the future was.

"How soon?"

"Very soon."

"I have something for you." She rushed back into the house and came back with an item in her hand. "I found this a few years ago, and I have always thought of it as a bit of a good luck charm. I want you to take it with you." She handed him a small notecard with a pressed violet and the word *Home* written on it.

"Where did you find this?" Thomas was taken aback. How in the world did she have this?

"A couple years ago or so, the girls and I were going on hols. We took the train, and this was on the floor when I sat down."

He was staring at it intently.

"Why? What is it, Thomas?" She sensed there was something wrong.

"You won't believe this, Viv, but my sister Mimi gave me this when I left Canada. I lost it somewhere on the trip over. I always felt terrible, thinking I had lost a piece of home. Now I know it was with you the whole time. It's like it knew you would be my home." He had tears in his eyes as he held it and thought back to that day. It seemed a lifetime ago.

"That means you were on the train. In those same seats right before us." Vivian was amazed. "Our paths have been intertwined longer than we even knew."

"I think you're right, Viv. Some things are just meant to be." He hugged her tightly and looked at the small card again. "I promise to bring it back to you unharmed."

"You better, Thomas Cooper. I am going to hold you to your word."

104

Chapter Thirteen

Thomas was summoned to the regimental headquarters for a briefing. Major Faulkes was present and surprised them all when he announced they had a very high-level guest coming to do an inspection later that morning.

"The men will not disappoint you, sir," Thomas promised.

"They better not, RSM. How is the waterproofing coming?" Faulkes asked, his back facing Thomas as he reviewed maps and notes on the wall in front of him.

"It's slow work, but we're ahead of schedule I believe, sir."

"Good. Right then. Let's go meet our guest."

"Shall I go get the men ready, sir?"

"No, come with me and some of the officers to meet him first. Then you can go get your men ready with the understanding of what to prepare them for," Faulkes answered. He finally turned to look at Thomas as he said that. His face revealed no clues as to who the guest might be, but Thomas knew it was someone of great importance if Faulkes was being somewhat secretive about it. "You cannot tell the men until they are sorted
for the inspection, RSM. Is that understood?"

"Absolutely, sir. I won't say a word until we are at attention and waiting for his arrival."

Thomas followed the major out of the building to a large tent that had been set up near the parade grounds. He noticed some of the other SSMs and officers had already arrived. The last were coming as he walked in with Major Faulkes.

"Attention!" he shouted. All the men turned and came to attention for their commanding officer.

"Thank you, gentlemen. At ease. I have spoken to some of you already and let you know we have a high-level guest arriving shortly to inspect and see how the 8th RECCE does things. Our reputation precedes us, and he wants to see what all the fuss is about. I will ask that you not share with your men who our guest is until they are on the parade grounds. As you can imagine, we want to keep knowledge of this visit off the radar. I'm sure you have put together that there is a big operation imminent. I will share with you that we were not part of the initial operation, but we will be part of the follow-up."

They all cheered at that.

"No offence, sir, but it is about bloody time they used us properly." RSM Finlayson lifted his chin as he spoke, and the others nodded in agreement.

"You are not wrong, Finlayson. The truth is our boys are stuck. They got off the beaches and things were not the bed of roses they expected."

"So, we're going over to finish it up, sir?" Thomas asked.

"That we are, Cooper. That we are." Faulkes patted Thomas on the shoulder.

The door swung open, and a group of MPs and junior officers entered. "Attention!" one shouted.

Everyone stood up and saluted, waiting to see who the important guest was going to be. Some senior officers came in next and lined the far wall like some rehearsed parade. In walked Field Marshal Bernard "Monty" Montgomery.

"At ease, men. I have some exciting news for you. You are officially on standby. In a few days, you will be landing on Gold and bloody well taking back Caen and Falaise. What say you?"

The room was filled with a deafening roar of cheers. "Herewae! Herewae!"

The 2nd Division and the 8th Recce broke camp and began moving from their locations around Aldershot to their embarkation assembly locations in the east docks area of London. Thomas and his men were loaded onto Landing Ship Tank 154 and towed out from the London docks by a tugboat.

"Stow your gear, and let's find the galley," Thomas instructed.

"Coop, they have pillows!" His SSM laughed. "Pretty posh."

"Well, enjoy it while we have it." Thomas laughed back.

The food on the American ships exceeded any they'd had so far in the war, and having an assigned bed was a comfort they weren't going to have time to get used to. There were card games planned for later to help distract the men, and Thomas promised to give them all a chance to win his money.

After ensuring the soldiers were cared for, Thomas ascended to the deck, seeking solace and a smoke. He gazed out at the tranquil harbour as the distance grew from the safety of the shore. The sky, a canvas of shifting shades, transitioned gracefully from the warm tones of the day to the mesmerising silver glow of night. He found himself wondering if he would see it again, wondering if he would see Vivian or meet his daughter.

Dear Ace,

We are certainly not being idle around here. Lots to keep busy. I won a few hands of poker. Turns out I am pretty darn good at it. I am enclosing some of the winnings for Viv and the baby as well as some in her letter to spread it out a bit. Some is foreign, but I am sure it will spend just as well if not better than our pound notes.

The commanding officers had a lovely retreat recently. They decided it was worth bringing a few more of us out. The food is the best we have had all war. It sure is nice to experience the finer things once in a while.

The weather is predicted to be clear, with a beautiful blue sky for the next few days. There is the most beautiful sea view ...

Thomas and his men were greeted with grim faces when they arrived at the small village of Trace-sur-Mer on what they were calling Gold Beach, the centre of the Normandy invasion. It was the beach the Americans were using as the planned staging point for the next push. The allies had not made the progress they expected on D-Day, and a month into the operation, Montgomery had severely underestimated the retaking of the vital villages of Caen and Falaise.

From the harbour, the men watched in awe as HMS Rodney fired her sixteen-inch guns in support of the forward troops. Thomas witnessed the huge shells disappear over the horizon beyond the treeline. Fleetingly, he wondered where they were landing. Thomas connected with his Commanding Officer Major Grey and was given their orders to work inland. They had expected a battle, but the beach was a picture of utter confusion.

As they organised their gear to move inland, the Major came over to Thomas. "RSM, be ready to strip it down to what can be carried. We're being shifted to support the 2nd Division on foot when we get inland." He looked grim.

The 8th Recce was an armoured division and trained differently than regular infantry. It would be hard on the men. Thomas didn't argue, however. He understood if the Major was asking that of them, he had already argued against it, and it was just what they needed to do. In the end, that was what they were all there for—to get the job done.

"Right. Will I need to pick a couple lads to stay behind with the wagons? They'll need to be kept watch over and then brought up to us eventually, ya?"

"No. The wagons will go with you. Just be ready to adapt quickly to foot travel," replied Major Grey, looking off into the distance at the cliffs and hilltops. "It's not gone well, Coop. Between these Hitler Jugend and the panzers, we didn't expect, I'm not sure how we will take back Caen."

"Well, sir, it doesn't really matter how. We just will. No choice." Thomas patted his officer on the arm and smiled slightly. He never shared what his commanders told him. They relied on his ear as much as his judgement.

Major Grey gave a small smile back. "You are right there, Tommy Boy. We've got the best reinforcements possible. Full grit. We will help them get the job done indeed." He paused and looked at the hilltops again. "Indeed."

Thomas glanced at his crew. It made him uneasy to all be stricken off service and then stricken back onto service with the 2nd. They were a small, tight-knit group of squaddies. He knew all soldiers looked out for each other, but it was different with one's own men. They were his responsibility. His boys.

Movement caught his eye just above the treeline. He realised, with a sickening feeling, what it was.

"Take cover!" he yelled as the Luftwaffe strafed the beach. Men, who had been trying to remove the waterproofing from their equipment, jumped for cover or hit the ground. A few raised their rifles and tried to inflict any damage they could to the plane as it flew past. It went out over the sea towards the ships. Anti-aircraft guns scattered shells up into the sky as three more planes appeared.

Men ran in all directions for cover and a better position to fight back. Thomas ran to the nearest Bren Carrier and waited. Looking over the edge of the vehicle, he could see the planes coming back around.

"Moore! Help me with that 50 cal!" he shouted at the young corporal huddled beside him on the ground.

He was rattled and didn't know what to do. Thomas' order cleared his mind. He jumped into the Fox with Thomas and launched into action beside his RSM. They moved in unison, predicting each other's movements, and got the gun loaded and ready as the planes began their second pass. They took aim at the one closest to them.

"Fire!"

Their rounds missed. In their haste to return fire, they had forgotten to aim off. The plane shifted its path to meet them head-on.

"Fire! Shoot it! Get that bastard!" Thomas yelled as the Bren Carrier lurched from the recoil of the 50.

The shells burst from the gun. They watched, mesmerised, as the tracer rounds made their way up to punch holes in the fuselage of the plane. The pilot realised too late he was in their reach and tried to pull up, but he couldn't. Pieces of the wing, cockpit, and pilot collided with the ground.

Thomas and Moore stood frozen, staring at the burning remains of the plane. Shaken, they looked down to see the heap of brass at their feet from the spent shells. Nodding, they set to chucking them out of the carrier, grateful they had upgraded to the 50 instead of relying on the standard-issue Bren.

The sound of a second plane exploding as it hit the water mere feet from the SS Rodney made them jump. Thomas and Moore were ready to strike again and were relieved to see the retreat of the two remaining planes.

"Thank you," said Moore.

"Why? What for?" Thomas looked confused.

"If you hadn't got me to move, I'm not sure I ever would have again," Moore answered. He had felt himself beginning to cower, to try and save himself over others. He knew the act of taking down the plane, his first real contact with the enemy, was a turning point for him. Every soldier had that turning point where they had to react. Thomas had taken him through it.

"You seemed to move pretty damn fast from where I was sitting." Thomas laughed and slapped the young man on the back. "Well done. Well done. Let's go check in and see where we stand now."

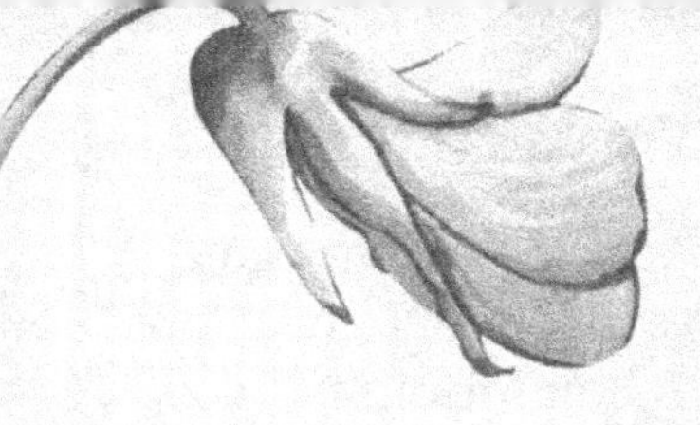

Chapter Fourteen

After three days of fighting, C Squadron had requested an urgent replenishment of resources. Fuel consumption had been much higher than expected due to their constant tactical manoeuvring.

"Sir, the replen has been set. Permission to accompany the men and oversee it." Thomas sensed the men may have been fatigued, and he wanted to check in on them.

"Granted, RSM. It will be good for you to stretch your legs, eh?" The major knew Thomas missed being with the men. He was an excellent soldier and leader. He had tried to give Thomas a promotion and was shocked when he politely asked not to be given the lift in rank. He knew if he did, he would not be able to keep a close eye on his lads, and for Thomas, that was something he just didn't want to give up.

"Yes, sir. It sure will. Thank you." Without missing a beat, Thomas turned and made for the crew to finalise the instructions for that night.

The convoy moved out at midnight, snaking its way along the main supply route, or MSR, to the grid C Squadron's SSM had provided on the radio. The drive
was slow but uneventful. The sky was clear and the stars

bright. Thomas thought about how the sky looked the same there in the countryside of France as it did far away in Ardoch, Ontario. In an odd way, it was comforting to know his family back home and Viv in England were all sharing the same sky together, even if they were what felt like worlds apart.

The convoy reached its location shortly before zero two hundred and quietly set up. Once completed, the Squadron Quartermaster Sergeant radioed 1st Troop to move forward to his location. They moved through quickly and dispersed back to their harbour area. The SQMS radioed for 2nd Troop to move in. They too progressed smoothly through the replen, stocking up on their desperately needed fuel, ammunition, water, and food, and 3rd Troop prepared to move forward.

Thomas wanted to get things done as quickly as possible. He understood and was keenly aware they were a prime target, literal sitting ducks. He jumped in to help with the ammunition truck to move the men through faster. He was getting concerned with the increasing level of noise of the 3rd Troop. Their lead wagon, commanded by Corporal Moore, was having carburettor issues, and the driver had to keep gunning the engine to keep it moving. The percussive popping sounds echoed insistently through the trees they were using as cover.

The early summer sunrise was beginning to break the horizon. The midnight sky turned plum violet, orange, and red as he heard the unmistakable retort of a German 88-millimetre gun. His heart sank as the first round crashed into the rear of the replen just as he was about to hand Cpl Moore another box of Bren gun magazines.

"Take cover!" he shouted, and the men instinctively did as best they could. He knew the artillery were on target. The next hit would be fatal. Moore grabbed Thomas by the arm and dragged him into the noisy lead wagon still holding the box of 303 ammunition.

"Get the hell out of here!" Moore yelled at the driver.

Thomas looked back and watched with a sense of horror.

Shells hit the ammunition truck, sending rounds in every direction. The troop leader's wagon was consumed by the twisted, curling waves of fire as red-hot shrapnel tore through the truck he had just finished refuelling from. Thomas shielded his eyes from the sudden brightness and the intense heat of the fireball. The wagon veered hard to the right as Trooper Franks, the driver, raced through the forest in the wash of morning light. He couldn't see where he was going, but he knew it needed to be as far as he could get from the caravan that had been hit hard. The jolt caused Thomas to lose his balance. Still holding the box of Bren gun ammunition from when Moore dragged him into the wagon, it smashed against his temple. Everything went dark.

116

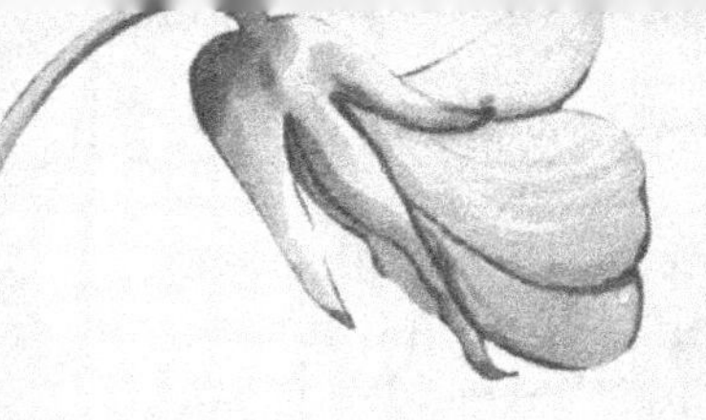

Chapter Fifteen

Thomas winced as he touched the bandage on his head. Bloody metal box. He was more fortunate than the troop leader and his crew, though. The whole lot had essentially disappeared before his very eyes, vaporised in the explosion of the fuel truck. The vision brought Thomas back, and he became fully alert.

"Report, Moore. What's our situation?"

"We lost the boss and his entire crew as well as Sergeant McDougall, sir."

"What about supplies?" Thomas asked.

"I consolidated all supplies with the three remaining vehicles and cross-decked fuel to the troop sergeant's vehicle."

Thomas sighed. They hadn't been able to get fully replenished before they were hit and had to hightail it out. He was impressed by how far Moore had come from that first contact on the beach. It seemed like a lifetime ago. He made a mental note to recommend Moore for the troop sergeant's position when he returned to headquarters. Knowing the men were without their leader, Thomas got on the radio to HQ to send the situation report.

"Sunray, this is Sunray Minor. Come in." He tried several times to reach Major Grey to no avail. He got no answer. Assuming the worst, that RHQ had fallen, he decided to take command of 3rd Troop for as long as he needed to.

Thomas knew the men under his command had been under pressure, with several days of unbroken contact. He needed to find a safe spot to offer them some rest. He looked at his maps and saw a location that might work.

"CPL," he called out to Moore. "I want you to recce here as a hide location." He pointed at the map. "Check and see if it's suitable."

Moore looked at the map. "Yes, sir." He then set out on the friendly side of the hill. A short time later, Moore radioed that the location was suitable and secure.

"Trooper, get ready to move to these coordinates." Thomas and the men did a quick equipment check and set off towards Moore's position, with the third vehicle following.

Moore saw them coming, and being careful not to make themselves visible, he guided the two vehicles into defensive positions. It was important they were prepared for any further attack. The Germans would know they hadn't been successful in taking out the entire squadron and could be looking for them. The three crews turned off their engines but stayed mounted. They needed to do a listen and make sure they hadn't been observed moving into position.

Satisfied there was no immediate threat, Thomas gave the order to stand down. "Baker, set up sentries, and tell the men they can dismount once they are posted."

"Of course, sir." Baker was a trooper and grateful to feel like there was some relief coming. With the sentries posted, the crews dismounted and began repairing the battle damage to their vehicles and equipment.

They were already exhausted from several days of contact.

"Moore, tell the lads to get some grub into them. We have a bit of a lull for now, and we are secure," Thomas called.

"Yes, sir. On it." Moore delivered the message, and compo

packs quickly came out. The mood became sombre as they all thought back and reflected on the last twenty-four hours. It was the first time they'd had to take stock of what had happened. They had lost friends, some of whom they'd come to rely on for the past three years. No one spoke much from their fatigue and thoughts. As they ate, and sentries were rotated, they realised just how hungry they were. They had made it further than a lot of others before them, but they wondered what lay in store for them with a new leader.

Thomas called in his crew commanders. "I understand the frequency-code book was in the troop leader's vehicle. Do you have confirmation of this?" Without the frequency codes, they would have no way of knowing how to reach RHQ and report in.

"That's correct, sir," replied Trooper Conners. "We can make an educated guess and start there."

"Sounds good, Conners. It's at least a start, eh?" Thomas smiled grimly. "We can go with the assumption the rest of the crews are heading here." He pointed to his map. Before he had left to oversee the replen, he and Major Grey had discussed the longer game plan as they prepared to join the fray for Caen with the 2nd Battalion. He had a pretty solid idea of where they would go if everything else had gone according to plan. "The Major was planning on heading there before all hell broke loose yesterday, so we'll stick with that plan for now."

The men nodded in agreement.

The sound of fighting was ever-present around them. It was distant and sporadic so not of immediate concern. They were not disturbed by it. The contours of their map indicated to their left the land sloped down towards farmland, with thick hedgerows between them and the open fields. They had learned the hard way that what farmers had grown to protect and shield crops was also an excellent location for German ambushes. The field was devoid of crops and resembled a barren desert, with craters like the surface of the moon where mortars had fallen short of the village. In the distance, they could see the Odon and Orne rivers and the remnants of the village. They were to secure the bridge and crossroads leading in and out of Caen. That was a vital travel route for the Germans and allies for supplies. It was also pivotal to them moving forward to secure Falaise and eventually Berlin. The success of the war was linked to the retrieval of Caen.

Thomas needed to keep the men focused to keep their minds off their losses. Looking at his map, he saw there was a major junction about 1.5 kms away.

"Moore, we still have a war going on here. See this junction?" He pointed to the map again. "We can use this time to gather some intel. I think this junction could have some strategic importance to enemy troop movement. What if we mount an observation post? We can send two guys at a time, two hours on and four hours off, with binoculars, book, and pencil. Get them to log any movement they see."

"Yes, sir, sounds good. I will go let the men know." Moore was walking a little taller. He knew he had to step up, and there was no way he would disappoint his RSM.

"Hey, sir! We got the carburettor fixed on the wagon. Quiet as a noisy mouse now." Trooper Franks, the driver who had got them safely away from the convoy when it was attacked, grinned from ear to ear.

"Well done, Franks." Thomas gave a nod. He knew Franks felt it was his fault that the replen had been compromised. The noise of his wagon had given them away. It was good to see him smile again.

CPL Moore came running up to Thomas. "Sir," he said excitedly, "the Observation Post reports a Panzer IV broken down on the junction. It seems to be having transmission problems. The crew was dismounted, and they're working on it. The back decks are up."

Thomas understood their excitement. The chance to capture a Panzer IV was an opportunity they wouldn't want to miss.

Hurriedly, he grabbed his Sten gun and headed up to the OP to check it out for himself. Sure enough, there it sat. Engine decks up, off to the side of the road making use of the scant cover afforded by the trees.

"So, what happened?" he asked the troopers.

"We heard what sounded like a bucket of nuts coming down the road. Then, we saw the white smoke coming out of it as it rolled to a stop where it is now. The transmission is probably buggered. The crew have been working on it for about two hours now. Lots of shouting in German." The trooper chuckled a bit. "What do you think, sir, should we try and capture it?"

Thomas was already forming a plan in his head as the trooper asked the very question he was thinking. He needed to discuss it with the crew commanders first.

"Keep an eye on it. If it moves, I want to know," he said as he moved back to the hide position.

When he got back, he quickly called in his crew commanders. "All right, we have an opportunity with a short window." He relayed what they knew about the panzer. "Any ideas on how to capture it or take it out?"

Cpl Moore looked at the other commander and then back at his RSM. "Well, sir, we have the element of surprise and a PIAT."

"The PIAT?" Thomas looked at Moore, expecting he had said the wrong weapon.

"Yes, sir. The PIAT. In anti-tank training, our instructor showed us that in Tunisia, they discovered a sweet spot on that Panzer IV. If hit right with the PIAT, it will take out the crew and the tank in one shot."

"Are you sure, Moore?"

"Absolutely, sir," Moore replied confidently.

"All right then, CPL, you have the job. What is the rest of our plan?"

Thomas and the two corporals quickly thrashed out a plan, involving a dismounted attack.

"We can leave a Bren with the OP crew for fire support while we move in on foot." Thomas ran his finger along the path on the map he intended for them to follow. "We can use the ground and the hedge grove for cover to get within striking distance of the Panzer IV."

The men received the news with enthusiasm. They were eager to get back in the fight and settle a score or two.

Within twenty minutes, the men had dismounted two Brens and camouflaged the vehicles. With each soldier carrying their personal weapons and as much ammunition as he could, they set off to drop the first Bren with the OP and brief them on the plan.

Using the dead ground as cover, they slowly made their way down towards the Panzer IV. The shot had to be taken from the front, which made the approach difficult. The tank crew's attention was focused on the engine and transmission located at the back of the tank.

Despite knowing they had cover from the Bren at the OP, the approach was still nerve-wracking. They had no way to know if the turret was being manned or not.

"I'm going to need to get into position over there." Moore gestured to the end of the hedgerow.

"We need to get positioned to support you, Moore," Thomas whispered back. "You need as much behind you as we can give to distract them so you can get off the shot."

"Okay. Give me a signal when you're ready then." Moore tried to smile bigger and more confidently than he felt. The plan had seemed easier in his head when he was telling his RSM back at base camp.

Thomas gave him the signal. He didn't hesitate. As he ran out of the corner of the hedgerow to position himself, one of the tank crew saw him.

"Achtung!" he yelled, raising the alarm. In response, one of the crewmen reached for his MP40 and fired a burst towards Moore, hitting him in the arm and chest. He dropped to the ground with the PIAT in his hands.

"Moore!" Thomas shouted as he saw the young man crumple to the ground.

The OP saw Moore fall and opened fire with the Bren gun. The rest of the men fired on the tankers. Realising they were facing more than just the solitary Moore, the panzer crew dove into the turret in an attempt to man their tank.

Thomas saw the loaded PIAT merely feet away from him. He knew if the tank crew got mobilised, they were all dead, so he raced towards Moore and picked up the PIAT.

"I sure hope you're right about this, mate!" he shouted as he raised the PIAT to his shoulder and took aim. He could see the turret traversing slowly in his direction as he sought out the aiming point Moore had described. The turret was now squarely on him, and it was now or never. He watched the 303 rounds from the Bren hitting the turret as he pulled the trigger on the PIAT.

There was a flash as the rounds hit the tank directly under the mantlet where the turret joined the hull. For a horrible moment that seemed to last a lifetime, Thomas thought he had missed.

"Sir!" screamed Moore. "Run!"

Thomas reached down to pull Moore up.

"No, you don't have time. Go! Go now!" Moore pushed Thomas away as Franks and Parker from his crew arrived to help. Together, they dragged Moore to cover as the ammunition inside the tank began to explode. Thomas had not missed after all.

It took a few minutes for him to hear the cheering of the men. When he gathered his wits, he looked back at the tank. It was engulfed in flames. The turret was hanging uselessly off to the side. He scanned the area quickly to make sure there were no other enemy soldiers around and saw CPL Moore laying on the ground. There was a large bloodstain on the young corporal's uniform, but he was still alive, his breathing shallow.

"I was right, eh?" Moore said.

"I guess there will be no living with you now." Thomas laughed. "Well done, lad. Well done." Thomas took a look at Moore's injuries. Miraculously, only one bullet had hit him in the shoulder. "Looks like you'll live to tell a grand version of this tale." Thomas took out the med pack to cover up the wound. It wasn't a serious one, but they still needed to stop the bleeding.

The sound of metal tracks, a group of them in fact, could be heard approaching from the west. Thomas and his men exchanged glances. He nodded and motioned for them to step into position to defend themselves again. Just as Thomas put a fresh magazine in his Sten gun, Trooper Franks jumped up and down.

"It's okay, sir! They're ours!"

Thomas's relief was audible, and he allowed himself to relax his grip on the Sten as a column of M4 Sherman tanks came into view. He slumped slightly and patted Moore on the arm. "See that? The cavalry has arrived."

The tank commander in the first Sherman opened his hatch and looked at the smouldering Panzer IV. He called out to Thomas with a thick Geordie accent, "What the hell have you blokes been up to then?"

They all laughed. Moore smiled and lay back down. He knew they would be okay.

Love Always

Chapter Sixteen

Thomas and his men had managed to find their way back to their regiment with the help of the British tank commander who had come across them at the site of the panzer win. As the wagons made their way through the edge of town to their new coordinates, he thought back to the 16-inch guns that had been firing from the beaches. Bombers had flown over the area the day before to help clear the way for their arrival.

Caen lay ahead of them, virtually levelled. The air was full of the smell of death. The remains of cattle, soldiers, and civilians littered the ground, resting in their final positions as life had left them. Some looked peaceful, asleep on their backs or sides. Others lay in crumpled heaps, twisted and broken. Some missing limbs and faces, split open in a ghastly display for the world to see of the fragility of the human body. It wasn't the blood that made the air smell so damn awful. It was the voiding of the bladder and bowels as the people died that fouled the air. Bodies ravaged, ripped open by the assault of bullets and mortars and left behind in the chaos of battle. Still, they needed to press forward.

"Try to breathe through your mouths and just focus on the task at hand," Thomas instructed the men.

They moved in silence. There were no words for what they were witnessing. Nothing that Thomas or anyone else could say to make them feel better that it wasn't them lying on the ground. They would mourn and care for the dead when they had time.

2nd Division had hunkered themselves at the edge of town, waiting for Thomas and his men before starting the next stage of their attack. Thomas found Major Grey.

"How are you holding up?" he asked, knowing it wasn't great just from the grim look on Grey's face.

"We've lost a lot of men. This hasn't been the walk in the park they expected."

"Never is. Where do we stand? Who is in position?"

"We have three tanks set, four squads moving into positions now, and a sniper moving into the corner window of that building." Grey pointed to a building that was barely more than rubble. "We had to pick something close enough that we could give some cover but also had enough height for advantage." Grey sighed deeply. "Not much left with any height advantage as you can see."

They all looked at the village. There weren't many buildings that hadn't been at least partially struck and damaged.

"We heard there was a panzer." Grey glanced up at Thomas and gave him a wry smile.

"Yeah. Well, it was one of the unexpected delights on our way back to you, sir. Brits gave us an escort. The Geordie tank commander thought they should try to keep us from getting ourselves into any more trouble." Thomas smiled a bit, then frowned. "Cpl Moore was hit in the shoulder, but the medic says he should be fine. They shipped him off to get some proper care. I'd like to recommend him for promotion and a military medal, sir. When he gets back, of course. He's really gathered himself up and proven himself."

"I heard you were pretty on the ball yourself, RSM." The major grinned.

"Thank you, sir, but I really only finished what Moore

organised."

"Right, well, we are ready to press forward now you've all arrived. We're sending C Squadron in first, RSM."

Thomas looked at Major Grey with some surprise. "First, sir?"

"Yes. You're still warm, and it will enliven the rest when they see the squadron carry forward."

"Yes, sir." Thomas would have liked to see his men get a brief reprieve after having just travelled and taken on that panzer, but he understood the major's point of view. His men still had some adrenaline rushing that they could use to their advantage.

"All right, Coop, pass on the plan to the SSMs. Let them know we will move at zero thirteen forty hours." Thomas nodded and left to find SSM Robinson.

"Hey, Coop! Heard you blew up a tank!" SSM Robinson patted Thomas on the back when he saw him. "Should have known you'd get yourself into trouble after we lost you at the replen."

"Technically, it blew itself up." Thomas laughed and greeted his friend back. They had known each other for most of their careers. Robinson was a good, level-headed soldier. Easy to rely on. "The Major wants us ready to move out at zero thirteen forty hours." He got to business. They didn't have time to catch up. Thomas relayed the plan and left Robinson to communicate it to the rest of the men.

He refilled his canteen on his way back to RHQ to support Major Grey. "The men will be saddled up and ready to go as advised, sir."

"Good. Let's move into position, RSM."

"Yes, sir." They got in their wagon and moved off to their first position for RHQ.

"All right, Coop." Major Grey took a breath and nodded at Thomas. "Engage."

Thomas spoke into the radio, "All squadrons, this is Sunray Minor. Ready positions." He gazed up and over the scorched and pitted rolling hills behind them. There was still a hint of the rich farmland that once covered the region. The sky was clear and bright blue with only a wisp of clouds. The sun was warm on his face, and he closed his eyes to soak it in for a moment.

Such a beautiful place to die, he thought to himself.

The battle for Caen had begun.

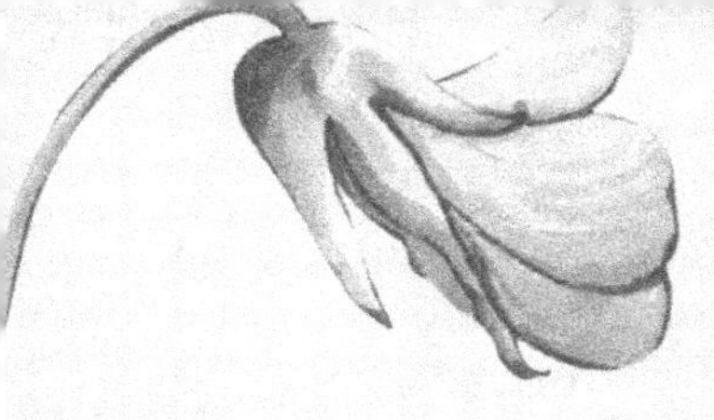

Chapter Seventeen

The small garden had not suffered despite Vivian's not-so-green thumb. She looked around her with a sense of pride. Her brother Bryant had managed to plant and grow quite a nice assortment of vegetables in her little patch in the rear of her parents' home in Tottenham. He was teaching her how to care for the plants and gave her a small patch to work with, under his supervision, of course.

He's a very patient teacher, Vivian mused.

The vibrant greens of the plants clashed with the stark grey, brown, and black of the scorched walls of houses and buildings around them. They had been charred from fire and ruin at the hand of the incessant bombings by Germany. Peas clung thickly to the twine she had strung across some sticks. She snapped one off and placed it into her mouth. It was crisp and sweet. She closed her eyes as she crunched happily on the shell and through to the sweet round peas inside.

Her belly rolled and stretched. She reached down to rub it, massaging her baby bump with delicate and affectionate stokes. Her child, Thomas's child,
responded to the happy calm of their mother. It didn't matter to Vivian if the child was a boy or a girl so long as they were healthy and well.

They would be moving to the house in Farnham in just a few more weeks. He wanted her to be safe and knew London would become an ever-increasing target for the Luftwaffe and the VK buzz bombs. He couldn't bear the idea of her being hurt, and with her carrying his child, it was even more crucial Vivian be kept safe.

The frequency of the bombings had been increasing as of late, leading many to speculate about an impending attack on the shores of Southampton. In fact, the frequency had grown to at least one bomb every hour. Most were taken down by the anti-aircraft guns and barrage balloons, but far too many reached their marks.

The scream of the air raid siren broke through the tranquillity of the garden. She was momentarily unsure of where she was or the significance of the noise. Even before the siren reached its peak, she could hear the drone. The buzzing of the VK bombs. How much longer would it last?

A sickening dread hit her. While they could be heard, there was usually no threat. It was when they stopped making noise, they became a true danger. That was when they were dropping from the sky, seeking their target. Seeking to destroy roads, bridges, and homes. Seeking to take lives and evoke terror. She could hear the drone of the bombs and the siren blending in with the anti-aircraft guns. The sounds blurred, creating a syncopated orchestra of cataclysm.

Terror lifted in her chest, and her heart pounded. Viv ran towards the house. She needed to get inside for her greatest safety. To get away from the potential shrapnel of crumbling walls and shattering glass. The risk of the house being hit was less than the risk of something around her being destroyed and her being without cover.

As she ran toward the house, her father appeared in the door, calling for her. "Viv! Come on!"

At that moment, she lost her footing and stumbled. She saw her father's face drop as she fell forward onto her swollen stomach.

"Viv!" he cried out, running towards her. But there was no

chance to reach her in time. Vivian had already hit the ground, belly first, with a horrifying thud. He helped her up and half-carried her into the house.

Her heart was pounding in her ears. She could barely hear her father, but understood he was telling her to hide under the bed. He helped her down onto the floor, but she couldn't fit. That was when she felt the warmth on her legs.

She looked at her father as she touched the inside of her thigh. He went ashen when he saw the blood on her hand.

"Right then." He took a breath. "Let's get you to the hospital. Seems my grandbaby has plans to come early." He smiled at Vivian and squeezed her hand, trying to feel as calm as he hoped he looked for his daughter's sake.

The streets were sheer madness as people ran for cover. Emergency vehicles swerved around pieces of burning buildings that had broken away or fallen into the road as they collapsed. One of the bombs had hit an apartment complex just two streets away. Bricks, glass, and wood had been turned into weapons in their own right as they crumbled and erupted into the surrounding streets.

Wallace was normally a very quiet and reserved man. He wasn't known for taking action or being a hero. But in the face of his daughter and unborn grandchild needing him, he rose to the occasion. He saw an ambulance hurtling down the road. He stepped into the lane, knowing they wouldn't stop for a mere hand in the air as if he were hailing a cab. He closed his eyes momentarily, expecting he would be struck. When the impact failed to happen, he opened them and saw the terrified eyes of the driver.

"Ah ya outta ya fookin' mind?" the driver yelled at him. "Do we not have enough dead and wounded without ya jumpin' in frontta me?"

"My daughter!" Wally yelled. "My daughter needs to get to the hospital!" He motioned towards Vivian, who was leaning against a lamppost. Her face was white with fear.

The attendant saw her swollen belly and the blood running down the inside of her leg. "Got an add-on. Hold tight!" he yelled at the driver while jumping out of the cab. "Let's get her in the back." He helped Vivian into the back of the ambulance and then jumped back into the cab.

Wallace didn't move until he saw the medics had placed Vivian inside. Knowing she was as safe as he could make her; he moved out of the way to allow her to be taken to the nearest hospital for care. As he watched the ambulance drive off, he finally surrendered to his fear and collapsed to his knees, sobbing in the middle of the street. He prayed for his daughter, his grandchild, and for all of London as they fought to survive the damned war.

The tanks began pulling out through the lines. Machine-gun fire could be heard three hundred yards away from the right of C Squadron's position.

"C Squadron to Sunray Minor. We have machine guns to the right of our position. Moving to intercept. Over." Trooper Franks advised RHQ and Thomas.

"Roger, C Squadron. Friends on the left report two other subunits. Keep status advised. Over." Thomas made a series of marks on the map, noting the known movements of all troops and what was happening at each location.

"Sunray Minor, C Squadron. Be advised our friends on the left had to withdraw from Toronto and have met up with us on this side of the river. Over."

"Roger that, C Squadron. Over."

Thomas wished he was with them. He knew they were facing a hard go. There were strong enemy counterattacks with tanks and infantry. The Germans had been well prepared. As the voice of RHQ on the radio, it was as close as he could get to them at the moment.

"A Squadron to RHQ. Any information on the bridge?"

"RHQ to A Squadron. Not yet. Stand by for the signal then move towards Toronto." Thomas checked on the position of the other squadrons.

"LO to RHQ, any of your people on the right flank?"

"No, LO. You are clear to move forward on the right flank."

The battle was escalating. German tanks were moving in.

"C Squadron arrived at position 777004."

"C Squadron, proceed." Thomas knew their orders were to blow the bridge. Their own location began to take artillery. They were on target, but they needed to move.

"Major, they are not on us quite yet, but I suggest we move before they acquire us," Thomas called out to the major.

"Agreed, RSM. Let's go." The major didn't waste any time. They scooped up the maps and communication equipment and jumped into the wagons.

"RHQ moving to Woodshire." Thomas alerted the men RHQ would be moving to their new position.

"C Squadron at 793052. Bridge blown, sir, but still in enemy hands."

"Roger that, C Squadron. When our new friends arrive, Recce to the southeast. Watch for sniper fire."

Thomas and Grey arrived at their new location and quickly opened up the maps to update their information as it poured in for each of the squadrons.

"C Squadron, carrier of new friends, has arrived. Moving to 743983."

"Roger that, C Squadron. RHQ now at Woodshire."

The ambulance lurched as it sped towards the hospital with Vivian. It already housed four other people wounded from the bombings.

"Here! Here! Lay her down," cried out a woman who was bleeding from head and arm wounds. "I don't need to be laying down. She does!" The woman moved to sit beside the other passengers in the back and helped Vivian to lay down.

"Thank you." She smiled meekly, but she was scared. There had been very few moments during the war when she had been genuinely frightened. At that moment, with her child at risk, she was more scared than she had ever been. What if something happened to wee Viv? What if … she couldn't bring herself to finish the thought.

The ambulance lurched again, and everyone had to grab hold of something to keep from being thrown.

"What's your name, pet?" The medic was taking Vivian's blood pressure.

"Viv … Vivian Waltman."

"I'm Stan." He paused to smile reassuringly at her. "Looks as though you're going to be a mum in short order, eh?" He patted her arm and touched her abdomen. "How far apart are the contractions?"

"I'm not sure. I haven't had a chance to really count. I fell trying to get into the house when I heard the sirens," she explained. "The baby, will she be, okay?" Vivian looked up at the medic and back to her baby. She ran her hand over her belly, trying to soothe her unborn child.

"Oh, I see," said Stan. "How far along are you then?"

"Just over seven months. It's too early for her to come."

"Well, too early or not, this baby seems to have decided it's their time. You said she. You think you're having a girl then?"

"Her father is convinced we're having a girl. He's in France…" Her voice drifted away.

"Ah, right. Well, we're almost at the hospital. They'll take good care of you both."

"Do you have any other children, Viv?" The woman who

had given up the cot in the ambulance touched Vivian's arm and smiled.

"No, this is our first." She tried to smile back, but she could still feel the warmth of blood between her legs and knew it was not a good sign it hadn't stopped.

"I'm Diane Christianson. My husband Will is in France, too. He's due to come home soon. He's a trooper for the 2nd Armoured Division.

"Thomas is Canadian. He's with the 8th RECCE."

"8th RECCE, aren't they armoured?"

"Yes, they are." Vivian knew Diane was just trying to distract her from the situation. The ambulance continued to bounce and careen down the roads. The driver could be heard swearing as he dodged traffic and debris.

"Well, small world, Viv. Wouldn't it be something if they knew each other? What a story that would be." Diane laughed, and Vivian couldn't help but feel a bit uplifted. Thinking about Thomas being with someone sort of familiar was comforting.

"We have two children. Our son Matthew is thirteen, and our daughter Isabelle is eleven. They are my joy."

"We can all use more of that," Vivian said weakly, though Diane was successful at making her feel calmer. She was trying to breathe evenly. The contractions were not that close together. Under normal circumstances, she would not have even left for the hospital yet.

A sharp pain struck Vivian, and she let out a startled yelp of pain and fear. She looked up at Diane, not able to hold back the tears as they flooded from her eyes.

Diane grabbed her hand tighter. "Look at me. Focus on me. Breathe with me, Viv. Breathe with me." Diane touched Viv's forehead to soothe her. "It's going to be okay. You will both be okay."

"We're here!" shouted Stan. Vivian sat up. "No, no, Viv. Let us help you." He took her arm and climbed out ahead of her. Diane held her other arm as they assisted her into a wheelchair.

"You're in good hands now," Stan said as nurses and doctors swept in on the group coming out of the ambulance. "Name is Vivian. Premature labour, bleeding, and contractions. They're not close but becoming steady," he told the nurse as he handed Vivian over. He touched her shoulder. "Take good care now." He gave her one last smile and jumped back into the ambulance, slamming the doors shut behind him. The vehicle was off again.

"Vivian, was it?" the nurse asked as she rushed the chair towards the front doors of the hospital.

"Yes," Diane answered for her, not letting go of Vivian's hand. The blood from her wound had dried and matted in her hair and on her face and neck. It was still dripping from her arm, though.

"I think we best get you a chair as well," the nurse said. She had been so focused on Vivian she didn't realise Diane was injured.

"Viv needs you more. This is her first baby."

"Diane …" Vivian looked at her new friend with urgency. "Please go get looked at. You've had a serious injury. We will be fine. Find us when you're looked after." Vivian squeezed Diane's hand and released it as the nurse wheeled her away.

Diane stood in the middle of the emergency room. People were rushing in every direction. The sound of crying and moaning surrounded her as she finally became aware of her own injuries, and she was no longer focused on Vivian and the baby. She felt the throbbing in her arm and reached up to wipe away some of the crusting blood that was pulling at her eyebrow and eyelid.

"Name?" a nurse asked as she quickly assessed the severity of Diane's wounds.

"Diane Christianson," she answered automatically.

"You need some stitches, Diane, but you'll be okay. Come with me, and we can get you taken care of."

She followed the nurse who cleaned away enough of the blood that she could stitch up the wounds on Diane's scalp and shoulder. Her shoulder needed more than the nurse had initially anticipated, but the cut wasn't too deep.

"There's a basin there if you'd like to try and clean yourself up a bit more, luv. I'm sorry but I've got to tend to others now."

"Don't worry about me, dear. I can sort this out." Diane did as best she could to clean her face and arm, then went to look for Vivian.

"C Squadron is under enemy mortar fire about ten south of 793052. Can you put something onto them?"

"Taking action, C Squadron." Thomas got on the radio to the artillery leader. "We need an immediate retort to 793042."

"Sir! Enemy burst coming over!" Sgt Keene shouted to Thomas and Major Grey.

They held their breath. It fell short.

"C Squadron, report," Thomas called out.

"C Squadron, report friendly relief sir but two casualties."

Thomas and Grey looked at each other and frowned. They continued to respond and advise their men until C Squadron called back with their recce report.

"C Squadron to RHQ. Bridge secured. Four prisoners. Enemy in slit trenches 807096 to 803096. Enemy in the house and movements indicate a possible HQ."

"Once the house is secure, gather it up and bring it back."

"You got it, sir."

"We don't have any beds left, so you'll need to stay here for now." The nurse helped Vivian onto a plank that had been laid over the top of a bathtub. A makeshift surface to at least get her off her feet. "Let's take a look." The nurse started by listening to Vivian's stomach and pressing it, trying to get a sense of where she was in her labour. "I'm going to need to take off your panties to examine you."

She winced as she tried to help the nurse remove them and pull down her stockings.

"Right, well you aren't dilated much, and we can't have this baby arrive just yet. We're overrun. Give me a moment. I'll be right back." The nurse left the room and came back a few moments later with a second nurse and some rope.

Vivian looked at her, confused.

"I am going to tie your legs shut. We need to hold back this baby."

Terrified, Vivian protested, but the second nurse held her legs while the first tied the rope tightly around her thighs and calves.

"We will come back and check on you."

"But what if …" Vivian tried to ask what to do if the baby started to come while her legs were tied shut, but the nurses were already gone. She took a deep breath and let it out, then she gathered herself and tenderly touched her belly. The baby moved to meet her hand. "I'm here. Don't worry. I'm here. I won't let anything happen to you." She softly hummed a lullaby.

A stab of pain swept through her, and she felt a fresh flow of warmth escape her body. "Ahhh!" she cried out, her body twisting in the ropes. She focused on slowing her breathing and spoke to wee Viv, "Your daddy will be surprised to hear you arrived so early. He can't wait to meet you. I wonder if you'll look like him. Do you have his nose? We will have a big story to tell him when you arrive, won't we, my darling?" Vivian rubbed her stomach, concentrating on keeping herself calm so the baby would respond in kind.

Another pain ripped through her, much stronger and longer than before. It had only been five minutes. A wave of panic swept over her. The baby couldn't come yet. Her legs were tied shut. She tried to undo the rope but couldn't maintain the position she needed to reach the knot for long enough.

The contractions kept getting closer and steadier. She could feel her baby struggling inside her. She reached for the knot again.

"Aaaagh!" she screamed as she kept working and tried to breathe through another contraction.

"All divisions, RHQ moving to 687141. C Squadron, proceed."

Thomas and the major needed to move forward to ensure they didn't lose track of their men, or the enemy didn't gather them in their sites again. They quickly moved out.

As they sped to their new location, the driver was shot and killed instantly. The armoured car ran into a truck that had been shelled. Thomas, the liaison officer Wagner, and Grey bailed out of the wagon and took cover behind it.

"Sir, are you hit?" Thomas shouted over the engine.

"Grazed, Cooper. Just grazed. You?" Grey took stock of his bearings and sat down with some force.

"Nothing, sir. I'm fine." Thomas saw his CO crumple and moved to his side. "Sir, let me take a look."

He could see blood seeping through Grey's jacket already. He tore open the coat to get a better view. The wound to Grey's abdomen was bleeding dark, almost black, blood.

"I think you need to just rest a minute, sir. Wagner and I will sort out the Germans and get us back on track. Press this." He placed a cloth over the wound. Grey screamed but took hold of it. Wagner nodded at Thomas that he was ready.

The knot was beginning to loosen, and Vivian tried not to move her legs as she had another contraction.

Breathe, just breathe. You can do this, she thought to herself. She kept humming the lullaby while working on the knot.

Finally, it gave way. She fell back, exhausted and sweating. She didn't have long to wait for the next contraction, but at least she'd be able to move her legs and feel some relief as she powered through it.

"I think we're just dealing with a couple of good shots behind that fallen wall." Thomas pointed just to the left of their location. "I think the Bren could clear them out."

"I leave it to you then, Cooper. You had that great success with the PIATs after all." Wagner slapped Thomas' shoulder.

"I'll draw them out, and you cover me."

"I can cover your six from here." Major Grey gasped as he lifted the weapon into his lap and positioned it as best he could, using the side of the armoured car to support it. Thomas nodded to him and helped position the Enfield for his CO. Wagner grabbed his Sten gun and waited for Thomas to get into position with the Bren.

Vivian lay back on the hard wooden plank, gathering her strength. She knew she wouldn't have long until the next contraction. "I hope you're not always this impatient." She smiled at her belly. "You are strong, though. I can feel you kicking and pushing."

The next contraction came just as Diane rushed in. "Viv! Thank God, I found you!"

Vivian sighed with relief. She was no longer alone.

"What did they do to you?" Diane asked as she pulled the rope out from under her. It was still loosely wrapped around her legs.

"They didn't want the baby to come before they were ready," she tried to explain.

"Are they mad? They tied your legs together?! Did they honestly think that would stop the baby?" She contained her anger. Her friend needed her. "Let me take a look, okay?" Diane pressed Vivian's stomach and felt around. "Viv, your baby isn't turned. Do you understand? The baby is breach."

Vivian nodded. She didn't know how Diane seemed to know so much about delivering babies, but she somehow instinctively trusted her. Besides, what choice did she have? There was no one else to help her.

"I'm going to go get a few things to help us. I'll be as quick as I can." Diane could see the renewed fear in Vivian's eyes and tried to smile. Vivian nodded again and shut her eyes as another contraction gripped her young body.

Diane was back before the next contraction with hot water, a scalpel, and cloths. She examined Vivian again.

"You're almost fully dilated, but I'm still going to need to make some space for the baby to come because she's breach. Okay, Viv?"

"Will she be, okay? Just tell me she'll be okay," Vivian begged Diane.

"If she is half as strong as her mother, she will be perfect." Diane wiped Vivian's forehead with a cloth as she began another contraction, gripping her friend's arm for support. Breathing. Humming.

Thomas nodded when he was ready. Wagner bolted toward some rubble, which was still smouldering from being torn from its original position as the back wall of someone's home. Thomas opened fire as the Germans tried to shoot Captain Wagner as he made for cover. He didn't need to have perfect aim with the Bren. It was a big gun, and even a minor hit would stop someone enough to make them think twice before taking another shot.

"Wir geben auf! Nicht schießen! Surrender! We surrender!" two soldiers called out from behind the rubble they had been using for cover. They put their hands in the air and gestured, repeating, "Surrender! Surrender!"

"Well, guess RHQ is going to be a POW site too, sir." Thomas looked over at his CO and smiled in relief.

Three Mustangs flew low overhead. They were brought back to the reality there were many other factors at play, and they needed to reconnect with their squadrons. Wagner stood watch over the German soldiers they had secured.

"Get on the radio, RSM. Determine where the lads are at," Grey said to Thomas.

"Yes, sir, but we also need to get you sorted." Thomas picked up the radio. "RHQ is moving to 637184. We need a medic when we arrive. All squadrons report."

Reports from all the squadrons and brigades came in "all quiet." They had been successful. Thomas wiped his brow and gave an exhausted smile to his CO. Caen was theirs.

"That's it, Viv. Breathe. Deep breaths. Long, slow, deep breaths. You can do it. Just don't push yet."

"AAAAHHHG! I need to push! I need to push!" The urge was primal. Her body told her what needed to be done.

Diane checked again and was relieved. "Viv, you're fully dilated, but I'm going to need to make that space for the baby now. Okay? I need you to bite this cloth for me." Diane handed her a piece of flannel she had rolled up. Vivian put it in her mouth and nodded she was ready.

"Okay, Viv. Just wait for me. I will be quick …"

Vivian let out a scream and bit down harder on the flannel as Diane made an incision on Viv's perineum to help make space for the baby to come through. Even with the incision, it would be a difficult delivery.

"Okay, Viv. I need you to listen carefully. Don't push until I tell you, okay? I need to help the baby a bit. Tell me when the next contraction starts, and I'll tell you when to push."

Tears were streaming down Vivian's face. She cried out as the next contraction surged through her.

"Not yet, Viv. Breathe." Diane reached into Vivian's body and slid her hand around the side to get a grip on the baby. "Okay. Now. Push, Viv. Push!"

Vivian gripped the sides of the plank she was laying on for support and pulled herself up. Outside the small room, people rushed around trying to help the wounded. There were stretchers and wheelchairs with people who were broken and bleeding. Crying. Moaning. Calling for help.

Vivian pushed.

"Again!"

She took a deep breath and pushed again, grunting and yelling as Diane pulled.

"One more, Viv. One more. You can do it."

Vivian closed her eyes. She could see Thomas's face. His smiling blue eyes. "Be strong. You can do this, Viv. I love you both so much," she heard him say. Taking another deep breath, she exhaled and pushed one more time.

"That's it! That's it!" Diane shouted. "It's a girl, Viv! She's a beautiful girl. You were right." Diane cheered as the cries of Vivian's baby filled the room.

Vivian collapsed back on the plank of wood. "Is she … is she okay?" she asked, out of breath and exhausted.

"She looks just fine. Here, see for yourself." Diane handed Vivian her tiny newborn daughter. Overwhelmed with joy, she couldn't hold back the tears.

"I can never thank you enough. I don't know what would have happened if you didn't come find us." Vivian grabbed Diane's hand and squeezed it and held on. Diane put her arm around Vivian and gave her a hug. Tears of elation and joy fell from their eyes.

"You don't need to thank me. Look at this beautiful little girl. That is everything I could ever need as thanks. I'll get a doctor or nurse to check on you. I'll be right back."

Vivian looked down at her daughter as she sucked on her tiny fist. Her fingers were long and slender. She had light brown hair with touches of gold. Her heart was so full and grateful.

"Welcome to the world, Diane Christina Vivian. You are already loved more than you can ever know."

Major Grey had been barely conscious when they left with him for the nearest hospital unit. Thomas gave his report to Colonel Jakes, who was overseeing command of the 2nd.

"Well done, RSM. Go grab some grub and some shut eye while we can."

"If you don't mind, sir, I would like to do a weapon check and see what the lads need before I grab some grub and maybe a scrub."

"Of course. I'm sure they will be glad to see you." The colonel walked off with his entourage, reviewing the results of the battle for his final report to his commanding officers.

We all report up to someone, Thomas thought to himself as he picked up his notebook and pencil and called a corporal to bring him a driver and Jeep.

Thomas enjoyed any excuse to go see the men. As RSM he didn't get the same opportunities to be in the thick of it, and truthfully, he missed that. The men liked and respected him as their RSM, but the job was different.

"Going to check the lads?" SSM Robinson called out to him. Oliver Robinson and Thomas had been together most of their career in the 8th. He was a level-headed man who could see the bigger picture without losing sight of the goal. Thomas trusted Robinson completely. They anticipated each other and worked seamlessly together.

"I am. Want to tag along?" Thomas asked.

"Always!" Robinson laughed and dismissed the corporal who had come to drive the Jeep.

Thomas and Frank were greeted warmly by the men of C Squadron.

"Sir, are they going to send Marlene Dietrich over for our RNR?" Corporal Ladner laughed and all the men joined in.

"Only the best for my boys." Thomas chuckled as he stood up and crooned the lyrics to "Lili Marlene." The lads all started cheering and singing along. Thomas had an impeccable German accent and switched back and forth from the English to the German lyrics. Marlene Dietrich was always a big hit, and the men needed some laughs.

As they walked back to the Jeep, Robinson was grinning from ear to ear, enjoying the light mood. "How is it that you are so fluent in German, Coop? If I didn't know better, I would swear you were German!"

"I guess I'm just really good with languages. Paid attention in the trainings. It comes in handy when we've been behind lines once or twice." He chuckled a bit, but it wasn't one of amusement. It seemed more deprecating and ironic.

"I've heard that some of our guys who have special language skills sometimes do extra recce. You know anything about that, Coop?" Robinson had heard that some of the men who were fluent in German had been given special assignments to provide close recce. Close enough to have contact with German officers.

"Yeah, I think I've heard about that, Robbsy. Be a pretty risky spot to get into, I think. Not for old dogs like us, eh?" He laughed and patted his friend on the shoulder.

Robinson wasn't convinced, however. He knew Thomas had been "borrowed" to other regiments with no real explanation. There had been rumours Thomas was part of a small special squad that took on operations that required more than silent observation at a distance, but no one would admit it had occurred. He decided to let it go.

"Best get back to RHQ and give the report." Thomas would have liked to stay with the men, but it really wasn't his place anymore. His presence would keep the men on edge, and they needed to genuinely rest that night. "See you at zero six hundred, gents." He waved as he climbed into the Jeep with Robinson at the wheel.

The men waved and popped the last bites of corned beef into their mouths. Thomas smiled at the greasy handprints on the bread. Who knew when they would have time to eat or rest again.

He got back to his bunk and slumped down onto it. He was exhausted. Forcing himself to eat, he unwrapped his sandwich. He thought about Viv and tears filled his eyes. He missed her so much. Loved her so much. Then, it struck him. Wee Viv had been born. He didn't know how he knew it, but he did. Thomas stood up and walked out of his tent. He gazed out over the hills. He got out his pen and some paper and wrote to her.

My darling Viv,

I am certain that word of the victory of Caen will have reached you by the time you read this letter. It was a hard-fought fight with many losses for a significant gain. This victory will give us a leg up on securing the end of the war. Our regiment had to forgo the comforts of our armour and fight alongside regular infantry. We got some good-natured razzing for that, of course. At times, the communication between our commanders was poor and probably led to more losses than necessary. It's a frustrating thing when egos get in the way of the safety of my men. The town has been obliterated, and many of the men are struggling and torn up by the loss of civilians.

Now that we are secure and have the high ground, the rolling hills as far as the eye can see have a new beauty despite the smell of death and decay. I can imagine what this place looked like before we all arrived, a place of lush hills and beauty. It's a place you would have loved, too, I think.

We are taking a much-needed short rest before the next push. I know it is too early, but as I sit here and write, I feel wee Viv has been born. I pray that it doesn't mean anything foreboding has happened. Please be safe, both of you. I am not sure what I would do if I lost either of you.

Love always,
Your Thomas

Vivian finished reading the letter as a single tear fell from the corner of her eye. She blinked it away. With the letter pressed against her heart, she smiled down at their new daughter. Diane contentedly slept in her mother's arms, oblivious to the events of her birth or the risks her father was taking many miles away from them.

"Well, wee Viv, it seems your father somehow already knows you are here. You are clearly connected by your hearts. We all are."

Viv placed the letter on the bedside table. As she kissed Diane on her tiny fingers, she carefully got up and placed the baby in her bassinet. She pulled her stationary out of the drawer and sat at the small desk in the room to write back.

My darling Thomas ...

Love Always

Chapter Eighteen

The journey through Holland for the next few days was quiet and uneventful, and no amount of rest or calm could prepare them for what they would discover in the village of Spier.

They had been told there was a Nazi encampment there and to be prepared for a low-level skirmish. It was the smell that reached them first. That awful smell. In the distance, they could see thick black smoke and assumed the Germans had torched their camp when they realised, they were about to be descended upon by the Canadians.

"RSM," Major Grey motioned with his hand, "let's stop here and send a recce team ahead to determine strength and numbers."

"Yes, sir." Thomas whistled and motioned to the men nearest him to stop. They passed on the instructions. "All right, we are going to hang back and send a small team ahead to recce up and report back. Sergeant Moore, feel up to leading?"

Moore immediately stepped forward. "Absolutely, sir. I will take my crew and go now."

"Excellent. Everyone else, make sure all your equipment is loaded up and ready to go. We need to move when Moore reports back."

Everyone nodded and settled into the motions of being busy while they waited. It didn't take long for Moore to return.

"Sir, may I speak to you and the major privately, please?" Moore's face was ashen. Corporal Nash was the colour of milk and looked like he had vomit all over him.

"What did you find, Moore?" the major asked.

"Sirs, first I want to report that there is limited resistance ahead. Two watchtowers, easily taken with our sniper, sirs. The guards are too bunched up and can also be taken down easily. The main building has no guards on it. Might be some inside. We could get close enough to see. They seem to be loading boxes into the cars and trucks. It looks like they're preparing to move out."

"That's good news, Moore. Well done. What's the rest of it then?" Thomas knew from Moore's demeanour he was agitated and upset. If the target was as soft as it sounded, it didn't make sense.

"It's a prisoner camp, sirs. It looks like there are hundreds of them."

"Do you think they will prove to be a problem? Will they attack us?"

"I don't think so, sirs. They don't look like they're able to do much. They are not in good shape."

"Damn Nazis. Starving their prisoners. We've heard about this. We will call for the Red Cross to start to head our way then. Best to have the supplies to help them ready as quickly as we can."

"There's more, sirs." Moore looked back at his men. Nash, knowing what Moore was going to say, vomited again.

Moore had been right. There was little resistance, and they gained control of the camp in a very short time. It was when they entered the camp, they fully understood what Moore had been trying to warn them about. The smell that had reached them miles away was inescapable. It was sour, and even thick cloths and a menthol grease under their noses couldn't hold it back.

The source of the fires was quickly ascertained. The gruesome clues of the purpose of the camp became obvious, and Thomas and Major Grey made their way to the headquarters to question the commandant.

"What is this place?" Grey demanded. "Who are these people, and why are they being burned by the hundreds in pits?"

Thomas translated with as much vehemence as Grey emitted.

"They are nothing. They aren't even dogs." the commandant spat on the floor.

"They are people. They are your prisoners. You have a responsibility to them even if they are your enemy!" Grey shouted.

"They are of no value. We should have just shot them all instead of wasting time burning them."

Major Grey asked Thomas to repeat what he had just translated. He could not believe what he had just heard the man say about the men, women, and children they had already seen in the camp.

"They are humans. No matter what else, they deserve to be treated with respect." Grey growled and turned to his senior men. "Gather all the papers they have so kindly organised onto their vehicles for us and check what is still left. Make sure we take anything that looks important."

"What do you want us to do with him?" Thomas nodded towards the Nazi officer.

"We aren't animals like them. We will hand them over to the 4th. They can decide what their fate is when they get here."

Thomas went to help oversee the securing of the camp. The men were overwhelmed with the sick and dying. "Sir! What should we do? We can't help them all, and the Red Cross is an hour out," one of the soldiers cried.

"Triage, private. If you think they can be saved, put a red cross on their forehead and move on. No cross, no transport." Thomas stopped to check on a woman on a bunk. The air was thick with the smell of urine and disease. She reached her hand up and grabbed his wrist with surprising strength. "What is your name, love?" he asked her in German.

"Eva." Her voice was hoarse and raw. "My name is Eva Olsson. Please, I don't want to die here."

"Eva, with a grip like that, you are not going to die any time soon." He gently put her hand back down and put a red cross on her forehead. "This woman is ready for transport," he called to the private, who ran over with a second man and lifted Eva onto a cot. They took her towards the back of a truck that was being prepared to take as many of the survivors as possible away from that evil place.

156

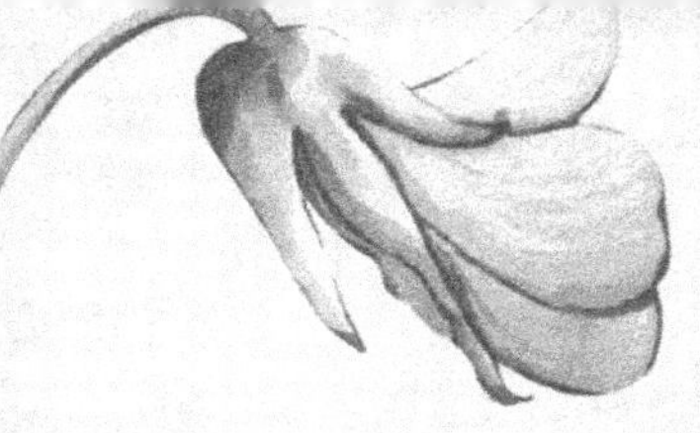

Chapter Nineteen

Thomas had not written to tell Vivian he was coming home. He wanted to surprise her. The end of the war didn't automatically mean the end of service. Thomas was assigned to the post-war occupation and rebuilding of Holland. He was finally fully and completely a civilian and eager to start his life with his family. He had managed to get a ride with his friend Fitzy, whose family had come to pick him up in Southampton. Robbsy had also jumped at the chance to grab a ride. They had a truck and plenty of room. Eager to get back to his family, Thomas had happily accepted the ride. He wasn't able to get leave when Vivian had written to tell him that their son had been born. Time passed in odd ways during war. At moments, it passed painfully slowly and then others, it passed at the speed of light. Knowing that it had been almost three years since the birth of wee Viv was almost unbelievable to Thomas. Now his son was already nine months old.

They pulled into the long driveway, and the farmhouse came into view, the sea sparkling behind it. His heart was racing as they drew closer. The truck stopped, and he jumped out of the back.

"Best of luck to you, Thomas." The two men hugged fiercely and slapped each other on the back.

"To you as well, Robbsy." Thomas watched the truck pull away and turned to finish walking up the last of the laneway.

He pushed open the gate, and a wave of emotion washed over him. There, in the front yard, was a sight that shook the breath from his soul. A small girl was playing happily with a doll on the grass near the front porch. He watched her play with pride and love in his heart. She had grown so much since he had last seen his daughter.

Then he heard her, calling to Diane from inside the house. He waited, his heart pounding in his chest until she emerged in the doorway. Her face was radiant with joy. For a moment, she didn't see him. She was focused on their daughter and the baby in her arms, his son.

But then, sensing his presence, she looked up and saw him at the gate. Her eyes widened in disbelief. "Thomas!" Her voice was both shocked and incredulous. She carefully put the baby down in the cradle near Diane on the porch, and then leaped into his arms, tears flooding down her cheeks. "Why didn't you tell me you were coming home?"

"I wanted to surprise you, and honestly, it wasn't a smooth transition, so I didn't want to tell you I was coming and then be delayed."

"I can't believe you are home. Home for good!" She kept looking at him and then pressing her face against him to check that he was really there. "Come see Diane and John." She led him towards their children. "Diane, look. Daddy is home."

Diane looked up from her doll at Thomas. She had his blue eyes and full lips. Definitely a Cooper. No doubt about that! She smiled and reached up to him, and he scooped her up off the ground and clutched her to his chest.

"Oh, my sweet girl. I'm so happy to be home. I'm so happy to see you."

Vivian reached down and picked up their son and faced him towards Thomas, still clutching Diane. "John, look, it's

Daddy." The chubby faced infant made a gurgling sound and wiggled in Vivian's arms.

She had written and told him his son John Henry had been born. His father was also John Henry. It was their tradition to name the first-born son after their grandfathers. Vivian had been proud to be able to continue their family tradition. "Did I get it wrong?" Thomas' reaction concerned her. He seemed taken aback, not pleasantly surprised like she had expected.

"No, darling, you didn't get it wrong. I'm just surprised you remembered that. I didn't remember even telling you." He pulled something out of his pocket. "I brought this back as promised." In his hand was the small note card with the pressed violet on it.

"I am so happy it got home safely and brought you with it."

Thomas wrapped his arm around her and pulled them both in as close as he could. His whole world was in his arms. He had never been so happy in his life. He was one of the lucky ones, and he didn't plan to waste one more moment worrying about secrets.

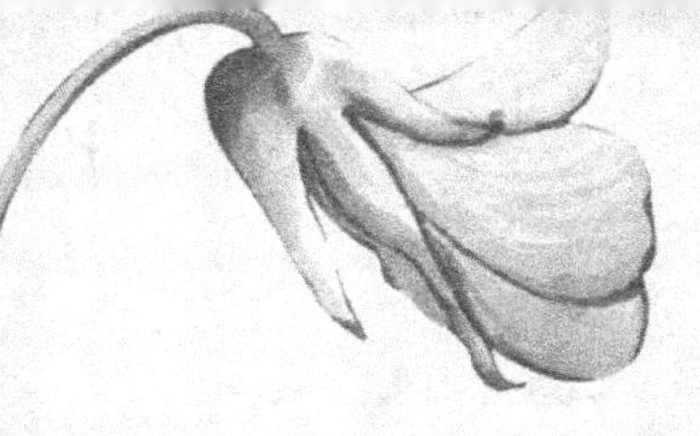

Chapter Twenty

The world had settled into the routines of post-war. London had been hard hit by the desolation of the aftermath of the war. Whole sections of the city had been levelled, and there was simply not enough housing to go around. Thomas and Vivian had moved back in with her parents. Rebuilding was top priority of course, and Thomas had been able to get a job overseeing some of the construction. The government had promised to build and then subsidise several large housing projects to help get as many families as possible settled into a more prosperous life.

"How is retirement treating you, Evelyn?" Thomas placed a plate of carrots to his left so Diane could spoon them onto her plate. He doted on her, but she was very independent and insisted on doing things for herself.

"Thank you, Daddy." She smiled up at him.

"I'm not sure I like it at all, Thomas. Leisure is not something I do very well, apparently," Evelyn replied.

"Mum, you've certainly earned it." Vivian was cutting up some of the carrots and the chicken on Jame's plate. He was two now, but he still needed his food to be cut up into safe sizes. She smiled as he stabbed the mashed potatoes with his

pudgy fingers and rubbed them around the plate while making satisfied noises. "Perhaps you need a hobby?"

"I suppose that's true. I'm just not sure what I'd like to do. I'm not one for garden parties or oil painting."

"You said you were thinking about getting involved with the housing council."

"Yes, yes. I went to a meeting last week. It could turn into quite a busy job. Lots to oversee and discuss as we try to get everyone housed again."

"So many are left without any place to live." Ace sighed deeply. "Seems rather unseemly to expect our lads to have no homes to return to after what they did to get us here."

They all agreed.

Despite Thomas having a job and the shared accommodations, life was still very hard in England. In many ways, it was harder than it was during the war. There were still rations on most daily items. The prospects were pretty bleak, and Thomas had spoken to Vivian about the possibility of returning to Canada.

"We could afford land and build our own home there, Viv," he had told her. "And it wouldn't be council housing either."

"What's wrong with council housing?" she had asked. "That's what you are helping to build. That's what is helping take care of our family, Thomas. Don't judge people because they are not as fortunate as we are."

"We live with your parents, Vivian. That's not exactly living the high life," he said with a scornful expression. He swallowed the last of his scotch and poured another. His drinking had increased steadily since he returned from the war. Her father had seen her worry. *Don't worry too much, Viv. Thomas has been through an awful lot. He has seen things no one should ever have to see and done things no one should ever have to do. He just needs to settle back into the regular world. He just needs to adjust to being safe again.* She knew he was right, but sometimes Thomas said hurtful things when he had been drinking. He had terrible dreams and would occasionally wake up crying and sweating. She promised to give Thomas some time and hoped that was all he would need to recover from the war.

"I see. Well, I'm sorry my parents' sacrifice is not up to your standards, Thomas. Feel free to buy us a fancy home in Mayfair with the fortune I was unaware we had available to us."

"Viv!" He had gone after her and caught up to her in the garden. "I'm sorry, Viv. I don't mean to sound ungrateful. You need to understand, it's hard for me to feel like I'm not properly providing for my family."

"Thomas, we are all proud of you. You work very hard for us, and you are a wonderful provider." She put her arms around him and her head on his shoulder. "This is all temporary, darling. It will get better."

They went back into the house and chatted about the project some more, but Vivian noticed the look in Thomas' eyes. He wasn't happy there, and she knew in her heart he was right. Canada offered more opportunities for them. If they stayed in London, they would never own a home. In fact, they may never even have a place of their own at all.

Vivian put Diane and John to bed in the room they shared with Bryant. He enjoyed the company and would read Diane bedtime stories. Vivian had to enforce a strict limit of two, or he would read to her all night.

Thomas had converted a small space that had been a landing at the top of the stairs into a bedroom for them. There was room for a bed and a tiny dresser, but the roof had a steep slant. They had to be careful sitting up in bed, or they'd hit their head.

Thomas slid into bed and lay on his back beside Vivian. She reached over and put her arm across him and her head on his shoulder. "You're right, Thomas. I wish you weren't, but you are. Our family will have better opportunities in Canada than here." Her voice cracked because while she knew it was true, she also hated the idea of leaving her family.

"Oh, Viv, I know this is hard for you." He shifted towards her and put his arm around her so they were wrapped together. "We don't really have a choice. I didn't fight that bloody war to have to live in a room with my in-laws. I want more than that for my family."

"I know. I know. What about your family? How will they feel about us coming back? How will they feel about me?" They still had not gotten married. In fact, they had stopped talking about it. It seemed unimportant at that stage, but that was when they were staying in England. If they were going back to Canada, well, that changed everything.

"I will write to them once we know for certain when we're coming. We will need to apply since I stayed here as a civilian. It shouldn't take too long though, darling." He kissed the top of her head. "They will understand, and they will love you almost as much as I do."

"It's a lot to take in, but we will be together, and together we can do anything." Even as she said it, however, she was not convinced his family would accept her and their children.

Love Always

Chapter Twenty-One

An envelope had come for Thomas while he was at work. It had only been eight months but when Vivian saw it, she knew what it was. Vivian decided to put the envelope up in their room. She didn't want to risk her parents seeing it before she and Thomas knew what it said. They had agreed it was best to not say anything to anyone until they knew for sure that they had been approved and they had a leaving date. Winston Churchill had referred to the mass exodus of British to Canada and other countries as *rats leaving the ship,* but it changed nothing. The prosperity being seen around the world was not being seen or felt in England.

When her parents and Bryant took Diane and John for a walk after supper, it wasn't unusual for Vivian and Thomas to stay back and tidy up and have some time alone. "Thomas, an envelope came today. I put it in our room when it arrived." She had been nervous to tell him about the envelope and waited for them to be alone.

"Okay. What is it?" Thomas could tell it concerned Vivian.

"I think it is the paperwork letting us know if we are approved to emigrate or not." Even though they were alone in the house, Vivian whispered to him as they walked up the

stairs to their bedroom. She had placed it in the top drawer of the dresser. Handing it to Thomas, she nervously waited as he carefully tore it open and read it to himself.

"We got approved!" he almost shouted it and Vivian's heart lurched in her chest. Until now, she hadn't realised how uncertain she still was about going. "It wasn't really an issue for me to return of course, but they have approved you and the children." He looked up as he said it and saw that she was smiling but it didn't reach her eyes. "I know you don't want to leave your family here, Viv. I love them too, especially Bryant. But this is what is best for *our* family."

"I think one of the hardest things of all is knowing that Bryant won't be able to come," she said flatly, he wouldn't be able to handle the trip on the boat. "Oh, Thomas, I know this is best for our family, but my heart is breaking for my dear Bryant. I am going to miss him terribly." He took her in his arms and hugged her tight as she wept.

Her parents and brother arrived back from their walk. Her father went outside to smoke his pipe while Vivian and her mother set out the tea. Thomas went as well. He didn't smoke a pipe, but he wanted to spend some time with Diane and John playing in the yard before they went to bed.

"Vivvy, you seem sad. Are you okay?" He was very attuned to his sister and incredibly empathetic.

"Oh, umm, I'm okay, Bryant." She avoided his gaze and knew he didn't believe her, but he didn't say anything else. The tea was ready, and she sent him to fetch their father, Thomas and the children.

Once they were all seated, she glanced at Thomas, and he nodded ever so slightly. Just enough that Ace and Evelyn noticed and were immediately alert. They sensed something serious was happening.

"Mum … Dad …" Thomas looked up at them both and took Vivian's hand. "We have something we need to speak with you about."

"Are you having another baby?" Evelyn hoped not since there wasn't enough room for everyone as it was.

"Erm, no. No, we are not having another baby," Thomas said.

Vivian spoke up, "We have been approved to emigrate to Canada." It felt loud in her head, but her voice was quiet.

"What? Canada?!" Her parents looked at each other with despair.

"No! No! No!" Bryant shouted. "No, Vivvy, you can't go to Canada. It's too far. You won't be able to help in the garden, and I won't be able to read Muffy bedtime stories." Bryant called Diane Muffy or Miss Muffet after her favourite story character that Bryant read to her almost every single night.

Vivian reached for Bryant's hand, but he snatched it away and ran outside to the garden.

"Give him a moment," Ace said when Vivian started to get up and follow her brother. "You need to give us a moment, too. This is something you have clearly talked about and had time to reason through. It's a shock to us." He sat back in his chair and looked up at the ceiling. He was trying to control his emotions and could feel a hopelessness invading his being.

"I don't understand, Vivian. Why didn't you tell us you were thinking about leaving?" Her mother stared at her with a pained expression.

"We were told it could take up to two years to get approved. It has only been a few months," she said.

"Well, it seems ridiculous Thomas has to apply for anything, to be honest. He's Canadian. You, as his wife, are automatically Canadian too, are you not?" The fact they had to even apply to return to Thomas' own home was shocking. "I mean, you were over here fighting for your country. For our country. What more do they want?" Her indignance seemed to have settled on that thought.

"I don't disagree with you, Mum," Thomas said cautiously. He knew his future in-laws were upset, and he needed to tread carefully.

Evelyn sniffed. "I, umm, I umm." She began to cry, and Vivian was so taken aback she started crying, too. In her entire life, she had never seen her mother cry. She went and kneeled beside her, hugging her and comforting her as best she could while being inconsolable herself.

Wallace took his wife's hand and squeezed it. "Okay ..." His voice cracked, but he held it together long enough to ask, "When are you leaving?"

"We have a two-week window to arrive in Canada on either side of the new year," Thomas said.

"That's only two months away. We better get organised then." Wallace had closed off his hurt. He needed to be strong for his wife and daughter. "I'm going to talk to Bryant and see if I can't help him understand this is what is best for you." He nodded at Thomas but not in solidarity. In dismissal. He did not want Thomas to follow him out to the garden.

He found Bryant sitting in the onions. "Did I do something bad, Daddy? Is that why Vivvy is leaving?"

"Oh, heavens no, Bryant! Vivvy loves you very, very much. She knows how much you love her back." Ace's heart was breaking for his son. "It's just that there's not a lot of work here or hope for a home of their own here. You see, when you have your own family, you want to be able to have your own house and garden for them. It isn't that Vivvy doesn't want to garden with you anymore. She and Thomas want to be able to have their own garden and their own kitchen."

"So, it's not my fault?"

"I promise you it is not your fault. I will get her right now, and she can tell you herself if you want."

"No. I believe you, Daddy. I just wish her garden wasn't so far away." Bryant hugged his father tight and then went back inside.

Left alone in the garden, Wallace watched the chickens scratch the ground and silently wept into the arm of his jacket.

There were a lot of plans to get organised for the trip, and Vivian was grateful for her mother's help. Evelyn was a skilled planner and organiser. She thought of every detail right down to how they would ship more things later— once Vivian and Thomas had settled down somewhere.

"Thomas, I want you to know, I respect you for this decision. As much as it breaks my heart that you're leaving, I know this is what is best for you and my daughter and grandchildren."

Thomas took Ace's hand and shook it. "I can't tell you how much it means to me to have your respect, Dad."

They weren't taking a lot with them, but they had still managed to fill six steamer trunks with everything they needed to start their new life in Canada. Diane had insisted on taking all her books, and Bryant had bought her a new one as a Christmas present.

"It's called *The Velveteen Rabbit*, Muffy."

"What's it about, Beeny?" she asked excitedly, not understanding that it would be the only time he would read it to her.

"It's about a stuffed rabbit, a toy, that becomes a real rabbit because the little girl loves him so much. It's one of my favourites." He showed her the book and pointed to the beautiful illustrations inside.

"Look, Diane, Nanny got you something to go with Bryant's book." Vivian had been holding onto her mother's arm as she watched her brother and her daughter enjoying a story together for the last time.

Evelyn choked back her tears and knelt in front of Diane. She pulled a stuffed rabbit out from behind her back. It had pink satin in its ears and a pink suede nose.

"Oh, Nanny! I love him." Diane hugged the rabbit tight, then hugged her Nan. "Look, Bryant, it's the rabbit from our new story!" She sat back down on the step with him, and he read her the story of her new rabbit and how he had been loved so much he was worn away in some spots and mistaken for being broken and damaged.

"I feel so badly for the people," Diane said to Bryant. "They can't see how beautiful the rabbit is. Only the little girl sees it."

"Yes, Muffy, only the little girl sees him for his true and wonderful self." Bryant hugged his little niece.

"Beeny, don't be sad. I will see you soon. Mummy says we are far away, but that means when we visit it will be long visits." She crushed him with a forceful hug around his neck. When she finally let go, he forced himself to stand with his mother and father as his Vivvy and Muffy prepared to drive far, far away to Canada. To their own garden he had promised to visit soon.

"I love you, Dad." Vivian's hands shook as she held her father's in hers. "We will see each other as soon as Thomas and I get settled. Mum promised you would come for a good visit." Her father nodded and pulled her into one of his enormous bear hugs.

"I love you, Vivvy. Never forget how much we love you and how proud we are of you. It takes a lot of courage to start a new life, and you are one of the strongest and bravest people I know. Second only perhaps to your mother." He tried to smile and ease the tension and emotion of the moment. It worked a little. Vivian laughed and hugged him again.

"Mum…" They had not words. The women could only hug each other tightly. Finally, they parted and held hands staring at each other for a moment before Evelyn let go of her daughter's hand and stepped back from her. Vivian understood and stepped back as well.

"Viv, we need to get going, love." Thomas took her hand and led her to the car where the driver was patiently waiting for them.

Nodding, she settled in beside her children in the back seat of the cab. Vivian turned to look out the rear window. She had to see them all one more time. Who knew how long it would be before she saw them again.

Her father stood strong and straight, tears streaming down

his face as he held onto her mother and brother. Bryant's sobs were audible, but he bravely stood tall like his father. Vivian held up her hand, and he held his up in return. For a moment, they both imagined they touched, and he felt comforted and calm.

Thomas reached out and put his hand on her back as they turned the corner out of sight. Evelyn watched the cab disappear, taking her daughter and grandchildren away. She was not an emotional woman or prone to public displays of her feelings, but in that moment, she felt a stabbing pain of sadness and loss. A sob escaped from deep inside her chest.

Love Always

Chapter Twenty-Two

Pier 21 waited patiently for the *Aquitania* to move into place at the dock. Thomas and Vivian stood at the railing, with Diane and John eager to see glimpses of their new country. The air was cold, and they could see their breath. January in Canada was already demonstrating to them how different it was than England.

Vivian nervously fidgeted with the collar of her coat, pulling the scarf up around her neck and ears.

"Is that snow, Mummy?" Diane excitedly asked, pulling on her mother's coat and pointing in the distance towards the dockyards beyond the main building. There was a coating of white that looked to have some depth in places. They didn't get this much in England.

"Yes, it is, dear." Vivian smiled down at Diane, who was trying to take in as much as her five-year-old curiosity possibly could.

"Cold!" huffed John as he hunched up in his coat. He didn't care for the cold. It wasn't that cold back home, and he wondered why they would move somewhere so obviously less pleasant.

"You will warm up when we get inside the depot." Pulling

John against him, Thomas rubbed his back to warm the small child up.

"How long do you think it will take to get through, Thomas?" Vivian asked.

"I honestly have no idea. There are an awful lot of people on this ship who need to move through the building. We will just be patient, I suppose."

Each deck was being cleared one at a time to manage the number of people inside the depot. From there, folks would need cabs to hotels or the train station to continue their travels. Managing the flow into the building also helped to manage the flow out as well.

Thomas, Vivian, and their little family were fortunate to be in the second group to be moved into the depot. As they disembarked, they found themselves in a room bustling with many other people carrying their own hopes and dreams for their future lives in Canada.

Following the lines and cues, they navigated their way through the chaos to the immigration desk.

"Welcome home, Mr. Cooper! You must be happy to be back safely and with a lovely new family as well. Congratulations." The clerk was a jolly man with a very round face and bulbous nose. His chair creaked despairingly every time he moved. "And what is your name, young man?" he asked John directly, showing him respect and offering his hand to shake.

"John Henry Cooper." While the confidence of the almost three-year-old was clear, his speech was not. The clerk understood the little boy nevertheless as he firmly took his hand and shook it.

"What fine manners. You are certainly raising fine children, Mr. and Mrs. Cooper." He smiled, impressed by how well-spoken John was for being so young. Turning back to the paperwork, he stamped some pages. "Welcome to Canada!" he boomed and shook Vivian's hand. "Where are you off to from here? I assume Kingston is your next stop, correct?"

"That's right, sir. Cooper Falls after that," Thomas proudly stated.

"Well, well. I didn't even connect it. A Cooper of Cooper Falls, eh?" The clerk's chair groaned loudly as he shifted again. "If you go through Exit C, you can get your ticket for the train. It is not far to walk, and you should be able to make the next one to Kingston. It leaves in about five hours. Your baggage should be out there as well. Once you have your train tickets, show them to the baggage clerks, and they'll get them brought over for you." He pointed towards a wall to indicate where the exit would be. "Seems like a lot, I know, but you made it this far without a hitch." The chair protested again as he leaned back and stretched. "Won't take you long to get it all boarded up. Have a good trip. All the best to you."

"Thank you for all your help." Thomas shook the clerk's hand, then helped Vivian gather their things. They had packed two smaller bags in case their timing was such that they needed to stay overnight in Halifax to wait for the train to Kingston.

As they stepped outside Exit C as directed, they saw the train ticket wicket. The line was not long, and they managed to purchase their tickets and arrange for their trunks to be sent over.

"I'm going to send a telegram to my brother to let him know we are going to be a bit ahead of schedule." The telegram office was near the boarding area for the train.

"Daddy, look at all the snow!" Diane scooped up a handful off the ground.

Thomas chuckled. "You will see a great deal more of it than this, my love. Wait right here, and I'll go send the telegram." He left Vivian and the children to be distracted by the snow.

"I need to send a message to Ardoch," Thomas told the clerk when he arrived.

"Right, you have the number?"

Thomas shook his head. He knew his brother's and parents' numbers, but not the pharmacy where the telegram would be going.

"What's the name of the place receiving it then?"

Thomas gave him the information, and the man behind the counter filled it in on the top of the form.

"Write your message here, and I will send it off for you," the clerk said.

Thomas hesitated. What should he write? It had to be short and to the point, but there was so much he needed to say.

Fynn,
ETA Kingston tomorrow 14:00. Don't tell family. Want to surprise them.
Thomas

He pushed the yellow paper and pen back across the counter. "Surprise, eh? Good surprise or not so good?" the man quipped. He shrugged at his own joke.

Good question, Thomas thought to himself, but he just nodded, smiled, and paid.

"Our message is sent. Let's go find our spot on the train!" Thomas said as he rejoined his family. He scooped up Diane and gave her a squeeze. "Are you excited to be on a train, Muffy?" Thomas used Bryant's nickname for her and playfully bounced her in his arms.

"Yes, Daddy, although I think John is more excited than I am. He's been asking loads of questions about how it works already."

His son had a mind for machines and how things worked. He had lost two radios to his inquisitiveness and examination of the inner workings of the devices.

"Well, maybe we can see if they'll show us the engine then, eh John?" he said.

John nodded with a great deal of enthusiasm, and they all laughed and made their way towards the train.

"Tickets please." The conductor stood beside the train steps. "You can sit anywhere in the next four cars." He smiled down at John. "Have your father find me once we are underway. I heard you talking about seeing the engine. I'm happy to show you, young man." He tipped his hat and handed the tickets back to Thomas.

"Thank you very much. That is very kind of you." Vivian smiled at him. Like so many others, he was struck by her eyes. Those golden and green orbs. They never failed to capture one's attention. He helped her onto the train.

"Of course, ma'am," he stammered slightly.

"How is this spot?" Thomas asked Diane as they made their way down the aisle.

"Oh, it's a fine spot, Daddy." She clambered onto the seat, her legs dangling over the edge.

"Here, treacle, let's have your hat and coat." Vivian helped her children take off their jackets and stow them with their bags in the storage above their seats. She had pulled *The Velveteen Rabbit* and a couple of toys out to help busy the children on the journey.

Thomas reached for Diane and pulled her onto his lap. She watched with keen interest all the busyness on the platform outside the train. The familiar movement was comforting, and she felt the warmth of drowsiness setting in and happily snuggled into her father, resting her head against his chest. Somewhere inside Vivian's pocketbook sat a card with a small violet pressed onto it with the single word *Home*. The sombre darkness of the snow-covered platform, depot, and city slowly gave way to rolling hills and meadows.

Love Always

Chapter Twenty-Three

"Thomas! Thomas!" Fynn called out to his brother, his long legs closing the distance between them.

"Fynn!"

The two brothers embraced in a fierce hug and held onto each other for a minute. It had been almost ten years since they last saw each other.

"Well, look at you! You have as much hair as me now!" Fynn had pulled off Thomas's hat and rubbed the thinning hair on his head and teasing him as though they were still children and not grown men. The two shared the same sparse hairline with more grey than ginger hairs left.

That was when Fynn noticed Vivian, Diane, and John standing behind Thomas, staring at him. Vivian was smiling, and the children held her hands tightly. Fynn looked from Vivian to Thomas, and the smile faded from his face. He was confused.

"Fynn, this is Vivian and our children, Diane and John." Thomas brought his brother over to Viv, who held out her hand.

"It's lovely to finally meet you, Fynn. Thomas has told me a great deal about you."

Still in shock, Fynn took her hand and shook it. "It's lovely to meet you as well, Vivian." He looked at Thomas with concern, then at the children. He crouched down to them, and John reached out his hand. "Good to meet you, John." The little boy's hand disappeared inside his uncle's.

He turned to Diane and asked, "Is it okay if I ask for a hug?"

Diane hesitated and looked up at her mother, who smiled her encouragement. Slowly, she stepped forward and reached out her arms to the uncle she had never met. He stood up with her, and she felt like she was being held by a giant.

"Vivian. My goodness. You are absolutely beautiful," Fynn said. "Thomas, let's take Vivian and the children to get some hot chocolate while we get your things and load them onto the truck, shall we? What do you think, Diane?"

"Hot chocolate?! Oh, Mummy, can we?"

"I don't see why not." Vivian wasn't sure why, but there was an unsettled feeling with Fynn. *I don't think he likes me*, she thought to herself.

With Vivian and the children settled at a table in a café nearby, Thomas and Fynn set off to collect their trunks.

"Thomas! What the bloody hell is going on?" Fynn demanded as soon as they were out of sight.

"Fynn, let me explain."

"It'd better be good. You brought a woman and children home with you, Thomas. You have a wife and children here! Why would you do this?"

"I know. The truth is, I didn't intend to ever come back, but we couldn't stay in England. There's no place to live and not enough   work.   Before   I   left,   Elise   knew."
"Knew what?"

"Knew that I was leaving her. I wrote to her and told her I had fallen in love with someone else. I told her about the children. She wouldn't divorce me, Fynn."

"Elise knows? She has never said a word, Thomas. It also doesn't explain why you wouldn't tell me or Mum and Dad. This isn't right. To bring Vivian like this. It's disrespectful of her and the children. Speaking of which … John? Your son's name is John? It's not John Henry is it, Thomas? Please tell me it's not."

He took a deep breath. He knew his brother was right about everything, and it was about to get worse. "The thing is, Fynn, Vivian knows about Elise, but she doesn't know about the children."

"Are you out of your fucking mind, Thomas?" Fynn rarely swore, but his anger swelled up and overtook him. "You're telling me you have told no one here about Vivian, Diane, and John Henry, I presume, and even better than that, Vivian, who has come all this way, thinks we know all about her and your children, but doesn't know that you have three children with Elise? Did I miss anything?" His voice was thick with disdain and disbelief.

All Thomas could do was nod.

"Well, you need to speak to Vivian before we get to the farm. She needs to be prepared because I can't promise Mum and Dad will be as polite and discreet as I've been with this news. Thomas, you are a selfish prick." Fynn turned away from his brother, picked up a trunk, and loaded the truck.

When they had everything packed securely, they came back to the café. "Uncle Fynn is going to have a visit while Mummy and I talk for a few minutes." Thomas took Vivian's hand and led her to the parking area near the truck.

"Thomas, what is it? Have I offended Fynn somehow? I can tell he doesn't like me. Is it because of Elise? He disagrees with you staying with me, doesn't he?" Her voice trembled. She knew something was very wrong.

"Viv, before I say anything, I need you to know I love you. I love you more than anything in this world. I need to tell you something, and you are not going to like it. Let's sit down over here." He guided her to the outdoor tables and bench nearby.

"Thomas, you're scaring me. What's wrong?"

"Vivian, I didn't tell Fynn about you or the children. I didn't tell my parents either." He waited for her to respond, but she just sat there, staring at him blankly. "Fynn was not expecting to see you today or the children. He didn't know I had left Elise. I wanted to let her tell people and be able to tell them what she wanted them to know. When she never did, I just didn't say anything either."

"And?" Her voice was flat.

"And? What do you mean?"

"What else, Thomas? If there is anything else, you need to say it now, or the children and I are getting on the next train back to Halifax and England."

Thomas knew there was no way around it. He had to tell her. "Vivian, I have three children with Elise: Hannah, Olive, and John—John Henry."

Vivian looked as though she had been shot. Her face contorted in pain, and her body reflexed backwards and away from him. "You didn't think, ever, not once before this moment, that perhaps I should know about this? Wait." She turned her head sharply to look at him. "John Henry?! Thomas! How can you already have a John Henry?"

"Viv, I know this is the most preposterous thing you have ever experienced. I should have just told you everything—all at once that first night we met. I'm a terrible person. I know that. I have done the worst thing I could. I've lied to you again." He tried to take her hands, but she snatched them away.

"I feel like I'm having déjà vu, Thomas. There were so many times you could have told me everything. Should have told me everything. But you didn't. You betrayed me over and over and over. Now I find out you've made me some sort of dirty little secret."

"Viv, no. No. That's not true," he pleaded.

"It is absolutely true. Not one person here knows I exist or that our children exist." Hot tears finally fell from her eyes, and she blinked them back, not wanting to allow herself to feel anything for him right then. "Why, Thomas? Why would you bring me here? Why would you do this to me? To us? To our children?"

"The longer it went on the less I was able to tell the truth. I didn't think you would come if I told you everything before we left London."

"That was my decision to make, not yours." She pursed her lips. "I need to think. I can't go with you today. The children and I will stay here for now. You can go home to your parents and tell them the truth or not. Honestly, I don't care. You need to find us a place to stay for a few days at least."

"Vivian, please, I ..." But it was hopeless.

She walked back to the children and to Fynn, with Thomas following behind her. When she started to tidy up the table, Fynn stood up and tried to awkwardly help. "Thank you, Fynn. I appreciate it." She put her hand on his and held it still before releasing it. Then, she turned to her children and forced a smile. In a light voice, she said, "Children, we brought so many things with us that the truck is overflowing. It's not safe for us to all go together. Daddy is going to go with Uncle Fynn and drop our things off. He'll come back in a few days for us. We're going to stay here."

Fynn pressed his lips together. He was not sure what was happening, but it was clear Vivian had no intention of coming with them to the farm that day.

"But Mummy, I want to see the farm. I want to meet Grandma and Grandpa," Diane whined.

"I know, darling, but it isn't safe, and we will do something fun while we wait. I promise."

"Umm, where are you staying with the children, Vivian?" Fynn wanted to help. He felt terrible for her and was still furious with his brother.

"Thomas is going to find some lodging for us now. Isn't that right, Thomas? I think he said there was a rooming house not far away." Vivian had no idea if there even was a rooming house in Kingston, but she felt it was a reasonable guess given the size of the city and the number of people who travelled through.

"Uh, yes. I'm going to go ask the conductor if he has any suggestions. I will be back in a few minutes. Fynn, do you want to come with me?" Thomas asked.

"Actually, I think I'll just stay here with Vivian and help her watch the children." His stare communicated his disinterest in helping his brother.

After Thomas left, they sat in silence watching Diane and John play on the swings and slide in the small park near the café.

"Vivian, I hope you know I'm not angry with you," Fynn said.

"Thank you, Fynn. To be honest, I don't know why you would be if you were." She met his eyes and held his stare. She had done nothing wrong, and it bothered her that she might be made out to be the villain. "I'm not sure what to think about anything right now, but I do know I'm not going to stand for any more lies."

"Are you going to stay in Canada?"

"I don't know. Please don't press me for a decision right now, Fynn. I know you mean well, but if I make one right now, none of us will be very happy."

Fynn sat back slightly to give Vivian more space. He admired her strength. He realised while watching her and his niece and nephew that he hoped they would stay.

Thomas had asked Vivian how much time she felt she needed, and she said one week. She would wait for him to come back, then she would tell him her decision.

They had a large room in a house near the lake. It was hard to imagine the body of water outside the house was just a lake. It was enormous, and even though it was winter, it still wasn't frozen over. The house had seven bedrooms, an enormous kitchen, and two parlours (or living rooms as they were called). Mrs. Wanda Lovett was a surprisingly young woman to own such a fine home.

"It belonged to my husband's family," she had shared with Vivian over tea in the sitting room. Her husband Seth had been killed in Sicily. "I don't need to rent out the rooms. I just like the company."

"I can understand that. It's a big house to be in all by yourself. Do you have any other family here?" Viv asked.

"No, it's just me. We didn't have any children before he left for the war. We hadn't been married long. I'm from Calgary, which is out west in Alberta." She added the last part in case Vivian wasn't familiar with the geography of Canada. "We met when he was doing some tank training on the base there. I could go back, I suppose. My parents, brother, and his family are all back there." Motioning around the room, she said, "But then I feel like I'd be leaving him, and I'm not quite prepared to do that yet. Also, I love living on the water. There's a peace that comes with it, even in the winter when the wind whips off the lake and against the house."

"Do you think you ever will?"

"Perhaps. I'm still young and would like to have a family of my own one day. I'm not sure another man would be comfortable living in my husband's home." The idea seemed to amuse Wanda, and she laughed.

"Perhaps not. Men seem to need their own rules for things," Viv commented.

Wanda picked up on the note of annoyance in her voice. "You can tell me it's none of my business, of course, Vivian, but why didn't you go with your husband and brother to your in-laws? It isn't that far, and I saw the truck. I think there was room enough to get you all in if you had wanted to."

Vivian was a very private person, and she wasn't sure how her new friend might judge her situation. It would be very easy to see her as the one in the wrong. Women often judged each other quite harshly rather than support each other. It could have gone either way. She decided to share part of the story and gauge Wanda's response from there.

"The truth is, Thomas hadn't told his family about us. He didn't really talk to them often, and I felt it was important that he go ahead of us and tell them and prepare them before we showed up. It would be the height of bad manners to show up with no warning. In-laws can be tricky enough without adding the shock of a surprise family to the mix."

"Oh, Vivian, you should know that it happens all the time. The war created some very strange situations."

Vivian was surprised to hear that.

"Honestly, men can be the daftest creatures on the planet. They just don't think things through sometimes. What they suspect is a simple matter can be an enormous one for everyone else, and what they think is enormous, well, frankly, no one cares one hoot." She poured some more tea into their cups, stirring in a drop of milk and a spoonful of sugar. "Don't let Thomas' male frailty and stupidity keep you from having a wonderful life here."

"Do you really think so? I feel so angry and humiliated, Wanda. Like he's ashamed of us."

"Oh, Viv. He's only ashamed of himself. I promise you that. There is also nothing wrong with allowing him to feel that way for a while longer."

Wanda was wise beyond her years, and her advice was sound.

Thomas arrived early on the seventh day. He hadn't slept or eaten properly the entire time they had been apart, and it showed on his haggard face.

"Daddy!" Diane and John shouted as they ran to him, jumping into his arms so he almost fell over.

"Oh, my goodness. I have missed you both so much." He clutched them to his chest and closed his eyes, breathing them in. When he opened his eyes, Vivian was standing before him. He set down their children and took a hesitant step towards her. He was afraid if he moved too fast, she would disappear or run away. "Viv." His voice was barely more than a thread.

"Daddy!" Diane took his hand and pulled him towards Vivian. "Mummy needs hugs, too. She hasn't seen you either." Her prodding was all the encouragement he needed, and he wrapped his arms around Vivian.

At first, she left her arms at her sides, reluctant to give in. She could feel his heart pounding in his chest. Slowly, breath by breath, she felt her love for him rush through her, powering her arms to rise and slide around his back.

"Oh, Vivian. I've missed you so very much. Please tell me you can forgive my stupidity and selfishness. Please tell me you are going to stay here with me." He spoke softly into her ear so only she could hear him.

Tipping her chin up so her mouth was at his ear, she spoke just as quietly, "Yes, Thomas, we are going to stay. I just hope your family will not blame me or think too harshly of me in all of this."

Thomas was overjoyed. "I have spoken to them. They understand the situation and know that I alone am the dolt to blame." His tone was humble.

"Time will tell, Thomas. Time will tell many things. For now, we are packed up and ready to go. I just need to say goodbye to Wanda."

Thomas picked up the bags by the door and called for the children to get their coats on.

"Yeah! We are going to the farm!" squealed Diane. "I want to pet the pigs, Daddy. I want to pet the pigs!"

Thomas laughed and agreed that not only could she pet them, but she could help feed them too.

"I feed pigs too, Daddy!" John called out. He was feeling left out of the fun. He didn't really want to feed the pigs. He thought they might be a little bit scary, but he didn't want to risk it being fun and not do it.

Wanda had heard the commotion and came into the front room to see her friend off. "I'm glad you decided to stay, Vivian. I hope you will keep in touch and let me know how you are all making out."

"I will. Thank you for letting us stay here. It was very helpful, and I enjoyed getting to know you, Wanda. You have been a good friend."

The two women hugged goodbye, and Wanda watched them pull away down the driveway.

"Bye, Wanda! Bye!" John and Diane shouted from the cab of the truck, waving frantically. "I shall miss Wanda," she stated. "She was my first friend in Canada." Her full lips pouted slightly.

"You will make many friends, Diane. Just you wait and see. This is the beginning of a great life with many friends, a yard of our own, and lots and lots of love," her father proclaimed.

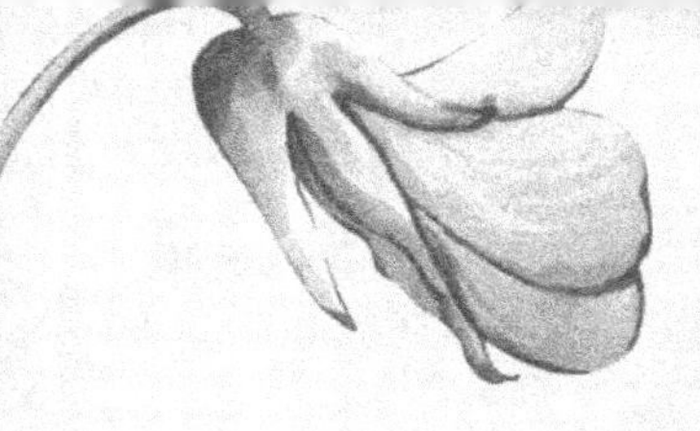

Chapter Twenty-Four

"Is that it, Daddy?" As Thomas slowed down, Diane pointed to a large, old farmhouse on their left.

"It sure is, sweetheart." He pulled into the laneway towards the side of the house where there was a small barn-like shelter with other trucks and machines underneath.

Vivian took in the enormous maple trees. There were also two willows in the front yard on either side of the porch entrance. They would provide a lot of cooling shade in the summer. On the far side of the house, there appeared to be an orchard, but she wasn't sure if they were apple trees or some other sort of fruit-bearing foliage.

A big black dog with a white blaze on his nose came lumbering out of the house towards the truck. He didn't bark but was very excited by their arrival.

"That's Patch. He's very gentle."

Vivian looked like she needed some reassurance.

"He certainly seems excited to see us." She looked out the window, and he jumped up on the door, startling her. "Oh! Goodness!"

Diane laughed. "It's okay, Mummy. He just can't wait to meet us."

Vivian waited for Thomas to come around to her door and push Patch out of the way so she and the children could get out of the truck.

"Patch! Sit!" Thomas commanded, and the dog did as he was told. His tail continued to wag furiously, and he made excited whining noises, but he stayed put.

"May I pet him?" John asked warily. The dog was a lot larger than he was, and while he wanted to pet him, he was also nervous the dog would crush him.

"Let me get a hold of his collar first, just so he doesn't accidentally knock you over." Thomas grabbed the dog by his collar and a little bit by the scruff of his neck and motioned for the children to come over.

Patch was in heaven. He was the centre of attention and getting all the love in that moment. Vivian smiled and relaxed when she could see how gentle the dog was with the kids.

"Well, you must be Vivian," a deep voice called out from behind them. They all looked up and saw a huge man with an oversized coat and fur-lined hat walking towards them from the front of the house. He could have been Fynn's twin if he were younger. It had to be Thomas' father, John.

"Yes. You must be Mr. Cooper. It's so nice to finally meet you." Vivian held out her hand.

"Oh, heck no. You can call me John or Dad, and I'm going to need a hug, not a handshake." He wrapped his arms around her, then stepped back to look at her. "Well, Thomas, you didn't explain well enough just how beautiful Vivian was. You tried, of course, but my goodness, you are lovely." His smile was infectious, and Vivian knew he meant it. "And who are these fine little people?"

"I'm Diane, and this is—"

"John too!" her brother cried out.

"You have the same name Grandpa." Diane proudly pointed out.

"Why, yes we do." He bent over and opened his arms, and they both ran to him.

Thomas looked at Vivian and mouthed the words *Thank*

you.

"We should get inside. May has cooked enough food for fifty people, and I think it's about ready." John's eyes twinkled, and Vivian could see he and Thomas shared the same-coloured eyes, though their builds and hair colour were not the same. Thomas was slimmer and fairer than his father as well. He carried both the children while Thomas carried their bags, and Vivian followed behind. Patch lopped along beside her.

The house smelled wonderful, and Vivian thought of the Sunday dinners with her parents and how scrumptious the house smelled on those days. A pang of homesickness hit her as she thought of them. It seemed like a very long time since she had seen them, even though it had only been a couple weeks. She hadn't written them yet to let them know they had arrived safely. She would do that tonight or tomorrow.

May Cooper was a few inches taller than Vivian with long, mostly silver hair pulled back off her face and gathered in a coil on her head. She had small brown eyes that darted from Vivian to the children, making Viv nervous. Her demeanour was not nearly as welcoming as John's had been.

"You have arrived safely, I see." She stayed in the door of the kitchen and did not come towards them. "How was the drive?"

Vivian felt like she was speaking to her, so she said, "It was quite nice. It's very beautiful here. It reminds me of the countryside back home quite a bit."

The two women stood across from each other. It was becoming a bit tense, so John put the children down and shouted, "Go greet your grandmother properly then." They ran towards her and hugged her around the waist, looking up at her.

"Well, aren't you a sight." Her eyes softened, and she reached down and hugged them back.

Vivian could feel the tension ease, but it was not quite as easy-going with May as it was with John. She did not insist she refer to her as Mum, for example, and only called her

Vivian, not Viv. It was clear she had words with Thomas, and he seemed to be overcompensating to be helpful around the kitchen.

They had a nice luncheon of chicken stew and homemade bread. May had baked two different pies and oatmeal cookies. She playfully slapped Thomas's hand away when he tried to sneak a cookie before they ate. "You'll spoil your appetite," she teased, and he gave her a hug.

It made Vivian happy to see how at ease he was with his family and how close they were. The pang of homesickness returned, and she wondered what her parents had for dinner that night, although they would be getting ready for bed soon with the time difference.

"I was going to take the children to see the animals after we eat. Is that okay, Mum?"

"Of course, Tommy. I imagine they'll enjoy the sheep."

"You have sheep?" Diane's eyes widened with excitement. "Pigs and sheep! Imagine, Mummy! Bryant would love it, wouldn't he?" The mention of her brother made Diane frown slightly. She missed him, too. "Will you help me write a letter and tell him all about them? I'll draw him a picture too."

"Who is Bryant?" May asked.

"He's my younger brother. He loves gardening and tending to animals. We didn't have this much space, of course, but he raised chickens and gathered eggs." Vivian enjoyed being able to brag about her brother.

"Do you have any other family?" she asked.

"Just my parents. My mother came from a very large family. She was the oldest girl of eleven children. My nan, Lottie, took care of me for a while when I was little. My mother works for Barrett's."

"Like the candies?"

"Yes! The very same."

"It's unusual for a woman to work after she has children. Do you plan to work once you're settled?"

Thomas interrupted, "Viv is going to stay home with the children."

"Well, yes, certainly until they're in school full time and more self-sufficient." But Vivian realised they had never discussed whether she would go back to work or not. She had assumed she would, but she didn't really know what she would do. It wasn't an option currently, especially since they didn't know where they would be living just yet.

Thomas looked at her with a bit of surprise, also realising they hadn't talked about it. He changed the subject a bit. "Viv's mom invented one of their most popular candies. The sherbet fountain. You know, the one with the liquorice stick in it?"

"Really? That is quite something. Your mother sounds like a very clever woman, Vivian." May sounded duly impressed.

"Thank you. Yes, she really is."

They finished up their meal and were tidying up when Diane and John tittered about the animals again.

"John, get your coat and hat." Diane ran to the door.

"We might need to figure out what else to call you so we don't get confused about which John we're talking about." May tousled the younger John's hair.

"Sometimes Daddy calls him Junior." The way Diane said the name made it sound like *Juhn-your*.

"That works. *Juhn-your* it is then." She pat his cheek and buttoned up his coat for him.

"Listen to your father and behave please." Vivian called to them as they scampered out the door after their father and grandfather.

"We will!"

"They are lovely, Vivian. They are so well mannered and spoken and clearly very bright." May brought two teacups over to the large wooden kitchen table along with the teapot, milk, sugar, and a small plate of the oatmeal cookies.

"Thank you, May. We always hope they'll behave when they meet new people or are in new places."

"I thought perhaps we should talk, Vivian." May poured the tea and glanced up at her.

"Yes, we probably should." Vivian poured some milk into

her tea and a small spoon of sugar. She stirred it and prepared herself for what would no doubt be a difficult conversation. "What would you like to know?"

"Well, how long do you think you will be staying with us?"

Vivian understood. They were not welcome to stay too long. "I'm not sure to be honest, May. I know Thomas has a job he is lining up in Toronto. They're building more of the underground here, and they need drivers. One of his sergeants lives in Toronto and has a basement apartment he is willing to rent to us when we're ready."

"Oh. I see. There was never a plan to stay here then?"

"No, there wasn't. We were just planning to stop here for a week or two so you could catch up with Thomas and get to know your grandchildren a bit. After all, you hadn't met them yet."

"Or knew they even existed until last week." May frowned at her cup.

"I'm sorry about that, May. I—"

"Vivian, none of that is your fault. It was up to Thomas to tell us, not you. I had some concerns that you would be staying here for a time, and that could prove complicated what with Elise and the children not that far away. We go to the same church. Well, when I go, we go to the same church. I'm not as committed as Elise is, I'm afraid." May realised that might have sounded rude. "I'm sorry. I don't mean to sound like I'm an atheist or anything. I do attend church, just not every single week. If you want to go, we can attend the later service. Elise is always at the early one."

"I think it would be wise for the children and I to forego church services while we are here." Vivian's voice was very quiet. The idea of running into Elise was bad enough, but their children, too? That would be unbearable not just for Vivian, but she imagined for Elise as well. "Does Elise know about the children?"

"Honestly, I'm not sure, Vivian. She has never said a word to us in all this time. Granted, she also stopped coming over for suppers and such. So, I'm guessing she must know at least a little of something. Certainly, she knows about you."

Vivian and May sat in silence for a long time. There was a lot to digest. Vivian found some relief in knowing that Elise at least knew about her.

"For what it's worth, I have never seen Thomas this happy. It pains me to say it because Elise is a good woman and a good mother. But there is a joy in Thomas I have never seen before. He never belonged on the farm. It just wasn't in his blood the way it is in John's and Fynn's. So as difficult as this has been, I'm also quite happy about it, Viv."

Vivian was so moved by May's words she reached out and gently touched the older woman's hand. "Thank you, May. That means a lot to me, and I know it will mean a lot to Thomas as well."

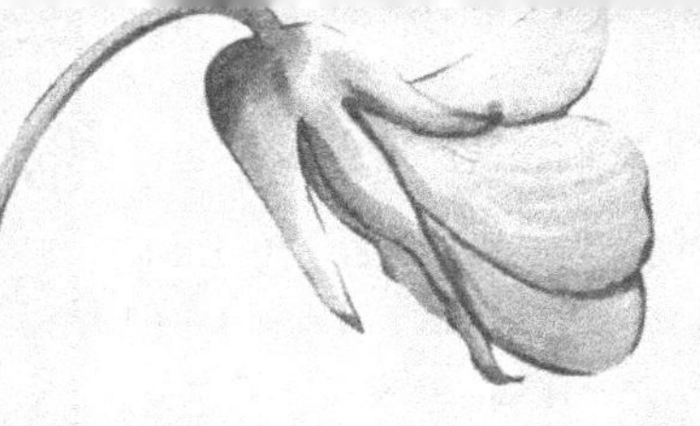

Chapter Twenty-Five

The basement apartment in Toronto felt quite grand compared to the tight quarters in Tottenham with her parents. Diane and John shared a room, and Thomas and Vivian made a bedroom space for themselves in the living room. There was even a small kitchen. Though it was a basement, they had large windows and a door on the back of the house that led to a large yard and a ravine with a creek.

Oliver Robinson, Thomas' SSM, and his wife Gloria owned the house. It was close to the base at Downsview. Oliver had decided to stay in the military after the war. He was a training officer. *Helping to train the next best generation of soldiers,* he had told them. He enjoyed it but was grateful he would never need to see active duty again or all the ugliness that went with it.

Gloria was what Thomas had called a *firecracker*. Not just because her hair was fiery red, but because she was a high-energy person and quick to put one in their place if they needed it. Gloria always had perfect makeup, including lipstick. It didn't matter the time of day or event. Her clothing was "smart looking," as Vivian's mom would say. It wasn't that she overdressed, she just liked to feel put together. She

had been very welcoming to Vivian, and they became fast friends. She showed her where to shop for the best deals on food and who to have things delivered from and who not to.

"Get your milk and butter delivered, Viv. It's less money and fresher than the glop at the store." She turned up her nose and made a face. "The meat at Mundy's butcher is better. He hangs it longer. Tyson's meat is always stringy or full of gristle."

Gloria also loved to cook and would make massive amounts of food and insist Vivian, Thomas, and their children join them. Oftentimes, Shelagh, their daughter, would take Diane and John back down to the apartment and watch them while the adult friends spent time together.

Shelagh was fourteen and in high school. She planned to be a doctor when she grew up. She had the brains and work ethic to achieve it. Diane and John adored Shelagh. She played games with them and read them books. She would never take any money from Thomas and Vivian for her time either. "Oh no, Mrs. Cooper. It wouldn't be right for me to take money. We're friends and neighbours. Besides, I love Diane and John. It's like I have a little sister and brother."

There was a short rap at the door, then Gloria could be heard calling, "Viv, the newspaper is here. Do you want to have tea and take a look together?"

"Come on in, Gloria," Vivian called back. "I'm just doing the lunch dishes." Using the term lunch instead of supper had been an adjustment, but Vivian wanted to embrace her new country and friends, so she used as much of the Canadian language as she could.

"Vivian, I have never seen someone do so many dishes," Gloria teased. She greeted her friend with a quick hug and kiss on the cheek. She then held up the newspaper. "Let's see what's available this week!"

Thomas and Vivian had been looking for property to purchase so they could build a house. Vivian hadn't told him yet, but she had drawn her own plans. She hadn't told anyone. She was sure they weren't sufficient, but it was fun to create the image of her future home in her head.

The ladies sat at the table chatting about the neighbourhood and day-to-day events while they scanned the classified advertisements for homes and vacant land for sale. Thomas was set on building their home themselves. "That way I know it was done right," he had said. It would also cost a lot less that way too.

"Viv! Look at this one." Gloria pointed her perfectly polished finger at an ad about halfway down the page. "They're selling a bunch of lots up in Willowdale. They're all about two or three acres each from the look of it. That would be perfect for you. It also isn't that far away from me, so we can still have our tea and visits."

Vivian read over the ad carefully. "It certainly sounds perfect!" She got out her map of Toronto and unfolded it on the table. "There isn't much around there according to this map. That partly explains why the prices are so low."

"I think you'll see it get developed quite nicely in a few years, Viv. The city has nowhere to go but north. The east and west are already getting too big. Look at the airport now! My goodness! It just keeps getting bigger and bigger."

"Oh, I don't mind that it isn't developed, but I do think you're right. People want to be close to things but not right in the city. This suburban life is becoming a real thing."

Vivian enjoyed talking with Gloria. She was smart and could speak as comfortably about the sale of beef as the economic conditions and public policies of governments and other countries. She was also a whiz with finances and in charge of all the money in her marriage.

A few weeks ago, she had confided in Vivian. "Don't say anything yet, but I might get a job at the bank on Keele Street. Shelagh is in high school now. She's very self-sufficient. It would be nice to do something for me." They didn't need the money; she had been quick to say. She just sometimes felt like a "wilted flower."

"What do you think of the terms they're advertising in the advert, Gloria?"

"I'd want to see the full details," she said, "but the rate seems very good. You would need a loan for the building materials themselves, and the bank normally only gives that out in chunks as they see you using it to build your house."

"I hope you do go get a job at the bank. You know more about these things than most people who work there already."

"Thanks, Viv. I find finance fascinating."

Together, they sketched out a plan of how much money would be needed to buy the land and build the house. "You'll need plans to be drawn up and approved by the city as well. That can be a bit pricey, even if you go with pre-done plans," Gloria explained.

"Wait here. I have something to show you." Vivian went to her bedroom and pulled out the rolled-up paper and brought it back to the kitchen table. "Is it cheaper if you can give the architect something to start with?"

"Usually, of course, but why?"

Vivian unrolled the paper, and Gloria's eyes widened in shock and disbelief. "These are excellent plans, Viv. Did Thomas draw these?"

"Actually, I did." There was a deep satisfaction in hearing the drawings she had made might be good enough for the city to approve.

"Vivian Cooper! You have been holding out on me." Gloria gave a low whistle. "Don't get me wrong, you're probably the smartest person I know. You can do complex math in your head for crying out loud. But this! This is something else altogether, Viv."

"Do you think the city would approve them then?"

"Viv, these are better than a lot of plans from professional architects. They will definitely get approved by the city. It's a lovely house. How did you come up with it?"

"Well, I just took the bits and pieces of houses I've liked and mushed them up and came up with this." Her hands made the movements of pressing something into a ball, then laying it open to reveal what was inside.

Gloria laughed. "Very technical indeed! Well, however

you did it, the layout has a smart use of the space."

Vivian happily showed Gloria the different parts of the house. The kitchen was connected to the dining room with an extra wide door so one could see people at the table while preparing meals. The entrance had a large closet for coats and boots, so they didn't have them hanging on a hook, and it made the space feel larger. Such simple, practical things but they would make a big difference.

"What does Thomas think of the plans?" Gloria asked.

"You're the first person I've shown them to."

"I am honoured! Thomas will be impressed." Gloria ran her hands over the plans again. "Four bedrooms?" She raised her eyebrow at Vivian. "Should I know something?"

"Not at all. I just thought it would be nice for Diane and John to have their own rooms, and it would be nice to have a room for guests when they come to visit." Her parents would love it, and with that much land, she could have gardens again.

Thomas had managed to get a job with the Toronto Transit Commission or TTC and had recently passed all his tests to drive the subway trains and streetcars. He took any overtime that was offered. When he arrived home, he would pull off his coat and shake it off before coming inside. There was always a lot of soot, dust, and dirt from the trains. Often, he would cough or sneeze, and it would be full of black specks.

Vivian heard the truck door close. She had been impatiently waiting for him to get home ever since she and Gloria had found the ad in the paper.

"There's my beautiful girl." Thomas hugged her tight and kissed her cheek as he came into the kitchen area. "I'm sorry I'm so late. They offered me a few extra hours, and I took them. Are the children in bed already?"

"You work so hard, Thomas. Sit down. I have a plate in the oven keeping warm for you." Vivian sat him down at the table and went to get the food from the oven. She had made something called meatloaf that Gloria showed her in a magazine. It turned out quite well for her first attempt, she thought.

"What's all of this?" He saw all the newspapers and the rolled-up paper.

"Gloria and I may have found the land!" Viv excitedly pulled over the newspaper that she had folded to the correct page. "Watch the plate, it's hot."

Thomas read through the ad and looked up at her with a beaming smile. "It sounds perfect! We should go see it tomorrow. I'm off for two days in a row. We can call them first thing in the morning."

"Oh, Thomas, I'm so happy you like it. I checked the map, so I could see where it was. There isn't much out there now, but it isn't far from Yonge Street, so you'll be able to get to work easily. Gloria thinks it will grow and become a very vibrant town. I have something else I wanted to show you." Carefully and with obvious pride, Vivian unrolled the house plans.

"Viv, this is a beautiful house. Where did you get these plans?" Thomas scanned them. There were so many innovative touches.

"I drew them."

"What? How?" Thomas was at a loss for words. "Viv! These are incredible." He jumped up and hugged her tightly. "You! You are fantastic. There's nothing you can't do, and you never cease to amaze me."

Vivian didn't think she could feel prouder of herself than she had when Gloria praised her work, but Thomas' words made her feel as light as air. "Thank you, Thomas. I wasn't sure they were good enough."

"Viv, they are more than good enough, and I love the layout. You designed such a great house. What is this here by the front door?"

"It's a large double closet with a shelf on the top for hats and mitts and a rack on the bottom for shoes and boots. Now they won't be in a messy heap in the hallway."

"Bloody brilliant!"

They spent the next hour looking at the plans and dreaming out loud about their future home that just became one large step closer to becoming a reality.

The next few months were spent clearing the lot and digging the basement. Thomas rented a tractor to pull the stumps out, but most of the basement he dug with a shovel after the rent on the tractor went up significantly. With all the houses being built, there was a greater demand for equipment, and they had a tight budget already.

"We should be able to move into the basement in a week or so. Once the floor is on the first level, it will be liveable, and Diane can start the school year with her friends."

"Are you sure, Thomas? We won't have water or a washroom yet." Vivian was not confident in that plan.

"Maybe not for the first month, but I can build an outhouse as a temporary measure until the plumbing is hooked up. The pipes downstairs will be done in a couple weeks." Vivian's face must have given her away because he quickly added, "It will be an adventure, Viv. Like camping. It's only for a few weeks at most until the plumbing and electrical get approved and hooked up. Besides, the money we'll save on rent, we can use to get the house done faster."

His boyish exuberance won out.

"Okay, Thomas, if it's just a few weeks, we can manage. It will be nice weather for a while longer."

"That's my girl! Kids! Kids! Come here. We have something to tell you."

Gloria, Oliver, and Shelagh were sad the Cooper family was leaving but very happy for them, too. It was an enormous move forward in the comfort and security of their family. Thomas had gone to the bank and received the next distribution of funds for the house. When he went to the building supply store, it turned out the demand from the housing boom wasn't just on tractors and heavy equipment. It was also on plumbing and electrical parts. The cost of the parts had gone up almost thirty percent.

"This is outrageous! I was here two weeks ago and priced everything out. That's what the bank based this last instalment on," he cried.

"I'm sorry, Thomas. The prices have gone up from my suppliers, and I must pass that on to my customers." Anthony Russo, the store owner, looked truly apologetic and embarrassed by the situation.

"What am I supposed to tell my wife? She agreed to move into the basement of our house because we would have plumbing and electricity before the fall. I can't afford both now." Thomas picked up his list of materials and stormed back to his truck and pulled a mickey of rye out of the glove box. Taking a deep swallow, he knew he had to figure out how to make it work. How could he ask his wife and young children to live in their basement with no lights or running water for, and that was the worst part, he wasn't even sure how long. Thank goodness he had bought extra lumber because it was cheaper to buy it by the truckload. "Think, Thomas. Think," he mumbled to himself.

The power had already been run to the house. Thank goodness he had gone in with four other neighbours to do that early on. At the time, he had almost not done it because they weren't ready for the power to be connected and wanted to use the money for other things.

"If I get all the electrical now, I can at least connect that, and we can have lights and some heat. The outhouse is not ideal, but it functions," he continued to talk to himself out loud and reason out a plan.

"You're back!" Anthony smiled, hoping he would be able to help Thomas out.

Thomas slapped his list down on the counter. "Yes," he said confidently. "I have a plan. I will take all the electrical on my list and as much plumbing materials as I can with whatever is left." He paused and then added, "How many square feet does the large canister of bituminous and each roll of tar paper cover?"

"How is the house coming along, Viv?"

Gloria and Vivian had started and managed to stick to a weekly tea visit. Vivian took the city bus with John after Diane left for school.

"We have a creek at the new house and lots and lots of wires!" John wanted to be part of the conversation and shared his current favourite things about the house.

"Well, that is wonderful, John."

"Mummy says not to touch the wires because they will bite me. I didn't see any teeth, but I certainly don't want to be bitten." He grinned, and his eyes disappeared behind his round cheeks.

"You're a good boy to listen to mummy. She's a very smart lady, and she will always keep you safe. I put out a puzzle in the living room for you. It's a new one. Maybe this one will be a challenge for you."

John ran off to see the new puzzle. He was very talented at them, and the new one was 1,000 pieces. He had put together a 500-piece in a few hours last week. He could see things and put them together and take them apart quite easily.

"We do. We hit a bit of a bump. The price of materials went up quite a lot so Thomas got what he could."

"What does that mean? What didn't he get?"

"Long story short, it means we don't have running water."

Gloria was alarmed. "But how can you not have water? You can't go much longer toting water back and forth from your neighbour's faucet, Viv. It's going to be getting cold soon. It already is and you are expecting again. That isn't good for the baby either." Vivian had shared about her pregnancy with her friend a few months ago. Thomas had been thrilled of course and told her not to worry about money. They would find a way. They always did.

"That was why Thomas decided to prioritize the electricity. We can have light, an electric stove, and an electric heater. I started using the wagon to carry the water jugs so that I am not putting too much strain on me or the baby. I promise to be careful."

"Vivian, I love you, but this is not a good way to live. How will you bathe?"

"We are connected to the stack, and because we have the electricity, the pump works to get the water to go out at least. Thomas put a tub downstairs and hooked it up to the drain. I can heat up the water, and the children can have a bath. We will still need to use the outhouse for the toilet for a while longer."

Gloria's eyebrow had not gone down.

"Honestly, Gloria, we're okay. It's not as posh as we would like, but even with the plumbing done, we wouldn't have much more than that."

"So let me see if I have this right. You are living in the basement of your house with the floorboards above you as a roof, a few plugs, and no running water until spring."

Vivian laughed. "Don't forget the bloody mosquitos! But yes, pretty much. Thomas was very clever. He got tar paper and bituminous to seal the floor so we won't have any leaks from rain or snow, and it will help keep the heat in a bit as well."

"Oh, well then. Pardon me. It's the bloody Taj Mahal." Gloria was trying to make light of things, but she was still concerned. Winters got harsh in Ontario. She hoped Vivian wasn't going to regret her decision.

Love Always

Chapter Twenty-Six

The fragrance of apple blossoms hung thick in the air. When they moved to Aurora four years ago, they had planted three apple trees and left the two original maples in place for shade. The children loved to climb them and hang off the branches. Mr. Morley, the back neighbour, had a massive weeping willow tree whose branches reached like hands over the fence, beckoning them. The boys would pretend they were Tarzan and swing across the yard. Mr Morley did not appreciate the level of fun to be had with mere tree branches and threatened to cut the huge limbs off his tree to prevent them from damaging it. The irony of cutting off large branches to prevent the use of the limbs was lost on him, but he never did cut the tree.

The years had been good to them. Thomas had been promoted several times at work. His seniority meant he was one of the first to select holidays or vacation time. They often looked back on those early days of building the house in Willowdale and laughed. Thomas could not believe Vivian put up with that first winter in the house. One of the coldest in memory, she had found ways to

keep them warm, fed and feeling like they were on an adventure and not living in a basement with just floorboards, tar paper and bituminous for a roof to keep out the weather.

As predicted, Willowdale had started to be swallowed up by Toronto. Aurora was a lovely, quiet small town and here they were, their children growing up so fast. Diane had just started high school. She was extremely bright and skipped a grade. Socially, Vivian worried that she was hanging around with the wrong crowd. She had started smoking and testing the patience of her parents with late nights and parties. John tried to talk to her, but she no more listened to him than she did their parents. *You can't put an old head on young shoulders, dear,* Vivian reminded Thomas when he would lose his temper with Diane. She hoped it was a phase and she would grow out of it. Thomas was not convinced. Phillip was older than Joseph by two years and Landyn by five, but it rarely seemed that way. Phillip loved jokes and silliness at the expense of his two brothers. They shared a room and Phillip borrowed Joseph's pristine clothes and shoes or boots daily to go to the barn where he worked in exchange for riding lessons. The items never made it back in the same condition.

When they had moved, Vivian was pregnant with Judy. Jess was just a toddler but was nevertheless thrilled to have a little sister. She treated Judy like she was a live doll, helping to dress her and care for her.

"What do you say to going for a drive tomorrow?" Thomas asked as Vivian came out the back door of the house.

"Here are." She handed him a *rye and ginger* and sat down beside him with her tea on the small patio. It felt good to sit down. Thomas still found the way she said *here you are* without the *you* endearing. "Of course." She loved their little road trips. They always came home with the oddest treasures. "That sounds intriguing. Where are we going?" He held out a folded newspaper. When she saw it, she frowned. "You want to move again?" Vivian asked as she took the paper seeing that it was folded to the real estate section.

"No, not move. I want to build a cottage on a lake." He pointed at an advertisement for lots being sold on a lake called Anstruther.

"I don't understand. A cottage?"

"A summer home. A vacation home."

"Can we afford it, Thomas?" Her worry was audible in her voice. They had been doing well, getting ahead again. The house in Willowdale was worth substantially more than the one in Aurora meaning they didn't have a mortgage. Vivian was hesitant to take on more debt when they could be saving instead.

"I got a good pay increase with the last promotion and can borrow against this house to get the money to build the cottage." He could see she wasn't convinced. "It would be good for the kids to have the lake and forest to explore. It will get Diane away from the riff raff she's been chumming with."

"I guess it doesn't hurt to go look." Vivian wasn't sure how much she liked the idea, but if it could help turn things around with Diane, she was willing to give it a shot.

"That's my girl!" He whooped. "We'll leave at about 6:00 a.m. It takes about two and a half hours to get there, and then we will have to travel for a bit by boat to get there."

"Wait … pardon?"

Thomas laughed and ran downstairs to gather some tools and things he thought might come in handy for looking at the property.

Love Always

Chapter Twenty-Seven

Vivian had not been very excited to learn her cousin Ava and three of her friends were coming to Canada to visit. Ava had always been an indulged and spoiled child and very unkind to Vivian. When she had received the letter from Ava saying that she was coming in July, Vivian did a rare thing, she called her mother.

"Mum, why in the world would she come to visit me? She has never cared for me." Vivian had asked Evelyn.

"Truthfully, because she wants a place to freeload from when she travels. She only goes to places she can stay free." Her mother was always very direct and had never approved of how Ava treated people. Her sister had raised an unscrupulous woman.

"What should I do then? We don't have the space for that many extra people. You have been to the house in Aurora. It's lovely but quite full of our brood."

"I don't think it matters, Viv. She will come regardless and for the sake of family peace, it isn't worth the fight. She probably won't stay at the house much anyway. She likes the nightlife."

"Well Aurora is not exactly known for its nightlife.

Perhaps they will end up staying in Toronto most of the visit anyway then." Vivian felt a bit more hopeful.

"I think you're right. They are not coming to visit you and the children. They want to have fun. I would suggest that you set some boundaries up front. They must buy their own liquor and do not let her use your car! She has crashed her parents' car so many times I am surprised it still runs."

Vivian decided against refusing to host her cousin and her three friends for the peace of the family as her mother had said. She was far enough away it didn't matter, but her parents and Bryant would be given a lot of hostility if Ava was snubbed as she would perceive it.

She and Thomas decided to finish off some space in the basement so their guests would have some privacy in their busy home. The lamps had been scavenged from the curb in one of the wealthy neighbourhoods. Two matching chesterfields that were also pull-out sofas came from a friend of Thomas's at work. Doug had been getting rid of them at the perfect time and was willing to trade them for some rototiller services Thomas did as a side business for extra money.

"It looks wonderful, Thomas. Thank you for doing all of this. I know it was an expense we weren't planning on right now."

"Now that it is done, I am glad we did it. Look at how much more space we have! Now Joseph, Phillip and Landyn can have a bit more privacy with their friends when they *hang out* as they say." The boys were all teenagers now. Joseph and his friends often got together and played guitar and sang songs together. Having them in the basement instead of the living room would afford everyone extra distance when they were in the early days of learning new songs and the sound was reminiscent of a wounded hound dog. Jess and Judy were not bothered that they still shared a room. They preferred it to being alone in the dark and thought having one more place they could tease their big brothers when they entertained would be a lot of fun.

Thomas was proud of the work he had done. He had added a gas fireplace in the corner. It was a charming touch if he did say so himself. He had been feeling a little out of sorts for a while and this project had given him some purpose. He knew Vivian was worried about her cousin's visit. He had never met her while they were still in England, but he had heard about how rude and unkind she was to people. He was happy to be able to help show off their beautiful home.

Vivian read his mind. "Even Ava will be impressed. Although, I really don't care if she is or not. I am so proud of our home and all the hard work you have put into it for us. Thank you." She put her arms around his neck and kissed his cheek.

Thomas had been on the night shift driving for the TTC and didn't have time to sleep before they needed to go get their company at the airport. He had a quick shower to freshen up and went to get changed. While they waited, Vivian told her youngest two children a bit more about Ava and some of the time she spent with her when they were teenagers.

"We would do our hair and then go to the park near her house and listen to the live performances. Ava was such a beacon of beauty. The boys just flocked to her," Viv said.

"I bet the boys flocked to you too, Mummy," Jess chimed in. She thought her mother was just about the most beautiful woman in the world.

"You are very sweet, Jess. No, I was very shy and happy to just listen to the music and be around the fun." Vivian hugged her daughter. "You will need to mind your brothers while your father and I go fetch Ava and her friends."

Jess and Judy made faces and giggled.

"We'll be good, Mummy. We promise. Don't we, Jess?" Judy looked pointedly at her sister. Jess was the one who would be more prone to bother her brothers and then squawk when they *thumped* her. Not that they didn't *thump* Judy. She just took it and kept quiet.

"All right, we will be back as quick as we can. The traffic on the highway is always so awful," Vivian complained.

"Honestly, I don't see the point in building bigger highways if they aren't going to take away the traffic congestion," Thomas remarked as he came back down to the kitchen. "Boys!" he shouted down the stairs to Joseph and Landyn. They shared a room with their brother Phillip. "We're leaving now. Watch your sisters, please."

There was a sound of a door opening followed by the reply, "Okay, Dad. We will." The door closed again. Thomas and Vivian glanced at each other with an amused look on their faces. They knew full well that door would remain closed until they pulled back in the driveway a few hours from then.

It didn't take long Ava to affirm her reputation. From the moment Ava stepped off the plane, she was a whirlwind of dismissive remarks and haughty glances. "My goodness, Vivian," she drawled, surveying the modest home with a critical eye. "I hadn't realized how … well frankly, simply you lived here."

Vivian forced a smile. "It's actually a lot larger than our home in England."

"It isn't so much the size as the way you decorate then, I guess." She turned to Thomas and beamed as she took his arm. "Thomas, dearest, what does a girl need to do to get a drink around here?"

Thomas flushed crimson. He knew Ava was trouble, but that didn't stop him from feeling an electrical charge go off inside him when she touched him. He hoped no one noticed, especially Vivian. "I am sure we can find you something." The blushing was subsiding. "Vivian, I am going to take Ava inside to make some drinks. Does anyone else want anything?" He took the orders, but declined the offer of help from Ava's friend, Maddy. The idea of being alone with Ava was thrilling. Her platinum hair reminded him of Marilyn Munroe although she was far more petite and delicate. She had a confidence that he found sexy.

Vivian took a breath and held her tongue. She had known to expect this. Ava was not just spoiled; she was a terrible flirt, too. An uneasy feeling rose in her stomach, but she pushed it back down. She trusted Thomas even if she didn't trust her cousin.

Ava's friends, Maddy and Greg, were equally snobbish and shared her disdain for Vivian's home. Leland, on the other hand, was full of compliments and gratitude for the hospitality. A slim, almost lanky young man who smiled and laughed easily, he had been a teletype clerk in the Royal Air Force and decided to leave and make a change. He had a great deal of knowledge and experience in communications much like Vivian. With communications growing and changing at a rapid rate, he found it exhilarating to keep up. He enjoyed learning and then teaching new technologies to others. He was considering moving to Canada and would be willing to accept any job necessary to be allowed to emigrate. That's why he had come with Ava and their friends, he wanted to see the country first-hand and see what it was like. So far, he loved everything about it.

"I think your home is charming, Viv. Your gardens are especially lovely. My brother would be jealous of all the space you have for roses," he said.

Vivian was relieved to have something pleasant to focus on. "They are all English roses. Thomas wanted me to always have a piece of home with us."

"That's a lovely thought." Leland pointed at a patch of flowers growing at the side of the house. "Are those lily of the valley?"

"Why yes, they are! They're my favourite, and they spread more and more every year."

Leland and Vivian continued to walk around the yard, discussing the different flowers, trees, and seasons.

Soon thereafter, Thomas excused himself to go get some sleep before his shift. "I apologise, but I have to work tomorrow before we start to officially enjoy your visit." He stumbled slightly as he climbed the stairs.

"All right there, Thomas?" Greg shouted out and laughed as Thomas stood still on the stairs for a moment to gather his wits.

"Right as rain, Greg. Don't you worry." His words were slurred. Vivian got up to help him.

"I think I will toddle off to bed as well. Night all." Vivian held Thomas by the arm and around his waist as they moved up the stairs towards their bedroom. The others bid them goodnight. Leland wondered how often Vivian had to help Thomas like that. He hoped it wasn't as often as it seemed.

The real trouble began the next day when Thomas came home from work. His eyes lit up at the sight of Ava, and Vivian felt that same pang of unease.

"Oh, Thomas!" Ava exclaimed, throwing her arms around him. "How delightful that you are home!"

Thomas grinned widely, holding her a little too long. "We can start to celebrate now. I have seven whole days off. Can I get us a drink?"

"Absolutely," Ava purred, casting a sideways glance at Vivian. "And do make it something strong."

As the days passed, Ava's behaviour grew increasingly intolerable. She openly flirted with Thomas, who seemed all too eager to oblige her. He fetched her drinks, doted on her every word, and treated Vivian like a servant in her own home. The children, Jess and Judy in particular, were not spared either.

"These children," Ava remarked loudly one afternoon, wrinkling her nose as Jess ran past with her sister, "are absolutely feral. Don't you bathe them, Vivian?"

Vivian bit her tongue, her cheeks flaming. "They were just playing outside, Ava. They're children."

"Filthy little animals," Ava muttered just loud enough for Vivian to hear.

The final straw came when Thomas suggested taking Ava to the cottage for a day trip. "Viv, you can manage here, can't you? The others want to take the train into the city for the day, and Ava doesn't want to go," he said casually, not meeting her eyes.

"Of course," Vivian replied, her heart sinking. She watched

them drive away, feeling a mixture of anger and helplessness.

When they returned, something had changed. Thomas avoided Vivian's gaze. Ava, however, did not. She grinned and carried on like she was the cat who caught the canary. For the remainder of the visit, Thomas completely ignored her and the children now and was completely focused on Ava unless he was asking Vivian to get them something. She felt like she was a server in a restaurant.

On the last night, Thomas didn't come to bed. In the morning, Vivian found him on the couch with Ava laying on him, their clothing askew, his pants unzipped. Empty bottles of rye and vodka were scattered on the table and floor. The intimate scene caught in her throat. Worried one of the children would see them, she reached down and touched Thomas arm to wake him. As he stirred, his hand moved over Ava's body, caressing her. When he realised where he was, his eyes shot open, and he froze for a moment.

"Viv, oh, sorry. We must have fallen asleep down here last night." He gently pushed Ava off him. What bothered Vivian most was that he didn't even seem bothered to have been found with Ava like that.

"Oh, Tommy darling," Ava purred, pretending to not realise Vivian was standing beside them. "You make the most delicious bed to lay upon." Then she looked up and smirked "Oh, Vivvy! I didn't see you there."

"Get up." Her voice was quiet but firm, her eyes glued to Thomas'. "Everyone will be up soon." Vivian's heart was pounding in her ears, and she could hear Ava giggling as she walked out of the living room to the kitchen to start making breakfast.

Vivian was quite happy that she was leaving and was sure Thomas would return to himself once they got back to their normal life.

"Uncle Leland, did you decide to move to Canada?" Jess asked as they all ate the breakfast Vivian had made while the others drank tea and chatted about the long trip home. Leland had quickly become part of the family and all the children were hoping he would stay.

"I sure have, Jess." He had been so impressed with the opportunities in Toronto, he had asked Thomas and Vivian to sponsor him to immigrate to Canada. "If all goes according to plan, I will be back in a months' time."

"Yay!" squealed Jess and Judy who jumped up and hugged him tight.

True to his word, Leland returned a month later. When he walked out to the baggage area where Thomas and Vivian were waiting, Vivian gasped. Ava was with him. Thomas did not seem shocked in the least and Leland seemed very uncomfortable. His greeting was a bit awkward, and he didn't shake Thomas' hand. Vivian knew something was wrong.

That evening, as they lay in bed beside each other in strained silence, Thomas finally spoke to Vivian. "Viv, I've decided I need a change."

"What are you talking about?" she asked, her voice trembling.

"I'm leaving," he said bluntly. "Ava and I … we've decided to be together."

Vivian's world crumbled. "What about us? The children?"

"They'll be fine," he replied, avoiding her tear-filled eyes. "Ava and I are going to go to Niagara Falls for a few days before we return to England."

"You're going back to England? You're going *back* with *her*?"

"Yes. Her father knows people who can help me get a job there. She has her own flat in London, and we will be living there."

Vivian's head was spinning. "I gave up everything to come here, Thomas. I lied to my family and friends. I have been lying all this time to our children. All for you!"

"I know, and I'm sorry for that, but Ava and I want to be together."

"You will regret this, Thomas. You're betraying your family for a selfish, greedy, spoiled brat. You have truly outdone yourself in the realm of idiocy and betrayal. You will leave us, your family, shattered and broken in your wake for the fleeting allure of Ava's superficial charms. The irony and almost poetic justice are not lost on me. You easily traded your devoted first wife and loving family for me—naive, gullible, and foolish for this life. A life you said you wanted. A life I thought was full of love and pride in what we built together. Bravo, Thomas, for setting yourself up to be discarded by a woman who can no more be happy or satisfied than you can."

With that, Vivian got up and walked out of their bedroom. She put on her slippers and quietly exited the front door. She didn't want to wake her family and have to explain why she was so upset. She needed time to collect her thoughts and decide how she would explain everything to her children.

Everyone was up early the next day. Leland needed to be in the city for his orientation and onboarding at legislative offices in Toronto. He could see Vivian was upset and had been crying.

"Viv, are you okay? I know Ava has done something. When she showed up at the airport in London, all she said was that she decided to come back here for another visit. She can be a viper." He held a cup of tea out for her.

Vivian sat down at the small kitchen table. The surface was chipped at the edges. She remembered how proud Thomas had been when he brought it home in the back of the car. Another scavenging treasure.

"Oh, Leland, no. I'm sorry to say I am not. I'm surprised Ava didn't tell you her plans on your journey back here." Her eyes were glassy as she looked up at him from the chipped table with her teacup.

"Her plans?" Leland got an uncomfortable feeling in the pit of his stomach.

"Why yes. Apparently, she and Thomas are going to have a lovely holiday in Niagara Falls before returning to London together."

"What?" Leland's voice was louder than he intended, and

he hushed himself as he continued to speak, "I can't believe that. Are you sure she isn't just trying to be spiteful?"

"Thomas told me last night after everyone was in bed." Vivian swallowed some tea. "I'll tell the children after they leave. He doesn't plan to come back here again." The last words came out as a choking sound.

"Viv, I, well, I have no words. I'm just so sorry." Leland reached out and patted her hand. He wanted to tell her she would be okay. That she was better off without Thomas. He knew it wasn't the time or place, but he also knew Thomas was making a terrible mistake. Ava was not worth what she was going to cost.

Vivian had gone to her room when Thomas and Ava were leaving for Niagara Falls. The boys had thought it strange Vivian wasn't going with them and looked at each other with concern.

"Why isn't Mum going with you, Dad?" Joseph, the older of the two boys, knew enough at sixteen to understand men and women didn't go on vacation together alone. "Landyn and I can watch the girls. We will do a better job of it this time." He wanted to try and give his father a chance to fix the problem.

"Thanks, buddy. But we have it all arranged."

Joe knew then what was happening, and it was not a vacation. He didn't hug his father or shake his hand. He looked him in the eye, frowned, and walked into the house, pulling Landyn and the girls with him. Something in his manner told his siblings to do as they were asked without question.

Vivian had called Diane and John and asked them to come over after she knew Thomas had left. Phillip was still at the barn and would probably not be home that night as usual. She asked Joseph to keep Landyn, Jess, and Judy downstairs so she could talk to Diane, John, and Sarah. Vivian would have preferred to just speak to Diane and John, but Sarah would know soon either way.

Diane was seven months pregnant. Vivian was worried

about telling her such upsetting news but was grateful Richard had not come as well. Her husband Richard was, as Thomas had said, *a giant child and not ready to have one of his own.* Diane and John were older than their siblings by several years and were usually told serious matters first. Vivian was relying on them to help deliver the news to the rest of her young family.

"So let me get this straight." John's voice was a quiet growl. "He is leaving you, and all of us, for that shameless slut?"

"John!" Sarah admonished him.

"I am not sorry, Sarah. This woman came here with an agenda to ruin our family. To hurt our mother." John stood up so quickly the chair he had been sitting on toppled over. Vivian gasped back a sob. "I am so sorry, Mum. I didn't mean to upset you more." He leaned down and wrapped his arms around her, placing his cheek on the top of her head.

Diane had remained silent throughout the entire conversation. Finally, she nodded her head and stated, "Well, if he thinks he's leaving without knowing what we think, he has another thing coming."

"What do you mean? He isn't coming back to the house." Vivian was confused. How would Diane tell Thomas anything if she wasn't going to see him?

"John and I will drive to Niagara Falls and find them. It isn't that big a place. We will take the extra car keys. He isn't going to need that damn car if he's going to England." Diane's voice was eerily calm and calculated.

John nodded and walked over to the bowl in the living room where they put keys and other important small items. He scooped them up and went to the door. "Ready?" he said to Diane.

"John, are you sure this is a good idea? Why not just leave it alone?" Sarah came over to her husband and touched his face. "I know you are hurt and angry. I don't want you to do something you might regret. That either of you might regret." She looked at Diane.

"Sarah, I know you're worried, and I love you for that, but

Diane is right. My father is not leaving without telling me to my face that he is a liar and a cheat." John hugged Sarah tightly, kissed her forehead, and held her for a long minute. The anger and hurt subsided briefly in that embrace. Long enough for him to collect himself and turn to his sister. "Di, I don't think you should come with me in your condition. It's bad for the baby." He took her hand and gave it a squeeze.

"John, I appreciate your concern. I will be fine."

"Di," Vivian interrupted. "I know you are upset and want to speak to your father, but it would help me if you were here when I speak to the rest of the family."

Diane saw her mother's face and simply nodded.

Once John and Sarah were out of sight, Vivian reached out and took Diane's hand and sobbed. "Di …" Her voice was so broken it was hard to understand what she was saying. "I need to tell you something else."

Vivian took Diane upstairs to her room and closed the door behind them. She didn't want to risk anyone coming in while she told Diane the story of her life with Thomas. "What I am going to tell you, no one else knows. Not even my own mother."

Diane nodded and didn't interrupt her mum as she unburdened the weight of the past twenty-five years. She told her daughter how she had become pregnant and how Thomas couldn't marry her because he had a wife who wouldn't divorce him. Vivian admitted how she had believed him, so they pretended to get married for her family and for the appearances of everyone in England.

"It seemed to go all right. After you were born, your father got us a house in the country so we would be safer away from the city and the bombings. Bryant came with us. Do you remember that at all?" Vivian paused and looked up at Diane. They both smiled weakly at the fond memory of Bryant's love of gardening.

"There's something else you need to know, Di."

Diane braced herself. What else could there be?

"Your father also had children with Elise, his wife. Three

in fact. Hannah, Olive, and John." There was silence, and Vivian waited patiently for Diane to process what she had just said.

"John? He has another son named John? How is that possible? Why would you name them the same?" She was incredulous.

"I didn't know. Your father told me it was a tradition in his family to name the firstborn son after his grandfather. So, I did that. I didn't realise there was already a John. When we arrived in Canada, I found out and I almost took us back to England. We stayed in Kingston for a few extra days."

"I think I remember that! In a big old house. The woman who owned it was really kind to us."

"Yes. That's the one. I decided I had been kidding myself that there hadn't been children in his marriage, and it was worth it to be with Thomas. I had already given up everything and moved here with you and your brother." Vivian sighed.

"So, you never told your parents you weren't married or about the other family?"

"No, I didn't."

"This other family, do they know about us?"

"Yes, they do. At least that is what I was told by your grandmother when we first arrived at their farm in Cooper Falls."

"Is there any reason to believe that Ava knows any of this? Would she use that against you now?" Diane's mind was racing in every direction. "Is that why you're telling me? Are you worried Ava would say something?"

"No. I don't know if Ava knows or not. I'm just so tired of the lies and had to tell someone. I had to tell you. I have carried this all this time. You are the only person I could ever trust with such an enormous secret, Diane, and it needs to stay a secret—at least for a while longer until I figure out what I'm going to do."

Diane nodded. "True. You don't want to do anything too rash yet. You need to make sure you have things in order. He must have told his boss he was leaving and given his notice."

"I don't know. I'm not sure how well thought out any of his plans have been, to be honest." Vivian slumped back against the headboard of the bed.

Diane pulled the pillows out from under the covers and propped one behind her back and the other under her knees.

"Do you think John and Sarah will find them?"

"Mum, I have absolutely no doubt they will find them." Diane leaned her head on her mother's shoulder, and they wrapped their arms around each other, both beginning to cry.

John and Sarah had made a plan that when they got to Niagara Falls, they would check the main roads first and fan out from there. John knew his father would have selected a decent hotel to stay at so he could impress Ava. He wondered if Ava realised just how little Thomas had to offer her. John would take his mother to see a lawyer as soon as possible to secure the house and any other assets they could.

"Johnny, would we be able to stop and get something to eat? Maybe a sandwich? I didn't have breakfast, and I know you didn't either." Sarah knew John didn't want to stop looking, but she needed a break to at least use the washroom and get something to drink.

"I'm sorry, Sarah. I didn't even think about that. Of course we can." He pulled into the parking lot of a local burger shoppe. "Let's grab something to eat and use the facilities. We can eat in the car and keep looking. Okay?"

Sarah smiled with relief and nodded as they got out of the car. "Don't worry, Johnny. We'll find them." If there was one thing Sarah was confident about, it was that once her husband put his mind to something, he would do it, no matter what it took.

When they got back into the car with their food and drinks in hand, they took a few minutes to organise themselves a bit. Sarah opened the wrappers and placed John's food on the seat between them so he could easily reach it. They ate in silence as John drove up and down the roads, scanning for his father's car.

"Which way next?" John asked Sarah as he took the last

bite of his hamburger while they sat at a red light.

"There's a hotel down there to the left. I can see the sign from here. Let's try that way." Sarah pointed, and John saw it too.

His heart raced as his body registered the presence of his father's battered brown station wagon, even before his brain fully realised what he was looking at. They had made the right choice. They had found him.

"I need you to stay in the car, Sarah." John parked behind the station wagon, blocking it in its place.

"Not a chance," Sarah said stubbornly. She got out of the car before her husband could argue.

John strode to the front of the station wagon and popped open the hood. He pulled a screwdriver out of his pocket and removed the distributor cap. "They won't be going anywhere even if we move our car," he declared with satisfaction as he held up the cap like a treasure.

"What do we do now?" Sarah looked around. She had become nervous since finding the location of Thomas's car.

"What the hell do you think you're doing?" They heard a shout from behind them and turned to see Thomas, red-faced, coming towards them. Ava lingered back a good distance, sensing trouble.

"What am I doing? Are you kidding me? What the hell are you doing?" John shouted back.

"John, this is none of your business," Thomas retorted.

"None of my business? You're abandoning Mum and the family for this … this home-wrecking whore?"

Ava sneered. "How dare you! Stay out of it, John."

Thomas moved forward and grabbed John by the shirt. "Apologise!" he yelled.

John grabbed Thomas by the shoulders and threw him to the ground. "I will not apologise for something that is a fact."

Thomas scrambled to his feet and moved to swing at his son again. John easily dodged his father's fist and stepped behind him. Smoothly, he shoved his father from behind and moved in over him ready to strike again.

"Do you have anything at all to say for yourself?" John demanded.

Thomas was silent, his face red with anger and embarrassment.

"You actually planned to just leave, disappear, and not tell us a thing?"

"I did. I see now that was unfair. I'm sorry, John. Ava and I are going to be together. I am going to go back to England with her. Our flight is in two days. I will call and tell you where to find the car at the airport, and you can come and get it."

"I cannot believe you would do this to my mother. She loves you. She gave up everything and moved here for you, and now you're leaving her here and going back?" John shook his head. "You are a genuine bastard. If you leave, know that you will never come near my mother or our family again." He pulled the distributor cap out of his pocket and threw it at Thomas, who was still on his back on the ground.

"Ava, you think you are so much better than everyone else. You aren't. In fact, you are proving right now that you are no better than a common whore, stealing the husband of someone you are supposed to care about. I can't wait for everyone in the neighbourhood and our family back there to hear what you did. You will be a pariah. I will make sure of it. You should know, he might be able to put on airs for a few days, but he has nothing. He lives paycheque to paycheque, and he is a drunk. Whatever twisted romantic fantasy you have created in your pathetic pea brain, you are in for a bitter disappointment. This…" he motioned to the two lovers, "is unsustainable."

Before Ava could think of anything to say, John took Sarah by the arm and led her back to their car.

"Johnny …" Sarah touched his shoulder.

"Sarah, I love you, but I just need to be left alone right now."

"Okay," she replied. "I love you, too."

The rest of the drive home was silent.

Thomas and Ava's holiday was a disaster. She seemed determined to prove that what John said wasn't true, that Thomas had money, and that he could take care of her. She demanded he buy her pointless things, then complained they weren't good enough. By the end of the trip, Thomas realised his mistake. He drove to the airport and put her bags on the curb. "Ava, this isn't going to work."

"I knew you didn't have a spine," she snapped.

"Actually, I think I'm finally growing one. Good luck to you."

"Fuck you, Thomas," she spat, slapping him hard across the face. "Where are you going?" she shouted as he turned around and walked away. "That's right. Go back to Vivvy, that dowdy cow, and your hoard of brats."

He stopped and walked back towards her with an anger on his face that made her take a step back.

"Say what you want to me. I don't care. But don't you dare say a word against Vivian. She's the best thing that ever happened to me, and I was an idiot who chased after a tasteless tart. Vivian on her worst day is more beautiful than you will ever be on your best day, Ava. Your ugly heart will eat you up and spit you out. I just pray Vivian will forgive me and take me back."

As he drove home, he felt a fear he had not expected. He knew he had hurt and humiliated Vivian. How could he possibly begin to fix what he had done?

When he walked into the house, Vivian was in the kitchen making a pie. It was something she could do with her eyes closed, and she was trying to distract herself. He watched her in silence. Even though he had come in as quietly as he could, she knew he was there. They still had an inexplicable bond. Her hands mixed the pastry until the ingredients were even and smooth but still crumbled to the touch. Finally, she looked up at him, her expression unreadable.

"Vivian," he began, his voice thick with emotion, "I'm so sorry. There is no excuse for what I did and how I hurt you and our children. Can you ever forgive me?"

Vivian sighed, setting down the dough. "You've hurt us all, Thomas. You hurt us for that … woman. Clearly, she showed her true colours and you have realised who she really is. You will need to explain this to the boys. I will spare the girls; they are too young to be burdened by the truth about their father yet."

He stepped forward, tentatively reaching for her hand. "I promise I'll make it up to you. To all of you."

Vivian looked at him, seeing the sincerity in his eyes. She nodded but did not take his hand. "One step at a time, Thomas. You should know, I told Diane everything."

At first, he thought she meant about the affair, but then he realised that she meant far more. "Viv …" He reached for her again.

She put up her hand and stepped back from him. "I needed someone to know who you are, Thomas. What you have done. What you are capable of. Diane won't tell the others, but you will need to talk to her and fix things with her, if you can. I want to be abundantly clear. This is the last time you hurt me or our family. I am not a spiteful person, but I will make sure that you are left with nothing if you lie or cheat ever again. You are going to sign papers that give me everything if you are ever this stupid and selfish again." She didn't wait for an answer. Nothing she had said was negotiable.

Thomas knew he had a long road ahead, but he was ready to fight for his family.

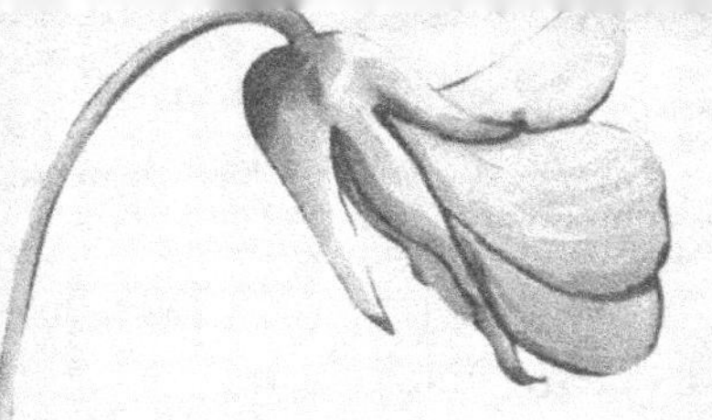

Chapter Twenty-Eight

It was the middle of the night when Judy tapped her father's arm. "Dad. Dad. It's Diane. She's on the phone."

It took him a moment to wake up enough to understand what Judy was saying. "Diane? Is she okay? Is it the baby?" He started to sit up.

"I don't think so. She sounds upset."

Thomas hurried down the stairs to the phone and picked the receiver up off the floor. "Di? Are you okay? Is it the baby?"

"No, Dad, it's not the baby. I just need you to come get me."

"Are you at your place?"

"Yes."

"Where's Richard?"

"He's here. Dad, I'll explain later. Just please come get me."

"I'm on my way, Muff."

"Thomas, what is it?" Vivian was coming down the stairs. Judy had told her it was Diane on the phone.

"I'm not sure, Viv. You stay here." Thomas ran back upstairs and grabbed a shirt. Vivian watched him back out of the driveway. She did not have a good feeling in her stomach.

Thomas stopped at the top of the stairs leading to Diane's apartment. There was an enormous man pounding on the door, screaming Richards' name. It was clear he had done something serious to anger the man that much.

"Richard! Richard Banner! Open this door, you son of a bitch! I'm going to fucking kill you!"

Thomas could hear Diane crying in the apartment. He wished he had thought to call the police before he left. He went back down the stairs without being noticed by the enraged man and knocked lightly on the door of the first apartment. He could hear noises inside but guessed the person was afraid to open the door. He didn't blame them.

"Hey! Hello? I know someone's in there. I need you to call the police. My daughter is in that apartment, and she's pregnant. I'm afraid that guy is going to hurt her." There was no sound. "Please. I don't need you to open the door. Just let me know that you heard me, and you are going to call the police. My daughter Diane is in danger."

"Diane?" There was a quiet voice from behind the door.

"Yes, my daughter is Diane Banner. She lives upstairs with her husband Richard, and this man is trying to break into their apartment."

"I'll call right now. I'm sorry. I didn't know it was Diane."

Thomas ran back up the stairs and halted at the end of the hall. He didn't want to come in too fast. This guy was far bigger than Thomas and looked like he knew a thing or two about fighting. "Hey there. Um, sorry. Can I help you?" Thomas walked slowly towards the man with his arms out.

"Get the fuck out of here, old man. This ain't none of your concern," he barked at Thomas.

"I can see that you're really upset. I don't know what's happened, and I'd like to help you, but right now, I really need you to calm down. See, my daughter lives in that apartment, and she's going to have my first grandchild any day now."

"That bastard is married, and his wife is having his kid?" For a moment, Thomas thought he was calming down a bit, but then the man turned and hammered on the door again. "You bastard! You fucking bastard! You screw around with my wife, meanwhile you got your own, and she's having your baby? Open this door, you fucker! Open this door!"

Thomas realised his approach was not making the headway he needed, and he didn't hear sirens yet. "All right, listen!" he boomed. "You are scaring the fuck out of my daughter. I don't give two shits about what he did or who he did it with. He's a son of a bitch. But you are going to stop scaring my daughter and everyone else in this building right now. Do you hear me? Get the fuck out of here. The police are on their way, and I don't give a fuck what they do to you. Got it?" Thomas hoped the man couldn't see he was shaking like a leaf inside.

The man's face changed from fury to shame, and he started crying. "I'm so sorry, sir. I would never want to scare your daughter, especially when she's having a baby. I'm so sorry."

Thomas moved closer and held out his hand to the man, lowering his voice. "Look, my name is Thomas. What's your name?"

"Kent."

"Okay, Kent. You are going to walk down to your car, get in, and leave. I can hear the sirens. I think more than one person must have called. So, you need to go." His voice was still low, but the firmness had returned. He steered Kent towards the stairs and looked out over the balcony to make sure he got in his car before he called out to his daughter.

"Diane!" He knocked softly so he didn't scare her more. "Diane, it's Dad. He's gone. You can open the door."

"Are you sure?" Her voice was trembling and afraid.

"Yes, Muff, he's gone. I'm sure of it. Let me in." The chain on the door clicked, and it opened. Thomas moved inside, then bolted the door shut again just in case Kent had a change of heart.

"Oh, Daddy! I was so afraid." She collapsed against him, sobbing.

"I know, my girl. I know. It's okay. I'm here. He's gone."

He stroked her hair and felt her start to calm down.

"Thomas, Dad. Oh, gee. Umm. Thanks for helping us out," Richard mumbled. "That guy was some kind of crazy, eh? I think we need to find a better place to live than this neighbourhood."

"Richard, my name is Mr. Cooper, and you would do well to stay away from me right now while I collect some things for my daughter."

"Dad." Thomas shot him a look, and he quickly changed to the formal name. "I mean, Mr. Cooper, Di doesn't need to go. Everything is fine now. Kent is gone."

"Diane most assuredly does need to come with me, and after what I just saw, she will not be coming back if I have anything to say about it." Thomas went into the bedroom and grabbed a few items of clothing, then went into the bathroom and snatched all the toiletries. He had no idea which things she needed or were hers, so he took them all.

"Di, come on. Don't go, Di. I love you. You know that."

"Richard, all I know is that you love yourself. This was the last straw. We are done." There was a loud knock at the door, and she jumped.

"Diane. It's Murphy from the police. Are you okay in there?"

Thomas opened the door. "Thank goodness you came, officer."

"Mr. Cooper." He nodded. "We got several calls that Diane was being threatened." He looked past Thomas and saw Diane standing there with her suitcase and Richard standing beside her holding her wrist. "Are you okay, Di?" Officer Murphy stepped into the room.

"That's Mrs. Banner to you, Officer Murphy." Richard tried to step between Diane and the officer.

"Dick, I suggest you step away from Diane. She's trying to leave, and you are not going to stop her. I wouldn't hate it if I had to arrest you."

Richard became visibly upset when Officer Murphy deliberately used the short form of his name. Murphy reached down and picked up the suitcase for Diane. "Do you have any other bags or anything you are taking with you?"

Diane shook her head.

"All right then, I'll give you an escort home to make sure nothing else happens. Have a good night, Dick," Murphy said.

Thomas helped Diane into the car while Murphy placed her suitcase in the backseat. He came around to Thomas' side of the car and held out his hand. "Mr. Cooper, anything I need to know?"

"Just that it looks like Dick," Thomas paused and smirked, "appears to be getting his just desserts for some poor choices. Thankfully, Diane didn't get hurt in the crossfire."

"All right then. If there's anything else, you call me, and I will come right over. I'll follow you back to your place and watch you get in okay."

"I'll do that. Thanks, Murph. You're a good man."

Vivian was waiting at the window when they pulled up and came running out in her pyjamas and robe.

"Oh, my goodness! Diane, are you okay?" She looked at Thomas, whose lips were pressed tightly together.

"I'm okay, Mom. Dad was a beast." It was the first time Diane had been able to say more than a couple of words, and as the shock wore off and she realised she was safe, she recalled her father's actions.

"A beast?!" Vivian looked from one to the other, and they both laughed. The stress of the moment was finally behind them, and the release of laughter was exactly what they needed. Diane put her head on her father's shoulder.

"Thanks for coming, Dad."

"Of course." Thomas sighed with relief. Officer Murphy had stopped and was waiting for them to go inside. He waved back to Thomas as he closed the door.

"I'll make some tea, and you can explain what in the world happened." Vivian went to the kitchen and put on the kettle while Thomas brought in Diane's bag.

"I wouldn't mind something stronger than tea please, Viv." Thomas' nerves were still rattled from the adrenaline rush of the night's events. Vivian hesitated but thought better of it. She didn't want to argue with Thomas about his drinking again in front of Diane, especially after what she had just gone through. She brought him his drink on the tray with tea and some peanut butter cookies she had made the day before.

Hot tea in hand, Diane explained Richard had been out partying as usual. He had stopped trying to hide the fact he was cheating on Diane. "It turned out that one of the women he was messing around with was married to some professional fighter or something."

"Kent?" Thomas inserted his knowledge into the story.

"Yes, Kent. The guy who was trying to break down our door while Richard hid in our bedroom closet."

"He what?" Vivian was still trying to wrap her head around it all.

"Yep, he was hiding in the closet, crying and wailing about how he didn't want to die," Diane said.

"Good to know he was so concerned about your safety," Vivian huffed.

"Well, thank God Dad arrived. He tried talking to him, and the guy was *not* listening, so Dad yelled at him. Shut the guy right up and made him cry! I don't know what would have happened if he got through that door." Diane threw her arms around Thomas's neck and hugged him tight.

"Well, we don't need to worry about it now. You and the baby are fine." He hugged her back, but he felt the same relief. "Tomorrow, John and I are going to go get the rest of your things and move you out. We'll need to do some rearranging, but you are never going back to him, Muffy."

"Thank you, Daddy." In the protective embrace of her father, Diane felt a turmoil of emotions. Her marriage had been over for a long time. She knew that, but the sadness was there just the same. The sadness had mixed with a different emotion though, and she was also angry because that man could have hurt her baby.

"Can I say something, Muffy?" her father asked. Diane nodded her head and put her teacup back down. "Did you see Richard's face when Murphy called him Dick?"

They looked at each other and burst out laughing again.

"I thought his head was going to explode," Diane joked.

"I was hoping he would put his hands on Murphy." Thomas knew Officer Murphy well. He knew him as Scotty before he was Murphy and long before he was Officer Murphy. He had been in love with Diane for years. It was clear from his behaviour that night he still had feelings of some kind.

Diane's face softened. "Scott is a good man. He always looks out for people. That's why he's such a great police officer."

Thomas and Vivian looked at each other and raised their eyebrows. Maybe something good would come out of tonight after all.

Diane had insisted on going with her dad and brother to the apartment to get the rest of her things. "What if he's there and starts something or claims you're stealing his stuff?" she said.

She had a point, so Thomas agreed to let her come. "If he's there, and it starts getting ugly again, you're leaving. We're bringing two vehicles, and you can take John's car, if need be, and we'll use the truck for as much as we can. If it needs to be multiple trips, so be it."

As much as Thomas and John would have liked to have had a few words with Richard, they were relieved for Diane's sake he wasn't there when they arrived.

"Where do you want to start, Muff?" John looked around the apartment. It wasn't the nicest place or nicest area for that matter, but Diane had somehow managed to make it look and feel warm and welcoming. There were a few things knocked over in Richard's attempts to hide the night before.

"Let's start with the baby's stuff. The crib and dresser."

Diane wanted to prioritise the baby's things in case Richard decided to keep her from being able to get into the apartment again at some point.

"Okay. Let's take the drawers out of the dressers and carry them down empty, then we'll put them back in on the truck. Makes the dresser lighter, and we'll save some space." John wanted to be as efficient as they possibly could and get his sister out of the apartment as fast as possible.

"That's a good idea, John." As efficient as John was, Thomas also liked that his plan decreased the weight of the items they would carry. He wasn't as young as he used to be after all.

They got to work. Diane pulled the drawers out of their two dressers and threw the few clothes she had in her closet into garbage bags instead of boxes. It saved time and space. She could fit more soft bags into the back of the car than boxes.

Once the crib and dressers were loaded on the truck, Thomas asked, "What about your bed?"

"It will never fit in the room with the crib and dressers. I'll have to get a single bed for now."

"How about this?" John was holding a stereo system.

"That's Richard's," Diane replied.

"Okay." John dropped it on the ground, and it smashed apart. "Wow. They sure don't make them like they used to." He smiled sheepishly at his sister. "Better his stereo than his neck." He frowned and paused. "After what he did to you, Muff, I'm sorry I didn't do something sooner."

"What would you have done, John? I wasn't listening. Everyone tried to tell me he was not a good person. I love you for that, but we all know I was blind and deaf to the truth for far too long."

"Well, not anymore," he said and hugged her tight.

"No, not anymore."

It didn't take much to get Diane set up in her old room. Her brothers and sisters took the news very well. In fact, Judy and

Jess were excited by the idea of the baby living with them. Philip had moved out and was working in Toronto for an electronics company. He and his girlfriend Fran had just announced they were going to be getting married. The speed of things seemed to support the rumours Fran was pregnant, but everyone was happy for them. She seemed to settle him down a bit. She had big goals in life and expected Philip to meet those expectations.

John had been married for two years to his childhood sweetheart Sarah. They had taken their teaching exams and were working at the high school in King City. All of that meant there weren't as many people displaced as there could have been, and there were, in fact, spare beds available to be used.

Diane set about decorating the room she would soon share with her baby. She had become a very proficient seamstress and made matching curtains and bedding for the crib.

"Di, can you make us curtains, too?" Judy and Jess were loving having their big sister home again.

"Sure, I can. We can go to the fabric store, and you can pick something out."

The younger girls were arguing about colours.

"It's okay. I'm sure we can figure out a way to give you both what you want. Maybe we go with something neutral for the curtains, then I can help make your beds extra spiffy," she suggested.

"Yay! Yes, please." the girls squealed with delight. "Thanks, Di."

A month had passed since Diane had moved in. She hadn't heard a word from Richard or his family.

"I get why Richard hasn't called. He knows he isn't welcome. But I don't understand Stewart and Corrine. Their grandchild is going to be born soon!" she said.

"They are probably too ashamed of him," Vivian offered.

"I doubt it. They don't have the most pristine reputations

themselves."

"That doesn't stop people from being judgmental and sanctimonious." Vivian was scooping oatmeal cookie batter onto the baking sheet when she heard Diane make a strange noise. "Are you okay?"

Diane was wincing and holding her belly. "Yes, just the baby moving a bit roughly. Took the wind out of me a bit." Massaging her stomach, she tried to breath and relax to ease the pain.

"Well, she's strong like her mummy."

"You and Dad both think I'm having a girl. Are you sure you're not just putting your own pregnancy on me?" Diane laughed.

"It would be possible if it were just me saying it. I could be wrong. But your father, he was right for every single one of you. How he knew I do not know, but he guessed correctly every time."

Diane winced again. "That was a bit more than a kick, I think."

Vivian stopped what she was doing. "Keep track of the time. Let's see if they are regular or if this is just a trick." She topped up Diane's tea, and they distracted themselves by talking about the curtains Diane was making for Jess and Judy's room.

"Mom, I know you won't like this, but I think I should at least call and tell Richard and the Banners that the baby is coming."

"It's your decision, and we will support whatever you decide." Vivian didn't care for the way Richard's family treated Diane, or their whole family for that matter.

Thomas decided he would call Richard first and see if he was even at the apartment or not. "Richard? It's Thomas Cooper calling." He paused to see if Richard was going to ask about Diane or the baby.

"Yah. What do you want? To break more of my stuff?" His voice was hostile, but Thomas knew that he was more nervous than cocky.

"Diane is in labour and having the baby. We are at the hospital with her now."

"Oh. Okay. I was just heading to the bike races. Maybe I can run by when I get back."

"Run by when you're back?" Thomas couldn't believe the man had managed to shock him yet again.

"Well, yeah. It's not like the kid will know I wasn't there."

"Diane will know. We will all know."

"Gotta go," Richard said.

Thomas was flummoxed. Yes, flummoxed. He couldn't think of a word that could express his frustration and confusion at once. Flummoxed sounded about right.

He came back in from the nurse's station.

"Did you get in touch with Richard?" Diane asked.

"No, sorry, there wasn't an answer," he lied. "I'll go try his parents in a minute. I just wanted to check in on you again in case there was any change I can tell them about."

"They're saying that I will probably have a long labour since it's my first, and I'm not very dilated yet."

"I'm not sure what that means except that you may be here for a while."

Diane chuckled at her father's lack of knowledge. "Dad! How did you have seven babies and still know so little?"

"Dads weren't allowed to be as involved back then. With you and John, I was in a different country fighting a war. With Joseph, I helped deliver him in the back of a cab. Although your mom pretty much told me what to do, not unlike a drill sergeant at that moment."

"Well, you looked like you were going to pass out. I had to do something to keep you focused." Vivian enjoyed teasing Thomas about how a man, who saw the worst parts of war, was so squeamish and couldn't handle a little blood and the birth of a baby.

It was nice to have time together with her parents, but it was even nicer to have someone with her while she had the baby. She didn't like to admit it, but the idea of single parenting was terrifying to her. Diane was overwhelmingly grateful for her family.

Doctor Williams and a nurse came in to examine Diane. Dr. Williams had been taking care of the entire family since they moved to Aurora.

"How are you holding up there, Di?" He checked her vitals.

"Pretty good, I think. The contractions are not awful, but they are steady."

"Oh, that's perfect for this stage of things. You are exactly on track. You probably won't even need us you are so on top of everything." He was very amused with himself and let it openly show. He had a wonderful, relaxed bedside manner that always put one at ease no matter how scared or worried one might be. "I see your mum and dad are outside waiting. They can come in and stay with you as long as you want. We're pretty progressive here."

"You're in good hands with Dr. Williams, Diane." The nurse smiled and nodded.

"Oh, I know it. He's one in a million, and we are all very grateful to have him."

In the waiting area, Vivian decided they needed to do as Diane wanted and tell her in-laws about the baby. "Thomas, I think we should go to the store and tell Stewart and Corrine that Diane is having the baby. Richard may be there, or they may at least know where he is," Vivian said.

"They don't deserve to know." Thomas's voice was curt.

"I don't disagree with you, but Diane feels they do, and it is not our place to tell her otherwise."

Reluctantly, Thomas had to agree.

"I'm going to go tell her where we are going and that we will be back as fast as we can," she said.

"We? You should stay here with Diane and the baby."

"I think I need to come with you and help keep your temper in check. You're still angry over the incident at the apartment."

"Incident? Incident?!" Thomas felt his blood pressure rising and realised it was exactly what Vivian was talking about. He closed his eyes and tried to settle himself down again. "I'm sorry, Viv. You're right. I need to keep my head, for Diane and the baby's sake."

Banner's Paint and Decorating was one of the oldest businesses in Aurora. It had evolved from being a mercantile-style store to the more specialised paint and paper store it was today. Stewart and Corinne had moved back into the apartment unit above it about a year ago.

Thomas parked at the back of the store. If Stewart and Corinne weren't inside, then they would be able to go up to the apartment through the back entrance with fewer people seeing them. He had agreed to let Diane's in-laws know about the baby, but he didn't agree to letting the whole world know how they and their son had treated his daughter and grandchild. Yet.

"Thomas … Vivian." Stewart Banner was at the counter with a customer. "Be with you in a moment." He had politely acknowledged them, but more for the sake of the customer in front of him than because it was the correct thing to do.

"Stewart." Thomas held out his hand as Stewart approached them after the customer left. There was no smile or sign of friendship. He didn't take the hand offered to him, and Thomas' eyes flared.

Vivian saw that Thomas was upset by his rudeness and intervened. "We wanted to come and tell you that Diane is at the hospital having the baby."

There was no response. Stewart stood looking at her as though waiting for her to say something that interested him.

Vivian was about to ask where Corinne was when she walked into the store. "Oh, Vivian, Thomas, I wasn't expecting to ever see you in our store. We don't have discount bins here." She came to stand beside her husband.

Vivian ignored the jab. "We just came to let you know that

Diane is in the hospital having the baby."

"Oh, I see. Do be sure to let us know what she has." A cruel smile curled on Corinne's lips as she walked away. Stewart followed suit.

"I take it you don't plan to visit her at the hospital and see for yourself?" Vivian called after her.

"After what she did to our son? I'm not sure how you can expect us to be concerned for her," Corinne spat at Vivian.

Vivian put her hand on Thomas' arm to keep him from saying anything or worse, hitting one of them. "As usual, Corinne, you have gathered your facts from a corrupted and purposefully deceitful source. Your son, after having had multiple affairs, finally put his boots under the wrong bed and nearly got himself, as well as our daughter and grandchild, killed in the process. So yes, she has finally left him."

"You are the one with the wrong information, Vivian. Besides, you would know all about affairs wouldn't you, Thomas?"

The smug look on her face fell away as Vivian stepped closer to her. She raised her voice. "Don't you dare speak to me or my husband like that ever again!" Thomas placed his hand on her arm in the same manner she had his, but he was more inclined to allow his wife the space she needed right then.

"It's okay, Thomas." She glared at Corrine. "Who do you think you are? The whole town knows you live in your dilapidated apartment above this nearly bankrupt store because your husband gambled all your money away and then lost your house because he messed around with the wrong woman, and they called his markers as a punishment. Like father like son. You walk around acting like you're better than everyone else, and you're not. You're a false Christian and a terrible person. God pays his debts without money, Corinne Banner. Just you wait."

Vivian turned to walk away, but she decided she had more to say, "How you have treated Diane and how you have encouraged Richard to treat her is a sin that you will all be asked to answer to. I hope that when that time comes, you're prepared for the very warm welcome you'll get where you're going. We are only here because our daughter felt it was important that you were included in knowing about her child. I will tell you this, if you and your lecherous, womanising charlatan of a husband do not ensure that your contemptible, carousing souse of a son, who can't even keep a job in his own parents' business, comes to the hospital to see his own child be born, I will make sure that the entire town knows it. People are long past being interested in doing business with the likes of either of you. Let's go, Thomas. You were right. They don't deserve to be part of our grandchild's life."

Thomas couldn't lie. He enjoyed seeing the fired-up side of Vivian. It didn't happen often, but boy when it did!

Vivian paused for one final thought as they left the store. "By the way, Stewart, you make yourself look sad and foolish wearing inserts in your shoes to appear taller. It doesn't matter how tall you make yourself. Everyone knows that you are a small, small man."

248

Chapter Twenty-Nine

Thomas and Vivian had arrived home from the hospital with Diane and Charleigh, and it seemed like there were an endless number of people pouring out of the house to greet them. Family, friends, and neighbours had all gathered to see Diane arrive with her baby and show their solidarity and support. She was moved to tears when they all cheered for her as she got out of the car and came forward holding her tiny bundle.

"Oh, Di! She is so beautiful." Judy and Jess had run over to get the first look at their baby niece.

"Welcome home, Di." Landyn gave her a big hug and lifted her up slightly.

"Watch the baby, Landyn!" Jess gave him a playful but also serious push. "Can I hold her, Di?"

"Of course, Jess." Diane handed her baby over to her younger sister who took her with great care and beamed with pride to be the first to hold the infant.

Judy was glued to her side, touching Charleigh's tiny little hands. "She is so small and sweet," she marvelled.

"Muff, let's take some photos. Come stand at the front of the house." John had a new camera and what better reason to

try it out than prolific photos of his baby niece and goddaughter.

"Oh, John, I look a mess!" Diane touched her hair and glasses.

"Diane, you have never looked more beautiful." John gave her a hug and kissed the top of her head. They had always held a special bond, looking out for each other since they were very small. Not that they didn't love their other siblings, but there was simply something magical about their friendship and relationship. They spoke to each other in a way no one else ever could or dared. "Besides," he gave her a gentle push, "who's looking at you anyway?" They both laughed at him quoting one of their mother's frequently used phrases. It didn't mean what it sounded like on the surface. It wasn't about the fact that you didn't *look good enough* so no one would want to look at you. The message was meant to say that you shouldn't concern yourself with the opinions of others and just be yourself.

"Mum, Dad." He beckoned them with his hand, lifting his camera to indicate he wanted to take pictures.

Thomas held his granddaughter in his arms as they posed for photos. His joy was displayed for the world to see. She was so tiny. So perfect. A lump formed in his throat as he looked down at her peaceful face. The baby knew nothing of the carelessness and selfishness of adults. Of his own cavalier choices that had hurt so many people. All she knew was the love surrounding her. He had not been there when her mother was born, and he realised that there was a great deal he would do differently with all his children if given the opportunity.

"I vow that you will always know that you are loved, Charleigh. I will always be here to keep you safe." His gentle promise to his grandchild appeared to be heard. She opened her eyes and looked straight into his. Time stood still as his heart lurched in his chest with the love he felt for the tiny, fragile being. Her eyes, a striking blue, seemed to hold the entire universe in their depths. He was mesmerised and captivated by their innocence and wonder. In those precious seconds, he saw a future with boundless possibilities.

One by one, people lined up to take pictures with Diane and the baby. Thomas stood back, watching his family and how much they all loved and cared for each other. "Vivian," he said, motioning for her to follow him. He wanted to speak to her privately. He had to get the words out while he could.

"What is it, darling? Is everything okay?" She noticed his eyes were shining with the tears he was holding back.

"Yes, yes, it is, Vivian Waltman-Cooper. Everything is more than fine, and it is all because of you." He held her face and kissed her.

"Thomas! What has gotten into you?"

"Vivian, let me say something and don't stop me, please. I have needed to say this for a very long time. Far too long and I don't want to miss this chance now." He let go of her face and held her hands, giving each one a gentle kiss. "Vivian, I have been such a fool so many times, too many times, and I have no idea why you ever showed the least bit of interest in me. From that first moment I saw you, walking down that aisle of the church, I loved you with more of my being than I ever knew was possible. I was not a good man, Vivian, and I didn't deserve you. For a long time, I lied to you, and yet, somehow ..." His voice cracked, and he paused. "Somehow, you forgave me. You have forgiven more than any woman should have had to forgive any man, never mind the man who loves her. You are everything that is good and kind and beautiful in this world, and I am utterly and completely sorry for every pain and humiliation I inflicted upon you." He kneeled before her, still holding her hands, and pressed them to his cheek. "I vow to you here and now that I will spend every one of my last days and breaths making it up to you. I will never let you down again. I will never let our family down again."

Tears spilled down her cheeks, falling onto their hands. "Oh, my darling Thomas, your words mean more than I can ever say, but I forgave you long ago, and long ago you showed me that you could and would change. Our past does not define us or our future. It merely helps mould us into who we decide to be." She pulled him up to stand in front of her again so she could look him in the eye.

"You are a good man, Thomas. For some reason, I don't think you ever believed that about yourself. You have always been worthy of my love. Your mistakes were just that—mistakes—and in the end, you always stood by me, by us." She reached up and held his face as he had hers and kissed him. They embraced, their foreheads pressed together, and arms wrapped around each other.

The sounds of laughter and jubilance floated to them as they stood together. "Let's go and celebrate our granddaughter. The next generation of Coopers." Wiping her face, she smiled and started to walk with her husband, still holding hands.

"No, Viv, a new generation of Waltmans. That is your doing out there, Viv. We owe everything to you. You are the strongest woman I have ever known."

Love Always

253

Chapter Thirty

The pain pierced his back, and he coughed violently. He sat for a long moment on the side of the bed, feet on the floor, hunched over and trying to settle his breathing. He knew he couldn't ignore it any longer. When he coughed, the blood was much darker, and it was getting hard to hide the telltale tissues.

"I was bringing you some tea," Vivian said. One of their simple pleasures was to have tea in bed with a cookie. A decadence, she called it.

Vivian stopped when she saw Thomas hunched over with the tissue in his hand. She rushed over, putting the tea on the side table and kneeling in front of him. "What is it, Thomas? How long has this been going on?" She knew in her heart he had been hiding it a long time, and it was bad.

"Oh, darling, I'm sorry. I'm okay. Just tired." His eyes were glassy, and his skin pale and clammy.

"You've been coughing for weeks, Thomas, and now I see that there's blood. You are not okay. I'm calling Dr. Williams."

"All right." He tried to smile weakly and failed.

If he was so willing to go to the doctor, it was clearly worse than she thought. Vivian pursed her lips.

Thomas felt some relief that she knew. He didn't need to keep the secret anymore. Truth be told, he'd had a terrible cough for decades from his smoking and the exposure to all the soot and brake dust in the subway tunnels. The blood had only been present for a few months, but it was worsening. It had started out a bright red, a fresher blood, then it turned almost black. At times, it had a green tint to it as well.

His back pain, though, he'd been having for almost two years. Pain medication only helped for short periods. His drinking had increased even more. He didn't understand that his drinking made it harder for the pain medication to work properly. Truth be told, it would have mattered anyway. He needed the alcohol almost more than he needed the pain medication. More recently, his doctor had increased him to something called Oxycodone. Dr. Williams had said he needed X-rays and tests. Thomas had so far managed to talk Dr. Williams out of doing them.

The drugs had helped for a few weeks, but he had to be careful about taking too much. He didn't want Viv to realise he was using such strong medication. He tried to only take it at night and first thing in the morning. He knew it was more than just muscle pain—it went far deeper than that.

It had been only a few days since they had gone to see Dr. Williams. His office had called them in, and they sat waiting to hear the results. A photo of Williams and his wife in front of a small pond wearing rubber boots and rain jackets, a large yellow lab happily covered in mud sitting patiently beside him, waiting to run back into the pond, sat on the desk.

Vivian's grip tightened on Thomas's hand as Dr. Williams

walked in. He always had on a white lab coat with his stethoscope casually hung around his neck. He didn't say anything as he sat down and opened Thomas's file. Clearing his throat, he finally looked up at them.

Vivian was sure everyone could hear her heart pounding in her chest.

"I wanted to bring you in straightaway. We got back the results of your X-rays and bloodwork, Thomas." He ran his hand over the papers in the file in front of him. "There are shadows on the X-rays."

Thomas' heart sank. He had known what he was going to hear, but having the words spoken out loud hit him harder than he expected.

"What does that mean exactly?" Vivian leaned forward uncomfortably in her seat. She knew what it meant. She needed to hear it. To hear *the* word.

"Viv, Thomas, the shadows are indicative of cancer. There's more, though. The X-rays also show unusual spots in some of your bones, especially in your spine." He paused, knowing he needed to let the words sink in before he gave them too much information at once.

Clearing his throat, Thomas looked over at Vivian and squeezed her hand. "So, what do we do next?"

"Well, I've ordered a biopsy. We don't have the equipment at our hospital, so I'm sending you down to Toronto General."

"What does that entail?"

"Essentially, they will give you a general anaesthetic and insert a tube to collect a small sample of your lung tissue. They will also take a sample from your bones, probably from your lower back to decrease the risk of damaging them."

Thomas straightened up in his chair. "When?"

"You're scheduled in two weeks."

"Two weeks," Thomas whispered. He and Vivian stared at each other.

"Two weeks," they both whispered.

They sat in the car in Dr. Williams' parking lot, silently waiting to wake up from the nightmare. Vivian held onto the paperwork the doctor had handed them. It would get Thomas seen at the oncology department in Toronto and help determine just how extensive his cancer was.

The wind bit against the windshield of the car as the defrost fought back. Vivian struggled to keep her breathing even. Winter had come early that year, and the warmth of her breath formed small foggy clouds in the car. She didn't want to show how scared she was.

"I want to go up to the cottage before …" Thomas didn't finish his sentence.

"How would we get across? We don't know if the lake is even frozen."

"We can walk in from the Bass Pond side if we need to."

"Okay. We can call the marina when we get home and see what the lake is like. Then we'll know which way to drive in."

Vivian understood why he needed to see the lake. It was their place of refuge, of peace. Where they felt closest and where they had truly raised their family.

Thomas needed to see it one more time, just in case.

The parking lot was almost empty. It was the middle of the week in December. Not many people came up at that time of the year. Most of the lake was water access, meaning one couldn't get to the cottages when the ice wasn't solid in the winter. There had been almost no snow, but the temperatures had been unseasonably cold. It had been called an "artic freeze." All it really meant was the miracle they had needed had happened, and the lake froze early.

They had decided to tell the family when they got back. Vivian kept silent about what they had been told along with the upcoming appointment. Their children thought it was a bit crazy to be going to the cottage for just one night.

"It's awfully cold. Why not wait a few weeks? The ice will be thick enough to drive over," Landyn had said. While they were always up for a run to the cottage, it was bitterly cold and expected to get a little warmer after Christmas in a couple weeks.

"Your mom and I just want to give it a visit. Been cooped up a bit lately. The cold air will be nice. Fresh!" Thomas hadn't been fully lying. He *had* been cooped up. Everyone thought he'd had a bad cold and a smoker's cough. After all, he had been hacking badly for over a year.

Thomas had packed two life jackets and some rope just in case they went through the ice. "Put this on over your coat just in case," he'd said as he tied the jacket around Vivian. "I'll carry the bag."

Mike, the owner of the marina, came out as they started to walk down the ramp towards the edge of the lake.

"Hey! Good to see you both. Lake is pretty solid. Are you planning to walk all the way up to your place? I haven't made it up that far to check the ice yet."

"Hey, Mike. Good to see you. Yep. Going to stay the night." He shook the man's hand and clapped him on the back. "Romantic getaway." Thomas laughed.

"Well, Viv, you're a better sport than my wife. No way she'd hike all that way for one night. In fact, no way she'd do the hike at all." He laughed back.

"Oh, it's not that far, Mike. It's good exercise. I've been stuck in the house the last few weeks. I'm looking forward to the leisurely stroll." They all chuckled, knowing the walk over was a bit more than a leisurely stroll. By boat, it took a good twenty minutes. On foot, it would probably be dinnertime when they arrived.

"Well, check in on your way out tomorrow so I know you got back safe."

"Will do." Thomas shook his hand again, and he and Vivian started out onto the ice.

Because it had frozen so fast, the ice was almost clear. They almost thought of risking the car, but they knew the ice at one end of the lake could be vastly different than the other. The direction of the wind and the additional currents at the north end of the lake meant it took longer for ice to form. Even in the heart of the season, there were several spots that were never safe to venture too close to.

Last year, in late January, the whole family had come up and drove across in the station wagon. The ice had been solid the whole way. When they got up in the morning, the lake had shifted, and there was a full gap of almost three feet between the edge of the ice and shore. A layer of water and slush lay on top as well. They decided to pack up and head straight back, leaving the car doors open in case they went through the ice, and they needed to bail out of the car quickly.

Without the snow, it was a lot easier to walk on the ice. The snow would have added more resistance and hidden some of the more concerning areas.

"Let's head straight to the far shore and then keep to it," Thomas said.

The cottage was at the north end of the lake and along that side of the shoreline. Following it would take them straight to the residence and keep them nearer to the safety of the shore in case the ice became irregular.

Vivian started humming and singing. Despite the cold, she felt strangely happy in the moment with Thomas. They had not spent much time alone together. Landyn was heading off to Europe in the spring with his friend for a few months before he went to university. Jess and Judy were both in high school and busy, of course. There was always someone at home with them, or they were taking their children somewhere.

Vivian suddenly started singing *Would You Like to Swing on a Star* and Thomas immediately joined in doing his best Frank Sinatra impersonation. The cold was helping to abate his coughing somehow, at least for the moment. He had taken some of the new medication Dr. Williams had given him, including some sort of puffer, before they had started across the lake. They always added extra animals to the song, laughing loudly with each new one the other added.

The singing continued. They were making good time because of the lack of snow. Linking arms, they pretended to skate in their big heavy boots. In the distance, they could see the point where their cottage sat just on the other side. They were almost there. Thomas was starting to slow down, his cough overwhelming him. He tried to cover his mouth but had to hold his chest at the same time, leaving himself exposed. Vivian tried not to show any reaction to the blood spatters that froze even before they hit the surface of the ice.

"We can stop and rest, Thomas. Let's just go sit on the shore for a few minutes." She moved towards the shore to direct him, and he waved his hand in a motion that indicated he wanted to keep going forward.

It took several minutes for him to stop coughing long enough to speak. "No, Viv, let's keep going. We are almost there. I can rest when we get inside."

Walking a little slower, Viv held onto him as they pressed on. They had to stop several more times. Fatigue from the walk had caught up to Thomas.

"There she is!" As they rounded the corner of the point, their cottage came into view. Thomas felt an elation at having made it and a small surge of energy. After he climbed up the shore, he collapsed at the bottom of the stairs.

"Thomas!" Vivian cried out, dropping to his side.

"Thomas!"

He coughed again and pushed her back slightly, not wanting the blood to get on her. It was black and clots the size of a silver dollar peppered the ground beside him. Vivian was feeling a sense of panic. She needed to get him up the steps and into the cottage for some shelter. At least then she could keep him warm, and he could rest properly. His coughing continued, larger clots covering the smaller ones.

"Thomas! We need to get you inside. Hold onto me, and we'll go up the steps. We can rest at the landing, but you must help me get you up." She took their life jackets off and put the bag over her shoulder.

Thomas looked up and saw the fear and determination in her face. He nodded and put his arm around her shoulders. She hadn't realised just how much weight he had lost. She had expected him to be much heavier and harder to support.

My poor Thomas, she thought. *What have you been suffering through?*

They made it up the steps to the first landing.

"Don't sit back down," she instructed. "Just lean against the wall. If you sit back down, it will be harder to get back up again."

Shifting her weight, Vivian lowered Thomas onto the stone wall he had built when making the stairs to the cottage. It was about hip high and only served to keep all the children who had grown up there from going over the edge. The concrete on the landing had Vivian's, Thomas', and Charleigh's handprints pressed into it. He had put it in with his last set of repairs that past summer.

Thomas motioned he was ready to continue up the last few steps. With great effort, he put his arm around Vivian's shoulders again and leaned against her.

His voice was hoarse but soft as he picked up their song where they left off.

Vivian joined in, understanding the distraction would help.

When they reached the porch, Thomas sat on the bench that also served as the railing while Vivian opened the door and carried the bag inside. She would go get the life jackets once they were properly settled. She came back out and saw him staring out over the bay, tears running down his face.

"Thank you, Viv." He didn't turn to look at her. He knew she heard him, and he could not bear to see her pain and sadness, nor let her fully see his.

"I will get the fire going and the kettle on. You sit and relax and enjoy our view." Vivian watched him a moment more before turning to go back into the cottage.

With the fire crackling, they sat to enjoy a cup of tea and the sheer peace around them. They had brought two cans of soup and some buttered buns. Vivian melted some snow to mix in. The water had been turned off when they closed up the cottage Thanksgiving weekend, and it would be far too much work to turn it back on and then close it all up again tomorrow.

Thomas's eyes were growing heavy. It had been a lot harder than he had expected to get there. He had taken his tablets, and he could feel them spreading like warm fingers through his body, but it wasn't enough. "I could use a proper drink, Viv." She didn't argue. She nodded and fetched them both a proper drink. *A short one* as she described how she made a drink. It meant long on rye, short on mix.

He finished his drink and carefully put his cup down, so he didn't drop it. Vivian took it and went into the kitchen to tidy up. He was fast asleep when she sat back down a few minutes later.

She stacked some more logs onto the fire and pulled the extra blankets onto them both as she settled in beside him for the night. There was no point in disturbing him. The couch would be comfortable enough for one night, and all she wanted to do was let him rest. She was already thinking about the long walk back tomorrow.

Vivian woke up to sunlight cresting over the trees. It was a glorious sunrise of oranges, reds, and purples. Not a cloud in the sky. Thomas was already out on the porch with his coffee. They sat in silence, savouring the scene before them, the aromatic coffee, and the butter biscuits.

"We better start packing up." Thomas sighed as he finished the last sip of his coffee. "It's going to be as long going back as it was coming." Patting her hand in his, he looked into her eyes. She still took his breath away all these years later, and he was back in that very first moment he saw her. Her eyes were as golden and jade green as they were back then, although she wasn't as naive.

She would see through me now, he thought to himself.

They packed and closed the cottage up again. No one else would be coming that winter.

Thomas stood on the ice, facing the cottage for a long moment. "I love you, Vivian. We have sure built a hell of a life together. I don't know what I ever did to deserve you, but I'm bloody grateful you never gave up on me, even when you sure should have."

Vivian came over and wrapped her arms around him, pressing their foreheads together. "I would never wish for any other life but this one, Thomas."

He looked up at the cottage one last time, then took Vivian's hand and started the long walk back. His voice was thick with emotion as he sang *Would you like to swing on a star* one more time.

"Mr. Cooper, I am Dr. Epstein. I will be performing your procedure today. Dr. Williams came down to make sure I do a good job." He smiled warmly at Thomas and shook his hand.

"Hello, Sam. I didn't expect you to be here," Thomas said.

"I like to keep an eye on my favourite patients." Sam smiled and squeezed Thomas' hand.

"Do you have any questions before we get started, Mr. Cooper?" Epstein asked. Thomas shook his head. "Okay then. Dr. Edwards is your anaesthesiologist. He's going to get us started."

"Mr. Cooper, I just want you to take nice, slow breaths as deep as you can, and count backward from ten, okay?" Dr. Edwards placed a mask over Thomas's face.

He nodded and took a breath. "Ten … nine …"

"Welcome back, Mr. Cooper." A bubbly nurse was checking Thomas's vitals as he groggily opened his eyes. "How are you feeling? Would you like a little water?"

Thomas nodded, and the nurse helped him sit up a little more so he could drink through the straw while she held the cup of water.

"I will let the doctor and your family know you're awake." She scurried off and was back quickly with Dr. Williams and Vivian.

"How are you feeling, Thomas? Any pain? I can get you something if you have any pain." Dr. Williams did his own quick check of Thomas' vitals and scanned his chart.

"I could use something, Doc. My back is sending knives through me," Thomas admitted. Dr. Williams nodded and told the nurse to bring him the pain medications.

"You came through the surgery well. We don't have all the

results back, but the initial biopsies have already been returned. One of the advantages to having your surgery in the best cancer hospital in the world, this is where all the biopsies from other hospitals get done. They have a team dedicated to tests just from this hospital." Williams paused as the nurse handed Thomas the small paper cup with the tablets and some water. He waited for her to leave. "I'm sorry, Thomas and Vivian. I don't have good news for you."

Vivian moved closer to Thomas and took his hand.

"The biopsy from your lung shows a very developed cancer, well into stage four. The oncologist feels that the cancer most likely started in your lungs and that it has spread from your lungs to your blood, which is why it is affecting your bones, specifically your spine. It is also why you're having such terrible back pain. They don't see this often. This kind of cancer attacks the bones, and essentially, they turn very porous and crumble. That is why it is so damn painful."

Thomas held up his hand to interrupt. "How long do I have, Doc?"

"I'm sorry, Thomas. Not long. We want to keep you here so we can at least keep you comfortable. We will move you to a nicer room, of course, but you won't be going home." Dr. Williams could barely utter the last words.

Vivian let out a sob. "Isn't there something we can do?" she begged. "Anything? I mean, Christmas is in a few days."

"I am so sorry, Vivian. All we can do now is make sure Thomas isn't in pain. The family can come and visit, of course. We will get exceptions made to the visiting hours."

"Sam, I know you would do more if you could." Taking the doctor's hand, Thomas clasped it with both of his. "Thank you." He let go and sat back in the bed with a sigh. "Viv, we need to talk to the family. Diane and John first. They can help break it to the rest of them."

Vivian nodded and went to get the eldest two children. Dr. Williams watched her walk away, chin up, eyes strong and clear, and he was once again amazed at the strength some people were able to muster when necessary.

Diane and Callum pulled into the parking lot of the hospital. Charleigh sat in the back with her bear. She had wanted to bring him for Grandad to help make him feel better.

"What if they won't let her in to see him?" Diane asked Callum.

"Good luck with that." Callum snorted. He had been married to Diane for just over a year now. The first thing he had learned when he met Thomas and saw him with Charleigh is that they were the light of each other's lives. "There's no way they will keep this child from her grandad. Right, pal?"

"Right!" Charleigh smiled. She didn't really understand who "they" were, or why "they" wouldn't want her to see her grandad, but if her daddy said "they" wouldn't stop her, she believed him.

The ride up in the elevator was very quiet. Her mom was breathing oddly, and Charleigh wondered if she was getting sick. Maybe the hospital did that. Maybe it made people sick. The nurse at the station smiled at them as they walked past but didn't say anything. Charleigh guessed whoever "they" were wasn't around right then.

"Grandad!" she called out as they came into his room. She clambered up onto the bed. Diane went to stop her, and Callum put up a hand.

"She won't hurt anything and look at how he perked up at the sight of her," he said.

Diane tried to relax, but she was worried.

"Grandad, Mommy told me you're sick, so I brought Tommy-Bear to help make you feel better." She placed the bear beside her grandfather on the bed. It was the bear he had brought back from England last year for her fifth birthday. He and Vivian had gone over for the anniversary of VE Day. He had asked her what she wanted for her birthday because they were going to miss it, and he wanted to get her something special. After all, it was her fifth. She had said all she wanted was a teddy bear. Nanny told her he walked all around London until he finally found one, he felt would be good enough for his Charleigh. She loved it. But of course, she loved anything her grandfather gave her, even the dimes or Jersey Milk chocolate bars that magically appeared in the enormous pockets of his TTC train coat.

"I'm feeling very poorly, but much better now that I get to see you and Tommy-Bear." His voice was quiet and raspy, but she sighed happily as she snuggled against him.

"Careful of all Grandad's wires," Diane told her, tears welling up in her eyes seeing them together.

"I will. Don't worry, Mummy."

"You just missed Leland." Thomas told them. "Good man, Leland."

"That's lovely, Dad. He mentioned he was going to stop in to see you at dinner yesterday. Found family, isn't that what you always say, Dad?" Diane smiled. Leland had very quickly become part of their family all those years ago after he first moved to Canada. He shared all their holidays and was even such a regular to the coveted family cottage on Anstruther that he even had his own parking spot at the marina. The corners of Thomas' mouth lifted as he thought about all the found family he had been blessed to have in his lifetime. "We won't stay too long, Dad. We don't want to wear you out, and Santa is coming tonight."

"I asked Santa for an Easy-Bake Oven. I'll make you a pie and bring it next time we visit." Charleigh said.

Thomas smiled. "I would love that. Raspberry please."

"Of course, Grandad. That's your favourite, just like me." She smiled at him and kissed his cheek.

Thomas quietly motioned with his finger that he needed the nurse. Diane quickly went and got her. She knew he was saying he needed more pain medication. The nurse came back with her.

"Hey there, Mr. Cooper. I'm just going to check everything and top you up here, okay?" She smiled kindly at the small child in the bed who watched her very carefully as she administered medicine into his IV.

"What is that for?" she asked, her big green eyes not moving from the nurse.

"It helps make sure your grandfather is comfortable and happy."

"Hmmm. Okay. Are you comfortable now, Grandad?" She looked at him with concern.

"Yes, my darling. I am." His eyes fluttered closed. "I'm a little sleepy though, and I'm going to rest."

Diane leaned over and kissed her father's forehead. "Get some rest, Dad. We'll be back on Boxing Day."

Callum pressed Thomas's shoulder. "See you in a couple days, mate."

"Love you, Grandad. I will bring you two pies if Santa brings me the oven, I promise." Charleigh kissed his cheek and let her dad lift her over the railing of the bed, so she didn't disturb him by crawling back down over him.

"Love you too, my girl." Thomas waved his fingers to her from his bed and drifted off to sleep.

Phillip decided to go see his dad on Boxing Day before heading back up to his mum's for the day. He had been having some trouble at his shop with a few employees and hadn't had a chance to get over since Thomas had first been admitted.

"Merry Christmas and Happy New Year!" he cheerfully called out as he passed a few patients sitting in the lounge, watching television as they waited for their own families to come visit them. They smiled and waved. Phillip had a contagious mirth about him. Like a giant playful puppy. He instantly cheered people up.

He was not surprised there were no nurses at the station. They were probably short-handed because of the holiday and no doubt very busy. He heard people talking in his dad's room and thought some of the family may have beat him there. Grinning in anticipation of seeing them, he walked into the room.

It was not his family talking, however. His smile abruptly disappeared. "Excuse me. Where is my dad?"

The doctors and nurses in the room did not hear him, so he spoke louder, "Excuse me! Where is my dad? Where is Thomas Cooper?" His voice echoed strangely in his head. He saw a nurse turn and move quickly toward him. What was her name again? Sabrina? Or was it, Margaret?

"Mr. Cooper, please, I am so sorry. Just wait out here for a moment." She tried to steer him out of the room.

"Why? What's wrong? Where is my dad?" Phillip pushed back into the room, and that's when he saw his father's bed. The sheet had been pulled up over him. The tubing and wires seemed to be dangling off the bed. "No! No! No! Dad!" he cried out like a wounded animal. "Please, let me see him. Let me say goodbye."

The doctors nodded and moved aside.

Phillip gently pulled the sheet down off his father's face. His eyes were closed, and Phillip almost thought he was sleeping. That they were wrong, he wasn't dead, right? "Oh, Dad. I wish I had gotten to see you just one more time." He leaned down and hugged his father and rubbed his cheek against his. It was cold and full of morning stubble.

He looked up at the nurse. "Has anyone called my mum

yet? Does she know?" He knew some of the family was planning to come down after lunch, and it was already 10:00 a.m.

"I'm sorry. We haven't called anyone yet. Do you want us to call, or do you want to do that now?" The doctor on call, Dr. Levis, led Phillip from the room to a small space near the nurses' station. The nurse brought over some water and handed it to Phillip.

"Is there a phone I can use? I think the news should come from me. How long ago do you think he passed away?"

"He passed through the night. He didn't suffer. He was in no pain. He would have just drifted off to sleep."

"Thank you, Dr. Levis. I will make sure I let my family know that." Phillip picked up the phone and dialled his parents' number. *I guess it's Mum's number now*, he thought to himself. He heard her pick up.

"Hello?"

"Mum, it's Phillip. I'm at the hospital. I'm sorry, Mum. I am so sorry. Dad is gone."

On the other end of the line, Vivian silently slumped to the floor. Diane, who had stayed over since Christmas Day, ran to her side and took the phone from her.

"Hello? It's Di."

"Di, it's Phil. I'm at the hospital. I am so sorry, Muffet, but Dad is gone."

He heard Diane's sob, a loud, guttural, painful sob, and the shouts of his brother Landyn and little sisters Jess and Judy in the background as they realised the news that had been delivered.

He sobbed with them, the phone against his ear, listening to them cry. He could see them in his mind, holding each other. Supporting each other through their own pain.

"Mr. Cooper." Not wanting to intrude, the nurse touched his arm to announce her presence. "I am so sorry to interrupt you. Your sister and niece were here a couple days ago. She left her teddy for your dad to keep him company. I thought she should have it back."

Phillip's eyes overflowed as he took the bear and clutched it to his chest. The last thing his father had touched. The very thing that had been his comfort as he passed. He nodded his thanks, then he roughly wiped his face and prepared to call the rest of the family.

The simple funeral for Thomas Cooper was well attended, and Vivian knew he would have been pleased. Many of the men who served under him and with him came. He was a well-liked and respected man.

He would not be laid to rest until the spring because the ground was already frozen. Vivian and her family sat off to the side of the chapel. She had not cried again since Phillip had told her he was gone. She had a family to take care of and many other demands of her. She remembered a day, a long time ago, when she had to pull herself together and take control of things. Many years ago, she had been told she was strong, and she could do it, to believe in herself, and dammit, she would do it again.

At the back of the chapel, a woman in an indigo-blue dress sat alone, mourning silently.

272

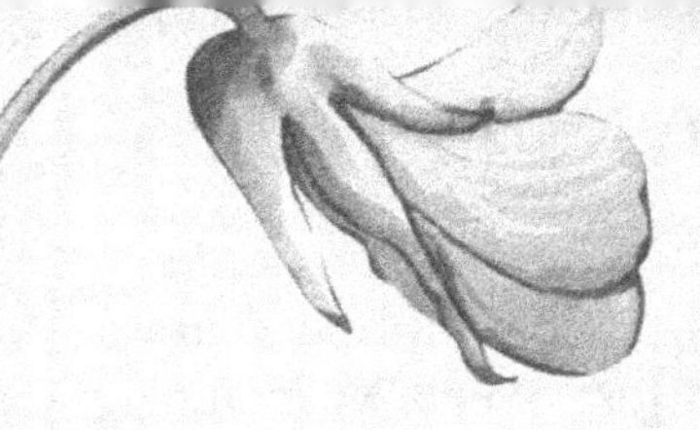

Chapter Thirty-One

As broken-hearted as Vivian was—she had just lost the love of her life— the reality was she needed to find a way to support her family and herself. Thomas' pension from the TTC would be helpful, of course, but she still had three teenagers to raise. Landyn was heading to university in the fall, and the girls wouldn't be far behind.

Diane pulled up in front of Robert Small's law office. It was located in an older building just off Yonge Street near the library. Vivian had asked Diane to come with her to help make sure she kept everything straight. Robert had called when he had received the last of Thomas' paperwork and asked for her to come in.

"Viv, I need to go over all of Thomas's estate matters with you. There are some, well, complications."

"Complications?" How could there be anything complicated about their estate? They didn't own enough property.

"I have his paperwork from the TTC. His pension and life insurance name you as the beneficiary."

"He had life insurance? I thought that ended when he retired?"

"Normally, that would be the case. With this particular policy, however, the coverage continues for up to ten years after retirement. Since Thomas retired just over a year ago, the policy was still in effect."

"That's great news, Mum." Diane took Vivian's hand and squeezed it. She knew her mother had not wanted to say anything, but they had all been concerned about how their mother would be able to keep her home.

"This is an unexpected surprise indeed." Vivian felt a surge of relief. It would take some of the pressure of going back to work right away.

"The pension also has you as the sole beneficiary and will have to be paid out in a lump sum. That is normal for all pensions. That brings us to the complication I wanted to talk to you about." Robert looked extremely uncomfortable, like he had been party to a crime and had been caught. "Thomas had a military pension as well."

"Well, yes, of course he did. He was an RSM when he left."

"Yes. I see all of that. He was in the civilian service for a time after as well."

"Yes." Vivian was confused. She knew all of this. Why was Robert so nervous?

He took a breath. "The thing is, Vivian, you are not the beneficiary of that pension." He sat there frozen. Not blinking.

"I don't understand. If I'm not his beneficiary, then who is?" Vivian's voice trembled slightly with a mix of confusion and apprehension.

"An Elise Cooper." Robert's eyes were glued to the papers scattered across his desk. What Vivian said next shocked him,

"I see." She took a breath. "That makes sense. She was his wife at that time, and he wasn't able to change it." Her voice was level and matter of fact. She knew who Elise was, of course, but this last reminder stung, nonetheless.

"Oh, Mum." Diane put her hand over Vivian's and looked at her mother sitting stoic and strong.

"I'm okay." she replied and pat Diane's hand in an effort to assuage her concern. We can talk more about this later, dear. I promise." Vivian gave Diane a small smile, but Diane heard the hurt in her voice.

"Okay, Mum. Robert, what else do we need to know?" Taking her cue from her mother, Diane straightened in her chair but did not let go of her mother's hand. She would not embarrass her.

"There is nothing about her in his will. Do you think there would be any effort to go after the estate at all?" Robert questioned.

Vivian had never considered that, but somehow, she knew the answer. "No. I don't think she's like that, and there isn't anything to try and take. She is getting the pension, after all. I think she will be surprised to be getting anything. He wasn't very good at supporting them while he was alive."

Diane jolted as if struck by electricity. She fixed her gaze on her mother, her expression a mix of utter shock and concern. She had rarely heard her mother speak against her father. This was a huge knock. "This is part of why I asked you to come with me, Di. You already know about Elise and the children. I didn't want the rest of the family to know all of this, certainly not like this anyway. You are the only one I have ever entrusted with this information."

Vivian was gripping Diane's hand. There was a panic in her eyes. "Please don't worry, Mum. I won't say a word." she promised.

"Thank you, darling." She sighed, her shoulders lowering slightly. "Robert, let's finish this up, please."

"I just need to get your signature on these few papers so we can get the pension and insurance released to you. I know the money will come in handy with all the expenses for the funeral and the house." He turned the small stack of papers towards her. "This first page just goes over all of the amounts."

"Thank you, Robert." Vivian quickly signed all the documents. Her signature showed a dedication to years of strict penmanship. "Is there anything else?"

"I hate to ask you, but do you have an address or phone number for Elise? I need to arrange to send her the paperwork for the military pension."

"I don't have it, but I can probably get it and call you with it. Would that be, okay? I'll have to call Thomas' niece. She might have an address or phone number for her."

Robert nodded awkwardly. "That works just fine."

Vivian stood up, indicating the meeting was done. She shook Robert's hand, nodded, and walked out.

Diane followed closely behind, still in shock from what she had learned about her father. Without a word, they walked back to the car. Diane wasn't sure where to begin.

Vivian exhaled sharply. "Let's take a drive up to Fairy Lake so we can talk."

Once they found a place to park beside the lake, Diane and Vivian sat in silence. There was a flock of mallard ducks sitting on the edge of the ice at the top of the waterfall. *How do they keep from freezing to the ice,* Diane wondered.

"Your cousin Adelaide is the one with Elise's address and number."

Diane nodded. "I figured as much when you said that you could get in touch with someone for the information. I cannot believe she never told any of us? We've been there several times. We took Charleigh last summer." Diane could only shake her head.

"She understood how hurtful it would be for everyone, including John, Olive and Hannah." It felt strange to say their names out loud.

"Does that mean that they have always known about us?" Diane was incredulous. The idea that an entire other family existed was hard enough to process, but to think that they had known about them all these years and kept quiet about it was inconceivable.

"Yes, it does." Vivian understood that Diane was reeling from this realisation.

"I feel awful for them." Diane looked out the window at the ducks again. A few were in the water now, paddling briskly in the frigid water. "Do you think they would want to meet?" She kept her eyes on the ducks.

"I'm not sure." Vivian glanced sideways at Diane. "But if that is something you want to do, I support you completely, Di."

"Thanks, Mum." Diane finally looked at her mother, giving her a soft smile. "I don't know what I want to do about it. I want to respect their peace and privacy, too." She was definitely going to need to think this through.

"I always knew the pension would go to Elise. It had to." Vivian's voice sounded tired. The kind of tired where you have carried something enormous for a long time, and you are finally able to put it down and let it go. "We were never married, and the laws were different back then. Besides, I honestly do believe she deserves to have it. I will always love your father with my whole heart, but that doesn't mean I can't also see that he was a flawed man." She didn't turn her head to Diane while she spoke. It was easier to focus on the ducks. "There have been times when I have wondered what my life would be like if I had never gone out with Thomas in the first place. What if I had never had any of you? What if I had never moved to Canada?" Her voice trembled. "But then I look at all of you, and how rich you have made my life. Oh Di, what a wonderful life I have! I know without a doubt that I would have happily endured so much more if it meant that I was given the gift of being your mum."

Diane reached for her mother, hugging her tight, crying together. Tears of grief for the loss of the man they loved, a husband, a father and a friend. Tears of regret for a family who had suffered a loss long ago and would never get the closure they may seek. Tears of anger and frustration for the lies and hurt Thomas had inflicted. Tears of overwhelming love for each other and the solace and council these two strong women relied on from one another.

Diane wiped her face and handed Vivian a napkin from the console of the car to blow her nose. Vivian sighed deeply then looked at Diane and said, "Never mind. Eat your cake, dear." And they both smiled knowing they could get through anything because they had each other.

Love Always

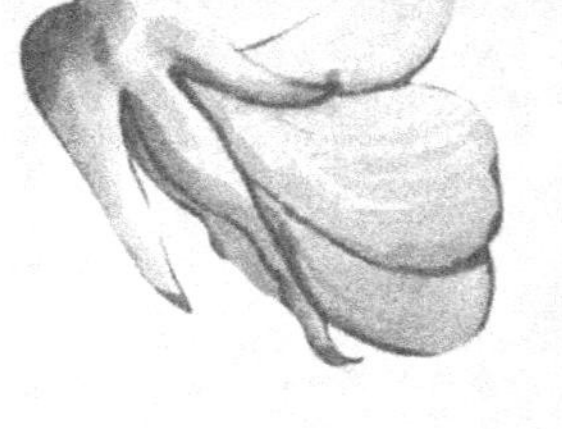

Chapter Thirty-Two

There was an inherent tranquillity and peace in the hushed atmosphere of the library, the occasional thud of books punctuating the silence as they landed on the counter by eager readers keen to satisfy their voracious appetite for words. Vivian enjoyed sitting in the nook and reading a few pages before she left for home.

"Viv?"

She looked up to see Joy, a woman her own age who she ran into at the library often. She was a petite woman with curly brown hair, a pointed nose, and glasses. Her face reminded Vivian of a small bird, perhaps a sparrow.

Vivian smiled. "Joy! Lovely to see you. How are you?"

"I'm very well, thanks." Joy sat down on the chair and put her hand over Vivian's. "How are you doing?"

Vivian was used to the sympathetic eyes and questions about her well-being. "I'm doing okay. Thank you for asking. I'm thinking I'd like to get a job actually."

"Oh, that's good to hear." The little bird's head bobbed, and she smiled kindly. "What sort of work are you looking for?"

"I'm not sure to be honest. I suspect secretarial work

or office work of some sort. It's been a good long while, so I don't know who would take me, especially at my age."

"Don't be silly. You're still very young. Do you have secretarial experience? I can keep my ears open and ask around at the schools."

"You're so kind. I would really appreciate that, Joy."

"I'd be happy to. We girls need to stick together." She laughed a little and tilted her chin down.

Joy was a secretary at an elementary school and had been divorced for almost eight years. She often spoke about all the activities she was involved in when she ran into Vivian and often invited her to join. Vivian never felt able to participate. Thomas liked her to be home with him.

"Listen, Vivian, some of my friends are coming over Saturday night to play cards. Would you like to join us? We do a little potluck, have a glass of wine and talk, a lot. They're a great group of gals. You'd fit right in," she said.

Without hesitating, Vivian answered, knowing it would be just what she needed. To get out and meet some new friends. "I would love to! What should I bring?"

"Maybe just some cheese and crackers. I have the wine sorted out. Let me write down my phone number and address, and you give me yours. That way we can keep in touch as well." Joy found a note pad and pen in her purse and wrote out her information, then handed it to Vivian to write out hers as well. "Well, that's just terrific," she bubbled. "I'll see you then, Viv. I'm so glad you can come."

"So am I. Thank you for thinking to ask me, Joy. It's just what I needed." Clasping hands, they both smiled, and Joy left.

Vivian sat back to read another chapter, but she was filled with so much happiness she couldn't focus and decided to head home.

Well Viv, she thought. *This is a step in the right direction.*

"Call me when you're ready to come home, Mum." Diane smiled as Vivian got out of the car, then added, "I'm really proud of you."

"For heaven's sake. Why's that?"

"Because you aren't afraid to start over and create a new life for yourself."

"Oh, darling, that is lovely, but I'm not starting a new life. I'm just continuing this one with a new route."

Vivian stepped up to Joy's quaint porch, the soft glow of the light welcoming her. She took a deep breath and pressed the doorbell.

"Oh! Hi, Viv! Come on in and meet the girls!" Joy's energy was inviting and invigorating, and Vivian felt instantly at ease. She turned and waved to Diane to let her know she was going inside. Diane waved back and watched her mum walk through a portal to her new life. A life of friends, of putting herself first, and of her own. She had never been happier for her mum. Diane turned on the radio and started to sing along with the music as she drove home.

Joy's living room was warm and cosy. Vivian was greeted by the other ladies already seated on the couch and chairs. They exchanged hugs and introduced themselves. The monthly "girls' night," as they liked to call it, was highly anticipated and enjoyed. Vivian felt an instant sense of belonging wash over her as she placed her cheese tray on the table and eased into an overstuffed chair.

"Your tray looks delicious, Viv." Paula, a short and rather stout woman with a booming voice, complimented her on her display.

"My daughter Diane helped me, if I'm to be honest." Vivian laughed nervously. Diane had brought over one of her larger trays for Vivian to borrow and helped her lay out the cheese and crackers in an appealing way. Then she helped her mum put some extra cheese in some tin foil to replenish the tray if required. She put the extra cheese and boxes of crackers in a basket.

"Well, it looks wonderful," Kathy said as she popped a slice of cheese onto a cracker and into her mouth. "Mmm! What kind of cheese is that?" She pointed to the one she had just eaten from the tray.

"It's a gouda. One of my favourites as well. I'm so glad you like it."

The evening continued with the ladies sharing stories of their families and getting to know Vivian and letting her get to know them.

"Vivian, you are a bit of a card shark! Joy didn't warn us." Ellen laughed.

"Well, we play a lot of Euchre at the cottage at night. There isn't a lot to do otherwise." She giggled, pleased with her success at cards and her new friendships. It felt good to be out, laughing and enjoying herself again. She had not felt so cheery in a long time.

"Do you like to sing, Viv?" Joy asked as she brought over a fresh bottle of wine for everyone and refilled their glasses.

"I love to sing."

"Oh! Then you should join us with the Sweet Adeline's this year." Ellen clapped her hands. "It would be so much fun. You'd love it, Viv!"

"What are the Sweet Adeline's?" Viv asked, a bit puzzled. She was nervous about committing to something they all were already a part of.

"Oh, it's just a lady's choir," Joy pipped. "We get together once a week to learn songs and practice. Then a few times a year we do little competitions."

"We're not actually all that good," Paula added, "but we

have a fun time anyway."

They all laughed, and Joy said, "It's probably *because* we aren't all that good that we have so much fun." The others all nodded in agreement.

"Well, I'm open to giving it a shot. What do you have to do to join?"

"You just sing a short song for the choir director so she can decide where to put you. I don't think anyone is ever turned down to be honest." Joy put her hand on Vivian's shoulder, realising she might be nervous. "Our director has a very welcoming attitude about our group."

Ellen started to sing *Baby Face*, and everyone joined in.

As they sang and laughed together, Vivian felt better about the idea of auditioning. It was already a lot of fun.

"So, how was it?" Diane asked as Vivian got back into the car.

"It was one of the best nights I've ever had in my life, Di. It was just what I needed." Vivian beamed and settled into the seat with a big happy sigh. "I think I'm going to become something called a Sweet Adeline!"

"Sounds great, Mum." Diane beamed back; her heart full as her mother sang *Baby Face* all the way home.

Love Always

Chapter Thirty-Three

"What sort of job do you want, Mum?" Diane asked as they looked through the classified ads in the Saturday copy of the *Aurora Banner*.

Vivian had decided she needed to get a job. Thomas' pension would cover the bills. His life insurance had helped pay for the funeral and a few other expenses. She didn't want to struggle, and she didn't want her family to feel like they had to take care of her.

"Well, it's been an awfully long time since I've worked, so I'm not sure, Di. I don't want to work in a factory, though." As they scanned the ads in the paper, they circled those that seemed like they might be worth looking at further. They would narrow them down after that.

The phone rang, and Judy answered it. "Oh, hi Joy! Yes, she's here. One moment, please. Mum, it's Joy for you." She held the phone out to her mum.

"Hello? Joy?"

"Viv, hi. How are you?"

"I'm wonderful, thanks. Di and I are just looking at the job ads in the paper."

"Oh!" Joy exclaimed. "That's why I'm calling. I wanted to

tell you that Aurora High is looking for an attendance secretary. My friend Carol works there. She said she would give your application to the principal, Harold Durham."

"Joy! That's terrific. I would love that. Where do I get the application?" Vivian was elated.

"I picked one up for you. I can drop it off later today if that's okay."

"That would be great. Do you have time for a cup of tea when you come by?"

"There's always time for a cup of tea." Joy laughed. "I'll be by around two o'clock. Is that all right?"

"Yes. I'll see you then. Thanks again, Joy." Vivian hung up and looked at her eldest and youngest daughters, Judy and Diane. "Joy says Aurora High is hiring an attendance secretary, and she's going to drop off the application for me a little later today."

"Oh, Mum, that would be perfect. The hours are good, and the school board is a very good employer. You'll have benefits." Diane gave Vivian a hug. "We should practise your typing skills some more." Diane had borrowed one of the electric typewriters from her work so she could help her mum practice in case she got an interview.

Vivian had been very diligent in her practising and had improved a lot. The electric typewriters were quite fancy. They automatically moved back to the starting edge of the page after reaching the margin. Diane was a marvel on the typewriter and had been giving Vivian some excellent pointers.

Joy arrived with the application in hand and a smile on her face as usual. She and Vivian had become good friends and spent a great deal of time together. She knew how important the job opportunity was to Vivian and was determined to help her friend in any way she could.

"Here we go! Let's fill it out together." She waved the paperwork in the air.

"Di, do you mind staying and helping us?" Vivian respected Diane's opinions on such matters and knew she would know how to word things best to impress the people who would be reading the application.

"Of course, Mum. I would be happy to help. I'll put the kettle on while you and Joy get settled at the table."

Diane went about making a pot of tea and put some cookies on a plate. She placed some cups on the table with the cookies while the tea steeped.

"How many bags did you put in, dear?"

"Two, Mum."

"Ah good. Don't want it as strong as old boots." Vivian nodded her approval and poured a little milk into the cups ahead of the tea. Then she poured a small amount of tea in to test its strength. "Lovely." It met with her approval, and she continued to pour and fill each cup.

They enjoyed their tea as they read through the application and discussed what to put in each section.

"How many words per minute do I type, do you think?" Vivian was worried she wouldn't meet the requirements for the position.

"I would bet you're up to seventy-five to eighty words per minute, Mum. Let's say eighty." Diane knew her mum would easily be able to reach that goal before any interview she might have.

"Are you sure? That seems like a lot." Vivian wasn't as confident.

"Oh, I'm sure you are as well, Viv," Joy piped in, eager to encourage her friend.

"All right then."

They kept the tea flowing as they filled out the rest of the application.

"This looks great, Viv. I'll take it over to Carol on my way home. She's going to bring it in with her on Monday and give it to Harold."

"When do you think, they will start interviewing?" Diane asked. She wanted to have an idea of when her mum would know if she made it through the first stage or not.

"I doubt it will be for a couple weeks. Harold is not all that organised." Joy shrugged.

"Well, we can wait a week." Diane motioned to her mom. "Then maybe you can call to follow up and see where he is in the whole process."

Joy bobbed her head in agreement. "That's a good idea. Shows you're serious about the job."

Vivian sighed and nodded. Her heart fluttered a bit at the thought, but she knew they were right. "All right then. Thanks again, Joy. Tell Carol thank you as well."

She felt grateful to have so many people trying to help her get the job.

Vivian had been rehearsing her song for weeks. She knew it cold, but she was still nervous. She would be so disappointed if she didn't make the group with her friends.

"Okay, next up is Vivian Cooper," Mathilda Maitland called cheerily. She did all she could to assuage anyone's nervousness. She had a very encouraging smile. "All right, Vivian. Whenever you're ready."

Vivian took a small breath and sang Anne Murray's Snowbird. Anne Murray was one of her favourite singers, and her voice was a great fit for the song. She finished her song and looked at Mathilda for some sign of how she had done.

"Wow, Vivian, that was really well done. I think you would be a wonderful addition to our group." Mathilda thumped the table enthusiastically.

"Really? Oh, my goodness. Yes, please. I mean, thank

you." Vivian was overwhelmed.

"Check in with Marion. She can give you the schedule for rehearsals and such. Tell her you'll be in the soprano section. Welcome to the Sweet Adelines, Vivian. You're going to love it!"

Vivian came out of the room almost bouncing with happiness.

"We assume you made it." Joy, Ellen, Paula, and Kathy all circled around her in a giant group hug.

"Oh, this is grand!" shouted Paula. "We're going to have so much fun. You'll love it, Viv. Just wait."

"Let's go celebrate," Kathy suggested, and everyone immediately agreed. Arms linked; they walked out together to celebrate their friend's success.

The phone rang insistently in the kitchen where Vivian was up to her elbows in flour. She expertly kneaded and rolled it out, perfecting her crust for the apple pie she was making for dessert.

She called out to Judy who was working on some homework in the next room. "Judy, can you grab the phone, please? My hands are full."

"Sure, Mum." She picked up the avocado-green phone off the hook in the kitchen. "Hello?"

"Hello, this is Harold Durham calling. Is Vivian home?" The voice on the other end of the line was deep with an air of authority.

"Why yes of course, Mr. Durham. She's here. Hold on one moment, please." Judy could hardly contain her excitement. She put the receiver against her shirt to muffle it. "Mum! It's

Harold Durham!" She excitedly held the phone out to Vivian as her mother wiped her hands on her apron.

"Hello, Mr. Durham."

"Vivian, I am so glad I was able to catch you at home. I wanted to call and offer you the job."

"Really? That's wonderful Mr. Durham. Thank you so much."

"You can call me Harold. I'll see you next Monday at 8:00 a.m. Congratulations and welcome to Aurora High Vivian."

Judy had gone to get Landyn and Jessica while Vivian had been on the phone and they watched her hang up, eager to hear what happened. Charleigh had been helping her Nan make a pie and was sitting at the table in the kitchen already. They saw a smile forming on Vivian's face as she absorbed the news. She turned back from the phone receiver and squealed in glee. "I got the job!"

Landyn's whoop of joy filled the air as he swept his mother up into his arms, spinning her around the kitchen in a whirlwind of celebration. The room was filled with cheers and laughter, the faces of her children and her granddaughter alight with pride and happiness.

"Congratulations, Mummy!" he cheered, his eyes shining with admiration.

Tears of happiness streamed down her face as she looked at her family, feeling an overwhelming sense of gratitude and accomplishment. She had taken one more giant step toward her new future.

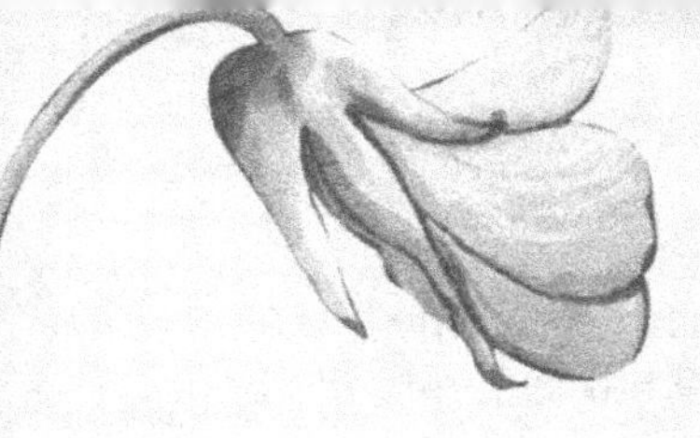

Chapter Thirty-Four

"Good morning, Mrs. Cooper. How was your weekend?" A lanky boy, about sixteen years old, with long wavy hair greeted Vivian as he came into the office.

"Good morning, Simon. I had a lovely weekend. Thank you for asking. How was yours?" She smiled broadly back at him. Vivian was a favourite among the students for her cheerful and kind manner. She gave them the benefit of the doubt when they got sent to the office. She never assumed the worst and always saw the good in them.

"It was pretty cool, thanks. I'm here for Mr. Durham. He wanted to see me first thing today."

"All right, well, have a seat and wait. He's with another student right now. He's popular this morning." She smiled and pointed to the chairs by the doors that lined the wall of windows. The office was often referred to as the "fishbowl" because of the bank of windows on three sides. It also had a glass ceiling that let in light and made the space feel bright and open.

Vivian loved her job and being able to interact with the students. The bustling of the hallways, the chatter, and the friendships she had built with her colleagues were truly satisfying.

Each morning, Vivian rose before dawn and quietly got ready for work. She would then make her way to the bus stop. She enjoyed the quiet of the early hours but found being held to the bus schedule very frustrating. Aurora was a small town and only had two buses. One went east and west and the other north and south. If she missed hers, the next one wouldn't come for thirty minutes.

"You should get your driver's licence, Mum," Jessica suggested at dinner. "It would save you so much time each day."

"I was thinking about that. I would need proper lessons, though. I've driven a car a few times, of course, but this would be different."

"Well, the school uses Apex Driving for their lessons. Maybe they have a good price. You should call them."

"That's a good idea. I'll do that today on my lunch break." The idea had formed in Vivian's mind, and she became set on it.

"Simon, have you taken your driving lessons yet?"

"I just started, Mrs. Cooper. Why do you ask?"

"I want to get my licence. I thought I would see what you thought of the company the school board uses."

"They're pretty good actually. There are four of us getting lessons at the same time. David Patterson crashed us last week." To emphasise what he was saying, Simon smacked his fists together and laughed. "Backed right into a parked car."

"Oh dear!"

"Oh, it's okay." he added quickly, "No one was hurt."

"Well, that's a relief. I'll give them a call and see what sort of lessons they have for adults."

"You'll do great, Mrs. C. You're very level-headed." Simon smiled and pumped his hand in the air to indicate his support.

Vivian laughed. "Well, thank you, Simon. I appreciate your confidence in me." Her determination was truly buoyed by the young man's words. She decided she would enrol in a beginner's driving course that day. No more delays and soon no more being restricted by bus schedules and the kindness of family and friends.

296

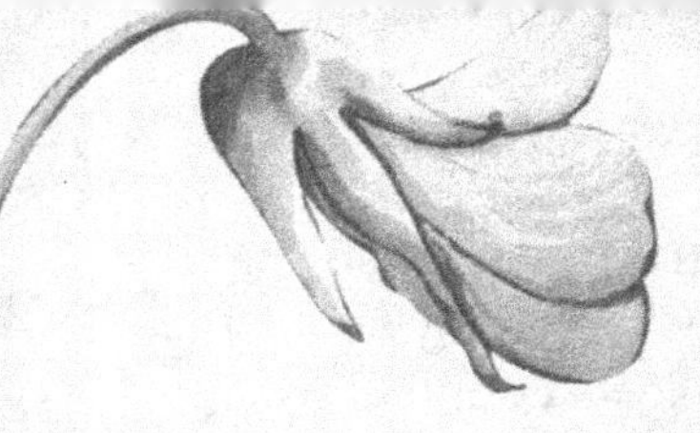

Chapter Thirty-Five

"Hello! Hello! Can you all come here for a moment? I've something I need to share with you," Vivian called out as she walked through the front door of her home. The entranceway was small, and she thought about how she might like to make some changes given she was working full-time.

Landyn was the first to appear, followed closely by Jessica and Judy, their curiosity piqued. "What's up, Mum?" Landyn asked, his brow furrowed in anticipation.

"I have a little surprise for everyone outside," Vivian replied, a grin spreading across her face as she led them back out to the driveway. Diane and Callum were waiting beside a small red Toyota Corolla, their faces filled with anticipation.

"Hey, Di! Nice car. Did you just get it?" They all came down and circled the vehicle, examining and admiring it.

Vivian interrupted before Diane could respond, unable to contain her excitement any longer. "Actually, it's mine!" she exclaimed, her heart swelling with pride at the shocked expressions on their faces.

Everyone stopped and stared at her for a moment, surprised. "What?" They were incredulous.

"Yep. Callum helped me. He checked it out to make sure it was in good shape since I don't know anything about the mechanics part of things. I got my licence a couple days ago and bought this car. What do you think?" Proudly, she opened the driver's door for them to look inside.

"Mum! This is fantastic. We are so proud of you!" Landyn shouted, enveloping her in a tight hug.

"Who wants to go for a ride?" Vivian asked, dangling the keys from her fingers as she settled into the seat.

"Shotgun!" Jess cried, and they piled into the car.

Diane and Callum waved as she backed down the driveway, bursting with pride.

"She's doing good, yer mum," Callum said, giving Diane a sideways hug.

"Yes, she is," Diane replied, a tear shining in her eyes. "Yes, she is."

Joy had become Vivian's best friend in a very short period. They spent a lot of time together going to movies, drinking tea, and encouraging each other to try new things. In fairness, Joy had much more experience being the adventurous one, but Vivian was a good student and catching on very quickly.

They had just been at their rehearsal for Sweet Adelines and were buzzing with excitement with the news they had all just been given.

"Can you believe we made it into the regionals, Viv?" Joy could barely contain herself. Their group had never done so well. "We're going to have such a great time!"

Vivian grinned; her cheeks flushed with exhilaration. "I know, right? I can hardly believe it! This is going to be an unforgettable experience."

They had walked from the rehearsal down the street to a new tea shop that had just opened. They were welcomed by the aroma of freshly brewed blends wafting through the air. The cosy interior enveloped them, and they settled into the seats in the corner near the large windows that overlooked the gardens and patio that would be opening soon with the nicer weather. The shop was busy, and the soft murmur of conversation and clinking cups was a peaceful backdrop to their excitement over the news.

They sipped their tea, and Joy leaned closer to Vivian, her eyes mischievous. "You know, Viv, since we're going to be in New York for regionals anyway, we should make a trip of it for ourselves and explore the city a bit."

Vivian's heart fluttered at the thought of visiting the bustling city for the first time. "I've never been to New York," she admitted, her voice tinged with nervous wonder. "It would be wonderful to see some sights and soak up the energy of the city."

Joy grinned at her friend's agreement. "Exactly! We could see a Broadway show, visit Times Square, maybe even take a carriage ride in Central Park. I've always wanted to do that."

Vivian's eyes lit up. "Yes! Let's do it. Let's do all of it." Since they'd agreed to the adventure, Vivian didn't want to waste the opportunity. "Diane can help us with the planning. She does that sort of thing for her work all the time."

"Oh, Viv! I can't wait."

The Aurora Sweet Adelines gathered in the arena parking lot to meet their director, Mathilda, and the coach bus they had hired to take them to New York for their competition. Many of the women were like Vivian and had never been to the city. They were excited for their adventure.

Ellen, Paula, and Kathy had decided to join Vivian and Joy and booked a stay a few extra days after the competition. It had turned into quite a trip. Diane helped them book four extra nights at the hotel where the competition was being held as well as tickets for *Guys and Dolls*.

"All right, everyone, let's get ready to climb on board and get this trip started," Mathilda called out. "Line up once Don, our driver, has helped you stow your luggage underneath the bus, and I will check you in."

The ladies all lined up, laughing and carrying on like a large flock of hens. The group chatted animatedly, their voices rising and falling as they shared jokes and stories of times they'd travelled before and what they thought their trip would be like. They clambered aboard, merriment echoing down the aisles as they found seats and settled in.

"Here, Viv, do you want the window?" Joy stopped at two seats about midway down the bus.

"That's okay. It's large enough that I can see, thanks."

The two ladies took off their coats and put them in the overhead compartment, then slipped into their spot. Once their small group had all settled near each other, Ellen pulled out a thermos.

"Girls, would you like some tea?" Fits of giggling ensued as they all said yes, knowing the "tea" was nothing of the sort. Paula pulled out crackers and passed them around as well.

"We are such great travellers!" Joy giggled, and they all agreed.

As the bus rumbled to life, everyone shrieked with excitement and burst into song, their voices blending together harmoniously, filling the bus. The rise and fall of the melody reached the friends and family who had dropped them off and the passersby as they pulled out of the parking lot.

As they approached the US border, Mathilda decided to address the group, "Ladies. Ladies," she called through the speaker handset. "We are about twenty minutes from the border. It would be really helpful if you all had your passports and identification out and ready for the inspectors." There was a loud cheer from the group upon hearing they were almost there. "It may be a good idea to seal up any, um, liquids that aren't meant to be open in a vehicle."

Mathilda's advice was met with a round of laughter and many heads nodding in agreement.

The border guards directed their bus over to the secondary area since they were a large group, and some were planning to stay longer than others. Everyone lined up alongside the bus, waiting for their turn to answer questions.

"Passport or identification please." The officer was quite tall and had a very easy-going nature about him. He wasn't anticipating too many issues from a group of women on their way to a singing competition in New York.

He looked down at Vivian's documents. "Oh, you're British? How long have you lived in Canada?" He looked up at her.

"Twenty-eight, almost thirty years."

"You came after the war then?"

"Why, yes, I did. My husband was a Canadian soldier. Better opportunities here for us and our family."

"My mom is from Newcastle. She was a clerk and met my dad when he was borrowed from his unit here." He smiled broadly at her.

"Oh goodness. Isn't that lovely! I'm originally from Tottenham, but we lived in Farnham for a time. It was safer outside the city."

"Small world. Is this your first visit to New York?" They had shifted to a comfortable conversation.

"It is. I'm very excited. We are going to have a bit of an adventure afterward for a few days and see some sights while we are all the way there."

He handed her passport back to her. "I hope you have a wonderful time, Mrs. Cooper. Be safe." He smiled and moved on to the next person in line.

Once they had all resumed their seats, the bus pulled out, and they were on their way again. A renewed vigour could be felt.

Patty, one of the girls who had been with the troupe since it was formed, started to sing *I Guess the Lord Must Be In New York City*. Everyone joined in, as the thermoses opened back up as they clinked plastic cups and munched on chips for the last leg of their journey.

The skyline of New York and its towering skyscrapers came into view as the bus rounded the final bend. There was an eruption of cheers and applause as they saw the iconic city come into view.

Vivian leaned forward in her seat, her eyes wide with wonder as she took in the dazzling lights and the bustling streets. She had never seen anything like it. The sheer scale of everything, even the energy of the city, left her utterly gobsmacked.

The ladies all took turns posing in front of the windows for pictures with the city in the background. As they pulled up in front of the hotel and conference centre where they would be staying and performing, Vivian felt her stomach flutter with nervous excitement.

"Let's check in and meet in the lobby in one hour for

dinner, ladies. We have a team meal tonight," Mathilda instructed before everyone got off the bus.

They went up to their room and couldn't believe their eyes. The enormous windows looked out over Central Park. It was truly a million-dollar view.

"Viv! Oh, my goodness!" breathed Joy as she gazed out over the city. "Did Diane arrange this for us? I think we're in a whole separate area from everyone else."

The room turned out to be a suite with a small kitchenette. There were two queen-sized beds in the main area and a king-sized bed in the separate bedroom that also had enormous windows and a view of the park.

"She probably did. My Di is one of a kind." Vivian knew Diane had taken care of every detail and had the travel agent she used for her company events get them a few extras.

"Well, this is certainly a bonus!" Ellen was holding a basket with two bottles of wine, some fruit, and chocolates. "It says, 'Welcome to New York' and it's signed by Monty Greenman, Manager."

"Oooooo!" They all shrieked and giggled hysterically as they held their faces and leaned into each other, gasping for air.

"We are so posh!" Ellen laughed. "Let's freshen up so we can go down and brag to everyone before dinner."

They took turns posing with the enormous basket in front of the window with the view of the park in the background.

After freshening up, everyone in the chorus gathered in the hotel lobby for dinner. They were then escorted into the dining area. A section of the restaurant had been cordoned off for them. While they were not all sitting at a single table, they were all together in one area. The restaurant came alive with the enthusiasm and excitement of the ladies as they found seats and began ordering.

"Are any of you going to have a drink?" Paula asked.

"Definitely!" Ellen responded. "We need to have a team

cheers after all." It didn't really take much to encourage them all to have one.

Once everyone seemed to be taken care of and the food and drinks served, Mathilda stood to make a toast, tapping her glass with her fork to get everyone's attention. "I just wanted to take a moment before our weekend starts to say how very, very proud I am of you all. Your hard work and dedication have been inspiring, and it has been such a pleasure to be with you all on this journey. When we started out, our goal was just to form a little group for ladies to be able to get out of the house and spend time together and enjoy each other's company. Well, we certainly have done that!"

There were several claps and happy murmurs of agreement.

"But here we are now, having made it to regionals!"

Applause broke out again.

"I want you to know that no matter how we score this weekend, I think you are all first-place winners, and I want you to enjoy this experience. Cheers to you all." Mathilda lifted her glass and motioned to the women before her.

"Cheers!"

After dinner, Vivian and her friends decided to change into more comfortable clothes and go for a walk. They wanted to see some of the 'city that never sleeps' and get some air before they settled in for the night. As Vivian and her friends stepped out of their hotel near Central Park, the vibrant energy of New York City enveloped them. The streets teemed with people from all walks of life, each with their own story to tell. Skyscrapers towered overhead, casting long shadows over the bustling sidewalks through the menagerie of lights.

"Can I get you ladies a cab?" The doorman held up his hand, and a taxi zoomed forward.

"How far is it to Times Square?" Paula asked. "Can we walk there?"

"Oh definitely. It's about a twenty-minute walk straight

down

Broadway." He pointed down the street. "Make sure you hold your purses in front of you. Pickpockets also don't sleep in New York." Each of them pulled their purses tightly against themselves with his warning and glanced at each other. As they made their way toward Times Square, the sights and sounds of the city surrounded them. Street performers dazzled passersby with their acts, while vendors peddle their wares on every corner. Vivian couldn't help but feel a sense of awe at the sheer magnitude of it all.

"Ellen, look at these sunglasses. They're calling your name.: Paula turned to Ellen, wearing bright pink sunglasses with jewels inlaid all around the edges. "Elton John would be in love." She laughed. They each put on a pair and posed for pictures before deciding to buy.

The intensity of the crowd seemed to grow exponentially with ever metre they got closer to Times Square. Neon lights illuminated the intersections, casting a cacophony of colours across the sea of people below. The iconic billboards flashed with advertisements for Broadway shows, movie premieres, and upcoming events, creating an electrifying atmosphere unlike Vivian had ever experienced.

The sheer scale of Times Square was overwhelming, with towering buildings rising up on all sides and throngs of people moving in every direction. Despite the chaos, there was a palpable excitement in the air, a feeling of being in the epicentre of something extraordinary. Posing and snapping pictures, the women savour the exhilaration of the heart of New York City.

"Look, Viv. Joy pointed to the sign for *Guys and Dolls*, the show they were going to see in just a few days when the competition was done. "Ellen, can you take our picture in front of the sign for the show?"

Ellen took their photo, then posed for her own as well. At the rate they were all going, they'd need to buy more film by the end of the day.

"We should probably start back. We have an early day."

Paula stood before them, having found an equally outlandish pair of sunglasses as the other two girls.

"I think we all need to find sunglasses now." Vivian laughed.

As they walked back to their hotel, laughter mingled with the sounds of the city around them. The lights of Times Square grew smaller in the distance but remained a beacon to them and a reminder of the adventures they still had ahead of them on the trip.

It was late when they got back to their room, and no one wasted time getting ready for bed. They settled in with almost no time passing, the rhythmic breathing of sleep heard throughout the suite.

Vivian lay awake, listening to her companions and relishing the friendships she had forged with the wonderful women who had welcomed her so openly and eagerly into their mix.

What a difference three years can make, she thought as her eyes closed, and she drifted off to sleep, smiling.

"We are after this group, ladies. Let's have a little warm-up." Mathilda led the group through a few vocal routines and some reminder steps of their medley. "Don't forget, I love you no matter how badly you mess up." She looked at them all sideways and cracked a silly grin. "Okay, we're up!"

The ladies walked out onto the stage and clasped hands. They gave each other a quick squeeze of support and got into their starting positions. They sang their hearts out with their *Hello, Dolly!* Medley an ode to Broadway that appropriately helped them get into a competition just down the road from

Broadway itself.

They sang in perfect unison, hands up and down and bodies turned as one. They knew they had nailed it, but they had to hold position until they were released by Mathilda, whose smile couldn't have appeared any larger if she had tried. She lowered her hand, and the audience roared their appreciation. They took their bows and moved off stage.

"That was the most amazing experience of my life!" Mathilda shouted. "Ladies, I have no words."

Everyone was hugging and congratulating each other. They just needed to wait until the end to hear their score and see how well they did.

"What do you think, girls? Do you think we'll place in the top twenty?" Esther, who was another of the original singers, was still in shock at how they executed their number.

"I heard Mathilda tell Rachel Murray she thinks it was a top ten performance!" someone shouted, and the group tittered and talked about who they thought they needed to beat, and why they may have done so.

Mathilda came back to the changeroom where they were all waiting for instructions. "Well, ladies! When I said I would be proud of you no matter what, I didn't expect that you would take it as a challenge to win this thing our first time here!" Everyone laughed and called out encouraging words.

"It's because of you, Mathilda!"

"We wouldn't be here without you!"

"That was simply mind-boggling!"

"Well." She smiled. "We can have something to eat but be careful of your dresses. Go back to your rooms and have a nap if you want. Be back in the auditorium to watch the last few performances by five o'clock, please. We have seats on the upper balcony sectioned off for us. If you're changing your clothes, please make sure you are back in costume for awards."

They had anticipated the awards would happen around 6:00 p.m., and it was only 11:30 a.m.

It took some time for everyone to move out of the dressing room. Vivian and her friends decided to go back to their room and change before going for a quick lunch together at the hotel. They didn't want to go far.

"Can you believe how well we sang today?" Kathy hummed happily as they made their way to the elevators.

"Positively our best performance," Ellen agreed.

"Well, if you're going to save your best, today was the day to give it." Kathy pressed the button to the elevator. As the door closed, they all sang their *Hello Dolly* medley again.

Everyone had gotten back into their costumes and makeup and met back in their seats in the auditorium. The last performances were wrapping up, and they were all having a hard time sitting still as they waited to hear about the awards.

"Good evening, everyone. My name is Jane Kennedy." There was a roar of applause, and Jane smiled modestly. "Thank you. Thank you. I am the president of Sweet Adelines International. What a competition!" She paused to allow for more applause and cheering. "We have had the most first-time groups of any year, and honestly, it has arguably been the most impressive competition we have ever had, and that is because of all of you." She pointed to the audience, who shouted out more cheers and applause.

"We love bringing everyone together in the sisterhood of music and share our passion not just for singing but for lifting each other up." She paused as a table was wheeled forward with tiaras and envelopes and trophies. "I imagine everyone would like to get to the awards." The room erupted, and she could be heard laughing into the microphone. "All right then. Let's get started."

There were several categories before theirs, and everyone patiently waited until it was their turn. "In tenth place, a first-time group who travelled a long way to join us!"

No one spoke. Hands were at their hearts and throats.

"The chorus from Westerville, Ohio!"

Their hearts sank, and many looked around in disbelief. Mathilda was surprised as well. She truly thought they had given a top ten performance that day.

"It's okay, ladies. My goodness," she said, "this is just our first of many times here. I am so proud of how well we did." Patting hands and shoulders, they settled in to politely listen to the rest of the awards.

"In sixth place, our returning champions from Memphis! Congratulations."

Many people were surprised by that. Memphis usually placed in the top three.

"In fifth place, again we have a first-time chorus from Aurora, Ontario." There was silence for a moment as they all looked at each other, unsure if they had just heard correctly. They won fifth place. Then they heard Mathilda shouting.

"Yes! Yes! Yes!"

They all jumped up and down as they were guided to the stage. Gathered together, they received their award, crying, hugging each other, clutching hands, and standing united in their success and joy.

As Vivian and her friends stood on that stage, basking in the glow of their win, they knew they had achieved something special together. After the awards, they left arm in arm, bonded forever in that moment.

The trip to New York was a dream come true for Vivian. They had, of course, had their big win as a chorus, but it was so much more than that. Staying on a few days after the competition, they had enjoyed *Guys and Dolls* and visited the Empire State Building and Statue of Liberty. They even did a carriage ride through Central Park as Joy had wanted.

They had arranged to take the train home. The station was enormous, and they felt very much like country bumpkins, wandering around trying to find their way to the correct train.

"Excuse me, sir? Would you mind helping us?" Ellen went up to a porter for assistance. They were feeling genuinely lost.

"Of course, miss. May I see your tickets?" He glanced at their tickets and smiled. "You're on the right track. Let me show you the rest of the way." He graciously led them to their train and compartment.

"Thank you so much," they chimed as they climbed up the steps. The porter reached down and helped Vivian with her bag, and she had a sudden flash of a different girls' trip and train so long ago. She could hear Fern calling out to her and the girls twittering as they climbed on board for their hols.

"Thank you." She smiled. Her eyes were still striking, and the porter couldn't help but notice. While the lines may have deepened, the sparkle in her amber and emerald eyes was just as bright and the smile just as sweet.

Vivian sat down in the window seat and looked out, scanning for a ghost. He wasn't there, of course, but the memory of that day was fresh. In her purse, unseen by the others, rested a small card with a violet on it and the word *Home*. She didn't need to look at it. She knew the paper was worn on the edges but the flower, having been properly preserved and pressed all those years ago, was still beautiful. She rested her head on the glass and watched the platform begin to move away as the train set off. The bustling city slowly gave way to the lush meadows and green rolling hills of the countryside.

Love Always

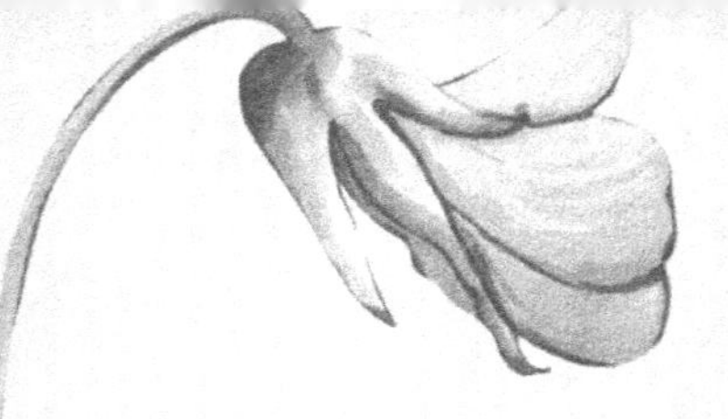

Chapter Thirty-Six

The water was hot, and Vivian had put lots of bubbles in. She'd had a long week and wanted to relax in the bath with some peace and quiet. She even had a glass of wine and a few candles going. Humming, she could feel the stress of work and life flow out of her and melt into the hot liquid.

Judy had purchased a bath pillow for her for Mother's Day so she could relax in the tub more comfortably. It was heavenly. As the bubbles started to disappear and the water cooled, Vivian began her grooming routine. She lathered up her legs and carefully shaved them along with her armpits. As her hand slid down the side of her left breast, she noticed something, and it stopped her cold. Frozen, she couldn't move her hand in case she felt it again.

Carefully, she put down the razor and lifted her left arm again. She ran her fingers slowly down her armpit and across the side of her breast.

Maybe it's a bug bite, she thought. She had been at the cottage, and there were a lot of mosquitos there.

She lay back in the tub, her mind racing. "Jess! Jess! Could you come here?" She decided to ask Jess to look and see if there was a mark from a bite.

"Ya, Mum? What's up?" In a house with one real bathroom and several girls, everyone was comfortable with their nudity. In a way, it was surprising given how modest Vivian was about such things, but giving birth to seven children, and the lack of boundaries kids had about personal space, seemed to have erased those concerns.

"Can you look at this spot? I have a bump, and I can't see if it's a bite or not." She pointed at the spot.

Jess looked but saw no mark. "I don't see anything, Mum. Is it sore?"

"No, not really. Can you poke it? See if you feel it, too?"

Jess reached around and pressed the soft skin. The moment her fingers found the lump, her eyes locked with Vivian's. Her heart sank.

"How long has this been here, Mum?" She tried to sound calm, but her heart was pounding in her ears so loud she couldn't hear properly.

"I'm not sure. I just noticed it." She reached for the towel. Jess handed it to her, and she stood up, wrapping herself tightly in the cotton. She needed to move. To do something. But what?

"Mum, what do you want me to do?" Jess was still in shock but knew her mum was a very private person.

"It's okay, dear. I'll take care of it. I'll call Dr. Williams tomorrow when the office opens and get an appointment." Vivian looked at her daughter's face full of concern. "It will be fine, dear. Don't worry." She gave her hand a squeeze before going into her room. She carefully closed the door behind her and sat on the side of the bed. Silently, tears ran down her face.

Oh God, she thought. *What if it's cancer? What about my family?*

Slowly, she put on her pyjamas and got into bed. She turned as she always did to Thomas' side and touched his pillow.

"Thomas, I need you."

She called to him with her mind and heart. As she lay in bed, listening for his voice and knowing she would not hear him, Vivian felt more alone than she had ever felt in her life.

"You can come around now, Viv." Mable, the nurse at Dr. Williams' office, called her from behind the desk. Diane stood up with her and followed her into the exam room. There was no way she was going to allow her mum to go through things alone.

"Here's a gown for you. It's easier for him to examine you if you put it on backwards so the opening is at the front. You can wrap it, so you feel more secure. Just take off your top and bra. You can keep on your pants. Doc will be right in." Mable smiled reassuringly and closed the office door.

Vivian removed her shirt and bra and folded them neatly in the small change room. She placed them on the circular stool and put on the gown. Stepping up onto the examination table, she waited for the doctor to come in.

Sam walked in with his usual flurry of energy. He was a man who was always in a hurry. He leaned against his desk and looked at Vivian and Diane. "I hear you're concerned about a lump on your left breast. Is that right?" He smiled kindly at Vivian. He had the ability to calm his patients in the most stressful situations, and her visit definitely counted as a stressful situation.

"Yes. I think it's pretty large actually." Vivian lifted her arm and pointed at the location of the lump.

"Well, it's always wise to get things checked out, but it's entirely possible it's a blocked lymph node or even a milk duct. Might seem unlikely to you after all this time, but the body can do some strange things that scare us for no good reason other than it can."

He patted her hand and gently helped her lay back on the table. "I'm just going to pull the gown down a bit. Can you lift your arm for me?" Vivian lifted her arm over her head and Dr. Williams carefully moved his fingers around her breast to examine it completely. "Let's just check the other side while we're at it and make sure we're thorough." He checked the other side as carefully as he had the first, then pulled the gown back up to cover Vivian and helped her sit up.

"Well, there is definitely something on that left side. I don't feel anything on the right. I'm going to send you for a mammogram of both sides though just to be sure."

He could see Vivian was trying to be strong.

"I don't want you to worry. As I said, it's not unusual for these to be an irritated or infected gland or duct. We will get everything checked just to be safe. I'll get Mable to call up to the hospital now and see when they can fit you in." He patted her on the hand again and left the exam room to let Mable know what needed to be done.

"Well, it's good to know it might not be anything to worry about." Diane smiled weakly at her mom as she got dressed.

"That is good to know. Hopefully, the mammogram will settle everything quickly."

As they came out of the room, Mable was just getting off the phone. "York County has a slot this afternoon if that works for you, Viv."

"Absolutely," Diane answered for her. "I can take her."

Mable handed her the requisition paperwork as she took her mum's hand and wordlessly led her out of the office.

They drove to the hospital in silence. When they arrived, Diane finally spoke, "I'll drop you at the door and go find a parking spot, Mum."

"I don't mind the walk, dear. It isn't very far."

"All right then." Diane smiled and kept driving past the entrance to the parking gate. They found a spot and started walking back to the main entrance. There was so much they both wanted to say but were afraid to acknowledge. So, they said nothing. No point in getting worked up over what might just be a clogged gland.

"Mrs. Cooper, you can come in now." Vivian followed the technician into the small room. The equipment was large and took up most of the space. "Is this your first mammogram?"

Vivian nodded yes.

"Okay. Well, it's not the most comfortable experience, but I will do my best to be as gentle as possible. I need to ask you a few questions before we begin for your file and history." Vivian nodded her agreement. "What is your date of birth?"

"July 30, 1920."

"Do you or have you ever smoked?"

"No, but my husband did. He passed away from lung cancer in 1972."

"I am sorry for your loss." The technician paused and looked up at Vivian. "He has been gone about eight years then?"

"Yes." Vivian was shocked to think of how long it had been since Thomas had passed.

"Is there any history of breast cancer in your own family? Mother, father, siblings, etc.?"

"Not that I know of. My father passed from a stroke. My mother got pneumonia and passed from that."

"Do you have polycystic breasts?"

"I don't think so. I don't know what that is. I have a flat nipple though."

"Probably not then. If you had it, you would probably know and would have noticed lumps before this. Has it always been flat or is that new?" She paused and looked up from her clipboard.

"Oh no, it's always been like that."

"Ah, ok then. Well, let me explain what we will be doing so it is a little less overwhelming." The technician explained she would be gathering up Vivian's breast tissue onto the plexiglass plate and then lowering a second plate onto the breast to flatten it as much as possible. It was important to get the tissue as smooth as they could to capture the best images.

Vivian nodded, held her arm up, and stepped closer to the

machine as the technician placed her breast and the side flesh onto the plate. It made her wince as her tissue was pulled and squeezed.

"Take a breath and hold it when I say. It's important you don't move while I take the pictures, okay?"

Vivian nodded, afraid to speak in case that extra effort moved something.

The technician stepped behind a wall and called out to her. "Okay, hold still." A buzzing sound could be heard from the machine as it took its pictures. "Okay, that's perfect. We're going to do a couple more. Stay still again."

The sound vibrated through the machine. The tech repositioned her breasts a few times, each image requiring they be pressed flat, and her breath held.

"Okay, Mrs. Cooper. I'm going to get the radiologist to look at these. Don't get dressed just yet in case any of the images are blurry, and I need to retake them. You can have a seat in the waiting area."

"How did it go?" Diane asked as Vivian came out to the waiting area still in her gown.

"The radiologist is going to take a look at them now."

"That's good then. It means we'll have answers quicker."

They tried to distract themselves by watching the television on the wall. *The Price is Right* was on, but they were watching and not seeing. Almost like machines.

"Mrs. Cooper, the doctor will see you now. Your daughter can come with you if you'd like." The technician smiled and led them to a small room past where she had just had the mammogram done.

Dr. Valley was already in the room waiting for them. He stood up and shook their hands as he introduced himself. "I have your images here," he said as he put what looked like X-rays up on the light box and turned it on. "This is your right breast. You can see here the tissue has no variations or clustering. Your left breast, however, is showing us something very different."

There was a sudden roar in her ears that sounded like the

rush of the tide. She closed her eyes for a moment, and the doctor paused, seeing her reaction. When she opened her eyes again, he continued.

Vivian heard every word, but it felt like she was in a different place and the doctor was talking through speakers. He was pointing at an area of her left breast image. It did look different than the right, but she still wasn't sure what she should be seeing.

"So, what does this mean, Doctor?" Diane interjected.

"It means that your mum has a lump, from what I can tell, about the size of a dime in her left breast. From the images, it looks like it's encapsulated. Which is good. Sometimes they look a bit like a shotgun blast with many small, almost seed-like tumours."

"Tumour?" Diane reacted to the word.

"Yes, we call it a tumour at this point. Even if it is benign, which it is still entirely possible that it is, we call it a tumour."

"What is our next step?" Vivian finally spoke as she lifted out of the fog, she had been in.

"We are going to schedule you for surgery as soon as possible to remove it. Once it is out, we'll be able to examine it and determine if it's benign or malignant."

"If it is malignant?" Her gaze was strong and steady.

"If it *is* malignant, your oncologist will create a treatment plan for you, depending on what stage it is and if any of the surrounding tissue is affected."

"Okay. When can you arrange for the surgery?" she asked.

"I'm going to go look into that now. You can go ahead and get dressed and then just wait here for me."

Vivian felt numb. The roaring in her ears had subsided, but she felt anesthetized. Diane was gripping her hand as they waited. Neither of them spoke, the silent elephant sitting between them.

The doctor came back in and sat down at the desk again. "We were very lucky. We can get you in in four weeks. Normally, we have to wait about eight to twelve weeks, but there was a cancellation. I'm going to send you up to oncology to meet with Doctor Spier. He has time now before his next surgery to see you and go over what the procedure will be and what to expect. Do you have any questions?"

"Should I be concerned with how fast you're getting me in to see the surgeon and have this procedure?" Vivian wondered if the efficiency with which she was being dealt with meant something terrible.

"Normally, you would be right to be worried. This is genuinely a case of good luck." He smiled.

"Right. Good luck." Vivian somehow did not feel like it was her lucky day.

"I'm sorry. I didn't mean …" His voice trailed off as he realised how flippant his comment had been.

"It's okay," Vivian replied. "Is there someone who can show us where we need to go?" She stood up, indicating the meeting was over, and Diane and the doctor followed suit.

"Yes, yes, of course. I will have the nurse show you the way."

Mornings at the cottage were Vivian's favourite time of day. She got up to start the coffee and opened a packet of butter cookies, a cottage staple. The fire had burned down, and the house was cool that morning. Vivian poked the coals and added a couple pieces of wood. It came back to life, crackling and sparking. The warmth in the room grew almost immediately. The gurgling and spurting noises of the coffee percolator were underway as well as she went to use the bathroom.

"Morning, Nan." Charleigh had heard her grandmother fixing the fire and making coffee. As always, they greeted each other with a warm hug and a kiss.

"Morning, dear. Coffee won't be long. Why don't you go get into bed, and I'll bring our coffee and bickies in a minute?" It was one of the rituals they loved most the quiet time together before anyone else was up, snuggled together in bed, drinking coffee and enjoying cookies, or "bickies" as they had nicknamed them.

"Okay, Nan." Charleigh went to her grandmother's room and got into the big bed. It sagged in the middle a bit. They joked that one had to hold onto the side when sleeping in it, or they'd be sucked into the middle and crushed by Nan as she rolled over in her sleep.

"Here are." Vivian came in with two cups and a small plate with several cookies on it. She handed one cup to Charleigh and put the other down on the table beside the bed along with the plate. Pulling the pillows up so they could sit up and enjoy their coffee, she got back into bed and placed the plate on the bedspread between them to share.

Munching happily and drinking their coffee, Vivian put her cup down. "I wanted to talk to you about something."

Charleigh looked at her Nan and felt the shift from cheery coffee in bed to something more serious. "What is it?" She put her cup down as well.

"I went to see the doctor last week. I found a lump in my breast, and they very quickly took a look at it. They're going to do surgery next week to take it out."

"What does that mean? Is it cancer? Is it the same as Grandad's?" Large, worried green eyes stared at Vivian.

"We don't know what it is yet, but it is definitely not the same as Grandad's. His was in his lungs and all through his body. The doctors did a bunch of X-rays and scans and checked my whole body. They can only see the lump in my breast. So that is particularly good news." She pulled her granddaughter to her and hugged her tightly.

"What if it is cancer?" Charleigh said in a faint voice as if saying it aloud might make it happen.

"If it is, then we'll deal with it. Until then, it's just a lump.

Like a pimple, only inside. Okay? We can't worry about more until there's more to worry about."

"I don't want you to die, Nanny!" Charleigh cried, pressing her face into her grandmother's neck.

"I am not going to die, darling. I might need to have some extra surgery and maybe some treatments if it turns out to be cancer. I am not going anywhere. I still have too much to do."

She stroked the blonde hair of her granddaughter and prayed she wasn't lying to her.

"Hello, Viv." Dr. Williams pulled down his mask so she could tell who was talking to her. "I thought I'd join you today. Is that okay?" He smiled and squeezed her arm.

"Thank you, Sam. I feel better knowing you're here," she said.

"Hello, Mrs. Cooper." Dr. Spiers, her oncologist, called to her from the other side of the room as he looked at the films they had taken that morning in preparation for the surgery. "We're almost ready to go here. How are you?"

"I'm ready for this to be over with," Vivian answered.

"Well, that is no surprise at all. It's been a lot to take in these last couple weeks. Let's get that lump out of there and get you started healing up."

Vivian nodded in agreement. That sounded like the best idea she'd heard in days.

The anaesthesiologist placed the mask over her face. "Slow, deep breaths, Vivian." His voice was soothing. It sounded so familiar. Like Thomas. As her eyes closed, Thomas was there. She saw him reach out to her.

"It's okay, Viv. You will be okay. It's not time for you yet."

He stroked her cheek with his thumb.

"Thomas, I am so scared. I'm trying to hide it from the children, but I am. I'm scared." She wrapped her arms around him and pressed her cheek to his chest.

"Oh, my darling. I promise. You are strong. This is not your time." He kissed the top of her head, and she looked up at him. "I love you so much."

"I love you too, Thomas. I've missed you."

"I know. I've missed you too, but you have a lot more time and a lot more to do. I will be waiting for you, Viv. I will always be here." He leaned down and softly kissed her lips. The light became so bright it hurt her eyes, and she had to turn away.

When she looked back, he was gone, and her heart lurched in her chest. The agony of losing him was back, but she knew that pain meant she was alive, and that was a good thing.

"Mrs. Cooper, can you hear me?" A nurse was gently touching Vivian's shoulder, trying to rouse her. "Oh good," she said as Vivian's eyes opened slightly. "Let me get you some water."

She placed a straw in Vivian's mouth, and she took a small sip.

"I will go get the doctor for you, and he can let you know how it all went."

Dr. Spiers looked very pleased to see Vivian sitting up in her bed. "The surgery went very well. When we took out the lump, it was clear from the shape and colouring it was malignant. We sent it for testing, of course, to confirm, and it came back indicating what we suspected. What that also means is that to be safest, we had to take your whole breast, Vivian. I'm so sorry."

He sat on the side of the bed and put his hand on her arm, knowing the shock he had just delivered. "We also took some lymph nodes from your armpit as an extra precaution." He gestured to his own armpit to illustrate the point he was trying to make. "We have you bandaged up pretty tightly to control the swelling and drainage." She had begun to shift as she became more aware of how her body was feeling. "How is your pain?"

"I think it's okay."

"I've given the nurses a prescription, so if you have any pain at all, you let them know. It's best that you be as comfortable as you can for the first few days so your body can start to heal properly. We should have the results back from the lab soon on the lymph nodes and more details on the actual tumour itself. Once we do, we can talk about what other treatment, if any, we need to do next. Okay?"

Vivian nodded and reached for the water. He held it for her as she took a bigger sip than last time.

"Good. I'm going to go see your family now and let them know you've woken up and are doing well. We have a room waiting for you, and as soon as the recovery nurses think you're ready, they will get you moved up there, and you can get some more rest." He patted her arm and walked out in search of her family.

She knew they would be worried. If they had taken her breast, that meant the surgery had gone longer, and they would know what that meant. Dr. Spiers had prepared them for that. Hopefully, she was prepared for whatever would come next. For the time being, she needed a little more sleep.

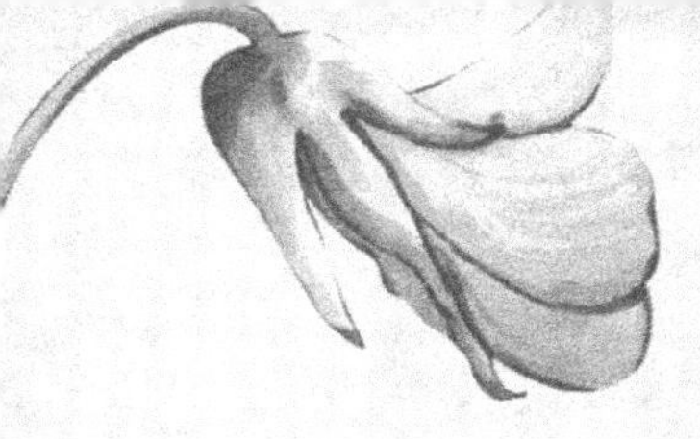

Chapter Thirty-Seven

It was Vivian's turn to host the ladies for their monthly card night. She found so much pleasure in those gatherings. Planning what she would make was something she looked forward to. Knowing she was selecting foods and treats for her friends that each of them wouldn't buy for themselves was a silly decadence they indulged on behalf of each other each month.

It had been a rough few months for Vivian and her family and she was looking forward to a lovely evening with her friends as a well-deserved break from all the stress she had been facing. Her diagnosis of breast cancer had been terrifying. Thankfully, the prognosis was excellent. She had finished her treatment which had only been radiation and no chemotherapy.

Her cancer scare was a wakeup call for Vivian. She realised there were a lot of things she still hadn't done and wanted to. After looking at her investments, Vivian decided she could afford to retire. Now she could travel with her friends and spend more time with her family. Life was too short.

Vivian was cutting up cheese to put out on her platter when Joy arrived, early as always. They enjoyed having a

pre-visit visit. Joy started putting out the trays and small side plates. Vivian enjoyed hosting because it gave her an opportunity to use her "nice things," as she was fond of saying. The dishes were one of the few items she had brought from England when she and Thomas came over.

She and Joy had both recently retired, and that night's card game was going to be a bit of a celebration for them as well. Judy had made her famous carrot cake with cream cheese icing for Vivian and her friends to enjoy. As she and Joy nibbled on some cheese and crackers before the other ladies arrived, Joy's eyes were bright with excitement.

"What if we go on a holiday to properly celebrate being retired?" Her voice was full of exuberant expectation.

"What did you have in mind?" Vivian was immediately intrigued.

"Well, Audrey retired to Spain last year. What if we go visit her for a few weeks? Her last few letters have begged us to come, and she says she has plenty of room for us."

The idea of going on holiday with Joy and her friends sounded like the makings of a grand adventure to Vivian. "I think that sounds like a great idea. Let's give her a call and find out what dates work for us to visit. How long do you want to go for?"

"Well, we are retired. We can go for as long as we want!" Joy shrieked a little bit.

"Well, let's see how long she's willing to host us then." They had no plans set, yet Vivian knew it would be a holiday to remember and cherish forever.

"Tell Judy she makes the absolute best carrot cake, Viv. Honestly! My mouth waters every time I think about it." Kathy meant it too. She had helped herself to three pieces and not small ones.

The ladies she spent time together and never cared about the pretence of worrying about their weight or the weight of the opinions of others. Ellen was equally as comfortable enjoying the sharp cheddar Vivian always made sure she had for her. It wasn't about showing off and having fancy things for each other when they hosted. It was about enjoying each other's company. Having said that, leftovers, if there were any, were always sent in containers with the more than willing guests.

"How are you feeling these days, Viv?" Kathy asked. "You certainly look well. You are already tanned!"

"I am feeling really well, Kathy. I was very lucky to not have chemo. I met a lot of people while I was getting treatments who had to get both. They almost all lost their hair. The chemo made them very sick and weak, too."

"It is a plague." Joy chimed in. "We are so grateful everything turned out so positive for you, Viv." She gave her friend a small side hug.

"I am grateful, too." Vivian smiled at her friends. "I am going to make another pot of tea." It wasn't that Vivian was uncomfortable talking about her cancer, she just felt that it was not worth talking about anymore. Talking about it gave it life and she didn't want it to live anymore. She was happy to commit murder on the cancer that tried to kill her.

"Tell us more about how it feels to be newly retired, you two." Paula sat back on the floor beside the coffee table. She always preferred to sit on the floor and somehow always looked so elegant doing so.

"Interesting you should ask, Paula. You might all be interested in our plan," Joy remarked.

Everyone looked at each other in anticipation.

"Viv and I were chatting earlier about seeing if Audrey might like to host us for a few weeks. She keeps asking us to come to Spain. Now we have the time, and it could be a celebration of our retirements and Vivian beating her cancer." she said.

"Oh, I'm definitely interested in coming. When will you know?" Paula sat up straight, and Ellen and Kathy nodded in agreement with mouths full of cake and cheese.

"Oh, girls! It would be so much fun if we all went." Joy

was excited to hear how the plan was growing.

"Does anyone know anything about the area Audrey lives in? What's there?" Ellen came back to the couch with her wine glass refilled and sat beside Kathy.

"I guess we'll need to do some research," Vivian suggested. "I have a CAA membership. I can get some travel brochures and information."

"If we each pick one thing we want to do or see, that would be a lot, and it would be a great trip," Joy suggested.

"That's very true, Joy. I'm sure we would have some things that we all want to do as well, so that would make it easier." Kathy added to Joy's idea.

"Vivian will need a beach or someplace with water." Ellen laughed, and everyone very quickly agreed, including Vivian.

"That's very true." She grinned. "I've heard that some of the most beautiful beaches in the world are in Spain."

"What time is it in Spain now?" Kathy wanted to start officially planning the trip.

"Far too early to be calling Audrey." After checking her watch, Vivian quickly calculated the six-hour difference. "Why don't we meet here tomorrow at eleven o'clock and call her then?"

"That should be the perfect time to call. Audrey will most likely be home for her own supper by then. Oh, Viv! Won't this be grand?!" exclaimed Joy.

Love Always

Chapter Thirty-Eight

The heat of the sun felt glorious on their faces as they stepped out of the airport in Alicante.

"Girls!" they heard a familiar voice shouting.

"Audrey!" they all shouted back as they saw their friend come running towards them. They smothered her in a group hug, laughing and talking a mile a minute.

"Goodness, it's so lovely to see you all."

Tears shimmered in their eyes from the happiness of seeing each other. It had been over a year since they'd last gotten together. Audrey had decided to move to Spain permanently when she retired. Some of her family from England had vacation homes there, and after using one for a month, she took the plunge and relocated. Her friends had been a bit shocked, of course, since it was such a big move and meant leaving everything, she'd established in Aurora and starting over.

"Let's get to the car and home so you can all freshen up," she said.

Audrey had borrowed her brother's station wagon. He had a big family who visited often and needed a large car to accommodate them. With the windows rolled down

and the radio playing, the reunited friends sang and laughed. Periodically, one of them would shout and point to something they passed like a church, the white houses, the orange trees, or the ocean. It was all so exciting and beautiful.

Audrey expertly navigated the narrow roads. At times, it seemed a single car would not make it through, but somehow, they did, much to the delight and amazement of the ladies in the car.

"How long does it take to get to your place, Audrey?" Paula asked.

"Only another twenty minutes, Paula. I'm so glad you decided to come. We were worried you wouldn't after everything." Several months earlier, Paula had gone through a very traumatic event. A man she went out with just twice started stalking her. She could sense there was something wrong with him and politely told him she wasn't interested in going out again. *My gut told me to stay away.* He found out that she called the police to lay a complaint after he kept calling her and showing up at her house and work. That's when he came to her house and forced his way in. She couldn't remember much after that except that *her girls* came to her rescue. They had come to pick Paula up for the movies. Her screams for help set them in motion. Without thinking, they ran into the house and according to Frank, the attacker, they all jumped on him and started hitting him. The arrival of her friends had kept her physical injuries from being too severe. The emotional toll was far deeper and would take more time. That's why her friends had been so pleased she decided to join them.

"I realised something after he beat me up." She looked at her friends and grinned. "I don't need a man to be happy. I have the greatest friends in the world. Will I find someone? Maybe. But it's not the priority it once was."

"Atta girl!" they all cheered so loud that people on the street stopped and turned to see what was happening in the car full of women with large floppy hats, sunglasses, and enormous smiles.

Vivian turned up the radio, and they all began singing along with *Girls Just Want to Have Fun*. It was perfect timing.

"You don't have as much on your itinerary as I thought you might," Audrey said as they sat out on the patio, enjoying the sun and some wine.

"Well, we wanted to do a lot of the same things." Ellen observed

It was true. When they had each shared the places they wanted to go, they all had similar lists. Kathy wanted to go to an orange grove and get fresh oranges. Ellen wanted to visit the Gothic Quarter in Barcelona. Joy wanted to do a sailing trip of some sort, and Vivian wanted to see the natural pools. They all had a wine tour and beaches on their lists, and since they had twenty-four days, there would be plenty of time to do everything they wanted.

"A couple of days to just rest and relax is the perfect start. We need to catch up." Audrey had not realised just how much she missed her friends. Her villa was a short walk to an unbelievably beautiful beach. The first few days were spent having a leisurely breakfast of coffee and tomatoes on toast or pastries before packing a lunch of empanadas, wine, and fruit and setting off to their favourite spot on the beach.

"I understand why you decided to stay, Audrey." Joy was leaning back on a chair, admiring the views around them. The ruggedness of the rocks and the colour of the water kept taking her breath away.

"You can always stay, too." She laughed, knowing none of them would. Their families were too important to them, and most of Audrey's were either there in Spain or still in England.

"Maybe we can visit more often." Joy offered.

"You are always welcome." Her friends beamed large, happy smiles at each other. "Where is Viv? Would she like some lunch or at least a snack?" Audrey covered her eyes and peered out at the water, trying to see her friend.

"Happily floating in the sea." Kathy said, pointing to the water.

They all laughed together. There were few places that made Vivian as happy as being in the water. She would float contentedly for hours if she could. It was so warm, and the beach was not particularly busy since they weren't in a touristy area. Most of the people were residents.

From her place in the water, Viv could see the girls spreading out a blanket to set up lunch, and she realised she was a bit peckish. Making her way to shore, the hot sand stuck to her feet and helped motivate her to move more hastily to the blankets they were sharing.

"Aren't you all pruney yet from being in the water, Viv?" teased Ellen.

"Oh definitely!" Vivian giggled. "But I don't care. I'll wrinkle up like a prune and still want to stay in the water. It's so warm and salty. I float so easily!"

"We're all looking forward to going to Les Fonts de l'Algar tomorrow." Ellen said as she put on more baby oil to help her tan.

"Oh, so am I. The pictures are so beautiful. I hope we're not disappointed. It is a bit of a hike, and I know not everyone enjoys that part, so I appreciate that you're all playing along." Taking a bite out of an empanada, Vivian leaned back on one arm, her legs stretched out as she gazed at the view. She held up her wine glass and with her best high-English accent said, "I wonder what the poor people are doing today."

They all clinked their glasses.

The heat made the hike to Les Fonts de l'Algar a bit challenging, but there were several spots where the trees and plants offered shade and cooled them down.

"The path is well marked. I wasn't sure how we would know where to go." Joy had been a bit nervous to go on the outing but didn't want to tell the others and ruin their fun. The landscape was quite rugged, but the path was clear and well maintained. There were even railings in some places.

They had stopped a few times to take photos, but what they

saw as they came around the bend to the opening to the water left them speechless. There were several waterfalls that spilled into turquoise pools. The vegetation was lush and thick and added to the privacy and beauty.

"Oh, Viv! You made a particularly good pick." Awestruck, Joy gave Vivian a side hug and started making her way toward the edge of the water. The rocky landscape reminded Vivian of the granite outcrops at the cottage.

Putting down their bags and towels, they all carefully made their way into the water. It was very cool and fresh.

"There has been some talk of protecting the area better." Audrey shared. She was almost a bonafide local now and had learned that many locals were against the tourism and resulting destruction.

"Well, I hate to think we're damaging anything, but I'm really happy we got to see it." Ellen was sitting on the rocks at the edge of the pool with her feet in the water.

The trip to the pools had been an enormous success. Everyone was tired from the day in the sun and the chilly water, but Kathy wanted to go back to one of the little canteens where there was live music. A short siesta seemed like the best solution to ensure they all had the energy to sing and dance and try and keep up with Kathy.

As they freshened up after their rest, Vivian laid out two outfits, unsure which one to choose. "What do you think, Joy? The green or the orange?"

"Oh, the green one. It makes your eyes even more gorgeous. The green almost comes alive when you wear it." Like everyone who met Vivian, Joy was always taken aback by her eyes.

"Green it is!"

The warm Spanish sun kissed their skin, and Vivian and her friends revelled in the joy of their holiday. Two weeks in, the signs of their enjoyment were evident—laughter lines etched around their eyes and skin glowing with a golden-bronze hue. Vivian, in particular, seemed to have flourished under the Mediterranean rays, her complexion ironically reminiscent of the Spanish ancestry her mother often spoke of.

They had decided to go back to a lively cantina they had visited a few times already. The vibrant sounds of music and laughter drifted through the air. Arm in arm, they chattered excitedly about the day's adventures, the breathtaking views, and the unforgettable experiences they'd shared thus far.

As they drew closer to the cantina, the pulsating rhythm of Spanish music infused them with energy. Without hesitation, Kathy, the most adventurous of their little group, broke into a spontaneous dance, her movements fluid and captivating. Laughing and joining in, Vivian and the others followed suit, their spirits lifted by the infectious atmosphere surrounding them.

Amidst the swirl of music and laughter, Vivian's eyes fell upon a figure standing near the bar. He was well over six feet tall, with broad shoulders and thick, wavy white hair. His gaze was fixed upon her. Her heart skipped a beat as she recognized him immediately. Aaron.

Shock mingled with elation as Vivian's gaze locked with his, their eyes meeting across the bustling restaurant. For a moment, time seemed to stand still as memories of their past together flooded her mind. Despite the passage of years, Vivian felt the bond they had shared return.

With a smile tugging at her lips, she broke away from her friends, her steps guided by an instinct she couldn't quite explain. Ignoring the curious glances of her companions, she made her way towards Aaron, her heart pounding with anticipation.

As she approached, Aaron's expression softened into a warm smile, and Vivian felt a rush of emotions flood her. In that moment, surrounded by the vibrant energy of the Spanish night, she knew their unexpected reunion held the promise of something truly special—to reconnect with her past and her youth.

"Viv!" He easily picked her up and spun her around. They embraced and held each other tightly as though it were a dream, and neither of them were real. "What are you doing here? I thought you had moved to Canada."

"I did. I still live there. I'm on holiday with some of my friends." She pointed to her girlfriends who had gathered together and were intently watching their every move. They all waved frantically and laughed.

"Who the bloody hell is that?" Ellen asked without taking her eyes off Vivian and the handsome man she was speaking with.

"Not a clue, but he certainly knows her, doesn't he?" Joy remarked. "I wish I did. Really though, are any of us surprised that Vivian would run into someone she knows all the way here in Spain?"

"Very true." Ellen waved her hand in the air to emphasise her words.

Vivian was someone who other people noticed. She just had an easy beauty that drew people to her, but then her kindness and the way she made everyone feel comfortable and safe around her made folks want to know her. It was rare they went anywhere and didn't run into someone who knew Vivian. It was also rare that the person was so obviously in love with her.

"Can I get you a drink, Viv?" Aaron steered her towards the bar. "What are you having?"

"Please." She nodded. "Wine. I think they called it Rioja."

Aaron motioned to the bartender and paid for the drinks. "Can we go sit and catch up a little bit?" He hoped his earnestness wasn't obvious.

"I'd love that. Let me just go let my friends know so they don't get worried."

"Here she comes. Be cool!" hushed Kathy as they noticed Vivian walking back over to them. "Oh, my goodness, Vivian! Who is that?" She couldn't contain herself, and the others laughed at her.

"Wow, Kath, way to stay calm and collected," Ellen joked.

"Oh, girls! You will never believe it." She looked back over at Aaron and smiled. "That's Aaron. I grew up with him in Tottenham."

"Whoa! Wait! What?" exclaimed Joy. "*That* is Aaron?"

"You know about him?" Audrey asked.

"I don't know much. I just know that Viv was engaged when she met Thomas and broke it off for him."

"Engaged! Vivian!" Audrey almost spit out her wine.

"I'm going to go sit with Aaron and catch up." Vivian was glowing. "Is that okay? Do you girls mind?"

"Oh, my goodness, Vivian! Of course not. We do expect a full report tomorrow, though." Kathy hugged her.

"You know the address to get back to my place, right?" Audrey confirmed.

"Yes, Audrey. Thanks, girls. I cannot believe we ran into each other this way." She practically ran back over to Aaron, and her friends watched as he put his arm around her, and they walked off to a private table at the back side of the bar.

"Well, Joy, it certainly seems like Aaron has never recovered from Vivian."

"Ellen, I think you are correct. I don't think I've ever had someone look at me like he's looking at her right now."

"Do you think she realises?" Paula interjected.

"Probably not. Vivian really has no idea the effect she has on people," Joy said, and they all nodded in agreement.

"Aaron, I still can't believe it's you. After all this time." There was a true comfort in seeing him again.

"It's such an amazing coincidence that we would be here at the same time like this. What brought you to this part of Spain?"

"Our friend Audrey retired here. She's actually from Bristol originally, and a lot of her family also retired here." Pointing to Audrey across the room, the ladies smiled and waved, clustered together, not even attempting to hide the fact they were intently watching the couple.

"Well, that seems like fate, doesn't it, Vivvy?" He smiled, laughed, and waved back at the ladies.

Vivian was caught off guard with the use of her nickname. There were only two people who had ever called her that, Aaron and her brother Bryant.

He noticed the flicker in her eyes when he said her name. "How long are you here for?"

"We've already been here two weeks and have one more left. We're going on a wine tour tomorrow. How long are you here for?"

"I also retired here. I have a villa not far away. It's near the beach. You know how I love the water." They had always shared that and used to speak of moving to a coastal town or village when they were married, after the war.

"You're so lucky to have such a beautiful retirement spot. I spend my summers at our cottage on a small lake. You would love it."

"I'm sure I would. I've seen pictures of some of the lakes in Ontario."

Nodding, she ignored the obvious details he seemed to know about her life. "Ontario is an incredibly beautiful province. I haven't travelled around Canada too much yet. The girls and I are planning a trip east again this summer for a few weeks. We went to Prince Edward Island two summers ago for a week. This year will be Nova Scotia and New Brunswick. We decided to drive and make the most of the places we stop, enjoying things along the way. Quebec City is beautiful as well."

"Parles-tu toujours parfaitement le français?"

"Pas parfait, mais suffisant pour s'en sortir." Her accent was impeccable, and he grinned.

"I will be going back to England in a couple days for my niece's wedding. So, it is very good luck we ran into each other tonight."

"It is so funny we haven't run into each other before tonight. We've come here a few times," Viv informed him.

"I don't come out often. My brother and his wife wanted to

have dinner out before they go back tomorrow. It's their daughter Alison who is getting married, and they need to be back to help with the arrangements."

"Where are they now?"

"They went back to the house after dinner. I had the good fortune of deciding to stop in here for a short drink." They fell into an easy conversation about Spain and travelling.

"You haven't asked me what you really want to know," Aaron remarked, his voice soft yet filled with meaning. He leaned back in his chair, his demeanour relaxed as he motioned for another glass of wine.

Vivian furrowed her brow in confusion. "What do you mean?" she asked, her curiosity piqued.

Aaron gazed at her. "About whether I married, had a family, and all of that," he explained, his tone gentle yet tinged with vulnerability.

A pang of regret pierced Vivian's heart. She hadn't thought to ask about such important aspects of Aaron's life. "I assumed you had, of course," she replied softly, a hint of remorse colouring her words. "I always wanted the best for you, for you to be happy." Eyes locked, the energy between them shifted. They both felt it.

"Oh, Vivvy, you are a dear. I did marry for a time. We never had children. Her name was Vanessa."

"She passed away?"

"Yes. She had a stroke and died almost instantly. Merciful really." His brows furrowed together. "We were only married for three years, and I never married again. I decided to just be a great uncle instead and focus on work."

"I'm so sorry for your loss, Aaron. That must have been terrible. I lost Thomas almost twelve years ago to cancer. It was already too far gone when they discovered it, and he died within a month."

He reached out and took her hand in comfort. He could see how much it still hurt her and wanted to ease her sadness. "I'm very sorry for your loss, too." They sat quietly for a moment. "Do you have someone now, Vivvy?"

"Oh heavens no. I'm like you. I decided to focus on my family. I got a job, my licence, and these girls." Motioning to her friends with her hand, she looked over at them and felt such a fullness seeing them. What a blessing they had been to her.

"It's clear that you are all very close." His hand shifted on hers to envelope it as he leaned forward. "I know it's a crazy thing to say after all this time but seeing you … I never stopped loving you."

Vivian couldn't believe what she was hearing. "Aaron, I honestly don't know what to say."

"I know you don't feel the same way. I'm not so foolish as to think we would be able to just step back into a life together. I just wanted you to know."

Vivian was surprised by the sadness she felt at his words. He was right, of course.

"Will I be able to see you again before you leave, Vivvy?" He studied her as he deliberately used the name again. He wanted to see if it reminded her of their connection the way he hoped it would.

"Aaron, I—"

He squeezed her hand, stood, and came around to her side of the table, not letting go of her. She stood to meet him.

"Vivvy, it's okay." He smiled and touched her cheek. Tenderly, he cupped her chin and kissed her soft, full lips.

Her lashes fluttered closed, and she held her breath. For that moment, they were both lost to a memory of another day when she said goodbye to him.

He pressed his forehead to hers and sighed deeply. "I will never stop loving you with my entire being, Vivvy, and I will never stop wanting the very best for you." He led her back to her friends, fingers laced together. "I hope you all enjoy the rest of your holiday."

He then kissed her forehead, touched her cheek with his thumb one last time, and walked away.

After Aaron left, her friends tried to find out more, but Vivian didn't share much. They were left disappointed but knew there was much more to it all than Vivian cared to admit. She didn't see him again, and they enjoyed the rest of their trip. Audrey made them all promise to return the next winter. They had already planned some excursions for their next visit.

The airport was busy when they arrived. Kathy had insisted they come three hours early just in case there were any delays getting through security.

"Perhaps someone will be here waiting for you, Viv," Audrey suggested with a strong hug.

"I'm afraid that ship has sailed, Audrey, and I think it's best if you don't interfere."

"If that's what you truly want, I won't interfere. I promise." Audrey was not convinced Vivian should just close the door to something with so much promise, but she would honour her friend's request.

With tears in their eyes, they gave final farewell hugs to Audrey and passed through the gate to return home.

342

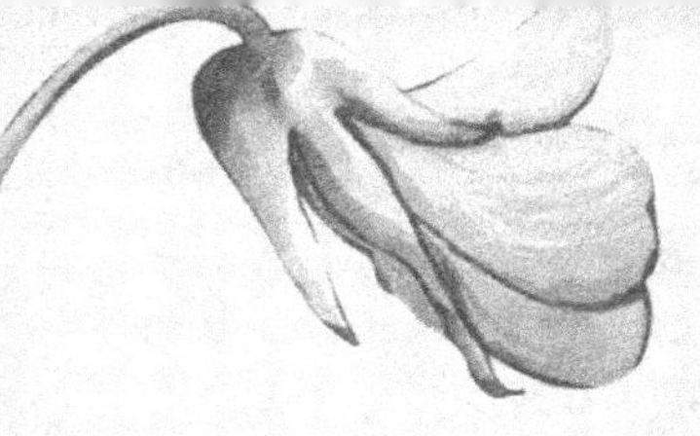

Chapter Thirty-Nine

As the sun dipped below the horizon, casting a warm glow over the tranquil lake, Vivian sat on the deck of their cottage, a cup of tea cradled in her hands. The evening sky was ablaze with hues of orange and pink, a breathtaking backdrop to the peaceful scene unfolding before her.

In the distance, Vivian could hear the familiar hum of a small boat engine, signalling Charleigh's return from her summer job at the marina. A sense of pride swelled within her as she watched her granddaughter navigate the waters with confidence.

As Charleigh docked the boat and made her way up to the cottage, Vivian greeted her with a warm smile, her heart overflowing with love. "How was work?" She lifted her face, and Charleigh leaned down to kiss her nan's warm cheek.

"It was good. Terribly busy with people heading home, of course." Sundays were always busy at the marina. Most of the lake was water access, and the marina was the necessary central hub for anyone coming up who didn't have road access. "What do you want for dinner, Nan?"

"How about just spaghetti and meatballs?" Vivian suggested. "Your mom left us some of her homemade ones."

"Ooo! That is a very good idea." Diane's meatballs were delicious and highly coveted. She often made them in big batches so she could leave some for Charleigh and her grandmother.

Together, they prepared dinner, their laughter filling the air as they reminisced about summers of the past and eagerly discussed Charleigh's upcoming journey to university.

"I'm really excited for the journalism classes." Charleigh had always wanted to be a writer. She'd been writing the column for her high school in the local paper for the last three years. She planned to become a photojournalist for *Equinox* magazine, travel the world, and save it.

"When do you and your mom leave?"

"Two weeks! I'm not sure how we will fit everything into the car." They chuckled. Diane's friend was renting Charleigh a room in her basement. They would spend a couple days visiting with her friend and getting Charleigh settled.

After dinner, they retreated to the deck, their cups of tea in hand. The night was alive with the soothing symphony of chirping tree frogs and the rustle of leaves in the breeze, a symphony of nature.

"Charleigh, I know you know how proud of you I am. You have worked so hard, and it has paid off." Vivian felt a lump in her throat and swallowed hard. Her words were like a warm blanket for Charleigh.

"I do know, Nan." She gave her grandmother a hug and stayed leaning against her on the bench on the deck.

"I have something for you." Vivian shifted slightly to pull an envelope out from behind her. She handed it to Charleigh, who sat back up and excitedly took it. Carefully opening it, she pulled out a card. It had a delicate violet pressed onto it and the word *Home* written underneath in elegant handwriting.

"Oh, Nan!" Charleigh cried, tears immediately flooding her eyes and spilling down her cheeks. "It's lovely."

"There's a little story that goes with it." Vivian told her

granddaughter the tale of how she had found the card on the floor of the train when she was going on holiday with her girlfriends all those years ago and how it had in fact belonged to Thomas. She told Charleigh how she kept it for years and gave it to Thomas when he went off to war and how he kept his promise to bring it back safely to her. "I want you to take it with you to school, as a reminder that you can always come back home, that you always have a place with me no matter what happens or where you end up."

"Thank you, Nanny. I promise to bring it back safely too." In that moment, surrounded by the sound of the waves softly cresting against the shore and the wisping of wind, Charleigh felt the enormous love and respect she had for her Nan overflow. They had always had an unshakable bond, far beyond grandparent and grandchild. The future was bright, and both of them were excited to see what it would bring for Charleigh.

346

Chapter Forty

It had been growing more difficult for Vivian to manage her house and property. The laundry was in the basement and the stairs were hard for her. She had slipped and fallen twice. The whole family was relieved when Vivian decided to move to an apartment building designed for seniors in Newmarket. Charleigh visited almost every week when she was in the area for her work. She was in sales and Newmarket was part of her territory.

Charleigh always stopped at the bakery and bought two brandy snaps and a custard Danish. The former were for Charleigh and Aunt Judy who was often able to pop over while Charleigh was there. The Danish was Nan's favourite. Vivian made them a cup of tea and they would sit and enjoy their treats together and catch up or talk about the craziness of world events. The visits were never long enough, but they both looked forward to them every week.

It was Charleigh's habit to call and let Vivian know she had arrived safely home. She lived about forty-five minutes away near Barrie. When Charleigh made her
call, her Nan didn't answer. Something unsettling rose in her stomach. *She might be using the bathroom, relax.* She

thought to herself, waited a few minutes, and tried again. There was still no answer. Charleigh decided to call Judy.

"Hi Jude, It's Charleigh. I just called Nan to let her know I got home safe, but she didn't answer the phone."

"She doesn't have any of her activities today. She might just be in the bathroom." Judy suggested.

"I thought of that. I waited and then called back." She paused. "I know it isn't super convenient, but can you run over and just put my mind at rest? I am sure I am just being silly."

"I was planning to pop over to get my treat later anyway. I will just go now instead. I will call you and let you know everything is ok."

"Thanks, Jude. I just get worried."

"I know Char, me too. I'll call you shortly."

Charleigh was distracting herself making dinner when the phone rang. "Hello?"

"Char, it's Judy. I am with Nan now. She fell and it looks like she broke her hip."

"Oh no!"

"The paramedics are with her. They are taking her to the hospital. I will call you when I know more."

"Thanks for checking on her. Tell her I love her, and I will come down tomorrow."

"I will. Char," Judy paused.

"Yes?"

"Never doubt your gut. Thanks for getting me to go over early."

"Thanks, Judy." They hung up and Charleigh let out a big breath. Thank goodness her nan would be ok now.

Vivian had come home from the hospital after her hip surgery and Charleigh had planned her day so that she could check on her early enough to make sure she had breakfast, and then stay long enough to make sure her lunch was ready before she left. She tried the key once more, hoping that it would magically work this time. *I really need to get a new key.* When it didn't, she buzzed her grandmother's apartment. It rang twice and she heard her nan pick it up.

"Hi, Nan. It's Charleigh. My key isn't working again." she called out through the speaker in the lobby.

Her grandmother mumbled something and hung up. She didn't open the door. Charleigh's radar was immediately set off and she rang up to the apartment again. "Hi, Nan. It's ..." The phone clicked off.

Glancing around the lobby for any sign of a neighbour, Charleigh started knocking on the glass door to try and get someone to open it for her. She knew that the residents in the building were friendly and often helped each other out, but now, in the early afternoon, it seemed deserted. Her heart pounded louder with each passing second.

Finally, the glass door swung open, and a tenant she recognized stepped out.

"Charleigh, right?" the woman asked with a warm smile. "Here to see Vivian?"

"Yes, thank you," Charleigh replied, relief washing over her. She slipped inside the lobby, offering the woman a grateful nod.

"She's a tough lady, your grandmother. I'm sure she'll bounce back from the hip surgery soon," the tenant said as she exited.

Charleigh forced a smile and nodded, but her gut told her otherwise. She hurried to the elevator, her steps quickening with each stride. As she waited for the elevator, a support worker, in a sloppy uniform and unkept hair approached her.

"You Charleigh?" the woman asked, her tone brusque.

"Yes," Charleigh replied, impatient to get to her grandmother.

"Look, your grandmother isn't making an effort. If she can't even dress herself, we might have to look into other arrangements."

Charleigh felt anger flare up inside her. "I'll handle it," she snapped, stepping into the elevator as soon as the doors opened. She hit the button for the fourth floor repeatedly, willing it to go faster.

The doors opened, and Charleigh walked quickly, her heart racing. She reached the door of her grandmother's apartment. Thankfully, her key worked without issue.

"Nan?" she called, stepping inside.

Vivian was in her usual chair in front of the TV. She turned and looked at Charleigh. "Oh, hi dear. How are you?"

"I'm good, Nan. I couldn't get the door to open. Did you have trouble from this end, too?" She approached her grandmother and leaned down to kiss her cheek.

When Vivian spoke next, the words did not come out properly. They were random and mixed together. She looked confused and seemed to understand that her words were not matching what she was trying to say.

Charleigh knew there was something very wrong and suspected it was a stroke. Not wanting to upset or scare her grandmother, she made an excuse to leave the room.

"I forgot something in my car, Nan. I will be right back. I will get us a tea and our treat when I get back. Just wait there, ok?" She kneeled in front of her grandmother and tried to see that she understood what she was saying. Vivian nodded.

In the hallway, Charleigh took out her cell phone and called 911. "I think my grandmother has had a stroke. She can't speak properly and seems very confused." The operator took the address and some other information and told her to make sure someone could let the paramedics into the building when they arrived. Rushing back down to the lobby, Charleigh went to the office on the main floor and knocked on the door.

"Oh, it's you. Your grandmother ..." the worker started to speak, and Charleigh cut her off.

"Claire, right? What time did you go to help my grandmother?"

"Yes. Why?"

"I asked you a question." Charleigh was trying her best to stay calm but it was getting more difficult with each passing moment. "What time?!"

"About eight."

"It is ten now. Claire, it is ten now! My grandmother had a stroke. That's why she couldn't help you get her dressed. That's why she can't speak properly now, Claire."

"I, uh, I ..." Claire blinked and gaped at Charleigh.

"Yah, so if it isn't too much to ask, let the paramedics in when they arrive. I am going to go back up and be with my nan now." She started to walk away. "Oh, and Claire, I would consider what you might like to do besides this for work. Your incompetence, rudeness, and lack of compassion are not a good match for this job."

As she was walking back to the elevator, Charleigh called Judy, "Hi, it's Char. I am at Nan's."

"Oh hey. That's great. I am sure she is happy to see you. How is she doing?" Judy's cheerful voice flowed through the phone to Charleigh.

"Um, not good, Judy. I have called an ambulance. I think she had a stroke. She is not able to form her words properly."

"I'm on my way." Judy didn't need to know anything else right now. She needed to get to her mother.

The paramedics had arrived and were assessing Vivian when Judy arrived. She rushed over to her mother. "Mum!" She took her hand and kissed her cheek. "Are you ok?"

"Yes, dear. I am fine." Vivian's answer was clear, and she sounded very alert. Charleigh and Judy looked at each other. Judy was confused. "I'm going to put the kettle on, Mum. Be right back." She and Charleigh went into the kitchen to speak.

"She seems ok."

"I know." Charleigh whispered back. "It is very odd. Some things come easily, and then other things are completely missing. I think it is better to be safe than sorry."

"Absolutely." Judy nodded and hugged her niece. "Thanks for calling me, Char."

They went back into the living room where the paramedics were still assessing Vivian. "Who is this lady, Vivian?" The lead paramedic was a gentle spoken woman who looked to be in her early thirties.

"That's my granddaughter Charleigh." Vivian smiled at Charleigh who came over and held her hand.

"And who is this lady?"

Vivian looked at Judy and answered, "That's my friend Mary." The look on Judy's face told the paramedic that she was not Mary. Judy went to correct her, and the paramedic put up a hand.

"It's important you not lead her or give her any pieces of answers. That way we can determine what we might be dealing with better." The young woman turned to her partner. "Let's prepare for transport." He nodded and started organising the gurney Vivian was sitting on, tightening straps and making sure she was secure.

Stepping away from Vivian, she confirmed to Judy and Charleigh that it looked as though Vivian had had a stroke. "It is hard to say how serious, but they will run tests at the hospital to figure that out." She tried to sound sympathetic, it was hard to keep your emotions in check all the time.

"Okay." Judy turned back to her mother. "Mummy, the paramedics are going to run you over to the hospital to get you checked out. Charleigh and I will be right behind you. Okay?" Vivian nodded, but neither Judy nor Charleigh were sure what she understood at this point.

"We need to call Jess." Charleigh said to Judy.

"I have the number for her school. She is on a field trip to Medieval Times though so I am not sure how we can reach her. She doesn't have a cell phone."

"I will call the school. They can find a way to reach her."

"Okay. Let's head over to the hospital. We will need to have more information for the rest of the family. Have you called your mum yet?"

Diane's work had recently moved her back to Ontario from Edmonton. Charleigh was grateful she was so close now. Her mother was the rock of the family. Everyone turned to her when they needed help, especially when they needed kind but truthful advice. "I'll call her now." Charleigh dialled her mother's work number. She knew it by heart. "Hi, Mum, I'm with Judy. We are on our way to the hospital with Nan. It looks like she had a stroke."

"I'm on my way." Diane responded and then asked, "Are you okay?"

"I am right now. I need to stay focused for Nan." Charleigh answered truthfully.

"Okay, hun. I will be there as soon as I can." They hung up and Judy handed Charleigh the number for Jess' school.

"Good morning, Rogers Public School. How can I help you?" The voice on the other end cheerfully answered.

"Hi, my name is Charleigh Smith. Aunt Jess Cable is a teacher there. She is on a field trip with her class today and I need to reach her or get a message to her. It is really important." Her voice was calm even though she didn't feel that way.

"Oh, I'm sorry, I am not sure how we could reach her until they get back."

"I know it's difficult, but her mother is on her way to the hospital. We think she had a stroke. We need to get a hold of her somehow."

"Oh wow! Ok, I'm so sorry. Let me get the principal and see if he can help you."

Charleigh spoke to the principal, but he also had no way to reach Jess. "I will meet her at the bus when it arrives back. They should be here by two. I'm sorry, I know that isn't what you need to hear right now." He apologised.

"Unfortunately, there isn't much we can do about it."

Judy and Charleigh found Vivian in the emergency room. She was relieved to see them but still didn't know who Judy was. The nurses and doctors came and went, all asking questions that Vivian was not able to answer properly.

Finally, a doctor came in to give them an update of their findings. "Vivian, I am Dr. Munroe. How are you feeling?" he spoke to her with a kind and patient voice.

"I am not sure." Vivian answered. She was very confused why she was there.

"That's completely reasonable. You have had a stroke, Vivian. We are going to be admitting you for some more tests and to keep an eye on you. Do you have any questions?" He smiled and pat her hand when she shook her head and turned to the girls. "We are getting a room arranged now and they will take her up as soon as it is ready. I understand she just had hip surgery. Do you know what blood thinners they have her on?"

"They discontinued the blood thinners when they discharged her yesterday."

"Yesterday? Well, that isn't very long to have been out of here, Vivian. Do you like it that much?" He joked with Vivian but was concerned by what Judy had said. Normally, the blood thinners were continued for a varied length of time after a major bone surgery to lower the risk of blot clots. "I am going to order a few scans and see if we can determine if there are clots anywhere just for a precaution." He already knew what he would find.

Dr. Munroe left and the three women were left to try and talk but not increase Vivian's stress with her struggle to speak. They had started her on some medications that should help to improve her condition.

"Thank goodness you went to visit Mum this morning. You are two for two, Char."

"I spoke to Claire, one of the workers in Nan's building. She was very rude and unhelpful."

"She's mean." Vivian spoke and the other two women almost jumped; they were so shocked.

"What do you mean?" Judy asked

"She's mean to everyone. She yells at us. Calls us names." Vivian told them.

"Mum, why didn't you say something before? We would have done something."

"Because she's mean." Vivian shrugged. She wanted to say more, but her words were still failing her.

"Well, we know now, and we will do something about it." Judy was fuming inside. How dare someone who works with elderly and vulnerable people be so cruel.

There was a bit of a flurry of noise outside the small emergency room they were waiting in. They heard Jess's voice asking where to find them. She appeared at the door frantic and worried. Judy and Charleigh burst out laughing. She was wearing a mediaeval style ball gown, crown and several fake pearl necklaces.

"The queen!" Judy was still laughing.

Realising the sight she must be in her costume; she broke out laughing as well.

"I must be very sick." Vivian piped up and they all looked at her wondering what she meant. "To be visited by the queen I mean." At first, they were all stunned that she had just made such a witty joke when she had been struggling with her words so much. The combination of the relief that she was showing improvement and the humour of the joke itself caused them all to all erupted into hardy laughter.

356

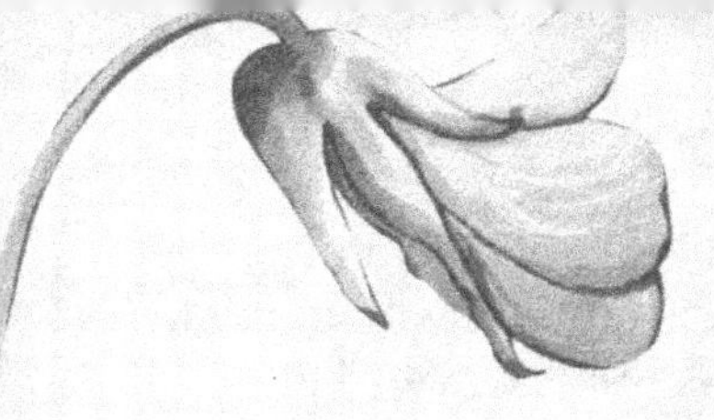

Chapter Forty-One

Vivian was waiting in her room when Charleigh arrived. After her stroke, it had been too hard for Vivian to manage on her own. It was a painful decision, but everyone had agreed it was best for her to move into the retirement home not far from Jess and Judy's homes. They were her primary caregivers, and it made sense to ensure Vivian was as close to them as they could manage.

"Mum, if you are not ready to move, we won't force you, of course. We want you to be happy wherever you are," Jess had said as they finished the tour of the third retirement home.

"You girls always have my best interests at heart. I know that. I think I like the second one the best. They seem to be willing to let me do the most to make the room my own." Vivian could see that her daughters were torn about Vivian moving, and she needed them to know it was time. "I think that at this stage of my life, I have earned being waited on."

"Well, it certainly is a lovely place, and the staff seemed very kind and friendly."

"Let's go back and sign me up, or whatever they call it." Vivian laughed.

Charleigh signed the visitor log and took the elevator up to Vivian's floor. She saw the usual guests out in the main area, watching television or reading a book. She waved hello to two men playing chess. Aside from the odd person talking, the retirement home was very quiet.

"Hi, Nan," Charleigh called as she came over to her grandmother and kissed her cheek and gave her a hug.

"Oh, hello, dear." Vivian hugged her granddaughter back and smiled up at her.

"What have you been doing since I saw you last week, Nan?"

"Not much, dear. They had a fitness thing. We don't really move. We stayed in our chairs, so it seemed a bit pointless to me. We did some crafts. It's all just to keep us busy."

"Well, no one wants to just sit around bored all day, and I bet the fitness is better than you think. Just moving your arms around is good for you to get your heart pumping."

"I guess. They don't really give us a choice, so I try to make the best of it." Vivian shrugged and made a bit of a face.

Charleigh laughed. "What would you like to do today? I can take you out. We could go down to the park or the library."

"I actually wanted to do some spring cleaning and organise these photos. I was thinking it would be nice to give them out to everyone when they come to visit." Vivian pointed at a box beside her bed.

"I'd love to help you with that. Spring is always the best time to clear out the clutter. Let's get you comfortable, and I'll pull them out and make separate piles."

"That would be lovely, dear. Would you go see if we can get some tea?"

"Of course, Nan. I'll be right back. I'll give you a few to start with, okay?" Charleigh placed a few photographs on Vivian's lap for her to look at while she went and fetched them their tea.

Vivian and Charleigh spent the day organising the photos, but listening to Vivian relive the moments in the photos was what made it so special.

"Oh my, look at this! This is me and Joy when we first joined Sweet Adelines. I had no idea back then she would become such a dear and important friend. Never underestimate the value of the women in your life, Charleigh. If it weren't for my girlfriends, I would have been very lost and lonely after Thomas died. They supported and helped me through some of the worst and some of the best moments. I got to live a whole second life." Vivian showed Charleigh photos of them in New York, Hawaii, and Spain.

"Look, Nan. You're so fancy in this picture! Where are you going?"

"That was our first Christmas party after we came to Canada. We were still living in the basement of our house we were building in Willowdale. That's Gloria. She was my first real friend here. She was always so made up." Vivian laughed. "That first winter was terrible. We didn't have running water, and I had to cart it from the neighbour in big jugs. If I had told my mother how we were living, she would have come and got me and dragged me back to England. I never told her any of it."

"That's understandable. She was your mum. She wanted you to be happy but also taken care of."

"She loved it here when she came over to visit. By then, we had the house finished, of course."

"They never thought of coming over permanently?"

"They would have loved to, but they couldn't leave my brother behind. He wouldn't have been allowed over because of his disability. It would be so different now. He might not even be thought of as having much of an issue today." She reached into the box and pulled out some photos. "Look here, this is Bryant." She showed Charleigh several pictures of a young man. "He loved to garden, and he was really quite good at it. During the war, we were in very good shape because of his gardens. This here, this is us at Piccadilly

Square. I went to take care of my mum's affairs after she died. I also went to see him, and we went to the park. He loved to go on adventures, as he called them."

"What happened to Bryant after you left?"

She was silent for a long moment, staring at the photo. "I don't know. I stopped getting letters a long time ago, and no one ever wrote to tell me why." Her fingers ran over the faces in the photo, touching the ghosts in the photo. "He had such lovely handwriting. I should have gone back over and found out where he was when the letters stopped. Maybe I didn't want to know. It feels nice, in a way, to think that your little brother is still tending to a garden somewhere rather than the alternative that he is gone. Don't you think?"

"Oh, Nanny. I am sorry. I hope I didn't upset you."

Vivian touched her granddaughter's hand, still holding the photos of her brother. "Oh, Charleigh, it's okay. There are too many things to remember with a smile than to linger on the ones that hurt." She placed the photos in the pile for Charleigh to keep. "Look at these ones of all the weddings we have had!" She moved away from the older pictures and focused on the ones of her children and grandchildren and, and even more recently, great-grandchildren.

"We may need a larger box for your mom," Vivian teased. "Three marriages and not one decent choice in the lot."

"Nan!" Charleigh roared with laughter. "I thought you liked Roy." Diane's third husband Roy had not won any praise when she moved to Vancouver and then Edmonton with him before they came back to Ontario.

"I would never hurt your mom, nor should you, but Roy is a lazy man, and he has managed to do very well at doing nothing. It's catching up with him, and your poor mom will be left holding the bag again."

"Do you think Roy will leave and go back out west?"

"No, and not because he loves your mom but because he would have nothing if he moved back. He likes having nice things, even when he doesn't earn them."

Charleigh knew her Nan was right. She loved her mother,

but Diane had terrible taste in men. Her uncle John had told her once that if Diane was in a room with a million wonderful men and one bum, she would find the bum.

"Let's stretch our legs a little and get some more tea." Vivian needed a break from the photos.

She pulled her walker over, and they took a stroll down to the main area and sat at a table. One of the caregivers came over and asked if they needed anything. "A cup of tea would be lovely, dear."

Charleigh and Vivian sat and drank their tea and talked some more about the family. Charleigh told her how John and Anna were enjoying their new school, and Rikki was going to daycare two days a week.

"It is good for her to be around other children. It's important for her socialisation. It isn't easy though, working and having children, but I think it's important to always have your own money. Women should always be able to choose whether they want to stay in a marriage—not have to because they have no other option."

"I agree. I'm actually looking at what might be involved in going back to school for teaching."

"I think that would be a wonderful idea. You'd be a wonderful teacher. You're creative and smart. It's the best of both worlds. You'd get to be off during breaks with your family and have a stable job and security. In case you ever needed it." Vivian exchanged a meaningful glance with Charleigh. Sometimes, she understood so much more than words could say.

"James is doing well?" she asked.

"He does very well in school and has a nice group of friends."

"He's a deep thinker that one. An old soul."

"He sure is." Charleigh enjoyed how connected her Nan was to her children. It was a mutual adoration society.

"I think he will change the world. He is so smart. Very advanced for his age. What about my girls?"

"Anna told me to give you butterfly kisses."

"Aw yes, she is such a little darling." Vivian's eyes twinkled at the thought of receiving butterfly kisses from her six-year-old great-granddaughter. "She has an adventurous spirit. Try not to hold her back, even if she terrifies you, which I think she might." Vivian nodded her head slightly, smiling as she thought about her great-granddaughter and her energy and spirit.

"I will try to always encourage all of them to be true to themselves, but I think you are right. She's a daredevil. She told me last week that she wants a motorcycle when she gets older, and her husband can stay home and watch the kids!"

"Oh, I can see it too. I can just see it. Rikki has it in her too, but she is still so little. It's too early to know for sure, except for how stubborn she will be. She gets that from you." A cheeky grin formed on Vivian's face.

"Hey!" But Charleigh wasn't upset. First, her nan was teasing her, and second, it was absolutely true.

"It's not a bad trait in a woman. We need to stand up for ourselves more in the world." Vivian added and nodded to herself. Charleigh was always impressed by how progressive and aware her nan was.

When they returned to the room, the first photos they saw made them both laugh. "The tradition of bathing in the cottage! You were the first. We could make a whole album just from this tradition, I think," Viv said. They found multiple photos of different babies sitting in the kitchen sink getting a bath. Chubby legs and toothless, grinning round faces abounded.

"Here is one of you floating in the lake, Nan. I have never seen anyone who can literally just sit and float like you do in the water."

"I'll tell you a secret. It is all in the buoyancy." She giggled and patted her own bottom.

"Look at you cross-country skiing! Remember how you and mom used to ski together around the lake?"

"We were terrible at it and spent more time helping each other up out of the snow than actually skiing."

"Well, you certainly enjoyed it."

"Yes, yes, we did. Oh, look at this one. Landyn and Joseph with their waterski trophies at the marina after the regatta. That Lee family always thought they were so good with their fancy boat and skis, and our boys beat them every year with our Canadian Tire skis." A triumphant sound erupted from her.

"The cottage has certainly always been your happy place."

"In the beginning, I hated it. The bugs were ferocious, and it was a lot of work just to get there and then double the work to do any chore or job. Cooking, cleaning, oh my. I did not enjoy it."

"But you did it anyway."

"Yes, I did it anyway. The kids all loved it so much up there, and it had always been Thomas' dream to have a cottage. Once we had running water and an actual toilet and shower, I loved it. I think it is how it brings us all together. No matter who is single or married or who has children, the cottage is where we all still come back together."

"That's very true. I think that's why I have such a love of the water and just being around it."

"I am sure it is. You were raised at that cottage from the time that you were a week old, and as soon as you could, you would spend the entire day in the water, jumping off the rock and swimming back in. We joked you were part fish. You would get mad when we made you come out, even though your lips were purple."

"This is one of my favourites." Charleigh handed a photo of her grandfather to her nan. He was sitting on a lounge chair with a chipmunk perched beside him, taking a peanut out of his hand.

"Oh yes, that is a good one. He spent days training them all, then was furious when they ate his garden. He tried everything to keep them out."

"This one is of him in the garden at the cottage. Look, there's chicken wire all around it." Vivian and Charleigh shared fits of laughter as they talked about how Thomas would come up with plans to keep the animals out of his garden, and in the end, they always found a way.

"I think we're about done with the photos, Nan. That was a respectable job done, I'd say!"

"Goodness, that was a lot of work. Can you put the ones I picked out on my board, dear?"

Every time one of the family visited, they brought updated photos of grandchildren. Vivian had a cork board installed so she had more room to display the pictures. There were some recent ones of Landyn's family at the cottage and Joseph's boys' graduations from university and their PhDs.

"We certainly have a handsome and smart lot, don't we?" She sat back in her chair, enjoying being able to look at all her family. "You know, I've had a very good life, Charleigh." Vivian spoke softly but very clearly. "I really am ready to go."

Charleigh was taken aback. "Nan. Don't say that. I'm certainly not ready for you to go."

"We all go sometime, my darling. It's been a rough year. I broke both hips and had a stroke and landed here. I'm tired, and I'm ready. Look at all the memories and accomplishments I have had." Vivian reached out and gently squeezed Charleigh's hand. "I love you. I will always love you, and I will always be with you. I promise."

"I know that, Nanny. I love you too, but I still need you to stick around a while longer."

When Charleigh got into her car to drive home, she wanted to call her mom and two aunts and tell them about the conversation she'd just had with her grandmother, but she didn't. It would upset them, and it would change nothing. As her Nan had said, *there are too many things to remember with a smile than to linger on the ones that hurt.*

With summer over and everyone back to school, Jess had gone back to her routine of visiting her mum on her way home after work. "Hi, Mummy. How are you feeling today?"

It was very unusual for Vivian to still be in her bed when Jess came to visit. She went over to her and leaned down to kiss her cheek. Vivian moved her head to kiss her cheek back, but she didn't open her eyes.

"Are you okay, Mum?"

Vivian murmured a yes, but Jess was very alarmed. "I'm just going to get a tea, Mum. I will be right back."

The nurses' station was at the end of the hall, and Jess felt like it kept stretching away from her, like she was not getting closer to it no matter how many steps she took.

"Hi, umm, I just went into my mum's room, and she's not really responding properly. Did she take something? Is there something wrong?"

"Jess, I'm sorry. I didn't see you come in. We just had a briefing, and I was leaving to call you and Judy." The nurse behind the counter stood up and came around to the front. "Let's go into my office to talk."

Jess could hear someone crying out, "No. No. Not my mum. Please no." And then she realised it was her.

The nurse had given Jess her office to use to make her phone calls. "Di? It's Jess. I'm at Mum's. I think you should come. You don't need to break the speed limit, I'd but come now." Then she called Judy and Charleigh.

Charleigh picked up the phone in the car on speaker. "Hey, Jess. Rikki and I are just on our way down to visit Nan. Are you going to be around?"

"How long until you are here, Charleigh?"

"Maybe ten minutes. Why? Do you need me to pick something up?"

"No. That's okay. I will see you when you get here."

Charleigh knew something was wrong. She walked into her nan's room and saw her mom and two aunts standing near the bed. It had been raised a bit.

"Nanny!" Rikki squealed with delight and ran to climb up onto the bed with her great-grandmother. "Hi, Nanny. I love you." Her little voice was full of sweet innocence and pure love as she spoke and planted kisses on Vivian's cheeks.

"I love you too, dear." Her voice was so soft, and she moved her head slightly to kiss Rikki back.

Diane, Jess, and Judy all let out a sound that mixed pain and happiness.

"Hi, Nan. Love you." Charleigh leaned over and kissed her grandmother's cheek.

Again, Viv turned her face and returned the kiss. "I love you too, dear."

Charleigh understood. The look on her mother's face. The tears running down their cheeks. They didn't need to say it, but she needed to hear it. "How long?" She mouthed the words.

"Let's talk in the hall, hun." Diane walked out with Charleigh, and Jess and Judy watched Rikki. "The family are all on their way. We haven't been able to reach Joseph. He's in North Bay for work and is in a meeting. His phone is off. Landyn and Lauren will pick Grace up and bring her with them. John, Sarah, Philip, and Marie are all on their way as well."

Charleigh nodded. "I'm going to call Gordon and have him pick up Rikki."

One by one, Vivian's children arrived. One by one, they told her they loved her and kissed her cheek. One by one, she kissed them back and told them she loved them, too. Joseph had still not arrived, but they at least knew he was on his way.

"Leland, I am so glad you made it." Landyn clapped the elderly man on the shoulder. An honourary member of the family for decades, Leland came as soon as Jess had called to tell him Vivian didn't have a lot of time left.

"Of course. Of course. Anything for your mum. How you holding up then?" Leland got teary as he talked to Landyn and got an update on Vivian's condition. He went in to see her. "Hi Viv, it's me, Leland." Vivian's eyes moved behind the eyelids in response. "I know you decided this is the time to go and I understand. You need to rest. You have worked hard your whole life, Viv. You deserve this rest. You raised a beautiful family that I am so proud and honoured to have been allowed to join. Thank you, Viv. I will never repay you for all you have done for me. I love you and I am really going to miss you." The last words were barely audible. He squeezed her hand one more time and went to collect himself in the men's room.

Each of them had taken up a post around their mother. Talking to her, sharing stories, laughing at all the incredible moments they had lived with this woman they called Mum and Nan.

Vivian's breathing was becoming shallower and more laboured.

"Do we know where Joseph is? How much further he has to go?" Diane asked Grace.

"He called about an hour ago and said that he was just over an hour away. He should be here very soon." Grace took Diane's hands, and she could tell Grace was worried Joseph wouldn't make it in time.

"She will wait for him, Grace. Don't worry. She will wait for him." Diane squeezed her hands and went back to stand beside Charleigh, who was sitting and holding her grandmother's hand. "You should go for a walk, hun. You need to move a bit. You've been sitting there for hours."

"I'm okay, Mom." Charleigh smiled weakly at her mother, holding back a fresh flood of tears. Landyn came back into the room and rubbed Charleigh's shoulder lightly and gave her the same teary half smile.

There was a flurry of activity in the hall. "He's here. Joseph is here," Grace called out, and he swept into the room to his mother's side.

"Hi, my mummy. I'm sorry I'm late. I love you," his voice trembled as he kissed her cheek.

Vivian's eyes fluttered but didn't open, and she turned her head to return his kiss, a faint smile on her lips. "I love you, too," her voice barely audible.

There were sobs from everyone, knowing she had managed to say goodbye to each and every one of her children and her granddaughter.

"Viv, Viv. I am here, darling. I have waited for you for so long."

"Thomas! Oh, Thomas. I have missed you so much, my darling."

"Oh, Viv. Look at our family. Look how beautiful and happy and well they all are. I'm so proud of them. I am so proud of you, darling."

"Thomas, I am worried about them."

"Of course, you are. But you don't need to be. They take after you. They are strong. Stronger than they know yet, and you will always be nearby."

A stillness settled in the room.

Vivian's last breath faded, and the realisation hit them all like a fist. Diane turned from the room, and a guttural sob exploded from her chest. They each said goodbye one last time and moved to the hallway. Except Charleigh, who stayed sitting beside her nan, holding her hand.

Diane and Lauren, realising that Charleigh was still in the room, came back inside. "Char, you need to let her go, hun. She's gone."

"It's okay, Mom, Lauren. I am just going to wait with her until whoever it is who comes for her, comes for her. I just don't want her to be all alone. She has always been there for me, and now I'm going to stay with her until they take her away."

"That's very true." Lauren squeezed Charleigh's hand and led Diane out. "She's okay, Di. She just needs her time with

Mum.”

Charleigh closed her eyes, allowing the tears to finally flow without resistance as she laid her cheek on her grandmother's hand. “Oh, Nanny, I love you. I am going to miss you so much,” she whispered. She placed something in her grandmother's hand. The fragrance of her Nan's perfume filled Charleigh's nose, and she felt their connection.

“She will be okay, Viv. I promise. She is so like you. Oh, my girl. I have missed you.” Thomas touched the blonde hair, and Charleigh looked up. “Look, Viv, she knows we are here.”

“Oh, Thomas, she does. Thank you.” Vivian wrapped her arms around her granddaughter one last time. Then she took Thomas' hand, and they walked away, reunited forever. Vivian was holding a small card with a pressed violet and the word *Home* on it.

About The Author

Michelle Brown, a proud mother of three remarkable young adults, discovered her calling as a writer under the nurturing guidance of her fourth-grade teacher, Mrs. Wales. Inspired by literary luminaries like Margaret Lawrence, Margaret Atwood, Alexandre Dumas, Harper Lee, John Irving, S.E. Hinton, and Aldous Huxley, Michelle's passion for storytelling blossomed.

While books have always held a special place in her heart, Michelle draws profound inspiration from her love for nature and water, finding peace and creativity along sandy shores or beneath the canopy of ancient trees. Her fondest moments are those spent with family, sharing laughter and forging memories amidst the beauty of the natural world.

Driven by a deep-seated commitment to human rights and social justice, Michelle infuses her writing with empathy and a keen understanding of the human condition. Her work reflects a desire to provoke thought and inspire positive change, addressing pressing societal issues with both sensitivity and insight.
Michelle Brown's writing journey is a testament to the transformative power of literature and the enduring impact of those who encourage and nurture creative expression.

www.ingramcontent.com/pod-product-compliance
Lightning Source LLC
Chambersburg PA
CBHW072042190726
48294CB00005B/1359